Max Kinnings is Head of Subject in Creative Writing at Brunel University in London. He is also a screenwriter, and is currently adapting the Ed Mallory novels into feature films. He lives in Oxford with his family.

ALSO BY MAX KINNINGS

Baptism

SACRIFICE
Max Kinnings

Quercus

Dedicated to the memory of my father, Terry Kinnings

First published in Great Britain in 2013 by

Quercus Editions Ltd
55 Baker Street
7th Floor, South Block
London
W1U 8EW

A CIP catalogue record for this book is available
from the British Library

ISBN 978 1 78087 182 0
EBOOK ISBN 978 1 78087 184 4

This book is a work of fiction. Names, characters,
businesses, organizations, places and events are
either the product of the author's imagination
or are used fictitiously. Any resemblance to
actual persons, living or dead, events or
locales is entirely coincidental.

10 9 8 7 6 5 4 3 2 1

Typeset by Ellipsis Digital Limited, Glasgow

Printed and bound in Great Britain by Clays Ltd, St Ives plc

10:15 AM

11 Blenheim Terrace, Belgravia

Someone was playing Christmas songs. It was one of those compilation albums with pop hits: Slade's 'Merry Christmas Everybody' and John Lennon's 'Happy Christmas (War is Over)' interspersed with a few orchestral numbers. It was loud enough that Ronnie could just make it out in the cold London air. In an hour or two he would probably be able to smell turkey roasting. That was bound to make him feel homesick. As it was, the triple time that he was earning sweetened the fact that he was away from the family. A few more days like this and he would be able to take them away for New Year.

Ronnie had never worked on Christmas Day before. Considering all the years he had spent in the paras and then his time at Omega Security after his return to Civvy Street, it was surprising that he should never have spent at least one year out of his forty-six at work. He thought about the opening of the presents back home in Bromley. They would have started by now. It wasn't so far away. As he looked towards the south-east, across the rooftops of Belgravia, he thought that it was probably only about nine or ten miles as the crow flies. It was very different from this neighbourhood, of course. Someone once told him – or he'd heard it on the news, maybe – that this part of London was some of the most expensive real estate in the world. The house had to be worth a mint. Twenty-five, maybe thirty million, had to be. Crazy money. There was no point in being jealous. It didn't mean the family that lived in it were any happier. Far from it, if the headlines were anything to go by.

Ronnie's two colleagues on the job, Paul and Roger – Roj – didn't seem too bothered to be working on Christmas Day, either. Good money was always a sweetener. Paul was in the garden, securing the perimeter. Roj was patrolling the terrace at the rear of the building. What Ronnie didn't know was that both his colleagues were dead. Paul lay in a puddle of blood on a path between two flower beds, his neck almost completely severed by the cheese wire that had been pulled through it; Roger was face down on the terrace, the top of his spinal cord eviscerated by a hunting knife. The man who had killed them both was now on his way to find Ronnie.

There would be time to put a call in to the family later. Maybe just before one o'clock when his wife, Trish, was hoping to have the turkey done. He shouldn't really, but it would only take a couple of minutes. Ronnie paced across the roof terrace, moving away from the shadow cast by the chimney stack. He shut his eyes for a moment and enjoyed the winter sun as it shone down on him. Maybe he could get a last-minute deal and take the family somewhere hot. The Canaries were pretty warm at this time of year – or North Africa. Tunisia, maybe. They had had a great time there a couple of years before. He'd look into it when he had the chance.

Ronnie didn't hear the footsteps across the roof terrace until they were almost upon him. He spun around and was confronted by a man dressed in black wearing a balaclava. Taller than Ronnie, who, at six feet two, had always considered himself large, the man punched him hard in the face, a blow that sent him reeling backwards. Before he could reach for a weapon or take any evasive action, his attacker had struck him again and pushed him with such force that he was thrown over the low wall on the perimeter of the roof terrace. He fell through the cold winter air, arms and legs flailing, until his trajectory was brutally interrupted by the spiked, wrought-iron railings at the front of the house, four of which passed through the middle of his body, erupting from his back in a neat, evenly distributed row of bloody exit wounds.

06:17 AM *(four hours earlier)*

V.I.P. Lounge, Heathrow Airport

Lily Poynter walked a couple of paces behind her parents. When she was little, she had walked ahead of them when they went anywhere together as a family. At some stage in her teenage years, she had started walking behind them. Maybe she was no longer as eager as they were to reach their destination. She knew it might look childish and petulant to walk behind them but she didn't feel part of their world. She enjoyed the feeling of being distant from them. Any separation was welcome, even just a few feet of air. The amount of time she had spent locked up with them in the past three months had only served to amplify her feelings of resentment towards them. They had given up any pretence of civility towards each other long ago. It had barely survived the first week in Zurich, where they had relocated – fled, more like – after one of the more spectacular of the financial collapses of recent years, namely that of her father's hedge fund, Stanmore Partners.

She knew her mother liked her to dress smartly when they were travelling by private jet and that's why she had made a point of wearing her black leggings and hoody top, just to piss her off. What was the point of being able to travel by private jet if you couldn't wear what the hell you wanted? Her mum was such a snob. So was her dad but he had other things to worry about now. Like how to stay out of prison. There was talk of Ponzi schemes and what made the media come on so hard was the lavish lifestyle that her parents had chosen to flaunt. Where other people at the top of the financial heap had kept their heads below the parapet during the storm, Lily's mother and father had continued with their conspicuous consumption. The press liked nothing more than a downfall and, with apparent losses as enormous as those of Stanmore Partners, this was shaping up to be a clusterfuck of epic proportions. Despite running away to Switzerland, a drip feed of revelations ever since the story first broke had ensured the continued interest of the public on both sides of the Atlantic.

Lily watched her parents stiffen as they approached the exit. In the rarefied environment of the first-class lounge, they felt safe, cocooned from the outside world and its attendant hostilities. Out there, beyond the doors, their safety was diminished. As they stepped into the cold air and her mother looked back at her with that little pout of annoy-ance – *keep up, Lily* – her father looked around, checking for photographers, the 'scum', as he referred to them. But he was in luck, there weren't any, and the car was right there ready for them. It was a massive black Mercedes. If she had a pound for every massive black Mercedes she had travelled in during her life, she'd probably have enough to hire one.

With the luggage stowed in the boot, their driver steered them through the light Christmas traffic towards central London. She watched him. He was slightly pasty but not unattractive. About thirty-five. Tall, slim; not a typical chauffeur's build at all. He had that quiet unobtrusiveness that all the best chauffeurs employed: spoke when spoken to; didn't offer an opinion unless it was invited. But when they joined the M4 from the airport feeder road, she caught him looking at her in the rear-view mirror. Right into her eyes. He looked away again immediately but it was enough to allow Lily to fantasise for a moment that he was checking her out. In truth, she knew that he probably considered her a spoiled little rich girl. Everyone else did. There was nothing she could do about it. What is it about being rich through no fault of your own that means that all your worries, troubles and insecurities are somehow invalidated? She hadn't sought this life. It wasn't as though she had been party to anything that her father had been involved in and now stood accused of. She had read all the charges that were laid before him in the court of public opinion and they were bad. If he had done half of what they said he had then he deserved to go down for a long time. Some of it was pretty inconclusive; some of it was less so. The media were enjoying his discomfort but they weren't the source of the hate-filled diatribes. These came from the badlands of the Internet via social media. She couldn't use Twitter and Facebook like her friends did, or even have an email address that contained her name, because she would receive hate mail and abuse. Most of it was directed at her father but some of it was directed at her. She had been threatened with various punishments, many of them sexual and a couple of them just plain sick. Her father had insisted that they report them to the authorities and she had done so. But once she had changed all her online identities, most – but not all – had stopped.

It wasn't the trolls, however, that frightened her. They were just misfits and losers. It was the hackers, the members of activist – or 'hacktivist' networks – who could pry into every aspect of her life. She knew that, however many times she changed her online identity, she was unlikely to fool any of them. She knew they were out there; they were always out there, watching and listening. No one was safe. But only certain people were of interest to them. None of her friends were. Their fathers hadn't been accused of fraud on an industrial scale that had made headlines around the world. It meant that her life was different from theirs even though her close friends never referred to it for fear of upsetting her.

It was still dark. The motorway rose on to the elevated section approaching Hammersmith and the lights of London stretched away ahead of them. It was good to be back in London. She watched her father. He sat in the passenger seat in the front. Staring ahead through the window at the approaching city, he picked at a hangnail on his thumb. It was the only sign of the turmoil that she knew was taking place within. For a man who had made a living out of betting on the future, the uncertainty that he and his family now faced was not something that could be processed without extreme stress. The papers had gone from discussing the possibility of him doing jail time to taking it as read that he would. It wasn't as though she was pleased that her father was facing an imminent fall from grace. She had too much to lose. It was the ever-increasing feeling that he had brought most of his problems on himself through his arrogance and greed. It was as though the man she remembered from when she was a little girl had been a different person. He was successful in those days but he wasn't poisoned by the world in which he worked. But that man was long gone. She hated the world of high finance and, as she watched her father staring through the windscreen at the approaching city, she thought that he was probably beginning to hate it too.

06:49 AM

Fortis Green Road, Muswell Hill

Ed Mallory took a big lungful of air as he stepped out of the back of the police car that had delivered him to the stronghold. It was probably all in his mind but he felt sure that he could taste something in the air that activated a chemical memory of the time he had spent in Muswell Hill. He had been living here at the time of the Hanway Street siege in Kensal Rise, a memory that he returned to on a daily basis not least because it was the negotiation that had cost him his sight. Up until that day, his years in Muswell Hill had been happy. He'd loved the woods and the open spaces around Highgate and Alexandra Park, loved seeing London in the distance and feeling that little bit removed from the urban grind. Being blind, these matters didn't seem to concern him as much as they once had. Maybe they should do; maybe he should make more of an effort to regain some approximation of his former life. But, even after fourteen years, he didn't seem ready to begin the journey. His former psychiatrist had despaired of his inability to achieve any level of acceptance of his condition. As far as she was concerned, Ed was wilfully obstructing his own healing process. He probably was and, as though in confirmation of this, he had stopped seeking advice from the medical community.

Ed was taken through to the negotiating command centre. It smelled like all the rest: cheap coffee and residual cigarette smoke. Smoking wasn't allowed in negotiating cells, as it once had been, but it clung to clothes and tainted the breath of some of the cell's occupants. He was introduced to the other members of the team. It was at moments like this that he wondered how he must appear to people. His face was scarred; the worst damage was around his eyes, which were concealed behind sunglasses as always. It wasn't vanity that made him consider his appearance but a sense of the effect that it might have on others. What he dreaded was that people looked at him and felt pity. He wanted no one's pity and his suspicion that others might feel it fuelled what he knew his former colleagues had referred to as his off-hand manner. Being awkward or difficult was not something he did consciously. These traits, combined with the black clothes that he always wore, were all part of his ongoing refusal to conform to the role of the victim.

He said, 'Hi,' to each of the other members of the negotiating cell in turn, each welcome of a uniform tone and volume. He had not worked with any of them before, which was unusual. Maybe it was something to do with it being Christmas morning but he couldn't help but feel that the negotiating team had been thrown together with the primary criteria being availability rather than any sense of team chemistry. But that suited him fine. It felt good to be back on the job. At least, he wanted it to feel good. He had been looking forward to this for months. But dreading it too.

Leaving the force had come at a difficult time. Although many of his former colleagues had assured him that he was going to be on their speed dial when his style of psychological insight was required in a negotiation, the phone hadn't exactly been ringing off the hook. He had supplemented his earnings with some lectures and seminars. The corporate work had gone down well and the money was good. His insight into negotiating techniques in hostage situations appeared to fascinate the business community. And he enjoyed the work. To a degree. But he was afraid that he was becoming a *former* hostage negotiator. He might be able to survive financially on the speaking circuit, but psychologically he would struggle.

The negotiating cell co-ordinator was a man called Keir. He sounded young and the soft skin on his palm as they shook hands confirmed this. Ed wasn't one of those people – and he had met other hostage negotiators who were – who found it difficult to work with and defer to a younger person.

Besides, Keir sounded like a good co-ordinator. He was calm, unhurried and organised: all qualities that should have re-assured Ed. But Ed found it difficult to allow himself to be reassured. It was an unusual sensation but he was feeling, not scared exactly, but anxious. He had been lucky that morning. A situation had arisen and he was available. He couldn't afford to screw this up and, if for no other reason, it had him a little spooked. It wasn't something that he couldn't cope with – he had been doing this for long enough to know how to deal with his own psychological demons – but he felt jittery nonetheless.

'Raymond Stolton is sixty-five years old,' said Keir as he began his briefing. Ed had already been given the basic details but it was good to have these fleshed out. 'He's a retired plumbing supplies manager.'

'Successful? High self-esteem?' asked Ed.

'Doubtful; it was early retirement. Company went down. He's had a couple of failed marriages, had a bit of a drink problem.'

'Had?'

'That's what we've got. Anyway, he's quite lucid; basically wants to know what his legal situation is, having shot and killed Ryan Howell, the seventeen-year-old accomplice of his hostage, Aiden Carver. If he doesn't have a clear, public assurance that he won't be prosecuted for killing Howell, he's going to kill Carver.'

'Hanged for a sheep as a lamb,' said Ed.

'Exactly.'

'What about weapons?'

'One shotgun, as far as we can tell.'

Keir went on to tell Ed about the layout of the house and Raymond and Aiden's location in the hallway. Without being able to refer to notes, Ed had to retain as much information as he could. Within moments, he was going to be negotiating with this Raymond, a man he had never spoken to before in his life. A total stranger. He was going to speak to him and try to persuade him to give himself up. It was something he had done many times. It was what he did and it should have felt natural.

Ed slipped on the headset and a call was put through to the house.

'Hello?' The voice on the other end of the line was frightened, suspicious.

'My name's Ed Mallory; I'm a negotiator. I'm here to try to resolve this situation.'

'I told that twat earlier. I told him that I'm not going to give this little shit up unless I'm home and dry.' The voice belonged to a Londoner but Ed couldn't narrow down its origins any more specifically than that.

'This is Raymond who I'm speaking to, is it?'

'Who the fuck else would it be?'

'OK; I can call you Raymond, can I?'

'Call me Ray.'

'OK, Ray. What do you mean when you say that you're not going to let Aiden go free unless you're home and dry?'

'I'm not going down for this.'

'There's no one saying that you will.'

'He attacked me in my own home. I did what anyone would have done.'

'Of course, but with the greatest respect, Ray, this isn't the best way of going about the necessary discussion. We need to check you over, make sure you're OK. You've been through a terrifying ordeal. When that's all done, we can talk about the legal implications.'

'No way. I want this sorted now. This little fuck isn't so clever anymore. You should see him. He's shitting himself.'

'I understand why you feel vengeful, Ray. But this isn't the right thing to do. You need to let your hostage go and then we can talk.'

Ed heard something on the line. It was the sound of a bottle of something being up-ended into a mouth. It confirmed Ed's suspicions that Ray had been drinking.

'I know what'll happen here, Mr Negotiator. I walk out of here and then the police will get hold of me. There'll be a court case and some clever, stuck-up public-school wanker will start tearing me apart and, before you know it, I'll be inside when this little shit is out mugging old ladies.'

'Will you answer me something, Ray?'

'Go on.'

'Are you drinking?'

'I've had a Scotch. I bloody needed one.'

Ed settled into his seat and tried to relax. He might as well get comfortable because he felt sure he would be there for quite some time.

07:02 AM

Lemon Road, Shoreditch

Lucas's face was twisted into a sneering, hate-fuelled grimace. He hated the pain in his arms and shoulders as he pulled up on the bar. Hated it, yet also loved it. With each strain of exertion he was getting stronger, his muscles were getting harder. Every day, he spent long hours at the computer. All that time sitting immobile in front of a screen was enough to make a body go soft. Lucas didn't intend to allow that to happen. He was twenty years old, old enough for a sedentary lifestyle to begin to take effect on his physique. Like any warrior engaged in combat, he had to make sure that he was battle ready. He wasn't alone in this; he was one component of a much larger machine.

His muscles burned as he attempted another pull-up and succeeded. He was at one more than his previous best of twenty-nine. When he had first started his fitness regime earlier in the year, he had never imagined that he might be able to do thirty pull-ups. At the time, he had barely managed ten. Yesterday and the day before, he had attempted the thirtieth but failed each time, his arms shaking with exertion and losing their battle with the force of gravity. But today he felt more confident. As he pulled up for the thirtieth time and the veins bulged in his pock-marked forehead and his face became screwed up tight with exertion, he groaned the word thirty and, as he surrendered to the laws of physics, he kissed the bar. Dropping to the floor and landing on his bare feet, he whispered, 'Yes,' and punched the air. Managing to do thirty pull-ups for the first time was a good omen for what lay ahead.

Lucas wiped his face on a towel and pulled on his vest and sweatshirt. He slipped on a pair of trainers over his old football socks, did up the laces and made his way over to the desk in the middle of the room. The building in which they were squatting was an old office block. Building developers were hoping to renovate it and make it into luxury flats but they appeared to have run out of money, which meant that Lucas and his friends and fellow activists got to stay – for the time being, at least.

Lucas reached down to the bottom drawer and took out a revolver, clicked open the chamber and ran his thumb across the six bullets. Closing it again, he reached back into the drawer to take out the box of ammunition. He had never fired a gun before. But how hard could it be? He knew where the safety catch was, had read about how to handle it. Everything was on the Internet if you looked for it. Everything.

Lucas checked that the safety catch was on, slid the gun and the bullets into the side pocket of his jacket, which hung on the door. He pulled on the jacket and walked through into the open-plan area of the office. There were lots of workstations, all sectioned off from each other into little boxes like a battery farm. But their former occupants were long gone, their services either no longer required or required elsewhere. And now he lived here, surviving – flourishing, even – in the wreckage of capitalism.

What he was going to do today would be the start of an ongoing campaign of direct action. Lucas's brothers and sisters around the world had closed the first chapter in the narrative that he was helping to shape. The movement had grown organically so far. Their anonymity was crucial to their survival. The concept of a leader was anathema to what the organisation stood for but, nonetheless, Lucas was, if not a leader, then a pioneer. Non-violence had served its purpose. There were other methods available now, methods that could be – indeed, should be – deployed for the first time. What was the point of going to all the effort of building a mass movement and taking sides against the military-industrial complex if you weren't prepared to win? Lucas and his colleagues needed to let the enemy know that they were not going away. If that meant that some people had to die so the movement could gain momentum and show its commitment, then so be it. That was OK. It was justified. He wasn't the only one who felt like that. There were others. Peaceful protest only worked up to a point. But this was a war and in war there are casualties.

07:54 AM

Blenheim Terrace, Belgravia

Graham Poynter so wanted to be surprised, he so wanted there to be no scum outside his house. He would know if there were any in a few moments when the driver steered the car around on to the terrace and he would have a clear view. If the coast was clear, it would be a rare bit of good news and might just signify that the bastards were beginning to lose interest in him.

If he looked into the wing mirror from where he sat in the front passenger seat, he could see his wife, Helen, and her stony expression in the back. She wasn't enjoying this any more than he was. She was looking tired. The past few months were enough to make anyone look tired. He could do with a holiday. Those trips they used to make to Anguilla and Mustique – what he wouldn't give for one of those now. He'd never really appreciated them at the time. Wasn't life always like that?

Graham turned in his seat and glanced back at Lily. She was sitting there staring out of the window. He had a sense that she knew he was looking at her but she didn't look around, didn't acknowledge his presence. As always. It was tough on her too. She had done nothing wrong, nothing to bring this about. Yet she was suffering – if not as much as him then something close. When the fund had first collapsed and before they realised the full implications of what had happened and how it might effect their lives, Lily and Helen had provided him with comfort and support. But as the weeks in Zurich became months, he could feel that support begin to ebb away. Now they had started to treat him with little more than undisguised disdain, as though they were actually beginning to believe all the lies and untruths that were hurled at him. But as much as he felt like running away, and to a certain extent he had run away by taking off for Zurich with his family, he also knew he had to come back and face his opponents. If he was going to have his reputation attacked from all sides, then he was not going down without a fight.

There they were. He saw them as soon as the car turned the corner: anoraks, puffa jackets and cameras. As the car pulled up at the kerb, he already had his door open. No point giving the bastards a moment more than he had to. With his face set to 'grim', he opened the back door for Helen and Lily as the driver pulled cases from the boot. Graham wasn't surprised to find himself back in the sodium glare of publicity but it didn't make the reality of it any less shocking.

So much for the new press agent. He'd told Graham that coming back on Christmas Day was a clever strategic move to lessen media attention. Graham would speak to him later – Christmas Day or not. Graham could feel his bottom lip start to wobble. Oh, Jesus, not now. This was getting out of hand. Alone in his own home, that was fine. Worrying, but fine. Now he felt as though he was going to lose control of himself in public. That would spell disaster. He clenched his jaw and tried something of a sneer as they made their way inside the house. The air shimmered with flashbulbs as a security guard ushered the three of them towards the front door.

It wasn't just the mainstream media, though. It was the anti-capitalist weirdos and the hacktivist whack-jobs who targeted him personally. His email account had been hacked numerous times. False social media identities had been set up in his name. Some of them were harmless enough and spouted supposedly satirical drivel but others were more sinister. And a few were downright scary: people threatening to attack him and his family and fantasising about doing so. The police were contacted; they claimed to be monitoring the situation. That wasn't good enough for Graham. Hence the security.

There were three of them, all suitably large and scary-looking. He was glad the scumbags would see them and hopefully photograph them. It would send a message. In all areas of his life and business, Graham Poynter was ready for a fight.

photographer and that it would send a message. In all areas of his life and business, Graham Poynter was ready for a fight.

07:55 AM

11 Blenheim Terrace, Belgravia

Helen Poynter looked up at the house as the car pulled up outside. She used to love it so much. It was one of the finest houses on one of London's most exclusive streets. But that wasn't why she loved it. She wasn't that superficial. It was the oasis of calm that it provided. It was big; the rooms were large. The double-glazing – triple, in places – made it the quietest house she had ever lived in. It was also secure. Graham had invested in state-of-the-art security features even before all the trouble at Stanmore Partners. She had always felt safe there. Had, past tense. Not anymore. Now, she felt insecure, frightened, hollow. This house, along with everything else they had collected over the years, could be swept away. She had seen it happen. The events of that September had changed their lives but the amount of vitriol that had been levelled at Graham and them as a family had been out of all proportion to what they were supposed to have done. She was not profligate and spoiled, as the papers tried to make out. She knew many wives who were far more high maintenance and spent far more money than she did. It was just unfair, but, more than that, it was nasty. Graham was a businessman. He had always done what he felt was right for the company, his colleagues, employees and, most importantly, his investors. The world was in crisis; Graham had been caught out by the markets. It wasn't as if he was the only one.

The house had provided an easy target. There it was, worth as much as the turnover of some medium-sized companies. And they owned it outright. Details of the renovation project they had undertaken had been leaked to the media. She hadn't been too bothered at the time. What pieces were written were focused on the imaginative nature of the interior design and the quality of the fixtures and fittings rather than the cost. But now it was all about the cost. When opining on the collapse of Stanmore Partners, newspaper columnists tried to outdo each other with their fake outrage at the Poynters' consumption.

But it wasn't all about the fund. Their problems, hers and Graham's, had started during the supposed good times. She sometimes wondered whether he suffered from some sort of medical condition. Obsessive–compulsive or Asperger's, perhaps. He never stopped, never switched off. If it wasn't for the fact that he was so successful, his behaviour would be considered borderline psychotic. He was locked in a perpetual competition of the most intense kind. Everyone was a competitor. The way to win was to make the most money. It was as simple as that. If he wasn't talking about making money, he was talking about other people making money – 'other people' meaning competitors at other banks and funds. It was difficult being married to a man like that. She always knew it would be, but there were plenty of compensations. And she had her own job, bringing up Lily.

As Lily had grown older, she and Graham had started to lead their own lives. The sheer geography of their domestic life was conducive to this. Factoring in Graham's overseas trips and the time she and Lily spent at the house in the Cotswolds, it was often upwards of a month that would go by without them spending a night together under the same roof. But although the arguments they used to have were often vicious, they were nothing compared to the ones since September. Locked away together in Zurich, their arguments were the only time she and Graham had really communicated. Lily was having her own problems, embracing teenage alienation with all the passion and intensity that she had embraced all the other phases of her life.

She knew the figures would be there outside the house when they arrived. Graham had seemed to think they wouldn't be, because of the time of year. But she knew they'd be waiting for them. Christmas Day wasn't going to put them off. They could smell the blood in the water. She didn't like the shark analogy when describing people like that. Sharks were way too beautiful and graceful in design. Graham called the people who made it their business to follow them and try to pry into every corner of their lives scum. But what they really were was parasites. She didn't mean it pejoratively, although she hated them well enough. It was the fact that they couldn't help themselves. As soon as the would-be host had entered the public domain and sides were taken, opinions formed, then they were fair game. The parasites' own survival depended on their success at feeding off the host.

When feeling particularly under attack, Graham would say that the scum would grow tired and move on – and he was right – but what he failed to mention was that they would only move on when they had bled them dry, or attempted to. There was the blood analogy again. It couldn't be helped. She looked at the faces that turned towards them as the car pulled up at the kerb and Graham swore under his breath. Their features were impossible to see, being partially obscured by cameras. But she could see their expressions well enough. There was no malice, no hatred. It wasn't personal for them; they were just doing their job.

They probably lived in the suburbs, did their work, filed their pictures, came home with a clear conscience and slept soundly at night. Two weeks somewhere dull and over-crowded every summer. Kids at the local state school. And as much as she resented them and their intrusion into her life, she also realised that, in a strange sort of way, she also envied them. Sometimes she wondered what she might have done if she hadn't married Graham. She nearly married a man called Damien. He was an actor. He'd done a couple of things in the West End but he was struggling. He was a great lover, much better than Graham, if truth be told. Graham, however, was going places. Even when she first met Graham and they were both in their mid-twenties, he was earning at least double what her father was. She hated the thought of struggling. Damien lived in a small flat near Brick Lane. Graham lived in a four-bedroom apartment just off the King's Road. She cheated on Graham a few times with Damien; couldn't help herself. But she always knew whom she would end up with. There was no contest. She was born to live the life that Graham could provide. Yet she often thought about Damien. He didn't amount to much, career-wise. He ended up lecturing at a drama college somewhere and doing some acting in commercials in his spare time. The last time she saw him was on an advert for car insurance. He still looked good.

As Helen stepped from the car, she maintained her blank expression, just as she knew Graham and Lily would be doing also. Even the muttered statements of 'spoiled bitch' and 'rich cow' that were directed at her from the scum were spoken without malice. It was tactical; nothing more than half-hearted attempts to make her angry and possibly respond, all the while providing more emotionally engaging pictures that could be sold for a higher price.

The cameras flashed and didn't stop flashing until they were ushered inside by the security guards that Graham had hired and the heavy front door was closed after them. It might as well have clanged shut and a key on a rattling key ring turn in the lock. The tabloids had referred to their home as 'sprawling', 'opulent' or 'palatial', but it didn't feel like any of those things now. It felt like what it was: a prison.

08:00 AM

Negotiating Cell, Fortis Green Road, Muswell Hill

'Ray, listen to me. I'm not a policeman. I'm not a lawyer or a barrister. I'm here to help resolve this situation so that no one gets hurt. That's it; that's my job. I can't say what's going to happen to you as regards the guy you shot but what I do know is that what's done is done. You were in a frightening situation; you were threatened in your own home by intruders. What you did in the minds of the legal system—'

'The fucking legal system. That's what all this is about, isn't it?'

'Not necessarily; you might not even get prosecuted. But I'm trying to be honest with you. You'd rather that, wouldn't you?'

'Yes, of course I would.'

'Well, these are the facts. The chances are, your case will go to court and you'll have to defend yourself. If you killed someone in the middle of the night because you were frightened and panicked by intruders, the chances are you'll be looked upon leniently.'

'Will I do time?'

'No, not if you can show you were acting in self-defence. But, Ray, all of this depends on what you do now, not what you did earlier. If we put an end to this now then you're going to be viewed favourably. You'll have done the right thing. But if you don't—'

'I'll be raped in the showers, right?'

'I can't tell because I haven't seen a picture of you but I can't believe you're that gorgeous.'

It was worth a try. Humour – albeit weak – could sometimes shock a subject into seeing the futility of a situation. But it wasn't going to work with Ray. The booze he was swigging was making him belligerent. Ed needed to encourage him to stop drinking, otherwise anything could happen. Drugs of any form were always a negotiator's worst enemy. Human behaviour was difficult enough to fathom without the unpredictability of stimulants being introduced into the mix.

'You might think this is fucking funny but I don't—'

'Ray, I don't—'

'Well, what are you pissing about for then, eh?'

Ed could hear Ray take another swig from the bottle and from the sound it made, there was considerably less in it than there had been earlier.

'Ray, you need to stop drinking.'

'Don't tell me what I need to do.'

'Pouring that stuff down your neck might make you feel better in the short term but, take it from me, it's only going to make things worse.'

'I don't see how they could get much worse.'

'You have to understand that, up to this point, you've done nothing wrong. You've defended your own property. You've done what many of us would have done. So you really shouldn't be thinking this is any worse than it is. If you put the gun down and walk out of there now, then we can sort all this out.'

'No.'

'If you stay in there and keep drinking then things are more likely to get complicated. The chances are that you'll get more angry about what's happened and less likely to think straight and make an honest, informed decision.'

The sound of another swig came down the line before Ray said, 'I'm going to tell you how this is going to roll, all right?'

'Yes, OK.'

'You're going to find out my exact legal situation now. You're going to speak to whoever you need to speak to and you're going to get them to spell it out as clearly as they can and they're going to tell you whether I'm going to be prosecuted for this. Then you're going to tell me. That's all I'm asking. You owe me that.'

The line went dead as Ray hung up.

08:04 AM

Jermyn Street, Piccadilly

James was about five feet eight or so. He wasn't tall but he wasn't short either. He was good looking. That wasn't vanity; he could see how girls were drawn to him. A couple of them had told him that he looked a bit like Colin Farrell. He had a good build too: slim and wiry. However much he ate, he never seemed to put on an ounce. He hated fat people. How could you display your greed and lack of self-control so publicly for all to see? He supposed it must have had something to do with his metabolism. It was fast and burned off all the calories. He had always walked quickly. His mum said that he was always in a hurry. It was no bad thing. It wouldn't do to be late at the Radcliffe & Penny depot, not today.

For Radcliffe & Penny, it was probably the most important day of the year. All the vans would be out – that's what the controller at the depot had said. One thing he did like about the company was their policy towards the environment. They were almost completely paper-free when it came to their client documentation; he liked the way the van was a hybrid with one of the lowest CO_2 emission levels of any vehicle on the road. If he had to work for a corporate entity – even if only temporarily – then at least his carbon footprint would be as small as possible.

As James made his way inside the depot, he caught sight of his reflection in a window. He looked happy. He felt happy too. Today was a good day. The sun was in the sky.

James thought the distribution manager was looking hassled as he made his way towards him, but he also had the air of a man who knew that he was rising to a challenge and doing so successfully. The man welcomed him with a, 'Hi, Jim,' and started to talk him through the list of drops. James hated being called Jim but he would let it go.

'They're all pretty straightforward, really,' said the distribution manager with his London accent. 'The traffic shouldn't be too bad this morning. You're going to have to keep an eye on the time as you'll need to be back here at noon for a couple of cooked turkeys that have to be in situ before one. It's completely do-able.'

James nodded and muttered thanks as he took the list and made his way to the van, which was being loaded up with the Christmas fare. He had taken a look at the Radcliffe & Penny website when he applied for the job. The prices were obscene. Of course they were. You only had to look at the clientele. They wouldn't pay for it unless it was obscene. That wasn't to say that the food wasn't good. It was. It looked – and smelled – amazing. Potted Stilton, cheeses of every colour and place of origin, smoked fish, pies, fruit baskets, boiled ham, caviar.

Radcliffe & Penny were clearly good at what they did. It was a competitive market. They had a reputation for the quality of their food and they managed to deliver it to wherever it had to go to on time and in the right condition. Schedules were important. This was the real world. He had seen so many of his friends from uni get fired from their jobs because of shoddy timekeeping. The traditions of student life were something that would never go away but he wanted no part of them.

James sat down in the driver's seat and waited for the last few items to be placed in the back. As he adjusted the rear-view mirror, he caught sight of his face again – or part of it at least. The half-smile was still there. He clenched his jaw and pursed his lips to banish it. He had to get to work.

08:13 AM

11 Blenheim Terrace, Belgravia

While her mum made coffee, Lily sat at the breakfast bar with her dad. When they had decided to go to Zurich in September, Marie, the housekeeper, had been invited to go with them and keep house for them there but she had declined and had got herself a new job. Lily couldn't blame her. She had had to endure three years of escalating tensions in the Poynter household. It was enough to make anyone look for an escape. Her mum said they would get a new housekeeper now they were back but, in the meantime, they were on their own. Apart from the three goons, that was. Her dad had said they were from one of the finest security companies in London. But Lily didn't like the look of them. They appeared to be only too well aware of who it was they were employed to protect. They had seen the headlines; they had seen the accusations of high living. They knew they were on to a winner. One of them, the youngest but still in his early thirties, had smiled at her. He had intended it to be a reassuring smile, friendly, but it also hinted at attraction. He was quite fit: tall, sort of rugged. But not her type. She much preferred the nerdy type, couldn't help it. It seemed to be a curse. All the hearty, over-ambitious rugby types – the jocks – were attracted to her but she didn't like them. The geeks were so much more interesting but, like everyone else, they thought she was spoiled. When she had pointed this out to her friends, they had told her she was wrong; but their eagerness to tell her how wrong she was made her know she was right. It was so horribly, boringly predictable. Her father's wealth tarnished everything. It wasn't like having a famous dad, someone in a band or a successful writer. It didn't make her interesting. It aroused the worst feelings in people. It made them jump to lazy assumptions of her, judgements based almost purely on jealousy. Whatever happened to her in her life, however hard it might get, somehow her wealthy, privileged exist-ence negated the validity of her concerns, somehow disqualified them from being worthy of understanding. She didn't want sympathy; she just wished she had someone to confide in. Nieve, her best friend, had a privileged life – her father was a diplomat and her mother was a corporate lawyer – but it was different for her. Her parents weren't the subject of the nation's disgust.

'So, what shall we do for Christmas?' asked Helen as she put the tray with the coffee and cups on it down on the island at which Lily sat with her father. She had poured the coffee and sat down at one of the stools next to Lily before she got a reply.

'What are the options?' asked Lily, seeing as her dad wasn't going to offer a suggestion.

'Well, we could play some games after lunch, maybe.'

It wasn't worth even getting angry. Like they were ever going to play party games together like a normal family. It was beyond stupid, so Lily chose to focus on another part of her mother's statement and asked, 'What are we having for lunch?'

'I ordered some things from Radcliffe & Penny. Don't worry, I know you don't like turkey so I just got some cold meats, pies and salads.'

'Great.' Lily said it with just enough seriousness to make her mother suspect that it was sarcastic and but not enough to pull her up about it. 'Although I don't fancy a big lunch,' added Lily.

'Me neither,' said Graham, taking a sip of his coffee.

Lily watched her mother as she immediately latched on to her dad's response, which had been expressed in a tone of voice that had managed to trip an alarm in her mother's head. Whether rightly or wrongly, it had been perceived as hostile. Lily knew that her mum wouldn't usually be the one to start a row but she was in a constant state of readiness, should enemy manoeuvres become apparent. It was pathetic.

'What would you rather do then, Graham?' The use of his name was a giveaway. Her mum was spoiling for a fight. They hadn't had one for at least five or six hours, not since they'd got into the car to leave the house in Zurich. When Helen didn't receive a reply to her question, she asked another one.

'Would you rather go out to a restaurant? We could be photographed entering any number of restaurants, I'm sure.'

'Oh, Christ, Helen. Don't. All right?'

'What do you mean, "don't"?'

'It's Christmas Day. Everywhere will be either closed or fully booked. And yes, you're right, wherever we go, we run the risk of being followed and photographed.'

Even though it was her mother who had been using by far the more combative of tones, it was she who accused Graham of sounding angry.

'Graham, calm down. Let's try and keep this civil.'

'I'm not the one—'

Lily's stool scraped loudly on the kitchen floor as she pushed it back and both her parents turned to look at her as though they had forgotten she was there.

'I think I'll leave you to it,' she said.

Neither of them said anything, just watched her as she left the kitchen carrying her coffee cup. Grabbing one of her bags from the hallway, she started up the stairs. If she hung around for a moment she would probably be able to listen to them talking about her. They would discuss how alienated she was at the moment, how what was happening to the family was having a serious effect on her. Each would try to blame the other for causing her alienation without really giving a damn about her well-being at all. They just used her as a channel through which they could conduct further hostilities. When she reached her bedroom on the first floor, she could hear her mother's raised voice but she was far enough away from it that whatever she was saying was indecipherable.

Lily dropped her bag on the floor by the bed, put her coffee cup on the desk and went over to the window. The room didn't have much of a view. She had chosen it from all the other possible bedrooms on offer in the house for no other reason than it was the one that was located the furthest away from her parents' room. It looked out on to the house next door and almost directly into a child's room opposite. The child was probably about eight or nine by the look of the decorations on the walls. Lily only knew the child by sight because they never spoke to the neighbours, had nothing to do with them. But seeing the decorations and the toys on the floor made her nostalgic for her own childhood. She had loved Christmas when she was growing up. It was a magical time. But as far as she was concerned, this year, Christmas was cancelled.

She heard a sound from outside the window. It was loud enough to carry through the double-glazing. When she heard it again, she realised it was one of the goons down below on the terrace. He was clearing his throat. It was the one who had smiled at her earlier. Had he been watching her? There was no way he could have missed seeing her in her bedroom window. What a creep. She shut the blinds.

From her bag, she took out her MacBook Pro and opened it up. The broadband was as fast and reliable as ever and, moments later, she was online. She typed out a message to Nieve:

Just got back. What we doing tonight? Got to escape from my Ps. Driving me nuts. L x

She clicked *send* and lay back on the bed. It was going to be a tough negotiation with her parents but she had her argument all ready. She had been rehearsing it all morning on the plane. Her father would be as melodramatic as usual. He would say she was a kidnap risk. But her argument was that nobody would even know who she was, let alone what she looked like. The press hadn't been able to use any pictures of her since her dad had got his lawyers on the case. What pictures of her that had appeared had been pixelated. The first time it happened, she and Nieve had laughed about it. As it went on, it was less funny. The only picture of her that was on the web was taken when she was thirteen. She had completely different hair, no make-up, little-girl clothes. Her hair wasn't even the same colour as it was now. No one would recognise her.

If this approach didn't work then she had a backup. If her parents were so worried about her, she could take one of the goons as a bodyguard. That might work. The lecherous one who had been scoping her out would do.

She knew it would be tough to persuade them, but it had to be done. After all those weeks and months in Zurich, she needed a break from them, even if it was only for one night.

08:29 AM

11 Blenheim Terrace, Belgravia

Good security was all about instilling confidence in the client. A threat made by persons unknown was always frightening. The Poynters had been subject to a number of them over the past few months. It was up to Ronnie and his team to make sure the High Value Individual and his family felt safe. That was the most important task they had. Yes, it was good to be as unobtrusive as possible, but a constant outward visibility was also crucial. Graham Poynter's house was large. Its size was masked somewhat by its location in the centre of London. Each member of the team had his own sector to patrol. They could keep in constant contact via their digital walkie-talkies. Omega Security had invested in some nice kit in the past few years. Business was brisk. They were living through a time of fear and people were prepared to pay good money to feel safe.

Ronnie had had an argument with his cousin, Will, a couple of Christmases before. They had both had too much to drink and Ronnie had become angry when Will had suggested that the best marketing any security company could undertake was to scare its potential clientele. The more frightened people are, the more they will pay to keep their fear at bay. Ronnie had got angry because it was true. Thankfully their argument had soon been forgotten but his cousin's words had stayed with Ronnie. Every time he looked at Omega Security's marketing literature and website, he could see that scaring its potential customers was exactly what the company was doing. By its very existence, it was suggesting potential scenarios that its clientele should worry about.

Today at least, or for however long this contract lasted, Ronnie didn't have to feel as though he was exploiting people's fear. The Poynter family genuinely needed security. The money that Graham Poynter was spending on achieving that security was money well spent. There were people out there who wished him and his family ill. Yet, however much Ronnie knew that the Poynters had been threatened, the threats had, in all probability, been made my people on the Internet. The anonymity of the web always made people brave. Trolls felt safe to say whatever they wanted when hidden behind a mask. It's easy to threaten someone when you know that no one will ever be able to hold you to account for it. How many of those people would ever actually consider making the journey to someone's home to confront them physically, especially when there was the very real possibility that the person they were threatening might have made some sort of security provision? The chances were low. Ronnie knew that, statistically, it was extremely unlikely that someone would attempt to cause physical harm to the Poynter family. That wasn't to say that they should be anything other than vigilant and alert at all times; but, in reality, he knew that his presence there, and that of his colleagues, was really all just for show.

Ronnie was glad he had chosen to patrol the roof first. It was a stunning view over the streets of Belgravia. As he watched the people come and go from on high, he wondered what their stories might be. What had they done to live in this exclusive enclave? Was what they did worth so much more than what he did? These houses cost fifty times the price of his house, maybe more, maybe a hundred times. Was what these people did a hundred times more worthwhile than what he did? He had fought for his country, after all, defended his people. What had they done? It wasn't a rhetorical question; he honestly wanted to know. It was intriguing. He remembered reading *The Godfather* when he was a teenager. The quote at the start of the book had stayed with him ever since: 'Behind every great fortune there is a crime.' He could even remember the French novelist who Mario Puzo was quoting – Balzac. It was a great line. How true it was, he had no idea. The press certainly felt it was true in Graham Poynter's case. This made Ronnie feel better about the vast disparity in their personal fortunes. He might not have as much money as Graham Poynter – nothing like – but at least he could sleep at night.

08:32 AM

Negotiating Cell, Fortis Green Road, Muswell Hill

'Ray, listen to me, I want you to pour away the rest of the whisky. You getting drunk really isn't going to help things.'

'It isn't whisky anymore; it's vodka.'

'Whatever it is, can you please just get rid of it? Everything's going to be much easier to resolve if you're sober.'

'Whether I'm pissed or not doesn't alter anything.'

'Seriously, Ray, it does. The worst thing you can do is make difficult decisions when you've been drinking. I can tell you that from experience.'

'You a drinker too?'

'Not especially, but I've been involved in plenty of negotiations, many of which have involved people who have been drinking. Trust me on this: it never helps. It always makes things worse.'

'Things couldn't get much worse than this.'

'That's not true. You've been through a very frightening situation. You've been the victim of a crime—'

'And I've also committed a crime too, right?'

'I don't know that. You don't know that. We need to put an end to this situation and then we can resolve everything.'

'I'm not going anywhere until I've had assurances.'

Ray wasn't at the slurring stage. If anything, the alcohol was speeding up his metabolism. He was consumed with a jittery, belligerent confidence and self-righteousness. This might work in Ed's favour. If he could make Ray feel that what he had done was right and that he should fight to make the authorities feel the same, it might be beneficial to the negotiation. From his admittedly limited experience of Ray, he had managed to establish that he was a man who felt strongly about his 'rights'. A lifelong conservative, with both a large and a small *C*, he considered himself a libertarian – saw nothing wrong with keeping a gun in the house. It was his right to do so.

They were trying to make contact with Ray's ex-wife. She was the only family member, albeit an ex-family member, that might be available. But, even if they could get her to speak to Ray, Ed didn't hold out much hope of her being able to help. She was the mother of Ray's two beloved grown-up daughters, currently holidaying together in France, but it had been an acrimonious divorce and putting her on the line to her ex-husband might actually make things worse.

'Ray, I don't blame you wanting to know your legal

situation. It's totally understandable under the circumstances. But what you have to realise is that, whatever assurances I give you, it's impossible to prevent the law taking its course.'

'Well, fuck it then—'

'All I know is' – time to keep talking – 'holding Aiden hostage, like this, isn't going to help. The longer this goes on, the less likely it is that you're going to walk away free.'

'All I want to know is what's going to happen to me on account of the one I shot. The police must know. Either they're going to try to do me for it or they're not.'

'Ray, you know how this works; you're an intelligent man. It all has to go through the Crown Prosecution Service. A decision can't be made on the spot. The exact facts of the case need to be established.'

'Twisted, more like.'

'No, not twisted. The fact is, you haven't done anything wrong, have you?'

'No.'

'Well, in that case, you've got nothing to fear.'

'I don't have a licence for the gun.'

'OK . . .'

'The little bastard here will say that they were trying to give themselves up.'

'Were they trying to give themselves up?'

Ed winced as he asked the question. He was always guarded in a negotiation but, occasionally, lines crept out that hit the wrong note. He was worried that this was one of them. It wasn't up to him to decide the legality of the case. His job was to bring the situation to a close with the minimum loss of life. He worried that his question sounded as though he was trying to establish Ray's guilt. It was essential that Ray believed that Ed had no sway over the legal process.

Ray chuckled bitterly before he replied. 'This one will say that. The little bastard.'

It sounded as though Ray had kicked Aiden or struck him with the butt of the shotgun – it was difficult to say – but Ed heard a groan of pain. Ed had already asked if he could speak to Aiden but Ray had refused. Ray needed to feel that he was in control, and while Ed knew that at some stage he would need to wrest that control from him, now was not the time. He could hear Aiden's whimpers and that was enough to know that the hostage was alive and relatively unharmed.

'Ray. Listen to me. Everything that has happened up until now can be explained away in the light of the fact that you came under attack in your own home. But from here on in, I can't guarantee that will be the case. You need to come out. We need to talk about this. We want to hear from you what happened. All we want to do is talk to you, Ray.'

'OK, that's fine, Ed. I'll come out and talk to you.'

Ed didn't become hopeful when he heard Ray say this. It was obvious that Ray was building up to an impossible condition. Ed had conducted enough negotiations in his time to hear it coming.

'I'll put my gun down and walk out of the front door as soon as I get a cast-iron guarantee that I won't do time for this. Until such time as I get that assurance, there's no point us talking.' Before the line went dead, Ed heard a yelp as Aiden was struck once more.

09:13 AM

11 Blenheim Terrace, Belgravia

Graham took out his phone and spoke into it: 'Call Bob Rushwood.' Even saying the name made him feel a little sick. Bob was a man whose destiny was inextricably entwined in his. When things were going well – and how well they'd gone for nearly twenty years – Graham could overlook Bob's irritating demeanour. He would never be friends with Bob. Bob was an arsehole. But he could put up with him when all was rosy. Now, however, after all that had happened in the past few months, Graham couldn't even bring himself to think about Bob without feeling his innards contract and his blood pressure rise a click.

Back in the old days – just over three months ago – Graham would have made the call in front of Helen. Whatever the state of their marriage at any given time, he had had no secrets from her in terms of his business dealings. But now he felt the need to keep her away from what needed to be done. When he conducted business in front of her nowadays, it was as though she was listening to what he said and judging him. She commented on what he said sometimes. She would never have done that in the old days. So now, when he needed to talk about something important, he would move rooms and keep his voice down. Especially when he was talking to Bob.

'Hello?'

'Bob, it's me.'

'I told you not to call me on this line.'

'Just a quickie.'

'Oh, Jesus.'

'Where are you?'

'I'm not telling you.'

'Why not?'

Graham listened to Bob as he muttered a series of truncated expletives into the phone before he said, 'I'm in a rented house. I'm not going to tell you where on the phone.'

'OK; I'm sorry.'

'What do you want?'

'I just wanted to tell you that I'm back.'

'I know; you told me you were coming back.'

'Look, I can see you don't want to talk, so let's set up a meeting. Email me or something.'

'I will. Happy Christmas, eh?'

It was the most desultory and off-hand Christmas greeting that Graham had ever received and, for a moment, he felt like hanging up without responding. But he muttered a, 'Yeah, you too,' before finishing the call.

Graham couldn't understand it. When things were going well, the press spoke of Graham and Bob in the same breath. They were Stanmore Partners. It was the two of them. Graham was always the most high profile but that was because it was his job to be the company's frontman. He was better at the communications thing than Bob was. But this seemed to count for nothing when the company got into trouble. Bob kept his usual low profile and the media let him. It was like he didn't exist. Graham, on the other hand, had become the public face of the fund. Suddenly his private life was dragged into the open. The papers wanted to know what car he drove, the property he owned, the outrageous extravagances in which he and Helen indulged. They didn't seem to give a shit about Bob Rushwood. He was just the boring back-room guy, the numbers guy, and it was an image Bob was only too happy to encourage. Graham had allowed him to get away with it. But no more. It wasn't as though they had received different remuneration. They were compensated equally throughout the lifespan of the fund. So what if Graham had consumed his wealth more conspicuously than Bob had his? Whether Bob Rushwood liked it or not, Graham would ensure that they would fight, and possibly fall, together.

Bob Rushwood made himself comfortable on the sofa and propped the iPad against his knees. He tapped on the browser icon and the Google home page popped up on the screen. He typed his name into the text box and pressed the return button. The search results dropped down the screen. There was the usual Wikipedia page devoted to him that he had had an intern write for him a couple of years previously. It made no mention of Stanmore Partners' collapse, unlike Graham's Wikipedia page, which was updated on a seemingly daily basis and had already been the subject of a dispute about impartiality and mediation. Bob found a few references to himself on news sites but nothing of any substance. What articles there were appeared to be confined to profiles on financial blogs and online magazines concerned with the markets. In comparison to the amount of sites devoted to Graham, his web profile was miniscule.

It was something of a compulsion of late, scouring the web for mentions of himself. But unlike most people who indulged in a little 'ego surfing' – as he had heard it described – he wasn't hoping for mentions, he was dreading them. If his name could have been scrubbed from all literature, whether web- or print-based, then he would have been overjoyed. His anonymity was something that he guarded jealously and was the main reason for his anger at Graham for calling him directly on his mobile. Hackers could access anything nowadays. He changed his phone regularly; always bought pay-as-you-go rather than taking a contract. But he never felt safe. There were clever bastards out to get him and they never seemed to relent.

He shouldn't have answered Graham's call. The conversation had only succeeded in putting him in a bad mood. He had been hoping to escape from his troubles for a few days, take a small vacation. Graham Poynter had taken nearly all of the flak so far and Bob intended to keep it that way.

Bob scrolled down the page, surveying the search results. There didn't appear to be anything new. He considered doing a search under Graham's name but decided against it. Closing down the window, he opened up a video file he had downloaded and watched the night before of two women having sex. The scene was a little melodramatic but it would do. He had his morning all planned. After he was finished with the porn, he would start off with forty minutes of cardiovascular on the treadmill and the cross-trainer, then shower, sauna for twenty minutes or so, before taking another shower. Then he would get the call to the family out of the way. That would take about fifteen minutes or so and then he was free for the rest of the day. He might have a beer late morning. That sort of start time would worry him under normal circumstances – he was drinking more than he had in years – but it was Christmas. He had had the toughest year of his career; he deserved some down time. The next few days were a treat to himself. He had some movies he wanted to watch. Maybe a little more porn. He would make himself some lunch and just lounge for the afternoon. He had toyed with the idea of calling for a couple of girls. He hadn't had a threesome for a while. Maybe they could bring some coke with them? He hadn't had any of that for a while either. He worried for his heart. All the time he spent on the treadmill in the gym was nothing more than an attempt to assuage his fears on that front. The last time he had indulged in coke and hookers, he had spent the whole time trying to work out whether the pain he felt in his chest was a warning of an impending heart attack or just indigestion on account of the meze that he had called up from room service earlier.

The ultra-modern house that Bob had rented for his Christmas sojourn was in a quiet Hampstead residential street. It was accessed through a yard behind a tall electric gate. He had employed security when the news first broke of the fund's collapse but once Poynter had fled to Switzerland after he had become the focus of public opprobrium, Bob was pretty much in the clear. Following the fund's collapse, there were some hacktivists who had targeted him and tried to hack into his Stanmore Partners email account, as they had with Graham's. He had taken to using an anonymised email account for all his Internet transactions. He had been taking advice – expensive advice – from a number of Internet security specialists. It was a constant firefight against these parasites. You always had to try to stay one step ahead. As soon as you found yourself in the public eye then you were a target.

Bob's ex-wife, Marianne, and the children were in Florida for Christmas. He hadn't been invited and that suited him just fine. He chose the house he would spend Christmas in off the Internet and rented it through a corporate account that was unconnected to Stanmore Partners. No one else had been involved in the transaction apart from him and the rental agent – who was discretion personified – so no one would know of his location. He felt safe and secure. A housekeeper who would cook and clean had been included as part of the rental agreement but he insisted on being alone. He just wanted to take a holiday from his life, drink, maybe screw a couple of hookers and do what the hell he wanted for a few days with no one to answer to other than his own conscience.

09:24 AM

Mare Street, Hackney

The thirty pull-ups had made him feel good. Lucas enjoyed the sensation of his newly hardened muscles rubbing against the inside of his sweatshirt as he sauntered along the pavement. Once this was all over, maybe he would join a gym. Or better still, he could join a boxing club. He had always fancied himself as a fighter. He had done some judo at school but it was always boxing that had appealed to him. He was a decent size. Maybe middleweight or light heavyweight. He could look after himself. Not like some of those he worked alongside. They were proper geeks. But they seemed to stir up his paternal instincts. It appealed to him that he was protecting them in some way. They were conducting a fight that took place ninety-nine per cent of the time in virtual communities. But one per cent of it was something altogether different. That one per cent required direct action – violence, if necessary. Lucas liked the symmetry between the ninety-nine per cent and the one per cent. It fitted nicely alongside the organisation's terminology. Lucas was part of the one per cent that didn't believe the answers lay in non-violent protest.

Lucas turned off Mare Street into a side street and along the pavement to a garage lock-up. Whistling, a picture of nonchalance, he took out his keys, unlocked the door and stepped inside. The van was all bought and paid for. The road tax and insurance were up to date. He had a clean driving licence and no criminal record. There was nothing about him or the vehicle that could arouse any suspicion. Apart from one thing: the load space in the back of the van was filled from chassis-bed to ceiling with sacks of commercially produced ammonium nitrate fertiliser mixed with propane. There was a detonator too. But apart from its payload, the van was clean.

Lucas opened the door and climbed into the driver's seat. Starting the engine, he drove out of the lock-up. He couldn't be bothered to close the door. It wasn't as though he was ever going back.

09:25 AM

11 Blenheim Terrace, Belgravia

It was always the same when Lily used Skype. She ended up looking at the small image of herself in the corner of the screen more than she did the much larger image of the person – or people – she was speaking to. She hoped it didn't mean she was vain. She would ask Nieve what she thought. If she couldn't ask her best friend then who could she ask? But the moment passed. Nieve was far too keen to discuss the arrangements for that night.

'There'll be nowhere open. So we can head to Celeste's brother's place in Old Street.'

'Good,' said Lily, distracted.

'What about your parents?' asked Nieve.

'I'll tell them now.'

'Good luck with that.'

'I've just spent three months locked up with them in the most boring place on earth. If they don't let me go, I'll sue them.' Nieve laughed and Lily told her, 'I'll call you back.'

'Bye.'

Lily closed the on-screen window and shut the MacBook. She stood up and made for the door. It was now or never. As she made her way down the staircase, she could hear them in the living room, speaking to each other in that sullen, emotionless tone they employed when they were trying to be civil. It was imbued with a higher degree of mutual hatred than when they were shouting at each other. At least when they were rowing there was a degree of emotional honesty to it. The passive-aggressive stuff was just boring. But she had to suppress her feelings for a few moments, or at least until she had told them she was going out. She wasn't asking; it wasn't a question. She was informing them of her movements, that was all. She was ready for her dad's objections. She had run through a number of potential conversations in her mind and was ready for any of them, or as ready as she would ever be.

She didn't loiter in the doorway; it was better to show confidence. She walked through the door and approached the low table between the two opposing couches on which her parents sat. They both glanced up at her at the same time. They looked old and tired. For a moment, she felt like informing them of this, just to soften them up, but they had both had words with her recently about being rude to them.

'Nieve and her brother are going to collect me at eight.' Lily knew things were going to move fast after the opening gambit but she was caught off guard by the speed of her father's response.

'You're not going anywhere.'

'I'm seventeen years old. It's Christmas. I'm going to see some friends.'

'You're not going out, Lily.' This was her mother. She had expected her father's objections and had armed herself with a selection of responses to them. But her mother's objections she hadn't bargained on. She was looking up at Lily with that regretful smile. Like it was a done deal and she was oh-so-sorry about it. Well, it wasn't a done deal; Lily was going out. She ignored her mother and turned back to her father.

'Eight o'clock pick-up; I'll be back about . . . Well, late.' She knew she was pushing it with the 'late' line but she was all fired up. In for a penny, in for a pound, as her dad loved to say. Graham started to speak but she spoke over him: 'I'm prepared to take whatever precautions you want in order to guarantee my personal safety, but once that's sorted, I'm going out.'

It sounded good. She surprised herself at how well she had delivered the lines but unfortunately she had no more rehearsed material.

'Invite your friends round here,' said her dad. This she hadn't expected. Usually he was more than happy for her to conduct her social life off site, preferring to have the place to himself.

'No, we're meeting people.'

'Invite the people as well.'

This was too much for Helen, who looked at him as though he had grown a second head.

'I won't be too late. Just gone midnight, I would have thought.'

Lily's tactic was to keep talking as though their objections did not exist and she managed to maintain it until her father looked up at her and said, 'It's a no, Lil. I'm sorry.'

Lily could feel the anger rising. She had tried so hard to keep it down. She knew the argument was as good as lost when she started to speak and couldn't suppress her hostile, argumentative tone.

'Dad, I'm going out tonight at eight. That's it. If you want to stop me going, you're going to have to physically restrain me and, if you do that, I'll have you arrested. OK?' She had lost. As easy as that. The fact that she had lost was confirmed by the fact that her parents didn't say anything. They knew she had lost too. And, just to make things worse, her mother decided that now was the time to make one of her classically stupid comments.

'It's a family time,' she said.

The Radcliffe & Penny van pulled up to the kerb with James at the wheel. He climbed out, walked to the back door and opened it to check the address labels on the boxes inside. Finding the one he was looking for, he took it out, shut the doors and walked towards a large Regency house. He climbed the steps up to the front door and pressed the doorbell, which elicited a distant ringing sound from deep within. Footsteps approached and the door was opened by a young woman in her early twenties. She was fashionably dressed in flat shoes and skinny jeans, a polo neck and long hair pinned up to reveal a shapely neck and pretty pixie face.

'Delivery from Radcliffe & Penny,' said James as she looked at him with just the beginnings of a smile forming on her lips.

'Do I need to sign something?'

'Yes; here, please.' James held out the electronic signature console. She took the little stilo with slim, shapely fingers and scribbled her signature.

'Here you go.'

James pocketed the electronic machine and reached down to lift up the cardboard box, which she took from him.

'Thanks,' she said, the smile widening.

James smiled back and, seeing that she had her hands full, he reached out and pulled the door closed.

It was a killer smile. Her face had lit up. But there was something else to it. As he went back down the steps to the van, a vision was taking shape in his mind. They were undressing each other, casting their clothes off as the passion took hold.

'Happy Christmas,' he muttered under his breath as he climbed back into the van and banished the image with contemplation of his delivery schedule. Next stop, Chesham Place, Knightsbridge.

09:33 AM

Negotiating Cell, Fortis Green Road, Muswell Hill

There was something schoolmasterly about Keir, the cell co-ordinator. He smelled of spearmint and tweed. He was possessed of a calmness and concision that belied his age, which Ed guessed at being mid-thirties. There was something about the way that he spoke that made Ed think, rightly or wrongly, that he was wary of him. Ed's notoriety within the force had spread on account of the Tube hijack negotiation the year before. His exact involvement had never been established – at least not publically. If his name ever did crop up in a description of the operation – there were hacks knocking out true-crime books about it with varying degrees of seriousness – he was described as being part of a special forces operation and as such was not subject to the same forensic analysis as other aspects of the subsequent enquiry into the attack. But his legend within Scotland Yard and the world of hostage negotiation had grown considerably on account of that day, a year and a half before. He noticed that people treated him differently. Those who did know exactly what he had done respected him for the lives he had saved, but they also knew that the manner of his saving those lives reflected a dangerous maverick attitude that was bordering on the reckless. Some people warmed to that; others thought it worth applauding in hindsight but not to be encouraged in the future. Those in the latter camp – Keir included – were in the majority by a considerable ratio. Keir was a high-ranking officer from Thames Valley, an experienced detective and hostage negotiator, lectured at Hendon, all of that. And he was going to run a tight ship.

Ed got another blast of spearmint as Keir said, 'We tell him that he's not going to be prosecuted for acting in self-defence. That's true – to a point. But, at this stage, we tell him what he needs to hear.'

'That's not exactly what he asked for, though, is it?'

'Not exactly, but it's fair. If he did act in self-defence – as he claims – then, in that case, he has the law on his side. But if it is proved—'

'Or suspected,' Ed butted in.

'Or suspected that he didn't, then that will change things.'

'I worry we're going to get bogged down in legal detail.'

'Well, let's try it and see.' Keir spoke the words as though he might be suggesting areas of possible improvement in a pupil's school project.

'What if I overplay it?'

'What do you mean?'

'Well, what if I make it appear that he will walk free, regardless of the exact legal niceties.'

'We haven't had approval for that.'

'Well, if it gets him to walk out of the stronghold and end the siege then what harm has been done? You can blame it on me. I don't mind.'

Keir's voice raised in tone slightly for the first time. 'No, that's not a good idea.'

'Why not?'

'We can only follow the advice that we've been given.'

Ed decided to let it go. It wasn't worth arguing about. If he did, he would only be confirming his reputation of being difficult. He would behave. He would do the right thing. Besides, it might just work.

When the connection was made with Ray in the stronghold, he started his sales pitch.

'I've got some news for you, Ray. We've spoken to the commander and this has gone to the highest levels. I can assure you that you're not going to be prosecuted for acting in self-defence.' It sounded pretty good. Ray might have been searching for a get-out for his predicament and would clutch at it without dissecting its exact meaning. But this hope was shot down immediately with Ray's first question.

'Where's the proof?'

'I can get you proof if that's what you want, although the tape of this conversation will be made available to your legal counsel.'

'So I'll still need legal counsel?'

'Someone's died here, Ray. You're going to need legal representation but what we're saying is that you're not going to be prosecuted for acting in self-defence.'

'Self-defence as defined by who?'

Ray might have drunk plenty of whisky and vodka but he was not going to be fobbed off with half-hearted reassurances.

'Self-defence as defined by the ensuing investigation and the Crown Prosecution Service, I expect.'

'You expect?'

'Ray, I'm a negotiator. I'm not a legal expert.'

'But you're a copper, right?'

'Was.'

'Was?'

'I'm an adviser to the Met – a freelance negotiator.'

'So you're not even part of the fucking machine?'

Ed could feel Ray's emotional temperature rising. He needed to soothe things fast.

'Yes, I'm very much part of the machine. This is a police negotiation.'

'I want to speak to someone face to face. Someone who's in charge.'

'Ray, I'm in charge here. But if you want to speak to someone else then by all means we can arrange that.'

'All right; you'll do. I want to speak to you, face to face.'

'That's not going to be possible, Ray.'

'I don't give a shit whether it's possible or not. I want you in here in half an hour's time with a written statement that I won't be prosecuted for what I've done, otherwise this little shit gets it too, just like the other one.'

11 Blenheim Terrace, Belgravia

The French called it *'l'esprit d'escaliers'* – staircase wit – the things you wish you'd said as you're walking away from a situation. She'd thought of it so many times as she returned to her room after arguing with her parents, just like this. And the staircase wit only ever made her feel worse about whatever argument had just taken place because she always worried she hadn't fought as well as she might have. The problem her parents faced was that they just couldn't admit they'd screwed up. The great palace of miracles that was her father's career had come tumbling down and now they were left exposed in the glare of the media, floundering around in their own greed. She wished she'd told them she was ashamed of them just before she had turned around and walked out of the room. She had done once before; she would save it until next time.

When she arrived at her room, she flipped up the lid on the MacBook and put a Skype call in to Nieve.

'Hey, it's me,' she said as Nieve answered the call.

'How did it go?'

'What do you think?'

'Well, maybe they're right.'

'How could they ever be right about anything?'

'Well, if someone does want to get at your folks, you are a target.'

'Oh, not you as well.'

'Just saying.'

'OK, OK, I'm a social leper, I know it.'

'You know it's not that. Look, my folks want me downstairs for presents so I'd better go. Don't be pissed off. Call me later.'

'OK. Bye.'

Lily clicked off the call, rolled over and lay next to the MacBook, staring at the ceiling of her cell. They might as well throw away the key.

09:48 AM

Chesham Place, Knightsbridge

James knocked on the door. The woman who opened it was middle-aged, maybe fifty or so, but still beautiful. The day before, when he was making the deliveries, most of the people who answered the door appeared to be staff – housekeepers. But today, James thought, the staff were probably at home with their own families and it was the owners of the houses themselves that were coming to the doors.

She was dressed immaculately and she had a kind face. But despite her obvious wealth and lucky circumstances in life, it looked as though happiness was one commodity in short supply in her world.

When she scribbled on the signature console, she asked him, 'Are you working all day?'

'No, I finish at about three.'

'Good, well I hope you get to spend some time with your family.'

'Hopefully,' he said, knowing that he wouldn't.

He offered to carry the box into the kitchen but she said it was fine to leave it in the hallway. They wished each other a happy Christmas. As he walked down the steps from the house, he was stirred by very different feelings to the ones he had experienced at the previous house. He felt no lust but more of a burning curiosity to know the woman's story. What was it that had caused her to look so sad? She appeared to have so much, certainly enough to inoculate her against all the concerns and problems that others might feel. But everything was relative. As much as money might sweeten the bitterest of pills, emotions could not be bought. Shit still happened, even with lots of money in the bank.

James climbed back into his van and looked at the clock. It was 9:53 AM. He was ahead of schedule. He reached for the ignition key, then thought better of it and sat looking out of the window at the houses all around. He didn't need to be anywhere for a few minutes at least. There was no point rushing.

09:58 AM

Basement of 11 Blenheim Terrace, Belgravia

Being six feet six inches tall, Danny found it difficult to
achieve any degree of comfort in his hiding place. He could
neither stand nor stretch out fully in the confines of the
cupboard. But what it lacked in space, it more than made
up for in terms of concealment. Little would anyone realise
that behind the door of the fitted cupboard, in the darkest
part of the basement, was former S.A.S. senior N.C.O. Danny
McAteer.

The cupboard was empty and had seemingly never been
used. It was just another of those pricy little added extras
that the developers had included in order to relieve the
owners of the house of further cash. The same went for the
C.C.T.V. monitors that relayed black-and-white images of the
garden and various corridors in the house above. Danny
had heard one of the security team come down earlier to
take a look at them. The reality of what Danny was about
to do had been brought into needle-sharp focus when he

listened to the man as he looked at the console. He was whistling 'I Believe in Father Christmas' by Greg Lake. It was a guilty pleasure of Danny's. The best Christmas song. The turmoil that Danny felt, the guilt, the pain – both physical and mental – were almost too much to bear. But he knew how to suppress his feelings. He was on a mission. It was like the old days. Nothing else mattered. He had to blot it all out.

The security guard was long gone by the time Danny stepped out of his hiding place and made his way across the basement to the door which lead to the stairs up to the ground-floor hallway. Taking out his iPhone, he made sure it was on silent as he switched it on and waited for it to connect to a mobile network. There were four missed calls, all from his wife, Jan. He knew she would be trying to get hold of him by now. He opened up the web browser and clicked on the link which took him through to the home page of the bank account in the Cayman Islands. He tapped in his user name and password and the screen opened into the account. Five thousand U.S. dollars had had to be paid in to open it and that figure had confronted him on the few occasions that he had accessed the account in the past. But now the number had changed: to the five grand had been added two and a half million U.S. dollars.

Danny let out a long sigh. Up until this moment, he knew he could turn back. This entire mission had consisted of nothing more than messages and phone calls, planning, strategy and reconnaissance. It was all theoretical. But there, on his iPhone, was living proof that the theory had come to an end. Yet even now, even with the money in the account, he could turn back if he really wanted to. He would be putting his family in danger by doing so, but it was still possible if that was what he wanted. The fact was that he didn't. Throughout what was to come, he would think of Jan and Emily. They were the most important people now. Whatever he did – however emotionally gruelling it might become – he was doing all this for them, to make their lives better.

Danny walked over to the C.C.T.V. consoles and checked for the positions of the security guards. There was one in the garden, one on the terrace that ran around the rear of the house and one on the roof. He opened the door and walked up the stairs. He stood behind the door set into the panelling under the main staircase. Having spent hours studying the layout of the house from the plans he had been provided with, his orientation within the building had become almost second nature. He listened at the door for a moment and then very slowly opened it a few inches, just enough to peer out. There was no one in the hall. He could hear voices from the living room and the sound of a television tuned to a news channel.

Stepping out of the doorway, he pulled the door shut after him. Thankfully, he paused for a moment and listened again. If he had not done so, he would not have heard the soft footsteps coming down the stairs. It was Lily Poynter, the daughter. By the time she turned to take the final flight of stairs, Danny was back behind the cellar door listening to the soft padding sound of her bare feet on the tiled hallway floor. Danny managed to watch her through a crack in the door and saw that she was wearing a tracksuit and carrying a towel. She was on her way to the swimming pool, which was accessed via a door leading off the kitchen.

Danny stepped out from behind the door once again, closed it behind him and made his way across the hallway.

10:02 AM

Lyall Street, Belgravia

Lucas pulled up next to a police minibus. He looked at the driver; he didn't look much older than him. The bloke's boredom was clear. Given the choice between driving a police van around the West End on Christmas morning or having a lie-in and waking up to presents and a turkey dinner, it was clear where this guy wanted to be. Lucas, on the other hand, didn't want to be anywhere else. He was happy right where he was. Unless the police van had sniffer dogs in it, of course. But it didn't; it was just a minibus; there were no cages. It was an eventuality that he hadn't really considered, having his cargo detected by passing sniffer dogs, but thankfully he wouldn't need to consider it now, as his journey was almost at an end.

As the lights changed and he let the minibus pull away from him, he looked for the road sign on the right and there it was: Blenheim Terrace. Exactly where Google Maps had said it would be. He was pleased to see that there were a few parking spaces. He chose one in a pay-and-display bay, its regulations not in force due to it being Christmas Day. He was glad to be parked legally; he didn't like to break the law. It attracted attention. Anonymity was not just a tactical necessity, it made life easier all round.

Lucas climbed out of the van and shut the door. Everywhere was quiet. There was a family getting into a car further down the street. In the other direction, a woman was walking east towards Grosvenor Place. A car went past: a Jaguar. Nice car. Lucas yawned and stretched. He walked to the back of the van and opened up the door a few inches. The gap didn't need to be wide, just wide enough for him to reach his hand inside and switch on the remote control receiver on the detonator. With the red light winking off and on in the darkness, he shut the van door and locked up with the key fob. The door locks dropped into place with a thunk and the indicators flashed three times. Lucas glanced around – still no one about – and walked east along Blenheim Terrace.

10:07 AM

11 Blenheim Terrace, Belgravia

The pool heating had been on since seven o'clock that morning. The water should have been warm by now. Lily pulled up the leg of her tracksuit bottoms and broke the still surface with her foot. It wasn't quite as warm as she had hoped but it was fine. At least something appeared to be going right. She took off the tracksuit and put it on a sun lounger by the door to the sauna. She might fire that up later too. If she was going to be imprisoned in the house then she might as well enjoy herself. The tracksuit was a favourite – Juicy Couture. She'd had it for a couple of years and she could quite happily live in it, if allowed to. She shivered without it as she walked towards the pool in her swimming costume.

The inclusion of the swimming pool and spa in a conservatory annexe off the kitchen was one decision her parents had made in which she couldn't find fault. She loved swimming but she didn't like swimming with other people. Public swimming pools were hideous places with their disinfectant smell and pale, out-of-shape bodies always getting in the way. She knew she was spoiled. But what did spoiled mean exactly? Was it to be taken literally? Did it mean that her character had been impaired by over-indulgence? Because, if that was the case, it was only the massive houses, the swimming pools and the expensive education that had done it. There had certainly been no emotional over-indulgence shown to her by her parents. There was no chance of being spoiled in that regard.

She sat on the edge of the pool with her legs in the water while she pulled on her goggles and nose clip. She tipped forward into the water with a gentle splash and started to swim. Front crawl. Occasionally she would do a length in breaststroke or on her back, but mostly it was front crawl. She enjoyed the rhythm of the strokes and the flow that she achieved. She enjoyed the feeling of her face being submerged between breaths, all sound blocked out, just the rush of the water and the sight of the clear aquamarine against the turquoise-and-white mosaics of the pool walls and the powerful lights set into them.

Swimming lengths in an empty pool allowed her to slip into an almost trance-like state and always provided her with a sense of calm. It was her way of meditating. But this morning it was difficult. She was up to her fifth length and there were too many thoughts clamouring for attention.

Her stomach was tense after the argument with her parents. While, moments after the argument, she had wished she'd said more and been more vicious in her attack, now she wished she had said less. She had hurt them. They deserved it – sure they did – but it was pointless. All she had succeeded in doing by blowing up at them was to bring yet more angst and stress into all their lives. There was enough of that already. She had made a promise to herself when they were in Zurich that she would opt out of traditional family communication; she would refuse to speak the language of antagonism and incitement. She didn't want to be like her parents. The thought of ending up anything like them was abhorrent.

She had decided on Edinburgh University. She had gone up with some friends to the Fringe Festival the year before and had loved it. It was also far enough away from London to make it awkward for too many visits either by or to her parents. But before Edinburgh, she wanted to go travelling. She wanted to see the Far East and Asia. She was going with Nieve. They'd start off in Indonesia or Thailand and take it from there. She thought of it as a spiritual detox. She wanted to cleanse herself of all the bad karma that she had collected over the past couple of years.

10:08 AM

Negotiating Cell, Fortis Green Road, Muswell Hill

'He's scared and vulnerable – of course he is – but he's also drunk. He's full of whisky and vodka, which means that his thinking has been flooded with self-pity. He's living up to his sentimental vision of himself as an underdog: the little guy, rising up to be a warrior. He's also in shock. Killing someone does things to your mind. So we need to keep everything as simple and straightforward as possible. If I can go in there—'

'It's not going to happen, Ed.' Keir's calm façade was beginning to slip. He was speaking more quickly; he had started on another piece of gum and the spearmint was blasting afresh.

'But if that's what it takes . . .'

'I've asked the question. It's been discussed but we can't sanction it. That needs to be communicated to Ray.'

There was no point arguing. Without the go-ahead from on high they were stumped. Ed knew Keir was watching him. What he was seeing, Ed would never know. Ed felt his watch. The half-hour deadline that Ray had given him had expired a couple of minutes before.

'Let's get Ray on the line.' Ed pulled his headset into place. The call was answered immediately.

'Ed?'

He sounded desperate. Ray needed this situation to be resolved, one way or another, as quickly as possible. He was crumbling under the pressure. Ed knew things could go either way. If only there had been no alcohol in the house; if only they would allow him to go in.

'Yeah, Ray, it's me.'

'Well?'

'I'm not going to be able to come in and see you. They won't allow it.'

'Why?'

'The thing is, Ray, I'm blind, so I can't make my way in on my own. That means an officer has to come with me. If that happens, we would have to ensure you were unarmed. You would have to throw out the gun. Then I can come and see you.'

'Fuck that. Fuck it!'

'Think about it, Ray. This doesn't alter anything. I'm happy to come and talk to you but you can't be armed.'

'I'll throw out one of the guns.'

'So you've got more than one?'

'Yeah.'

This was significant. Earlier in the negotiation, Ray had refused to answer whether he had any other weapons. Now he was saying that he did. Either he did have one, or he was lying and he would throw out his only gun while hoping to prolong his negotiation with just the threat of another possible weapon. Ray didn't come across as the sort of man who would have more than one unlicensed weapon. The shotgun had probably been in the family for years. It was understandable that he might not have sorted out the necessary paperwork for it. Ed felt sure there was no other weapon. This was a good sign. Ray was, in effect, offering to put down his only weapon on the condition that someone came into the stronghold to talk to him face to face.

'Hold on, Ray, I need to speak to someone about this. You just stay on the line, OK? I'll be about a minute.'

'OK.'

At times like this, Ed couldn't help but feel as though he was working in some sort of call centre for the psychotic and desperate. He was the last call-centre operative some people ever got to speak to. If he couldn't resolve their issues, then no one could.

Ed signalled for the call to be put on hold and he pulled off his headset. But before he could speak, Keir was hissing at him. 'He's playing you, Ed. You're falling in.'

'Listen for a moment; he's only got one gun, I'm sure of

it. He throws that out, then he's disarmed and I go in and talk to him. This can work.'

'No, Ed. He puts his weapons down. He's telling us he's got more than one weapon, so we need to see that weapon too before any attempt is made to enter the stronghold either by you or anyone else. That's the deal.'

Ed didn't have time to argue. They were in danger of losing control of the negotiation. He signalled for the line to be opened.

'Ray, we need all weapons out before I can come in.'

'That's not going to happen.'

'Listen, Ray, with the greatest respect, I think me coming in there is a distraction. You've done nothing wrong here. Not yet. But if you continue holding Aiden hostage then you will have done.' Ed paused, giving Ray an opportunity to jump in, but he didn't take it, so he continued. 'Let's put an end to this now and get you out of there. I realise that you feel very strongly about your legal situation. So you need to allow yourself a platform from which you can voice those concerns. You can represent all the other people who have found themselves in this situation. You can be their spokesman. Now you owe it to yourself and to them to put an end to this.'

No reply. For a man who was so keen to communicate earlier, this was a worrying development.

'Ray, please respond. I need to hear what you want to do. I want to hear if you're going to stand up and be counted.

I want to hear you're going to fight for your cause and demonstrate to the people of this country that what you did in protecting your home was the right thing to do. Ray, please let me know you can hear me.'

There was silence on the line. There weren't any background noises. Was he even there? Ed shifted in his seat. This was a dangerous stage of the negotiation. It was essential that he kept calm and didn't allow any hint of desperation or exasperation to enter his voice.

'Ray? Are you there?'

'I'm here and I hear what you're saying. I know what you're doing. I've seen the films and T.V. shows. It all sounds great. But I'm not prepared to take the risk. I don't want to go down for this. You can have this little shit. You can have him; I'm past caring.'

Ed knew that as soon as his suspicions were alerted that a perpetrator was in danger of committing suicide, he should voice those concerns, get them out in the open.

'Ray, I'm worried you're going to do something silly.'

'It's not silly.'

Ed stood up. 'Ray, listen to me. We need to talk about you coming out of there and airing your grievances. Now, how can I make that happen?'

'You know how you can make that happen. You've known all along. I keep telling you. All I need is a cast-iron guarantee that I'm going to walk free. That's all I ask.'

'And I can give you that guarantee. You were acting in self-defence, so no charges will be brought.'

'But I have to go to court for that to happen, right?'

'Ray, I can't change the laws of the land. Facts have to be established and that process takes place in a court.'

'A court,' Ray repeated the word.

'But that court also provides you with a platform to express your concerns about the system; you can tell the world what you think about the law and how it should be changed.'

'And also risk going to jail.'

'Every time a defendant ever steps foot in a court of law, there's always a risk that the proceedings won't pan out as they might have hoped, but you've got the strongest defence that I can think of.'

Ray was going to do one of three things. He was going to walk out of the stronghold and give himself up; or he was going to commit suicide; or he was going to commit homicide and then suicide.

'Think of your daughters, Ray. How do you think they want to see this end? They want to see their dad walk away from this with his head held high, fighting for what he believes to be right.'

'They hate me.'

'Why do you say that?'

'Cos they do.'

'Of course they don't.'

'Their bitch of a mother has turned them against me.'

'I don't believe it.'

'Believe what you fucking like, Mr Negotiator. My life's fucked enough already and now I'm going to be made to go to jail for it. Well, no; this ends now.'

'Ray, talk to me.'

There was no reply just a shuffling sound followed by a click.

'Ray! Talk to me; don't make a rash decision that your kids are going to have to live with for the rest of their lives. Ray, are you there?'

There was a gunshot.

10:09 AM

11 Blenheim Terrace, Belgravia

Danny could hear the voices of the husband and wife coming from the living room. He thought the daughter was probably in the pool by now. As he opened the door to the garden terrace, he could only just make it out, but it was unmistakable: Slade's 'Merry Christmas Everybody'. There were excited children's voices occasionally piercing the music amidst the almost imperceptible background hum of distant London traffic.

Through the gap in the door he could see the target – the security guard – at the end of the terrace, looking out over the garden. He was approximately fifteen feet away. It was still early and he was being more vigilant than he would be later when the boredom would have set in; that was the problem with that line of work. He was facing outwards, looking across the garden, safe in his mind that any attempt to enter the garden would come from outside the perimeter.

As he turned and started to walk back along the terrace, Danny pulled the door to. In approximately ten seconds, the target would be less than six feet away from him as he passed the door on his patrol. All being well, he would still face the garden, allowing Danny a window of opportunity of no more than a second in duration in which to do what had to be done.

As he took the hunting knife from its scabbard, Danny counted down. His heart was thumping but all worries as to the morality of what he was doing had gone now. His mission had started and he was acutely focused on the task at hand. He knew that he didn't have time to prevent the target from turning around and seeing him, so he needed to make the kill before a weapon could be raised. He opened the door and moved fast. The target was in position, turning towards him as anticipated. Danny's forehead cracked against the man's face but, as the man's head recoiled backwards, Danny's hunting knife interrupted its trajectory and as Danny pressed his forehead harder and harder against his victim's, the blade of the knife cut through his spinal cord. To someone watching from a distance, it would have appeared as though they were carrying out some sort of social ritual – kissing, even. By the time Danny had finished crushing his forehead against the man's face, however, and driving the blade of the knife into the top of his spine, the man was dead and had failed to take any evasive action or make any sound.

Danny pulled the blade out of the body and lowered it gently to the ground. Moving along the terrace, he caught sight of the second target. He was standing in the garden, near the perimeter fence. Danny glanced up to check that he was not visible from the roof, then jumped over the balustrade into the bushes below. Crawling on his stomach across the soil, he managed to peer out at the target. In a few seconds, his patrol would bring him within striking distance. Danny waited. Twenty seconds, thirty. He took out the cheese wire and held it taught. He was lucky, the man came close to the hedge and before he realised that he was in trouble his neck had been severed to the bone. One more guard and the first part of Danny's mission would be at an end.

10:16 AM

11 Blenheim Terrace, Belgravia

Graham stood watching the news on the television, holding the remote control console as though it was a weapon and he might leap forward at the first sign of attack and beat the perpetrator with it. He always hogged it. He was flicking through the digital options on the B.B.C. News Channel, checking to see if there was any mention of their return to London.

'"Disgraced hedge-fund supremo returns to London with family" – is that what you're looking for?'

'Don't take the piss.'

'Are you secretly a bit hurt that you've not made the grade?'

He didn't respond.

Maybe she was losing her touch. '"Disgraced hedge-fund supremo upset that he didn't make the news—"'

'Shut up!'

She muttered, 'Prick,' under her breath, loud enough for him to hear.

Graham turned around, still holding the remote control console. He looked as though he would have liked to switch her off with it.

'Is that what we've come to? Muttering offensive remarks and comments? Helen, that's pathetic. *You're* pathetic.'

Yes, she still had it. It might have required a little outright abuse but she could still get a reaction from him. She didn't say anything, just stared him down until he turned back to the television, shaking his head, as though disappointed in her. Like he had the right to be disappointed in anyone. She would repress the urge to continue with the name-calling. She would wait until she had thought of something much more strategic.

She watched him standing there, his eyes flicking from the remote control to the television, but her surveillance of him was interrupted by the sound of the doorbell. One of the guards would get it, but force of habit made her look up. If a visitor stood back from the doorbell, they were sometimes just visible through the right-hand living-room window. As she looked through the glass, a large object crashed into the railings from above. Any confusion as to what the object was, however, was immediately banished by the blood erupting from it and splashing against the window.

'What the fuck was that?' said Graham as Helen jumped to her feet and stood next to him.

'Oh my God! It's one of the security guards,' said Helen. 'Has he fallen?'

'People like that don't fall.'

'Should we call an ambulance?'

'No.' Graham's voice had become whispery and high pitched. 'We get in the safe room and we find out what's going on from there.' Graham dropped the remote control console to the floor and rushed towards the door. 'Come on; we've got to go,' he hissed, as he turned back to Helen, who hadn't moved.

'But what about Lily?'

'She's in her room; we can get her on the way.'

Graham suddenly cowered and turned back. Heavy thudding footsteps emanated from the hallway as someone bounded down the stairs, taking two steps at a time.

'Who the fuck is that?' whispered Graham.

'One of the guards?' mouthed Helen.

Graham took her arm and pulled her through the dining room to the doorway. He put his head around the doorframe and, seeing there was no one there, he led Helen along the corridor to the narrow back stairway. Helen followed him up the stairs until Graham gestured for her to hang back as he checked there was no one on the first-floor landing. Content that all was clear, he took her hand and they hurried to Lily's room.

'Shit,' said Graham through gritted teeth when he saw the room was empty.

'We have to get her,' said Helen, without any attempt to lower her voice.

'Not so loud,' hissed Graham.

'She'll have gone for a swim.' Helen moved towards the door but Graham held her by the arms. He looked down at her, his eyes wide, pupils massive, every cell in his body vibrating with fear. Looking at him, she knew that she and Graham were going to react to the threat they faced in very different ways.

'We get in the safe room, now,' he said, his face only inches from hers, his breath metallic and sour.

'I'm not getting in there without her.'

'Yes, you fucking are.'

Graham wasn't tall and she would never describe him as athletic but he was strong enough to drag her along the landing into one of the guest rooms and what appeared to be a fitted wardrobe that was the entrance to the safe room. She resisted him, fought back and struggled as hard as she could.

'Get off me. Get the fuck off me!'

The nearer they came to the safe room, the less Helen cared whether she was heard or not. By the time Graham had the thick metal door open, she was shrieking at him. But he managed to give her a shove that sent her stumbling to her knees in the small room, which was illuminated by a harsh white light. Before she could get to her feet and try to stop him, Graham had slammed the door shut. She flew at him, punching and kicking.

'Open the fucking door.'

Graham pushed her backwards and she tripped and landed in a chair.

'Shut up!' She felt a spray of spittle as he shouted the words into her face. 'We'll get her. I just need to do this first.'

'You make one fucking call and then we get her.'

He nodded, snatching up one of two phone handsets set into a console on a small white table that ran along one side of the room. There were numbers written on a laminated noticeboard on the wall above the table. He read one of them, muttering it to himself as he dialled the number. He was shaking and sweating. She couldn't bear to look at him for a moment longer and turned away. It felt as though there was a great pressure on her chest. She couldn't catch her breath. The air was dusty and stale in the room. She had only ever been in it a few times before. The first time was when it was completed and then a couple of times when they were showing it off to friends. It gave her the creeps. Now she felt as though she might pass out. She took some deep breaths as she looked up and watched her husband as he started to speak into the phone.

'This is Graham Poynter. I'm calling from the safe room in number eleven, Blenheim Terrace. We need help immediately.'

10:16 AM

11 Blenheim Terrace, Belgravia

James stood outside another large, glossily painted front door and rang the doorbell, this one a large brass affair set into the cream paintwork. He could hear raised voices through the windows at the front of the house. A man and a woman were having an argument. A third voice cut across the two emanating from the living room. It was a shout from above and it was followed almost immediately by a movement to James's right which made him turn to see the body of a man slam into the spiked railings near to where he stood. Blood burst from the body, some of it spattering in warm flecks across his face. Dabbing at his cheek and seeing the red that came away on his fingers, he wiped his hand on his trousers. Glancing across at the body, he could see that the tops of four railings had passed through it. The body wasn't entirely still; one foot trembled and kicked out momentarily. But the man was clearly dead. James looked to see if anyone else in the street had been witness to this hideous spectacle. A car drove past but didn't stop. Someone was playing Christmas music nearby.

From within the house, he could hear footsteps along the hall and the door was opened from within to reveal a huge figure dressed in black paramilitary clothing and wearing a balaclava. The eyes stared down at James from the apertures in the tight-fitting balaclava. A fist smashed the Radcliffe & Penny box from his hands and it broke open, spilling its contents down the steps in a mess of expensive food. The man reached out, grabbed hold of James and dragged him inside the house, slamming the door after him.

10:22 AM

11 Blenheim Terrace, Belgravia

The only time her body touched anything solid was when she tumbled at the end of each length and pushed off from the wall of the pool with her feet. Lily loved the feeling of moving through the water. She couldn't remember how many lengths she had done. She had lost count after twenty. She was oblivious to the outer world, lost in her thoughts and the warm tunnel of water through which she slid.

She tumbled and pushed off from the end of the pool but, as she did so, a hand reached down and grabbed her by the ankle. The shock made her choke as she spun around to see a huge figure dressed in black and wearing a balaclava. Taking hold of her other ankle, he pulled her from the water so she was almost completely upside down before he lowered her to the side of the pool and threw her tracksuit at her.

'Put it on now. Fast.'

She was still coughing as she pulled on her hoody top and then the tracksuit bottoms. The man was enormous and the balaclava made him look as though he had stepped fully formed from a nightmare. He wasn't alone. With him was a man in his early twenties, dressed in some sort of uniform. His face was entirely emotionless as he stared at the ground. His eyes, however, betrayed his fear. He was a hostage too. She felt like throwing up.

It was difficult pulling on the tracksuit bottoms over her wet skin but, once she had managed it, she stood up and the giant said, 'Hurry,' and loomed behind her, encouraging her to walk faster with the occasional push.

'Stairs,' he said as he gave her shoulder a nudge with his hand.

Where were her parents? She couldn't hear anything. All was quiet. Maybe they had made it into the safe room. Maybe the giant had killed them already; maybe she was going to be killed now. It was impossible to think straight. It felt as though someone had thrown a switch and reality had gone haywire.

'Where are we going?' asked the man in the uniform, who was also being steered through the house with prods and nudges next to Lily.

'No talking.'

Lily knew where they were going. The giant took them up to the first floor, along the landing to her bedroom and then into the spare room opposite. He shepherded them to the fitted wardrobe doors that were intended to conceal the entrance to the safe room. He took out an iPhone and called a number. He raised the phone to his ear, waited a moment then passed the phone to Lily. As she took it, he said, 'Tell your dad to open the door, otherwise I'm going to kill you in ten seconds' time. After you've told him that, I want you to count down from ten to zero. Let's hope you don't make it to zero.'

10:28 AM

Safe Room, 11 Blenheim Terrace, Belgravia

Graham put down the telephone. The police were on their way. Whatever was going on out there, no one could get to them in the safe room. The whole thing might very well turn out to be something of nothing. The guy might have fallen off the roof. The footsteps they heard on the stairs might have been another of the security guards coming to investigate. But it didn't feel like it was nothing. It felt all too real. And where was Lily? Helen was screaming at him, as of course any mother would in the same situation. But he knew it was madness to go out there until he knew that the house had been secured. If there was someone out there who wanted to do them harm then going out to find Lily was foolhardy in the extreme.

'Graham, for Christ's sake, we've got to find her.'

'If there is something weird going on – and we don't know

that yet – then the police are going to be able to do far more for her than we can.'

'I can't believe I'm hearing this. Your own daughter . . .'

She would try to shame him, he knew that. He was prepared for it but he still wasn't opening the door.

One of the two phones on the console rang. He snatched it up.

'Hello?'

'Dad, it's me.'

'Lily.'

Hearing this, Helen stood next to him, holding her head next to the receiver so as to hear her daughter.

'Dad. Listen to me. You've got to open the door.'

'Yes, we'll open the door,' said Helen.

'Is someone with you?' asked Graham.

'Dad, if you don't open the door in ten seconds, there's a man here says he's going to kill me.'

'Lily!' Helen was going to become hysterical again. Graham pulled the phone out of her grasp. Since they had entered the safe room, he had felt some of his old fighting spirit return. He was going to beat these bastards. These scum-bags, whoever they were, they were bluffing. He hadn't installed a state-of-the-art safe room in his home just to open the door and let them in.

'Listen, Lily,' he said. 'You tell whoever's got you that, if they touch a hair on your head—'

'Ten.'

'Let me speak to them, Lily.'

'Nine.'

'What are you doing?' shouted Helen making a grab for the receiver. Graham turned away from her.

'Eight.'

'Stop counting down, Lily, and tell whoever you're with that I want to speak to them.'

A moment's hesitation and then, 'Seven.'

'Lily?'

'Six.'

'I know about the Anchorage account,' said Helen.

'Five.'

'If you don't open the door, I'll tell the police.'

'Four.' His daughter's voice cracked with emotion. But his mind was stuck. How did Helen know about the Anchorage account? No one knew about that. No one other than him and Bob Rushwood.

'Three.'

'Open the fucking door, Graham!' Helen's voice was little more than a screech. She was trying to force the door release catch but she was turning it the wrong way.

'Two.'

Lily's voice became faint. Graham couldn't move.

'One.' She whispered the word just as Helen managed to turn the handle the right way and the door clicked open.

10:30 AM

11 Blenheim Terrace, Belgravia

What would have been a 'zero', if she could have said it without choking, came out as a gasping sob. As the door clicked open and swung back, she fell into her mother's arms.

'What the hell is going on?' asked Graham from within the safe room. It was pathetic. Under different circumstances, she might have laughed. He was attempting his authoritative voice. She had heard him use it so many times over the years, both with her and her mother, and also business associates on the phone. It often seemed to work with people who didn't know him. It obviously did – his success was testament to that. But it didn't work with her. It just made him sound like a jerk and she had a feeling that the giant, who was ushering the delivery man into the safe room and then stepping inside and pulling the door after them, thought the same.

'Who are you?' Still the confident, aggressive tone in her father's voice but the question didn't even receive a reply. The giant shut the door and secured it. Lily sobbed against her mother's chest but she was watching her dad. He looked terrified as he came face to face with this enormously threatening physical presence.

'It's very important that you listen to what I've got to say,' said the man.

'I said, who are you?' Graham was convincing no one, especially as his question was accompanied by a wobble of the bottom lip. Rather than present a façade of strength imbued with an implicit threat that he might launch some form of counter-attack, he succeeded in doing nothing other than give the impression that he might very well burst into tears.

When he spoke, the man addressed him directly. 'Now, listen, Graham, I realise this is a stressful situation but you're going to listen to me and you're not going to interrupt, O.K.? Because you have to realise that you and your family are in extreme danger here.'

They were looking into each other's eyes. Graham looked down first.

'Have you got that?'

'Yeah, I've got it.' Her dad's voice was soft and reedy.

'Good. Now I'll get straight to the point. I've already killed three men this morning: the three security guards that you hired to protect you. As of now and until such time as you are relieved of the description by future events, you are my hostages. This means you will do exactly as I say. If you don't, then there's no question: you will die. Have you got that? I want each of you to let me know that you agree.'

The man stared at Graham, who nodded.

He turned to Helen, who said, 'Yes.'

'I'm nothing to do with this,' said the delivery driver. 'I don't know what's going on here.' The young guy spoke with confidence. His voice wasn't choked by fear and emotion.

'You're going nowhere. Do you understand?'

The man in the Radcliffe & Penny uniform nodded.

It was Lily's turn. She pulled away from her mother, stood up straight and, looking into the dark eyes peering at her from the holes in the balaclava, she nodded.

'Good. Now, this is what's going to happen. We haven't got much space in here but I suggest we spread out. You four take the chairs and sit up at that end of the room. I'm going to sit here on the table with the phones. We need to get comfortable because we may need to be here for some time.'

Lily, her mother and father, and the delivery driver shuffled along the room and sat on the small wooden chairs, their knees touching each other's in the confined space. The giant sat on the table. Throughout the entire hostage-taking, Lily had seen no weapon. He didn't need a weapon;

his size and strength were enough. On his back he wore a small rucksack, which he kept on as he sat on the table and picked up one of the phone handsets.

10:38 AM

Negotiating Cell, Fortis Green Road, Muswell Hill

'They're bringing him out now, Ed,' said Keir.

Ed didn't want to be there when they brought out the body. It was too painful. Negative resolutions to situations like this were always difficult but so much more so when the death was avoidable. Keir employed the tone of voice he probably used when talking to mourners at a funeral of a distant relative. It was telling Ed that he felt his pain. It was Ed's fault, after all. It was he who was talking to the subject when he shot himself. Ultimately, it was all down to Ed. Keir's smug demeanour made Ed keep his mouth shut. He knew from past experience that, if he pursued any form of conversation with Keir, he was in danger of saying something inappropriate. He knew if he had been allowed into the stronghold to talk to Ray face to face, he might have changed the outcome of the negotiation. And he felt sure that Keir's own reluctance to sanction the plan had soured its potential acceptance when discussed with the on-scene commander. Which meant that Ed couldn't help but feel that, if anyone should be getting the there-there, pat-on-head treatment, it should be Keir. Ed felt sure he could have saved Ray, but the fact that he hadn't was something for which Keir was determined to blame him.

'I can honestly say I don't think we could have done any more. Sometimes you just can't stop people killing themselves. We have no real idea of what issues were at work.'

Ed could have done without the lesson. He felt sure he had taken part in many more hostage negotiations than Keir. But even thinking that thought made him feel childish and wretched. He wasn't on the force anymore. He was a freelancer on his first job. He needed to keep his opinions to himself. There was no point alienating people who might provide him with work in the future. Pragmatism had never been a strong point. His unsolicited opinions had often got him into trouble in the past. He was determined that shouldn't happen now.

'You're absolutely right, Keir. We mustn't blame ourselves.'

What a two-faced bastard he was. But what the hell. It was Ray who consumed his thoughts. The poor guy had cracked during a situation that he was psychologically incapable of processing. Ed had no idea how he would have conducted the negotiation had he been allowed in to talk to Ray in the stronghold but he felt sure that the openness implicit in the gesture of going in there to speak to him in person would have allowed him to establish a stronger layer of trust. It may have been enough perhaps to make Ray realise what he was doing was a massive overreaction, enough perhaps to make him put down the gun.

'Ed.' It was a voice he recognised but its owner was going to tell him who it was anyway. 'It's Nick Calvert.'

Ed was transported to Leicester Square Tube station after the Tube hijack some eighteen months before, the last time the two of them had been together.

'Hi, Nick. What are you doing here?'

It wasn't Nick who answered him, however, but Keir who stood up and said, 'Thanks for everything, Ed. I'm sure I'll see you soon.' Unfortunately, that was probably true. There was bound to be an investigation and much tortuous analysis of what had taken place that morning.

'Yeah, *see* you, Keir.' It came out sounding more derisory than he had meant it to be, but he didn't care. He was far more interested in finding out what Detective Inspector Nick Calvert was doing there. He and Nick had had no contact since Ed had left the force. Ed liked to feel there was a good deal of mutual respect between them; they went way back.

As was always the way, Ed's hand felt weak within Nick's muscular grip.

'Ed, we've got a situation that I need to talk to you about.'

'OK, Nick. It's good to hear your voice and I'm grateful

for the visit, but you do know what's just taken place here, don't you?'

'Yeah, I hear it ended badly.'

'One hostage out but the hostage taker dead.'

'Oh, so not all bad. Anyway, listen, Serina Boise wants you down in Belgravia.' Ed felt sure that Nick Calvert didn't intend to sound heartless and dismissive of Ray's demise, just couldn't help but sound like the battle-hardened copper he was – a man who would do whatever it took to get the job done.

'What's going on in Belgravia?'

'Graham Poynter,' said Calvert. 'Know the name?'

'He's the disgraced hedge-fund guy who won't play the penitent. He's in Zurich, isn't he?'

'Was, until this morning. He's got plenty of security: three guards and a fortified safe room from which there were two calls this morning. The first one was from Graham Poynter himself, to say he was in there with his missus after one of the guards had fallen or been pushed from the roof terrace and ended up dead on the railings at the front of the house. The second call was from an unidentified hostage taker who is now in the safe room with Poynter and his wife and two more hostages – one of them the daughter – and he's saying that, if he sees any attempt to enter the house on the C.C.T.V. monitors in the room, he'll start killing his hostages.'

Ed couldn't help himself. He found his mind wandering from Ray's squalid death in his modest house in Muswell

Hill, a story that would warrant perhaps no more than a couple of inches in the local newspaper, to what was by anyone's standards a major situation that involved one of the most notorious and divisive characters in British public life. Not that it was fame or media coverage that attracted Ed to a situation like this. It was the fact that a hostage-taking like the one that Nick Calvert had outlined was one that required meticulous planning and execution, and the potential motives for which he couldn't help but find intriguing.

'To make things worse, when they turned up at the house, they found all three of the guards dead.'

'And Commander Boise wants me to do what exactly?'

'I don't know; I was asked to pick you up and report there with you. She wants the same team in place as on the Tube hijack.'

'Putting the band back together, eh?'

'Something like that, but only if you're up to it – after this.'

'And what if I don't feel up to it?'

'Ed, she's not going to want to hear that.'

Ed couldn't help a chuckle. He swallowed it almost immediately and it alarmed him how unhinged he sounded. 'I've just been speaking to someone who shot himself and you want me to jump straight into another negotiation?'

'No positions have been assigned within the cell, but she wants you there.'

'Well, it sounds as though I don't have much of an option.'

'No,' said Nick Calvert in his typically blunt tone. 'Shall we go?'

10:41 AM

44 Courtenay Avenue, Hampstead

Bob Rushwood looked at the clock on the iPad screen. It was still early, maybe too early. Then again, the sun was over the yardarm somewhere in the world. He would kick things off with a beer. Hopefully that would lift his mood. It was so difficult to relax after all that had happened. Dealing with Stanmore Partners' problems was bad enough without having to dodge the media's attentions, not to mention all the Internet trolls and activist nutters. Fuck them all. And that included Graham Poynter.

Bob returned to the sofa sipping at a cold beer from the bottle. Opening up the web browser, he clicked on the favourites folder and scrolled down to the link to the Charleston site. Its name made it sound strangely innocent. But it wasn't. He clicked through into the live webcam section and there were a number of smaller windows, each one containing a live stream of a young woman looking to camera in a greater or lesser state of undress. This was his menu. He would browse through the live streams. If he so wished, he could click on one of the windows and speak with a girl directly and make the necessary arrangements. He had been extremely cautious when he had first used the site and its facilities – paranoid, even. But the prices charged meant that the site and its owners and administrators could afford to be extremely discreet. He had used the Charleston site a few times but not since September and the fund's collapse. Everything had been too tense. He had felt as though he was being scrutinised too closely. But now he was going to treat himself: two girls – young, game. He would go for a blonde and a brunette, hire them all night. They could have a party.

One of the girls looking at him from the screen had short bobbed black hair and a mischievous expression. She was part oriental. Her name was written beneath her image: Mika. He liked oriental women; they reminded him of all those business trips to Singapore in the old days. The window enlarged when he clicked on it and Bob looked at Mika on the screen. She wouldn't be able to see him – or so it was claimed on the site – but, just in case, Bob had stuck a small piece of Blu-Tack over the tiny camera lens above the screen. He didn't want to take any chances.

'Hi,' she said and smiled. 'How's it going?'

He liked the way she tried to make her voice sound more mature than her age. She was probably no more than about nineteen, about the same as his oldest, Charlotte. But he wouldn't think about that now. Very off-putting.

'Hi, Mika.'

'Hi there. What's your name?'

'Graham.'

'Hi, Graham.' This appealed to Bob and he chuckled to himself. 'What's so funny, Graham?'

'Nothing,' he said, his smile withering as his thoughts turned to more carnal pleasures. His lustful imaginings were interrupted, however, when a phone started to ring nearby. There were phones on multiple extensions throughout the house so the ringing sound was almost symphonic. Who could be phoning the house? If it was a family member, they would have phoned him on his mobile.

'Sorry about this,' said Bob to Mika. 'I'll be back in a minute. There's someone on the phone.' Bob closed the browser on the iPad and left it on the sofa as he looked around the kitchen for the nearest handset. There was one mounted on the wall by the door. Bob walked across and picked it up.

'Hello?'

'Hello; this is Marcham Estates.' This was the company from whom Bob had rented the house. It was a man's voice. 'Our security team have had electronic notification that there has been an attempt to enter the house.'

All thoughts of what he and Mika and possibly one of Mika's friends might get up to that night were struck from

Bob's mind and he was suddenly alert and staring around the kitchen as though someone might jump out of a doorway or a cupboard at any moment.

'Well, I haven't seen or heard anything this end.'

'Whereabouts are you at the moment?'

'I'm in the kitchen.'

'The perimeter alarm in the yard has been tripped. Is it possible you could take a look outside?'

From the kitchen, Bob had a clear view of the 'yard', as the man from Marcham Estates had described it. It was, in reality, more of a walled garden, complete with fountain and numerous large, ornate stone pots. There was no sign of anything untoward. Nothing appeared to be out of place.

'I can't see anything. It all looks fine.'

'It could be that it's just tripped out.'

'What does that mean?'

'It's a laser system. It could be a leaf or a bird or something has broken the beam. That's all it takes sometimes.'

'Should I be scared?' It sounded stupid – childish, even. And it was patently obvious that he was already very scared.

'Not at all. We've got one of our guys in the area and he can be with you shortly.' Bob was thankful for the man's calmness. He sounded like he knew what he was doing.

'Can you be more specific on his E.T.A.?' asked Bob.

'Hold on a moment.'

Bob waited and listened expectantly.

'OK, I'd say no more than about five minutes. He's near Belsize Park.'

'Should I call the police in the meantime?' Bob's mouth had gone dry as he continued to look around the garden.

'If there's no apparent sign of any attempt to break in then you might want to wait as I think our guy can be there before the police. But it's up to you.'

'OK, I'll wait for your guy.'

'Right, well, I'll get him there straight away.'

'Good; you do that.'

Bob hung up and went to continue his surveillance at the back door that lead from the kitchen into the garden. The walls were high, about seven feet, and covered with creeping shrubbery. There was nowhere that anyone could be hiding. All the doors were locked so, even if someone had managed to get over the wall without him seeing them, they would still not be able to get inside the house.

His breathing was erratic; his heartbeat was an audible thump-thump. He pulled the dressing gown tightly around himself, wishing he had got dressed earlier. Looking around the kitchen, he turned towards the range – a large, catering-sized affair – and beneath it, a long drawer: the most likely home of kitchen utensils. Bob snatched open the drawer and surveyed the equipment. There were a variety of different sized sieves, some measuring spoons, scales, a whisk, some oven gloves and, as he started to move objects apart, his fingers curled around the long handle of a steel skillet. Then he saw the knives above the range, attached to the wall on a magnetic rack. He took the largest one down.

Holding the skillet in one hand and the knife in the other, he realised what a ridiculous figure he cut: pudgy and out of shape in his dressing gown, clutching his weapons. But looking stupid he could live with if it meant staying safe. He returned to the back door and took up position, waiting and watching the garden. How long had it been since the call? It had to be five minutes now, didn't it?

10:46 AM

Courtenay Avenue, Hampstead

The sound of a large, powerful motorcycle on Courtenay Avenue was unusual. This quiet North London suburb was more used to the purr of large luxury four-by-fours. But this being Christmas Day, people were ensconced in their homes, set back from the road, oblivious to the drama that was about to unfold in their midst. Lucas steered the big machine towards the kerb and killed the engine. Dressed in black leathers, he dismounted from the motorbike, pulled it back on to the kickstand and peeled off his gloves. Flipping up the visor on his crash helmet, he looked over the road to the high gates of the house that Bob Rushwood had rented for the Christmas break. He had only seen pictures of it on the Internet before. It was just possible to see the top of the house from the road. Rushwood had clearly chosen it for its safety and security. And booking it on the Internet under the name of an obscure company had clearly reassured him that he was keeping his location a secret. But what he didn't know was that, once Lucas had managed to access his email account, it didn't matter what false fronts he tried to construct in terms of his identity and location; Lucas knew exactly what he was doing, knew all his arrangements and could act accordingly.

Lucas took off his crash helmet and walked across the street. After his trip to Blenheim Terrace earlier on, he had returned to Shoreditch, changed into his leathers and picked up the bike. He enjoyed wearing the leathers. It wasn't necessarily the feeling of the leather against his skin – he wasn't into that sort of thing – but rather what it did to his appearance. It gave him a certain official air, as though he was wearing a uniform. The forces of the state had their uniforms with their shiny buttons, epaulets and serial numbers; his uniform was more anonymous.

Lucas walked up to the small console on the wall by the gate. He pressed the buzzer and stared into the camera mounted into the stainless steel fascia. The voice that came from the speaker sounded troubled and suspicious, and well it might.

'Hello?'

'Marcham Estates Security.' Lucas held up the forged security pass next to his face so that Rushwood could see it.

There was a buzzing sound and the high gate clicked open. He was in.

'Thanks,' said Lucas, pocketing the I.D. card as he entered

the courtyard, closing the gate after him. There were plants in stone pots and planters; there was a water feature in the middle of the courtyard but whatever it was – a fountain, possibly – the pump was switched off. The mosaic stone pattern on the ground was expensive. It probably added a few quid to the rental value, that alone. With its high walls, clad in creepers, and its exotic plants and tree, with a table and chairs on a raised area of decking, it felt like a secluded sanctum within suburbia. But there was something else as well – something oppressive. It was the walls. Anyone who wanted to live behind walls like these had something to hide or something to hide from. It made Lucas think of where he had grown up, his mother's tiny two-bedroom flat in Camberwell above a row of shops. People on the top deck of the bus going past could see straight into his bedroom. He had lived in that bedroom all of his childhood. It had felt as though his life was open to the world. But he had nothing to hide. Lucas's mother had worked hard all of her life. Her home was tiny and crumbling. It was constructed of different materials from a place like this. Everything here was solid and strong, looked as though you could take a hammer to it and leave no mark. What had Bob Rushwood done to deserve to live in a place like this? Lucas's mother had struggled to bring up her son single-handedly. She had had to fight to survive and to give them some sort of life. This man, on the other hand, had detected weaknesses in a market system and exploited those weaknesses in order to accrue as much personal wealth and benefit as he could. Whereas Lucas's mother had been paid poorly for her hard work, this man was lavished with obscene rewards for his recklessness and amorality.

He could see Bob Rushwood's head and shoulders framed in the back door of the house. Rushwood's fear was apparent even from across the courtyard. His cover story on the phone and his forged pass had been swallowed whole and, as Lucas approached the back door, Bob Rushwood was opening it for him. Now he could see him in his entirety, he could see he was wearing a dressing gown. There was a knife and a steel skillet on the work surface next to the back door. These were clearly Rushwood's preferred weapons should he come under attack. Lucas felt like laughing it was so comical, but he remained stony-faced for a few moments more.

'Thanks for coming so fast,' said Rushwood.

'That's OK; no problem.' And now Lucas did allow himself a smile. He was still in character. He didn't need to be. Taking out his revolver from the side pocket of his leathers, he pointed it at Bob Rushwood's foot and fired off a shot. It wasn't loud. It sounded like a book being dropped flat on to the floor. Bob Rushwood's screams, however, were loud. By the time they had reached the height of their volume, Lucas had shut the back door.

Looking ahead to the day's events, particularly this part, when he knew he would be required to actually start to hurt someone physically, he had been more than a little concerned as to how he might feel about casting himself as the architect of someone else's pain. But he needn't have worried. As he stood over Bob Rushwood's shrieking, writhing form, he felt perfectly calm and even a little excited.

11:12 AM

Blenheim Terrace, Belgravia

Commander Serina Boise had given specific instructions that no attempt was to be made to enter the building. The surrounding streets had been evacuated and tow trucks had been ordered to remove cars from around the house so as to provide greater access for police and special forces vehicles. A fully operational command centre for the nego- tiating cell arrived on the back of an articulated lorry. Photographers and news crews began to assemble. Details of what exactly was taking place were scant but the address of the massive police deployment did not go unnoticed and some of the photographers were the same ones who had doorstepped the Poynters earlier in the day when they had arrived from the airport.

The one detail that had been made clear was that a man's body had been photographed – from a distance – seemingly impaled on the railings at the front of the house. Editors were already obsessing over the issue of whether to publish the picture, while it had already started to appear on social media, providing a single grainy image of the unfolding event which had far more impact on the public mind than if the photographer had had the opportunity to light and frame the shot at leisure. The white stucco frontage of the house, when combined with mention of hostage-taking, provided a resonance in the minds of those who remembered the Iranian Embassy Siege in Kensington in 1980 and the iconic imagery of men in black wearing balaclavas abseiling down the side of the building with guns and grenades.

'Reports are coming in that disgraced hedge-fund C.E.O. Graham Poynter has been taken hostage with his family inside their central-London home by a person or persons unknown.' A story was starting to form and, along with it, the impatience and hunger for detail that fuelled the accompanying speculation. Less than an hour since Graham Poynter had made the call from the safe room in his house, 'news' had gathered momentum. Al-Qaeda had taken Graham Poynter and his family hostage; far-right extremists had taken Graham Poynter and his family hostage; Graham Poynter had taken his own family hostage; distraught at his own fall from grace, Graham Poynter had jumped from the roof of his house on to the railings below; Graham Poynter had been thrown from the roof of his house by a masked intruder; one of Graham Poynter's security guards had jumped to his death from the roof of his house.

As Ed arrived at the stronghold with Nick Calvert, the police officers deployed on the perimeter of the exclusion zone were buzzing with nervous energy. The demeanour of the one that Calvert spoke to through the open window of the car was borderline aggressive. Whatever else happened at that location throughout the remainder of the day, he was not going to be the officer who allowed entry to someone who shouldn't be there. Not content with a cursory glance at Calvert's I.D., he took the card and pored over it with a colleague. The scale of the hostage-taking was apparent to Ed by the sound of the helicopters hovering over the stronghold. He always found their close proximity to be stifling, the expectant thrum of their engines an ill portent of things to come.

Having proved his own and Ed's identity at the perimeter of the stronghold, Nick Calvert closed his window and parked the car. Ed climbed out and waited for Nick to join him and offer his arm before they walked across to the command centre.

'Great to have you here, Ed.' Serina Boise's voice was unmistakable but its tone was different from usual. It was authoritative and respectful as always. But it was also needy. As a barometer reading of the pressure that she felt, Ed found it was more than a little unnerving. She hadn't invited him here to act in a peripheral capacity. She wanted him right at the heart of the negotiation.

'Commander Boise.' Ed held out his hand and Boise shook it.

'Please, take a seat.'

Calvert steered Ed towards a hard chair as Boise sat down nearby. She smelled good: unperfumed and clean. She was wearing her uniform, he could hear the stiff material bend and crease as she moved.

'I presume Nick's given you some rough details of the situation here.'

'Yes, he has.'

'I want you both to listen to the following tape recording of the second call that was made from the safe room in the stronghold.'

The hum of a sound recording came through speakers nearby. A voice belonging to a female telephone operator said, 'Hello? Go ahead please.' The voice that followed was solemn. It was the voice of a man who was expressing himself with reluctance. There was an accent. Whoever the man was who was speaking, he came from Tyneside or nearby.

'As you are no doubt aware, I am calling you from the safe room in the home of Graham Poynter. I have four hostages with me who are as follows: Graham Poynter himself; his wife, Helen Poynter; his daughter, Lily Poynter and a delivery driver from a company called Radcliffe & Penny Fine Foods who was making a delivery here at what I'd guess you'd say was the wrong moment. Now, we are currently located in the safe room or panic room as it is sometimes called. There are C.C.T.V. monitors in here from which I can see all of the house. If anyone enters this building, then I will kill Lily Poynter.'

There was a woman's voice audible in the background. It didn't sound like a seventeen-year-old girl. It must have been the mother. The voice sounded desperate. There was a short pause in the monologue before the man continued.

'I repeat, I will kill Lily Poynter if I see any evidence of personnel entering the building. Any contact between us will be initiated by me. I will call you back in just over an hour's time at eleven thirty. That's eleven thirty, OK? Then I will give you further instructions. In the meantime, be aware that further attempts at communication with me will be rejected.'

The tone of the hum on the recording changed as the call was disconnected.

'So, Ed, that's what we're up against.' Ed liked Serina's posh can-do demeanour. She spoke as though she was talking about a leak in the stable roof which might need fixing. But it was as much her own coping mechanism as it was an attempt to keep the mood in the cell calm.

'I don't get it,' said Ed, thinking aloud. 'If you're going to take a banker hostage, you're clearly doing it for some sort of ideological reason. But this guy doesn't sound like someone who is acting out of passion for a cause. He doesn't sound like he even wants to be there. But he – along with

whoever's with him – is responsible for killing three security guards and now he's trapped there with no possible
means of escape. My hunch is it's him on his own but I'd
need to speak to him to establish more facts and build up
more of a profile.' He'd said it. All the way there in the car,
he had promised himself that he wouldn't make any suggestion that he was ready to conduct a negotiation, even if he
was called on to do so. But now, having heard the voice on
the tape, he knew he was hooked.

'We'd like you to speak to him too,' said Serina; and, with
that brief statement, she confirmed his fears.

'The thing is, less than an hour ago, I was involved in a
hostage negotiation that—'

'We know what happened this morning, Ed.' The woman
who interrupted him had a voice even more familiar than
Serina's. It was someone with whom he had spent many
hours in negotiating cells. It was Laura Massey.

'Hi, Laura,' he said, turning in the direction of her voice.

'Good to have you here, Ed.'

Ed knew there were others in the cell. Under normal
circumstances, he would have been more than a little
offended that there should be people there whose identities were not made known to him but, due to the urgency
with which Commander Boise had wanted to speak to him,
he had not given it any thought.

'Don't tell me,' he said. 'Des White is here too.'

'Hi, Ed,' said Des.

The team from the Tube hijack were back together. The cell co-ordinator was Laura Massey; Ed would be number one, Nick Calvert number two and Des White number three. While Serina Boise's intention was clear and honourable, Ed couldn't help but feel that it was misguided. He wasn't sure if he was in the right state of mind. If the situation earlier had turned out positively, things might have been different.

'It's good to be with you all again and I'm thankful that you think I might be able to help here, but I'm worried I'm not match fit.'

'We appreciate your concerns,' said Serina Boise. 'If there's any suggestion that you're struggling, then Nick or Des will take over. You just need to let us know.'

'What if I'm telling you now that I'm struggling?'

'Ed, I'd like you to speak to the subject first.'

Serina moved closer to him. Her adjusted posture and the softened tone of her voice attempted a form of intimacy. *You need to do this for me*, it was saying.

'The opening negotiation is going to be crucial and I want you to deal with it. Is that OK?'

She wasn't asking; she was telling. The fact that he was no longer on the payroll of the Metropolitan Police meant little. He could say no, but he didn't want to. As much as he questioned the tactical wisdom of using a number-one negotiator who had just concluded an unsuccessful nego-tiation less than an hour before, he also knew it was good to be back in a room with these people. As soon as he had heard the man's voice on the recording, he couldn't help himself, he was already thinking of tactics and constructing a potential negotiation strategy in his mind. But, just as the ideas were forming, so too was a gnawing fear in his stomach.

'OK,' he said.

'During the first exchange with the subject,' said Laura Massey, 'we should try to ascertain the well-being of the hostages, whether the hostage taker has accomplices, what weapons he has in his possession and then take it from there in terms of subsequent demands.'

Ed listened to Laura as she voiced the patently obvious. It was her own way of dealing with the stress. Procedure was something that wasn't just a means of providing a framework of knowledge and understanding, it also provided a crutch through which the members of the negotiating cell could keep themselves grounded within the complex psychological web in which they were trapped. Unlike the others, Ed didn't like to think in terms of the procedural framework of a situation. Maybe he should; maybe it would help. Then again, if he did, he worried that it might blunt his instinct and intuition, and without those, he had nothing.

11:13 AM

44 Courtenay Avenue, Hampstead

This was everything Bob had ever dreaded, the worst nightmare that his mind could conjure, and it was standing over him, dressed all in black leather, with a gun from which a shot had already been fired into him. All his meticulous planning and care over his own personal security had amounted to this. The pain was like nothing he had ever felt before. It felt as though the bullet had taken his foot off at the ankle. He knew it hadn't because he had looked at it as he writhed on the floor after the shot was fired. The entry wound was neat, just a black hole in the skin. It was now awash with blood but it wasn't the entry wound that he was concerned about. The exit wound felt as though it had pulverised his heel. He couldn't manoeuvre himself into a position whereby he could see it but, even if he could have done, he wouldn't have wanted to.

The first few minutes were the worst. It was probably the

shock. He had screamed, shrieked and cursed. But the pain had changed. If anything, it was worse than before, but it wasn't so intrusive, so all-consuming now. It allowed him to think. The fact he was still alive had to be a good sign. If this was just an intended assassination then he would be dead already. The man needed something from him. That allowed Bob an opportunity to negotiate. It allowed him an opportunity to try to stay alive. What worried him was the clear pleasure the man derived from his pain. He stood over him, watching him intently, absorbed, eager not to miss a moment of his own personal horror show.

'What do you want?' Bob had lost count of how many times he had asked the question, or variations of it, since the intruder had entered the house. Responses that he had had so far ranged from a total refusal to even answer the question to laughter. When Bob groaned and shrieked with pain, the bastard watched him, seemingly enraptured. He was only a kid, maybe twenty or so. It was impossible to know whether he was a messenger, part of a larger organisation, or just a lone wolf who had gained access to his personal information and details of his location. Impossible to know too whether he would be aware that in each of the rooms in the house there was a panic button. The one in the kitchen was located on the wall by the fridge-freezer. How he would manage to stand up in order to reach it, he would worry about when he got there, but all he could think of doing was trying to move towards it as fast as possible.

As he writhed on the floor, leaving a slick of blood behind him as he did so, he had managed to drag himself away from the back door. He was halfway there.

'Please, tell me what you want.' He didn't expect a reply, hadn't had one all the other times he had asked the question, so he was surprised when he received one.

'I want the password for the Anchorage account.'

'I don't know what you're talking about.' It was a knee-jerk reaction and it was a lie, of course. He knew very well what the Anchorage account was. It was his and Graham's 'ace in the hole': their insurance against all eventualities, including the collapse of the fund. Whatever differences they may have had personally and in the running of Stanmore Partners, on the subject of the need for some funds to be salted away well beyond the prying eyes of the Financial Conduct Authority, or even the police, they were in total agreement. Whatever fate hurled at them in the coming months, however poisonous their legal affairs might become, they always had the Anchorage account.

His captor circled him, his heavy leather boots creaking and squeaking against the tiled floor.

'Don't be silly; you know exactly what I'm talking about,' he said in his London accent. Apart from the shot he had fired from the gun, the kid hadn't made any attempt to hurt him or harm him since he had entered the house. But this all came to an end when he kicked Bob's wounded foot. It was as though the pain he had felt up until this moment was immediately rendered insignificant by what succeeded it. It was like an electrical charge that sent his entire lower leg into spasm. When he started to scream, it came out as nothing more than a gasp but, when he found his voice, the noise it made didn't sound human; it was altogether more primeval and animalistic. Fearful, however, of another kick, he knew he needed to speak.

'Fuck, Jesus! Listen, all I know is that the account was set up by my partner, Graham—'

'Poynter, yes, I know very well who your partner is. And we're going to deal with him too. But in the meantime, you're going to tell me the password.'

The man kicked him again but, thankfully, the blow struck his other foot. Under normal circumstances, it might have provided some discomfort but now it didn't even register, such was the agony he was already experiencing. But it wasn't meant to hurt him; it was a threat, a reminder of what would happen if he didn't comply.

'I don't have it; Poynter has it.'

'You're lying.'

Bob held his breath in a vain attempt to prepare himself for another kick. But it didn't come. The man placed his booted foot on Bob's injured foot and started pressing down. This aroused a different sort of pain, a pain that was lower-pitched and bursting, but equally unbearable. Bob tried to pull his foot away but it was trapped.

'Don't lie to me, Bob, there's really no point,' he said as he increased the pressure on Bob's foot.

'OK, OK, please.' The pressure was reduced but still the sole of the boot remained and, with it, the threat of further pain.

'Now, tell me the password or it's all going to get very painful.'

Bob's only instinct was to try to make the pain go away or lessen it in some way but, despite the agony he felt, he knew that his knowledge of the password might be the only thing that was keeping him alive.

'Listen to me, please; don't hurt me any more. Let's talk. If you want money, I can give you money.'

'Bob, you're not listening to me; I know everything about you. It's all there on your computers. All of it.' The boot was being pressed down harder on Bob's foot, creating yet another explosion of pain. 'The only thing that isn't on them is the password to the Anchorage account and, if you don't give it to me now, I'm going to kill you. You got that?' Bob was gasping with pain once more. 'And once I've killed you, I'm going to go and see your family in Henley when they get back from their Christmas holiday in Florida next Wednesday and I'm going to kill them too.'

11:29 AM

Negotiating Cell, Blenheim Terrace, Belgravia

'OK, Ed,' said Des White, attempting to repress the nervous tension in his voice. 'We've got an incoming call from the safe room in the stronghold.' Being the number-three negotiator, White was in control of communications into and out of the cell. Ed slid on his headset as Des White whispered, 'You're on.'

'Hello?'

'Hi.'

'My name's Ed Mallory; I'm a negotiator. Who am I speaking to?'

'I'm not going to give you my name.' There was the voice again: a definite Tyneside or Teesside accent.

'Can you tell me what this is all about?'

'I'm sure you heard my call from earlier.'

'I did,' said Ed. 'But you didn't issue any demands.'

'How do you know there are any demands?'

'Because that's usually how it works in situations like this.'

'All you need to know at the moment is that, if anyone tries to enter the house or meddles with the power supply or communications into the safe room, I'll start killing more people.'

There was a confidence to the man's voice. He wasn't fazed by speaking to someone like Ed. It was as though he had dealt with people like him before. When he told Ed that he was going to start killing his hostages, there was none of the bluster that usually accompanied such threats, none of the overly aggressive demeanour which is usually used as a means of convincing the perpetrator as much as anyone else that the threat is serious. When this man said he was going to start killing his hostages if any attempt was made to compromise his position, Ed believed him.

'OK; understood. But you have to make me understand a reason for why you're here and why you've killed the security guards.' Ed had thought hard about mentioning the security guards and decided he would. It didn't sound as though the hostage taker was agitated or emotionally fragile.

'You don't have to concern yourself with reasons at the present time. I'll keep you informed of everything you need to know as we go along. Is that clear?'

'Yes, it's clear, but you have to understand something from my side of things.' The man tried to interrupt but Ed talked across him. 'As I'm sure you're aware, your actions here this morning have meant there is a massive deployment of police and security forces. There is going to come a stage when you're going to have to tell me why you're doing this and I'm hoping we can have that conversation now before anyone else is hurt.'

'No one else will be hurt, so long as you keep your side of the bargain and ensure that no one tries to enter the house.'

'Can I at least ask what you're hoping to achieve by doing this?' There was no reply so Ed continued: 'I really think it's going to help us all if we develop some sort of mutual understanding.'

'I'm telling you nothing, although I will tell you this: I know how all this works.'

'How what works?'

'Your job.'

'Are you, or were you, a hostage negotiator?'

'No, but I know enough; so, come on, why don't you ask me about the condition of the hostages?'

'How are the hostages?'

'They're fine; bit scared.'

'Is anyone – yourself included – in need of medical assistance?'

'No, we're all fine.'

'What about the men working with you?'

There was a brief pause and then, 'No, they're all fine as well.'

Ed could hear that the subject was trying to wind up the call, so he thought he would try a direct question about his choice of hostages.

'Why have you and your accomplices decided to take the Poynter family hostage?'

There was a small humourless chuckle on the line before the Geordie-accented voice said, 'Why do you think?' and the line went dead.

In confirmation of the call's termination, Des White said, 'He's gone.'

'Let's think about this,' said Ed to the members of the negotiating cell as he pulled his headset down around his neck. 'Why does he want to take this family hostage?' And, attempting to answer his own question, he said, 'It can only be one of two things. Either he wants to try to extort money from Graham Poynter for a third party who will ultimately collect the money, or it's revenge born of some ideological grudge relating to Graham Poynter and what he represents. There can't be any other reason, can there?'

The silence in the cell signified that no one could think of one. Finally, Nick Calvert said, 'Maybe it's both of those.'

'Yeah, maybe it is,' said Ed, but already his train of thought had moved on. 'Laura?'

'Yes, Ed.'

'We need to get intelligence working on this. We need to focus on the anti-capitalist hacktivist networks. We need to know if there are any disaffected elements who have rejected non-violence and want to move towards direct action. We also need to focus on ex-special forces or military personnel in particular who might be involved, because, whoever this guy is, he has taken out three former soldiers single-handedly. He has to have undertaken advanced training.'

'You sound as though you think it's just him on his own,' said Nick Calvert.

'Did you hear him when I asked him if any of his men were in need of medical assistance? The way he said they were all fine? Maybe I'm wrong but I think it's just him in there. I'm sure of it. So we need to look at someone who is extremely disaffected with the financial industry, someone who is probably a member of some loose affiliation with others of a similar outlook, who is possibly an existing or former member of special forces.'

'We'll get them straight on to it,' said Laura.

'What I don't understand,' said Ed, turning towards Nick Calvert and Des White, 'is why he's taken the fourth hostage. The family, sure, but the delivery driver from – what was the name of the company?'

'Radcliffe & Penny,' said Des White. 'It's an upmarket catering company based in Knightsbridge. Very expensive stuff.'

'Do we have the delivery driver's profile yet?' asked Ed.

'Not yet,' said White. 'But we will have soon.'

'Maybe the hostage taker was worried that he didn't have enough hostages to bargain with successfully,' said Ed. 'And when another one was presented to him, he took him.'

'But, in that case, he could have taken one of the security guards hostage,' said Serina Boise from the doorway. Ed had forgotten that the on-scene commander was listening to their deliberations.

'Too dangerous,' said Calvert. 'If he is on his own then he's not going to want a highly trained ex-military individual with the hostages. The Radcliffe & Penny driver, on the other hand, is probably as terrified as the members of the Poynter family and not a risk in the same way.'

'So, Ed,' said Commander Boise. 'How are you going to play things from here on in?'

'Well, our man's created a bit of theatre here. He wants everyone to know what he's doing. This is a targeted form of terrorism. It's making a spectacle out of Graham Poynter's fear. It's making an example of him. The sort of person who wants to go to all the trouble of doing this – killing three men in the process – is going to have no qualms about killing Poynter and his family. As far as the next stage of the negotiation is concerned, I'm going to be completely honest with you, it's going to be difficult. My feeling is that this guy has created a situation in which he intends to do some serious harm to Graham Poynter and/or his family. He knows he's not going to walk free from this, so the only benefit he can derive is ideological, not financial.'

'There's something else you need to be aware of,' said Boise. 'We have intelligence regarding the safe room in which they're all located. It would appear that, once the door is locked, it has its own air supply which is pumped through from a filtration system installed in the cellar. We can break into the system and pump gas into the safe room, which could knock out the occupants in a matter of seconds.'

This information was greeted with a couple of approving murmurs in the cell, one of which came from Calvert and one from Laura Massey. But the mention of gas troubled Ed. . He couldn't help but be reminded of children's television shows like *Batman* and *Star Trek* in which knockout gas was a staple.

'The name of the gas' – asked Ed – 'it's not Kolokol-1, is it?'

'It's a derivative. Why?'

'That was the gas they think was used in the Moscow theatre siege of 2002. I don't need to tell you how that turned out.'

'I know; over a hundred died from the gas alone,' said Boise. 'I'm fully aware of it.' She seemed tetchy that Ed had mentioned it. However well developed the plan was, it was clear that she favoured its use. 'That was a theatre' – she continued – 'a large space the exact volume of which was almost impossible to estimate. This is a small room, the dimensions of which we have to the cubic millimetre. There's also a fortunate coincidence at work here because Scotland Yard has only recently commissioned research at University College into the use of this gas and the initial findings are that, with the correct calculations, it can work. They feel that, due to the safe room's sealed construction and ventilation system, they can almost completely recreate laboratory conditions in which the outcomes of their trials have proved extremely positive. They believe that, once the gas has been released, the occupants of the safe room will be rendered unconscious in a matter of seconds.'

'Matter of?' said Ed, not caring if he sounded prickly. 'Can they be any more specific than that?'

'Less than ten, they think.'

'And how are we going to get anyone inside the basement to rig up the gas, when our man is watching all the C.C.T.V. cameras in the safe room?'

The tetchiness in Serina Boise's voice melted. She clearly felt confident about this part of the plan. 'There are no cameras in the basement itself so, in order to access it without entering the house via the traditional means, we're going to knock through the wall from the house next door. Although worth countless millions, these are terraced houses and everything's interconnected to a degree, cellars and basements included. So, now you've heard the plan, what do you think?'

'It's got to be worth a shot,' said Nick Calvert.

'Yeah, I agree,' said Laura Massey and Ed heard another murmur, this one from Des White.

'What do you think, Ed?' asked Boise.

'Well, I can see the plan's appeal. Why go through a

lengthy and potentially extremely difficult negotiation when we can close this down right now and no one gets hurt?'

'So what are you saying?'

Ed responded to Boise's question with another question: 'Are you putting this to a vote?' He knew she wasn't. That's not how things worked. A negotiating cell wasn't a democracy.

'No, but I need to know what you, as first negotiator, think.'

'Well, in theory, I like it. If we can knock out the perp in seconds, before he can employ whatever weapons or explosives he might have with him, then all well and good. But it's also dangerous, and something that we haven't considered is there's an outside chance it's a trap.'

'What, you think that he might have engineered all this to kill the team that goes inside to get him?'

'He has killed three already,' said Calvert.

'No, I don't think that's what he's doing,' said Ed. 'The three guards were collateral damage while he made his way to Graham Poynter and his family. I just get a sense from talking to him that he knows exactly what he's doing and he will have researched the safe room and know its strengths and weaknesses as a location from which he can conduct his operation and issue his demands. On balance, I think you've probably got to go for it, but I'm glad it's not me that has to make the decision.'

'It's not me, either,' said Boise. 'This is a decision that will ultimately be made by COBRA.'

'COBRA?' asked Ed. 'Why are they involved?'

'This is a major incident. Graham Poynter is a controversial public figure. There are far-reaching political implications, so all we can do is wait and hear what they decide.'

Ed thought of the members of COBRA, the Prime Minister and whichever Cabinet ministers he decided to include in the briefing, being dragged away from their families on Christmas Day. It was the one day of the year that they might have hoped for some respite from the rigours and pain of government. Now, however, they would be called upon to decide how best to deal with this sudden attack against the home and family of Graham Poynter, a man whose destiny was in some ways inextricably linked with their own. What judgements and opinions would they be calling on when they made their decision? And would they, even if only in their subconscious, find themselves experiencing a moment of spiteful pleasure at the thought of what was taking place? Poynter had brought this all on himself, right? Yet they might also feel a creeping sense of fear – paranoia, even – that if the barbarians at the gates, the anonymous forces ranged against them, could get to Graham Poynter, a man with all his wealth and security, they would in all likelihood be able to get to them too.

11:30 AM

44 Courtenay Avenue, Hampstead

'How do I know that you won't kill me anyway?' While his captor's voice maintained its calm monotone, Bob's voice was screechy and terrified.

'You don't.'

'So why should I tell you the password? What's in it for me?'

'If you tell me, you'll live. So will . . . Marina, is it? And Alexander and Charlotte are the kids, aren't they?'

Each time his captor released the pressure on his foot, Bob was sliding himself along the floor. It would appear that he was trying to move away from the source of the pain – and he was – but he was also dragging himself that bit closer to the panic button by the fridge. He still had no idea if he would be able to utilise it, or even if he should try, but he felt himself being inexorably drawn towards it.

The more pain the kid inflicted on him, the more the bastard seemed to enjoy it. Bob had no frame of reference in terms of how to negotiate with such a person. He had negotiated with thousands of people all over the world, some of them psychotic or even psychopathic – there were plenty of those in the world of finance – but he had never dealt with someone like this before.

'How can I trust you?'

'You have no choice. And don't think about giving me the wrong password, because I'll be checking.' He took an iPhone from a pocket in his leathers and held it up for Bob to see. 'Each password is approved in sequence. You know that, right?' He did know it. Each password would be approved one after the other until both had been approved, at which point the online banking dashboard could be accessed and, from it, money could be transferred anywhere in the world. Hearing the full extent of his captor's knowledge made him realise he was fighting a losing battle. The Anchorage money was as good as gone already. All he could do now was try to stay alive. If he was going to do that then he had to divulge the password.

'Before I tell you the password, you need to take me to a hospital. Once I'm there, I'll tell you what it is.'

'No, that's never going to happen.'

'But you have to guarantee my safety, otherwise I might as well just let you kill me. At least I know you won't get the money.'

Before he could make any attempt to object, the gun was raised and a bullet fired into his left leg. It felt as though someone had taken a metal pole and thrust it through his thigh. The pain made him retch and choke as the burning taste of bile filled his mouth and throat. For a moment, he thought he might black out, but the agony was insistent of his attention and accompanying consciousness, and it held him locked in its grip.

'Tell me the password, Bob, or this is going to get a whole lot more painful.' The bastard was standing over him with his legs either side of him. There was no hope of making it to the panic button now. He had to take his chances and tell him the password. The pain and the shock had made him breathless; his chest was seemingly rising and falling involuntarily and he coughed and hiccupped as he spoke.

'Don't kill me. Please don't kill me. I'll tell you . . . I'll tell you the password.' The gun was pointing straight at his face now. The end of the barrel was only a couple of feet from him. 'Just promise me you won't kill me.'

'I promise I won't kill you. All I want is the password. Once I've got it, I'll let you go.'

Bob had no choice. At that moment in time, he would have traded all the money in the Anchorage account for the pain to stop. 'It's two, three, one, two' – the 23rd December, his mother's birthday – 'then capital T, followed by lower-case O, M, K, I, N, S. Tomkins' – his nickname for the pet cat,

Tom, he had had as a child. Just a random configuration of numbers and letters like millions of other passwords around the world.

The gun was withdrawn from his face and pocketed in the leather jacket as fingers tapped on the iPhone's screen. The pain from both the bullet wounds was so intense and all-pervading that Bob couldn't help but groan. His heart rate was fluctuating, palpitating as his temperature dropped. If he didn't get some medical attention soon, he knew he would probably die. With the password typed in, the bastard stood over him and watched the screen. The smile on his face was confirmation that the correct information had been supplied. Looking down at him, he said in a surprisingly warm and sincere tone of voice, 'Thanks, Bob.'

11:37 AM

Safe Room, 11 Blenheim Terrace, Belgravia

Danny replaced the receiver and looked across at the four of them at the end of the safe room. Only Lily, the daughter, held his stare momentarily before looking down. They had heard what he had said on both phone calls. They had heard him threaten to kill his hostages, starting with Lily, if there was any attempt to enter the house. The mother was cowed, emotional, distraught, and eager to communicate with him. The father, the big man himself, was conflicted. Part of him was relieved that the threat wasn't directed solely at him, but another part of him was only too aware of the danger he faced. Lily appeared to be the only one in the family with any guts. Even though her life had been threatened, she was not going to be intimidated, and she fired hateful stares at him. He would have liked to reassure her but he knew he couldn't. As for James, he had no idea what he was thinking and didn't much care.

'What is it you want?' asked the mother, unable to keep silent any longer. She stared at him through dewy, tear-filled eyes.

'I can't tell you.'

'You've got to tell someone, some time.' Graham had managed to regain a little of his composure.

'For your own safety, you really need to keep quiet.' But as the silence resumed, he started thinking about the security guards again. Maybe he should allow his hostages to speak to him and question him. That way, he wouldn't have to think about those three men. They were men like him. They were going about their work, trying to earn a living after their days in the military had come to an end. It was possible that their paths had crossed over the years. The only consolation he could manage to dredge from the situation was that the most difficult part of what he had to do was over and the mission was that little bit nearer completion. What he needed to do later, while difficult from a tactical point of view, wouldn't trouble his morality any.

11:39 AM

Negotiating Cell, Blenheim Terrace, Belgravia

Ed's opinions on the science of hostage negotiation varied. While glad that it was finally getting the recognition it deserved, he didn't like the way that it was hijacked by others in order to inform their own disciplines. Not that it stopped him earning money from talking about his experiences. Since he had left the force and gone freelance, he had to do what he could to get by. The business community in particular often paid large sums for negotiators to come and talk at corporate events. The inherent danger and underlying criminality of what was under discussion provided an extra frisson. What these awayday management types wanted to hear was the nail-biting detail of talking down desperate people. Whether they would actually take away anything from one of these events that they could utilise in their own everyday lives was a moot point but not one that seemed to bother them unduly.

Many of the same rules did apply in both hostage and business negotiations. But the context was all different and while business folk liked to feel that the arena in which they conducted their work was of enormous importance, Ed could never become excited about it. At some of the events he attended, he had been asked to consider hypothetical deals and case studies. Everyone was only too keen to try to find the correlative link between their own business practice and the world of law enforcement. It made them feel more worthwhile. It moistened the dryness of the subject. But as soon as figures and the intricacies of corporate policy were discussed, Ed would feel himself glazing over. How could this have anything to do with what he did? Yes, he was trying to persuade people to take a particular course of action but he was doing it to prevent them from killing or harming either themselves or others. It was all in the jeopardy, the risk. People in the business community, particularly men – nearly always men – got turned on by the concept of risk and its reward. It touched something deep down in their male psyche. A business deal, however, was a different sort of risk to the risk Ed encountered during a hostage negotiation. It was a soft risk; the risk he took was hard.

One of the key rules of hostage negotiation – and one that he had found himself expounding at various moments during his burgeoning career as a speaker on the subject – was that the negotiator should always try to limit the influence of emotion both on himself and the subject. The effects of emotion were often misunderstood even by psychologists and mental health professionals who should have known better. Its causes and its effects were subtle and uniquely personal. A person might react differently to the exact same event or situation from one moment to the next based purely on their emotional temperature. The influence of emotion on behaviour was one of the great unknowables of psychological profiling. What was known was that subjecting an individual to a surfeit of emotional stimuli, like that provided by a hostage negotiation for example, could spell disaster. For a hostage negotiator to go straight from one negotiation into another was – as far as his own experience was concerned – unprecedented. In the event that this situation was not resolved satisfactorily, it was something that would be pored over at the inevitable enquiry.

'COBRA have given us the go-ahead to use the gas,' said Serina Boise. She said it with conviction. In her mind – if not in Ed's – it was absolutely the right thing to do. It was an audacious plan. The hostage taker had utilised the security infrastructure of the house for his own ends. He was in a position of strength in that he had, in effect, created a stronghold within a stronghold. The reason for doing this was not entirely apparent, but as a tactic to keep himself out of the physical clutches of the authorities, it was a highly effective one. So, to turn his use of the safe room against him in such a simple and effective way was something that had to be considered. Ed couldn't help feeling, however, that a man who had managed to take the Poynter family hostage so easily with all the planning and reconnaissance it would have required would have considered all eventualities.

'There's something in the guy's voice, Nick; can you hear it?'

Nick Calvert was sitting next to Ed, close enough that Ed could smell his deodorant. It was one of those aerosols with an exotic name and promises to the wearer of added allure to women.

'What do you mean?' asked Nick.

'Maybe he's not the ringleader. What's ultimately driving this situation has to be ideology, yet he doesn't sound fired up with the zeal and passion you would expect.'

'But he's the one calling the shots,' said Nick. 'He's the one who killed the three security guards. He's the one who's talking to us.'

'Maybe he's just the sharp end of a much more complex weapon.'

'Well, let's hope we can find that out soon enough.'

Ed could hear the notes of concern in Nick Calvert's voice.

'You like the idea of using the gas?' asked Ed.

'I think I do, yeah.'

'You don't think the subject might have thought about its possible deployment?'

'Maybe he has but, on balance, I still think we should go for it. Especially if it can knock them all out really quickly, as they seem to think is possible.'

'Well, it's not for us to decide.'

Calvert lowered his voice as he spoke to Ed. Whether this was a signal that they might be overheard or just an unconscious affectation to enhance the intimacy of the subject matter was unanswered by the nature of the question.

'Is everything all right, Ed?'

Ed lowered his voice as he responded. 'I think so; I hope so. But you're going to watch my back, right?'

'Right,' said Calvert patting him on the shoulder. It was a gesture of friendship and respect and Ed appreciated it. But the opportunity for Ed to voice any further concerns regarding his operational abilities was terminated when Laura Massey spoke from the doorway.

'They're through the wall in the cellar and have accessed the safe room's ventilation system. They should be ready pretty soon.'

'That's good,' said Nick Calvert. Ed said nothing.

11:40 AM

44 Courtenay Avenue, Hampstead

Lucas loved the interior design. The kitchen equipment, the utensils, everything was top end. Even the panic button on the wall by the fridge had its own stainless steel housing to match everything else. Bob had been trying to get himself across the floor towards it and Lucas had allowed him. He knew he was never going to reach it, not since he had shot him the second time.

The floor was one aspect of the kitchen that wasn't industrial in its construction, being polished, honey-coloured wood. It was nice. It was all messed up from Bob Rushwood's blood now but that would wash off.

'You're going to let me go now, right?' Bob's voice was convulsed with pain. Lucas could almost feel sorry for him.

'I'm going to release you, yes.' Lucas was pleased to see the look of relief on Bob's face. Despite the reason for his intrusion into Bob Rushwood's life, he felt relaxed in his company. It was a relationship the likes of which he had never experienced before and he wasn't sure he wanted it to end just yet. There was no hurry now. He had done what he had come here to do. He had the password; he could allow himself a few minutes of relaxation before he continued to the next stage.

Mounted on a flip-down console unit on the wall was a plasma television screen. Lucas walked across to it, pressed the power switch and on came the picture. Bloody carol singers. He tried another channel: a *Top of the Pops* rerun from the 1970s. Another channel: a film. A fourth and he had found what he was looking for. It was an aerial shot of a central-London location: big cream houses shining in the winter sun. On the ticker tape at the foot of the screen were the words, 'hostage crisis at banker's home'.

'Here, Bob, take a look.'

'You need to get me some medical attention now,' said Bob.

'Forget that for a minute and take a look at this.'

'I'm telling you, I'm dying. You need to do something.'

'It's your man, Graham Poynter.'

Lucas watched Bob, waiting for the reaction. Bob looked across, his face a mask of pain. 'What about him?'

'I told you we were collecting the other password.'

'You'll find it hard. He's got some serious security.'

'Not anymore he hasn't. Look.'

Bob couldn't see very well from where he was lying. Lucas

considered dragging him across the floor so that he was nearer to the T.V. screen but thought that it probably wouldn't be appreciated.

'Please, you need to call an ambulance. Please. If you don't call an ambulance for me, I'm going to die.'

'Here, Bob, keep it down, will you? I'm trying to watch this.'

Lucas turned up the volume on the television. What with Bob blathering away, he could hardly hear the news reporter.

'Please, just call an ambulance.'

It was no good, Bob wasn't going to let him listen and kept bleating on about getting an ambulance. Lucas flicked off the power, walked across to the worktop by the back door and picked up the steel skillet that Bob had left there next to the kitchen knife.

Basement of 11 Blenheim Terrace, Belgravia

As a scientific adviser to New Scotland Yard, Dr Samantha Barnes had always known there was a possibility she would be called upon to undertake an operation in an 'advanced position' – as her boss had put it. She had never anticipated something on this scale, however. The special forces soldiers had given her a flak jacket to wear and she had been driven along the deserted street immediately in front of the row of houses in an armoured vehicle. When it had come to a halt, the soldiers had accompanied her behind a bullet- and blast-proof screen and in through the front door of the house next door to Graham Poynter's. From there she was taken down into the basement where a breach had been made in the wall, allowing access to the cellar of the Poynters' home.

The hostages and hostage taker were situated in the safe room only two floors above. That it was Graham Poynter and his family who had been taken hostage was something she couldn't help but have mixed feelings about. Her husband, a professor of journalism at Goldsmith's College, had authored a book on the financial industry in the wake of the banking crisis and had written at length about Graham Poynter and his arrogant management style. Because of this, she had followed the story of Stanmore Partners' collapse with interest. Her husband's book had been published before the fund's downfall had hit the headlines and he had spoken to the publisher about possibly bringing out an updated edition or possibly an entirely new book which would chart the subsequent events. The tone of the book's content regarding Graham Poynter had been fairly damning but as balanced as one would expect of a serious piece of reportage. Nonetheless, when she had been informed of the exact details of what they wanted her to do, she had felt it only right to mention the family connection. She was told that it had gone along the line to Commander Serina Boise and immediately been dismissed as irrelevant. And here she was, being shown the ventilation system belonging to the man who her husband had researched so assiduously and whose life she was now trying to help save.

While fully aware of the magnitude of what she was about to undertake, she also relished the opportunity to use her own research in a real-world situation. If this operation proved successful, it would be the perfect validation of everything she had been working towards in the past three and a half years. If it was successful, it would pave the way for the use of incapacitating agents by law-enforcement agencies throughout the world. She had checked and re-checked her calculations. Too little of the agent and the hostages would be put at risk of the hostage taker harming them; too much agent and all the occupants of the safe room would develop hypoventilation, apnoea and eventually die if not provided with rapid ventilatory assistance.

So much was at stake that she was alarmed to see her fingers were shaking when she took the aerosol dispersal unit from its case and connected it to the ventilation system. She took a gas canister from another container and connected it to the gas dispersal unit. Turning to the commanding officer of the team who had brought her into the building, she said, 'OK, I'm ready.'

11:54 AM

Negotiating Cell, Blenheim Terrace, Belgravia

'If it was sprayed into your face,' said Commander Boise. 'You'd be out in about two or three seconds but, because it's being propelled into the room up a pipe, we're allowing for up to ten.'

'A lot can happen in ten seconds,' said Ed Mallory.

'I know that, Ed, and I'm aware of your reservations but you've got to see this is an opportunity worth exploring.'

'Yeah, I do, but we mustn't overlook the risk involved.'

'Of course not. No one's thought harder about this than me. It's my neck on the line if this all goes wrong.'

'It's worth calling the phone in the safe room before the gas is released,' said Ed. 'The perp may not answer it but there's a chance he will. If he does and I can engage him in conversation, it might buy us a couple more seconds before he realises what's going on. It might also provide us with an audio connection to the safe room. Hopefully, we can hear his and the hostages' reaction to the dispersal of the gas.'

'We've just got word from the basement of the house,' said Laura Massey. 'The gas is ready to be released. Paramedics are on standby. The S.A.S. team is in its start position at the rear of the building. We just need to give the go-ahead.'

'Thanks, Laura,' said Boise, her voice assuming a more steely, authoritative tone. 'Let's put the call through to the safe room, see if we can make contact.'

'Line connecting,' said Des White and Ed pulled on his headset as the others in the negotiating cell did the same. The ringtone chirruped in Ed's ears. After the first few rings, however, he knew the call would not be answered.

'He's not going to pick up,' he said. 'It's not like he's got far to go to reach the phone. You might as well go with the gas.'

'It's done,' said Serina Boise.

'Let it ring, Des,' said Ed. 'Our man's not going to answer but a ringing phone is still something of a distraction.'

Ed waited, listening to the filtered sound in his earpieces as the phone in the safe room rang out. There were muttered voices and the crackling of a walkie-talkie before Serina Boise said, 'The gas has been dispersed. It should have taken effect by now. The S.A.S. team will be on its way in.'

His and his colleagues' emotions were wound so tightly that Ed could feel the electricity in the room. The smell of pheromonal sweat in the air was strong as the members of the negotiating cell set the vinyl covers of the seats squeaking as they shifted nervously, listening to the ongoing ringtone in their headsets and saying nothing.

11:55 AM

Rear Garden of 11 Blenheim Terrace, Belgravia

The body lay where it had fallen not six feet from where the S.A.S. team huddled in their start position in the hedge adjacent to the terrace at the rear of the building. By the look of the boot prints in the soil around where they waited, it appeared that whoever it was who had killed the security guard had launched his attack on him from here. The victim had suffered massive blood loss from the wound in his neck. After all the time that Justin had spent in Iraq and Afghanistan, the sight of bodies in differing states of dismemberment and decomposition meant nothing to him. This one, however, looked incongruous. In a war-torn location, bodies were just part of the landscape, but here, in a carefully tended English garden with rose bushes and wisteria, a bloody corpse appeared so out of place as to make it border on the surreal.

Thermal imaging of the house had proved inconclusive.

The walls in old Regency houses were too thick for it to be effective and it was impossible to ascertain whether there might be others in the building besides the single perpetrator in the safe room with the hostages. Justin knew the other three men would be thinking about this too while they waited. There was always plenty of waiting. The waiting was the hard part. But maybe a little more of it today might not have been a bad thing. It was the most rapid rapid intervention he had ever been involved in and the plan of action once they were inside the house was far from conventional either.

When clearing a building, their training had focused on going from room to room. This was not an option for them now. They needed to get to the safe room as fast as possible. Initially, they had discussed abseiling down from a helicopter on to the roof but, once the configuration and location of the C.C.T.V. cameras around the building had been ascertained, it was decided that to go in through a door at the rear of the building was the best option. All being well, of course, the occupants of the safe room would be sleeping soundly. They needed to make an entry into the room in order to allow the gas to disperse as quickly as possible before providing medical assistance prior to the arrival of the paramedics.

Justin and the rest of the team had managed to snatch a few minutes in order to study the layout of the house. Ideally, they would have liked to rehearse the approach to the safe room within a mocked-up interior but sometimes such a luxury wasn't possible. As things stood, all they could do was deal with hostilities as and when they arose. It was once they were at the safe room that things got more difficult. It was a top-of-the-range construction with reinforced steel. Its entire purpose and function was to keep people out. If they had longer, they could have dismantled the door. Time, however, was another luxury they did not possess. They needed to get in there fast. They would start off with a small explosive charge and increase the size of the charge as required. What they would find once they had gained entry was something that no one could predict. The danger of using larger charges was that they might injure or even possibly kill the occupants – hence the paramedics who could be in position in a matter of seconds.

Justin's thoughts were interrupted by a crackle of static on the radio link as a connection was made. It could only mean one thing and this was confirmed as the command burst into his headset: 'Team A. Go! Go! Go!'

11:59 AM

Negotiating Cell, Blenheim Terrace, Belgravia

'It'll be coming through on that screen over there at any moment,' announced Des White to the members of the negotiating cell.

'I'll commentate for you, Ed,' said Nick Calvert.

It was the first time Ed had been part of a negotiation when live video was being streamed from special forces during an intervention. Everyone – apart from him – would be able to watch in real time as the S.A.S. team went into the house. For the second time that morning, technology had conspired to make him feel excluded from the negotiation process. The decision to put gas into the safe room was one that he thought extremely risky but, on balance, worth attempting. This, the sound and vision from the S.A.S. team, however, sounded like it was pure show business. They didn't need to see the advance of the S.A.S. team through the house. But even as he thought this, he also realised that his antipathy was probably no more than his subconscious attempting to ease the pain of his blindness. It was a trait that he knew was prevalent in many disabled people who struggled to come to terms with their disability. When faced with proof of your disability, you disparage, demean and belittle the cause of that proof.

Ed pulled the headset down so that it hung around his neck. He could still just make out the ringtone purring out of the earpieces as the phone in the safe room rang out. The other members of the negotiation team watched the screen. There was no sound on the video feed and Ed was aware of the sounds that his fellow negotiators made: Des White scratching his head; Nick Calvert breathing; Laura Massey clicking the clip on a ballpoint pen with her fingernail.

'Here we go,' said Calvert. 'They're moving across the garden and up the steps to the terrace.' He exhaled loudly, accompanied by what Ed presumed was a shake of the head at what he was seeing. 'There's one of the security guards. Poor bastard. Now they're through the door and inside. They're in the hallway. They're going up the stairs.'

12:00 noon

11 Blenheim Terrace, Belgravia

Justin looked down at the security guard lying where he had fallen on the terrace by the rear door to the house. Massive blood loss from what amounted to his partial decapitation had coloured the stone around where he lay. It was clear that he had been ambushed when someone had stepped out of the door on to the terrace behind him. His face was twisted into an expression of surprise and sudden realisation. As with the body on the lawn down below, it looked out of place in such a scenic, domestic situation.

Outside the closed door to the house, Justin signalled for the others to put on their gas masks. The perspex visor on Justin's gas mask was clean apart from a slight smudge above his left eye. Sweat, most probably. Checking that the others all had their gas masks in place, he pulled open the door and they went inside. All the years of training they had spent running through mock rescue missions at the

Killing House at S.A.S. headquarters in Hereford; all those rounds they had fired in order to gain total familiarity and 'muscle memory' with their weapons: it would all be called upon now.

Once inside the house, they moved down the corridor, past the back staircase. Justin aimed his C8 carbine up into the stairwell but it was clear. When they had planned their movements through the house earlier, they had considered going up the back staircase to make their way immediately to the safe room, but it was decided it would be better to use the main staircase, which would decrease the likelihood of sudden ambush. It would take a few seconds more but it would provide them with considerably more safety.

Moving out from the corridor into the large square hallway, they spread out and scoped out potential angles of attack. Once satisfied it was clear, they made their way up the main staircase to the first-floor landing, one side of which looked out over a banister rail on to the hallway down below. As Justin knew from the plan of the house, which he had managed to memorise in haste, the safe room was in a bedroom along the landing. The house was still and silent. Justin knew that, at the slightest sign of an attack, there were two more teams of four soldiers, Team B and Team C, on standby, one team in each of the houses either side of the Poynters'. The first-floor balconies of the three houses – in fact, all the houses on the terrace – could be connected using a ladder. Each team could be within the house in a matter of seconds. But, even though their close proximity was reassuring, Justin didn't think they would be needed. The hostage-taking bore all the hallmarks of a lone-wolf operation.

Moving along the landing, they passed one bedroom on the right but continued just beyond it to the room on the left, the guest room in which the safe room was situated. But no attempt had been made to conceal its location. The fake wardrobe doors were pulled wide allowing a clear view of the black metal door leading into the safe room. While two of them covered the corridor and the doorway to the bedroom, two of them unpacked the sticky bombs. These were bespoke explosives, developed to cause as much damage as possible around the door frame, including the locks and hinges, while minimising the blast within the room. With the explosives in place, Justin set the electronic fuse to ten seconds and they made their way back down to the landing where they hunkered down away from the mouth of the corridor to wait for the blast.

When it came, Justin felt a tremor in the very structure of the house itself. He hoped they didn't need a second blast to get through the door – that might put those in the safe room in extreme danger. They moved back down the corridor through the smoke and the unmistakable smell of detonated ordnance. He needn't have worried about using the second bomb. Although still on its hinges, the door was misshapen enough to allow a crowbar into a gap between the door and the frame. With the door levered open, Justin could see that all the lights in the safe room had been blown out by the explosion and even the powerful beams of the torches on their C8 barrels couldn't cut through the smoke.

It was a difficult moment. All four of them pointed their guns into the dark interior of the safe room. For all they knew, someone could be pointing a weapon straight back at them. It was impossible to tell. The only certainty they did have was that the phone was ringing. It was an old-fashioned sounding ringtone and it rang in his ears as Justin led them in. As his torch cut through the dispersing smoke, however, the situation became clear.

'It's empty,' he said into his headset, knowing that the members of the command centre and negotiating cell would be able to see for themselves soon enough on the live stream from the camera mounted on his helmet. 'Repeat: the safe room is empty.'

12:03 PM

44 Courtenay Avenue, Hampstead

Lucas did a final rep on the abdominal crunch machine in the gymnasium in the basement of Bob Rushwood's rented house. He had lost count of how many he had done in total but the muscles in his stomach were burning. His sweat felt sticky in his leathers but the exercise had had the desired effect, which was to expend the nervous energy he felt after his successful extraction of the password to the bank account from Bob Rushwood. At first, he had considered defecating somewhere, maybe on one of the sheepskin rugs that seemed to be part of an interior designer's running theme throughout the house. But he worried about the D.N.A. implications and, besides, he didn't need to go. The use of the gymnasium was more civilised as a means of calming himself and he had made sure to keep his gloves on, so there were no fingerprints.

It wasn't all about the money but the money was

important. It was funding for the cause. If all went well today, they would have funds with which they could recruit more members and expand their network internationally. They could support similar operations and open up multiple fronts in the war. The intention was to create a profile not unlike al-Qaeda's in terms of their reputation and the fear they provoked in people. But their own long-term aims would be entirely different, of course. They were not working towards some sort of new society based on rigid religious principles; they were hoping to ensure that a tiny percentage of the population took responsibility for their actions. They wanted to fight back against a cabal of individuals who had been holding the peoples of the world to ransom for far too long. If governments were not prepared to hold the financial markets and the people who ran them to account then he and his associates would do it for them. As with al-Qaeda, their principles were based on the propagation of fear. Someone had to try to stop the enemy looting the natural resources of the world and raping the money markets for their own nefarious ends. They would engage in targeted acts of terrorism: incidents of violent theatre that would grab the headlines and force their argument centre stage. If it took acts of extreme brutality against a small handful of people in order to scare others into behaving with a greater sense of morality, then so be it. Ultimately, they were working for the greater good. Bankers were forever talking about risk – they were drunk on it. It turned them on. Well, this was *real* risk. Instead of facing something abstract, like losses on the financial markets, at its worst, they would lose their lives. Faced with this as a possible risk, it would be interesting to see how many of the over-privileged ex-public schoolboys who littered the industry would step up and continue with their ongoing behaviour.

Lucas climbed out from the machine and glanced at his watch. It was time to go. He left the room that housed the gymnasium and walked along the hallway, back to the kitchen. He stepped over the body and went to the sink to wash his sticky hands. He turned on the tap before he removed his gloves then held his hands under the lukewarm water and splashed some on his face. He shook his hands dry, put his gloves back on and walked across to the large luxury refrigerator and the panic button that was mounted on the wall next to it. He pushed the button hard, once. The security company would take a few minutes to respond, by which time he would be long gone. Within the hour, the news would be out and another vital piece of propaganda would be flooding the media. Lucas made his way to the back door. Opening it, he turned to look at what the unfortunate security-company employee would see on entering the house, namely Bob Rushwood, sitting wide-eyed with his back against the island in the middle of the kitchen. Blood-soaked ten- and twenty-pound notes were protruding from his distorted mouth where Lucas had driven them with the handle of the skillet, breaking his teeth and choking him to death.

12:07 PM

Negotiating Cell, Blenheim Terrace,
Belgravia

'There appears to be some sort of electronic device attached
to the phone,' said the leader of the S.A.S. team, his voice
relayed through the speakers in the negotiating cell.

'We're going to need that connection,' said Ed.

'They want to send in the other S.A.S. teams,' said Serina
Boise.

'No!' Ed shouted the word. He didn't care how it sounded
and what effect it had on the morale of the cell. Events were
overtaking them. He had to make sure that the momentum
was slowed. It was at moments like this that mistakes were
made and lives lost. 'Tell them it's essential that they stay
in position. I need to speak to the hostage taker.'

Any worries Ed might have felt about sounding unhinged
were banished when he heard Serina Boise's voice. She was
the on-site commander and she sounded like she was struggling with her own rising panic.

'But Ed, he's not answering the bloody call.'

'He will answer, trust me. He won't have gone to all the trouble of linking the line in the safe room to a mobile phone if he doesn't want to speak to us. Please, hold back just for a couple of minutes.'

'Ed, this is no longer a police operation; the Ministry of Defence are now involved.'

'A couple of minutes, that's all I ask.'

'I don't know; I'll try.'

There was movement in the room, voices, instructions, mutterings. Ed tried to block them out and focused instead on the sound of the ringtone coming from his headset that had been providing a purring back-rhythm to the unfolding events of the past few minutes.

'Ed, they want to go in and they want to go in now,' said Serina.

'No. You promised me two minutes. He's there; he's going to answer.'

'It's not going to happen, Ed.'

'It's going to happen.'

Ed had never felt as unhinged and unbalanced in a nego-tiating cell as he felt now. If the call wasn't answered, he didn't know how he could react. The ringtone was taunting him; he was tired, he felt sick and his confidence in his own abilities was ebbing away. His mindset was so far away from what it should have been to conduct a negotiation, or to make any form of strategic decision, that his overriding impulse was to tear off his headset and get as far away from the command centre as he could.

'Ed, I'm sorry.'

'Don't be sorry, just tell them to hold back.'

How must he look to the other members of the cell, standing up, his scarred face twisted with nerves? There was more muttering coming from Serina's direction. And then it came. The purring rhythm of the ringtone that had infused Ed's senses for so long came to an abrupt halt and was replaced by the subject's voice.

'Hello?'

Ed pulled the headset from around his neck, up on to his ears. Everything was moving so fast that he had no time to collect himself for the next stage of the negotiation. What should he say to the hostage taker – wherever he was – now it was clear that an attempt to bring the situation to a violent end had already been attempted?

'Hello, this is Ed Mallory.' Ed's tone of voice took a swerve as he attempted to reduce its emotional temperature.

'Call off any further I.A. plans. Have all special forces stand down immediately, otherwise I detonate explosives and everyone I'm with ends up dead. Confirm!'

There was no point disconnecting the line and waiting for confirmation from Boise – or anyone. However messed up Ed felt at that moment in time, he was still the first line in the chain of command.

'Yes. Confirmed.'

'OK. Now, what I'm going to tell you needs to be carried out to the letter; got it?'

'Yes, yes.'

Ed sat down and leaned forward with his elbows on the desk. He had work to do, issues to consider, strategies to devise. His heart rate dropped a little. But even before he began to listen to the hostage taker's demands, he had made a discovery. The man had told him to 'call off any further I.A. plans'. The 'I.A.' stood for 'Immediate Action'. His use of the terminology was confirmation of his military training. Before Ed could attempt any further character profiling, however, he had to try to re-establish some form of rapport with the subject.

For the time being, at least, Ed was back in the game.

12:10 PM

Attic of 11 Blenheim Terrace, Belgravia

Lily had watched the giant earlier as he had unpacked the small electronic box from his rucksack and connected it to the telephone handset in the safe room. He was a man who clearly knew what he was doing; this wasn't just some lone chancer. His attack on her family had been planned meticulously and all the necessary equipment provided. He had an air of professionalism about him at all times. When he had opened the safe room door and ushered her and her parents and the delivery driver out into the spare room, she had allowed herself to hope they were being released. It was an irrational hope; she knew that. Why go to all the trouble of attacking their home if he was going to let them go? Any last vestiges of hope she might have had that their removal from the safe room represented some sort of release, however, were snuffed out as soon as the giant had led them up the narrow stairs from the first floor, up to the attic.

Once there, he had herded them to a position next to the door leading out on to the roof. There he had told them to stand in silence while he unpacked further equipment from his rucksack.

This wasn't electronic equipment, however, but some sort of metal collar. Her parents had remonstrated with the man as he started to attach it to Lily's neck. She had remained silent, numb with shock. It wasn't so much the collar that was the problem, it was what it was attached to – a small canister with a handle on the top of it. Any curiosity she might have had as to its exact purpose, and any hope that its purpose was innocuous, was put to rest when the giant told them, 'This is a hand grenade.' Immediately, her parents had started shouting and pleading and the man had told them to shut up. He said that any objections they made were placing Lily's life in even greater danger. He attached a thin chain to the grenade, which he connected to a leather strap around his wrist, not unlike a watch strap. But as much as her parents tried everything they could to stop the man doing what he was doing, their entreaties remained purely verbal. Neither of them attempted any physical intervention. The delivery driver, on the other hand, remained silent. He stood next to her as though frozen to the spot.

The explosion down below had been powerful enough to shake the building. Her mother had emitted a shriek and the giant had told her in a calm voice to keep quiet. Seemingly, the explosion had come as no surprise to him. Pulling on a headset over his balaclava, he tapped away on his smart-phone, which Lily could hear was vibrating from an incoming call alert which continued indefinitely. The metal collar that had been fixed around her neck was cold against her skin but gradually warmed up to become clammy and sweaty as they continued to wait. There was no heating in the attic but she burned with all the fear and discomfort of a fever dream.

Her mind was crowded with questions. Was there a rescue attempt in progress? Was that what the explosion was all about? It came from the direction of the safe room. Had someone tried to release them? Or was the explosion the handiwork of their captor? Every question that her mind conjured up went unanswered. As a coping mechanism, the asking of the questions was failing, so she tried to think of something else.

She used to come up here to the attic when she was little. She came up once with a friend who was staying over and they had hidden away for a couple of hours, concealing themselves behind some old furniture and refusing to answer her parents' increasingly frantic efforts to locate them. The prank had backfired when her mother had called the police, thinking that the two of them had been abducted. It was the first time she had ever seen her mother in tears. It was a strange experience. She had seen her cry plenty of times since then, especially in the past couple of months, and Helen was crying now as she hugged Lily's dad – the first time Lily had seen them have any physical contact in as long as she could remember. And, all the while, the iPhone continued to vibrate in the giant's hand.

12:12 PM

Attic of 11 Blenheim Terrace, Belgravia

Danny knew they would try to close him down sooner rather than later. An assault on the safe room was the obvious course of action, particularly if it was combined with an attempt to knock out the room's occupants with gas. Danny's training allowed him to think strategically about the situation, view it dispassionately and anticipate all possible eventualities. In all the years he had spent in the S.A.S. he doubted if he had planned anything as meticulously as he had this mission. This one was different. In other operations, all he had to lose was his own life. There was so much more at stake now. This was all about his own family.

Successfully completing a mission like this was all about having confidence in his own abilities. That confidence, tempered with acute concentration on the minutiae of what he had to do from one moment to the next, was the key. His conflicted morality and the final outcome of what he was going to attempt made that level of focus difficult to achieve. There had been distractions in the past, for sure. He had always considered the implications of what he was engaged in, probably more than he should have done. But the morality involved was largely intellectual in terms of his day-to-day activities. He was working for the British government and, ultimately, the British people. It was what he had signed up to do without hesitation when he left school. The morality of what he was doing was unimportant. This operation, however, had tortured his conscience to such an extent that he worried that he might lose his mind. So many times he had nearly walked away but, every time he thought he might, he had been dragged back by thoughts of the future – such as it was. The choice he was presented with was always an impossible one. When he had made his decision, it was final. Some people would have to die. The implications wounded him deeply but their deaths would not be in isolation. There were positive benefits – as there were in war – and so long as they outweighed the negatives then the strategy was justified.

That didn't alter the fact that there was so much that could go wrong. The mission was very tech heavy. He wasn't happy with the communications angle. It was decided that a connection should be made with the authorities. He had argued against it, suggested that it wasn't necessary in such a short space of time, but he had been overruled. He was told that the connection needed to be maintained with the authorities so that demands could be made and necessary stalling tactics deployed. It meant the use of specially modified smartphones, headsets and connection devices. These had been provided and he had spent plenty of time learning how they worked. In the past, he had always preferred operations that didn't rely on too much technical expertise, but all he could do was prepare as thoroughly as he possibly could and try to consider all eventualities. And one aspect of the operation he couldn't fault was the backup support he had received.

Reconnaissance was a bigger issue. Although provided with detailed plans of the property, he had been unable to rehearse any scenarios in a similar location. Another crucial factor that set this mission apart from others he had experienced was that, once it was under way, he was entirely on his own. The only interaction he would have would be with the authorities and their nominated negotiator. And one of the hardest parts of the operation, psychologically, was thinking of himself as the perpetrator, the hostage taker, the subject, the target. That was something he would never be able to assimilate in the long-term. But it didn't matter. There was no long-term.

Danny had anticipated that the second and third S.A.S. teams might enter the stronghold via the roof. They still might. But he had heard nothing – no movement whatsoever – so far. They might come across the balconies or even through the walls and he needed to make his move before they did.

The phone was vibrating in his hand as it had been for the past few minutes. The collar was in place on Lily's neck and the chain attached to his wrist. None of the hostages had presented him with any resistance. They were all terrified. None of them had been in a situation like this before. They were all desperate to stay alive. It was this will to survive that made them compliant. Danny looked at the screen and pressed the answer button with his thumb. Raising the phone to his ear, he said, 'Hello.'

It was the negotiator he had spoken to from the safe room, Ed Mallory. Aware of the fact that there was only one floor between him and an S.A.S. team, Danny knew he needed to move fast.

'Call off any further I.A. plans,' he said into the handset. 'Have all special forces stand down immediately, otherwise I detonate explosives and everyone I'm with ends up dead. Confirm!'

Ed Mallory confirmed and Danny told him he must carry out his instructions to the letter. Danny couldn't be certain, but Ed Mallory sounded more flustered than he had been when they had spoken earlier. It was probably something to do with the failed intervention.

'There is an explosive device – a hand grenade – attached to Lily Poynter's neck,' Danny told him. 'Do you understand?'

'Yes.'

'Attached to the pin on the hand grenade is a chain. The other end of the chain is attached to my wrist. If any attempt

is made to compromise my safety or well-being, the chain
will be pulled and the pin will come out of the hand grenade.
Please confirm your understanding.'

'Confirmed.'

'Do you need time to relay this to others further up the
chain of command?'

'No, that's fine. You're coming through loud and clear.
May I ask a question?'

'You probably want to know where we are, right?'

'Amongst other things.'

'Well, if there's a camera on one of the helicopters that
I can hear hovering above the building, you should be able
to see us at any moment.'

'I can't see anything; I'm blind.'

'In that case, you can tell other members of your team
to watch out for us. And remember, any hostile act that is
made towards me will result in the grenade around Lily
Poynter's neck being detonated. Are we clear?'

'We're clear.'

Danny disconnected the call before Ed Mallory could
attempt any further interaction. He unbolted the door,
leading out on to the flat roof, and kicked it open. The light
erupted into the dark interior of the attic as Danny pushed
his hostages through the doorway. He was careful with Lily.
The chain was approximately ten feet long; he made sure
there was enough slack that, should she stumble, the pin
would not be pulled out. It was essential, however, that the

authorities didn't feel they could risk using a sniper to take him out, thinking that he might fall without disturbing the pin.

When he had been up here earlier, his mind had been focused on dealing with the security guard and getting back into the house to find Lily and her parents. Now, however, he could see that the layout of the roof was exactly as detailed in the plans with which he had been supplied. There was a large chimney stack to one side and a low brick wall, about two feet high, ran around the perimeter of the lead-lined flat roof space.

The sound of helicopter rota blades throbbed all around. There were four, maybe five; he didn't count. Some of them would contain special forces – almost certainly S.A.S. They would be considering every opportunity to take him out while keeping the hostages safe. Logistics would be proposed and tested at all times. But so long as he presented enough of a threat to his hostages – and Lily in particular – then he would be allowed to live long enough to complete his mission.

'You need to stand here, in the middle of the flat roof,' he shouted above the sound of the helicopters. There was no question of any of them disobeying or being anything other than quietly compliant. Danny positioned himself with his back against the chimney, a stack which presented a brick cliff rising four feet above his head with a large stone architrave near the top that cast a shadow across him. This meant that he could only be in a clear line of sight – or as clear a line of sight as a sniper on a helicopter would require to take a shot – if the helicopter reduced its altitude considerably and positioned itself on the south and south-westerly side of the chimney stack. In the time it would take do so, Danny could take action by either moving into a more sheltered position behind the hostages or presenting an even greater threat to them. He felt horribly exposed. But that was all part of the mission. They were up on the roof for a reason.

12:13 PM

14 Spruce Road, Stockton-on-Tees

Jan had tried to keep smiling, for Emily's sake, but she had expected Danny home earlier than this and it was annoying that he couldn't phone her to let her know where he was. Today of all days. He had been typically vague about what time he would be back but that was not what had set her worrying. It was difficult to say exactly when it had all started – sometime in the spring, most probably. He seemed so distant and he was so sentimental. Tears would come to his eyes at the slightest provocation, especially if it was something to do with Emily. When Emily had been born, they had struggled with sleepless nights like all new parents and their tempers had frayed. They had had a few arguments. Nothing too bad. But for the past few months, there had been none. Danny had backed down from every confrontation. It was as though he didn't want to upset her, as though he knew something that he didn't want her to find out about.

She didn't seriously think he might be having an affair. They still slept together; everything was fine in that department. If anything, it was better than ever; he was so tender and loving. Even his lads' nights out had come to an end. He had vigorously defended his social life when they had first got married, told her that his friends were important to him. Mal and Stevie were friends from way back. They had grown up together. They were like brothers. But, even though he still saw them from time to time, the Friday nights in the Acton had been few and far between of late. So much so that when Mal, Danny's best man at their wedding, had phoned up one night to speak to Danny and Jan had answered, he had asked her if there was something the matter. Jan had tried to reassure him as best she could but there was no avoiding the fact that Danny had changed. They loved each other. She was confident of that. But there was something wrong and she had vowed to herself she was going to sort it out over the Christmas break. It was the first time in the past few years they had not been to either of their parents' for Christmas. It was going to be just the three of them – as a family. She had looked forward to it like no other Christmas for years. And now this.

She hadn't been happy about him going to London on Christmas Eve but he had said it was the only time that Arthur would be in London. Arthur was a name like so many others Danny used: a name without a surname or any other reference to his specific identity. She had never seen a picture of Arthur, didn't know anything about him other than he was one of a handful of men that provided Danny with employment. Danny had said he was meeting Arthur in a hotel in the West End. It had used to annoy her that he wouldn't be more specific regarding the exact details of the jobs he did. In time, though, she had learned to live with it. As Danny himself had said, it was safer for her and Emily if she didn't know what work he was doing; she would worry less too. One thing she had noticed, however, was that the meetings with the Arthurs of this world had been fewer of late and their income had suffered accordingly. When Emily was born, Danny had decided to try to pursue contracts exclusively in the U.K. but it was proving to be more and more difficult. The fact was, in his line of work, most of the well-paid jobs were in Africa or the Middle East. But even though he was worried he was going to have to start travelling again to find the work and be away from his family for sometimes weeks at a time, she didn't think that the change in his demeanour was down to that – or not that alone, anyway. There was something else.

When she tried his phone again, the ringtone came to an end and the phone company's standard voicemail greeting clicked in: 'The person you are calling is currently unavailable; please leave a message after the tone.' She was about to speak, about to tell Danny it was the third message that she'd left in as many hours, but there was no point. He would know she was trying to get hold of him. She didn't want to sound desperate, so she disconnected the call. Earlier, she had felt angry. Now that anger had begun to turn to fear. What if something had happened to Danny? When he was in the S.A.S. she had been given a number she could call if she needed to leave a message for him. Nowadays, she had nothing more than his mobile phone number. When he was saying his goodbyes the day before, he hadn't behaved like a man who was just going down to London for a meeting. He had held her and Emily tightly for a good minute, maybe more. There were tears in his eyes too. She hadn't thought too much of it at the time, just thought that it was part of his ongoing mid-life crisis that seemed to have become so much more marked of late. Now, however, as the minutes ticked by and there was still no call from him, she couldn't help but feel an increasing sense of dread.

12:17 PM

Roof of 11 Blenheim Terrace, Belgravia

The sound of the helicopters hundreds of feet up above them meant that, when he spoke, the giant had to raise his voice to be heard. 'Don't make any sudden movements, Lily; don't fall over; don't stumble or trip because – well, you know why.'

'Yes.' The word stuttered out from her shivering mouth. Lily was wearing no shoes or socks. Her feet had soon become numb as she stood on the lead of the flat roof.

'You're cold?' he asked and she nodded. The giant looked towards her parents and the delivery driver. 'Why don't one of you give her an extra layer?' It was the sort of suggestion a parent might make to their children when out for a family walk. It wasn't the sort of comment she expected from a man who had engineered her potential decapitation with explosives. His benevolent demeanour was in stark contrast to the threat that he presented. What sort of mind could at one moment secure a high explosive around her neck and threaten to kill her by detonating it, and the next enquire about her well-being?

Her parents looked so small. It was as though fear had made them deflate. They glanced at one another, trapped by their own helplessness, their faces drawn, their eyes confused. It was the delivery driver who moved first. He took off his jacket and put it around her shoulders. Then he asked, 'Can I give her my socks? She's got nothing on her feet.'

The giant nodded and the driver slipped off his shoes and pulled off his socks. He bent down to Lily and taking one foot and then the other, he pulled on the socks that were still warm from his feet.

'Here you go,' he said, his back to the giant. 'My name's James. This is pretty messed up, right?'

'Right.'

'Kill the chat,' said the giant but his voice didn't rise. He didn't appear to be angered by James's communication with her. It seemed that he felt no fear of losing control of his hostages. He was big enough and terrifying enough to feel secure in the situation that he had engineered. He wasn't expecting an insurrection and, if one came, he clearly felt certain that he would be able to put it down. He stood in the shadow of the chimney stack and looked at the smartphone in his hand while James pushed his bare feet back into his shoes and straightened up.

'She's still cold,' James called across to the giant.

Whereas, earlier, the van delivery driver had appeared as mute with fear as all of them, now he was gaining in confidence. Lily worried that this might be provocative, although she was thankful for his concern.

The giant looked across at him and appeared to wince a little. He shook his head momentarily and said, 'Well, why don't you put your arm around her then?'

Her parents didn't move. Lily felt sure that the giant's suggestion was directed at any of them but it was James who put his arm around her. He rubbed her arm, awkwardly.

'Touching,' said the hostage taker. He was behaving as though he was killing time, as though waiting for someone else to arrive. There was no reason she could think of for why he wanted to stand on the roof of their house, threatening her family, with no possible means of escape. He was trapped. The only reason that the full magazines of live rounds remained in the guns of the snipers that were surely pointed at him was the chain and collar around her neck and the implicit threat that it presented.

'So what are we doing here?' James shouted, as though following her train of thought.

The giant looked up from the iPhone again and his expression had changed. He wasn't angry, just hassled. He allowed his left hand – the one attaching him to Lily – to drop to his side. This took up the slack on the chain. Lily could feel it pull very slightly on the pin and she found herself leaning forward to reduce the tension.

'I didn't ask you to speak, so don't, you of all people. You're only here to make up the numbers. You're just an extra bargaining chip and utterly expendable. So don't push it.'

For a moment, Lily feared that James was going to say something else but he remained silent.

'We're going to be here for a little while,' said the giant. 'So I needn't tell you that this is a dangerous situation. If you want to talk to each other then do, but keep it down. I don't want to hear it.'

There it was again; he spoke as though he was genuinely trying to be amenable, as though he was some sort of public servant and what he was doing was in their own best interests. She didn't know if it had registered with any of the others but, to her, it was unmistakable.

Her father leaned towards her and whispered, 'It's going to be OK, Lily.'

'No, it isn't, Dad.'

'I'm so sorry you had to get wrapped up in all this.'

'What, your life?'

'Well, I'm sorry.'

'You're only sorry you got caught.' Lily looked across at the giant. He was staring straight at her, seemingly unconcerned about her ongoing conversation. It wasn't as though he could understand what she was saying. The helicopters' rota blades rendered words spoken at normal conversational volume inaudible even three feet away from the mouth that had spoken them. The giant was ten feet away. She looked away as her father's whispered voice raised in tone as emotion gripped it.

'This isn't me being caught, Lily. This isn't a fraud investigation.'

'I don't want to die, Dad.'

He didn't have anything to say to that, pulled away from her and looked up at the sky, gasping in the air, tears in his eyes. The helicopters hovered up above, their bulbous glass probosces staring down at them impassively.

'I'm sorry.' Her dad whispered it more to himself than to Lily. She watched him and she could see in his face all the self-pity that she might have expected and as much as she felt desperate for him, she also despised him.

'He's keeping us alive for a reason.' James didn't bother to lower his voice, didn't need to on account of the helicopters. Lily looked at him standing next to her. There was a thoughtful intensity to him that she hadn't noticed before. She liked that he had his arm around her. 'For every second that ticks by,' continued James, 'there's a greater chance that someone's going to stop him doing what he wants to do.'

'Like who?' asked Lily.

'Like me.'

'He'll kill you,' said Lily. 'He's already killed three security guards.'

Though speaking to each other, Lily and James both watched their captor when they spoke and he shared his attention between his hostages and the screen of his iPhone. Suddenly, his demeanour darkened. He shot them an angry stare. He tapped at the screen with his thumb and made a call. As he spoke into his phone, he pushed himself away from the chimney stack and moved towards them, winding the chain around his wrist, ensuring that he maintained the tension between his arm and the collar around her neck. Grabbing James's shoulder, he roughly pushed him to the ground, James's legs buckling as he fell forward on to his knees. The giant took out a huge hunting knife and held it against James's neck. Standing as close as he was, the words he spoke into his phone were clearly audible.

'Reinstate the Internet connection or I will cut the delivery boy's head off. You've got exactly one minute.'

12:26 PM

Negotiating Cell, Blenheim Terrace, Belgravia

'You've fucking cut me off,' the hostage taker's accent became stronger as the anger took hold.

Ed knew immediately what he meant. It was standard procedure for phone and Wi-Fi signals in the environment of the stronghold to be jammed to prevent any untoward communication between hostage takers and potential accomplices. What the tech guys had done was keep the phone reception in place but cut the Internet connection. Ed found it infuriating that he hadn't been consulted. He was the first negotiator; he was the first point of contact between the hostage taker and the rest of the world and he should have been informed of any key modification to the stronghold's communications access. But a decision as important as the timing of when to close down the Wi-Fi signal had been made and put into action without any consultation with him or anyone else in the negotiating cell.

'What do you mean, cut you off?' Ed was stalling, the fist that he had raised, knuckles tapping against his forehead was a clear visual sign to his colleagues that he was in uncharted territory.

'Don't play dumb, mate. The Internet – you've messed about with the connection.' There was the sound of movement on the line. When the voice returned, it was more antagonistic than before. 'Reinstate the Internet connection or I will cut the delivery boy's head off. You've got exactly one minute.'

The line went dead and, as it did so, there was an explosion of voices in the command centre; Ed's was the loudest and most insistent as he said, 'Why didn't I know we were going to cut the web access?' But it seemed as though that question had already been rendered redundant by the rapid advancement of the situation.

'They think they might try a shot,' said Serina Boise. 'They've got a sniper in one of the helicopters with a clear line of sight. As soon as there's some slack on the chain, they're going to go for it.'

Ed didn't care about rank and protocol anymore. The normal rules no longer applied. When he addressed Commander Boise, he used her first name. 'Serina, you guys better decide who's in charge of this incident. Is it the military or is it the police? Because unless someone can give me some guidance on this, I'm out of here.'

It was the first time he had ever threatened to quit a negotiation and it was scary how easily it came out.

'Ed, we have to try to resolve this with the minimum loss of life and if that means taking the hostage taker down then—'

'So this is a military operation now.'

'It's a combined operation; we're working together.'

'Thirty seconds gone,' said Des White, his deadpan delivery ratcheting up the tension more than if he had screamed the words.

'Let's at least put the Internet back on while they're trying to work out whether to shoot the guy.'

'But, if we do that,' said Serina. 'He'll move back into the shadow of the chimney stack and we'll have lost the chance.'

Ed pulled his headset from around his neck and slammed it down on the desk in front of him. He wanted to storm out but he knew that he couldn't. What a sick joke that would be: blundering into people and objects as he tried to find his way.

'I don't understand the hurry here.' Ed didn't direct his words at anyone in particular. 'It's almost as though we're forcing him into attempting further violence. You've got to give me more time. I can make a difference here.' Whether it was his renewed calm or the forcefulness of his words, he didn't know, but after a brief muttered conversation between Serina Boise and someone in the doorway to the command centre, she said, 'OK, let's put the Wi-Fi back on.'

'Fifty seconds gone and the signal's back on,' called out Des White. Ed counted down the seconds and knew with a cold certainty that, true to his customary efficiency, the hostage taker would call back on the dot. 'Subject calling,' said White as Ed counted the fifty-ninth second. He pulled his headset back on.

'Right,' said the hostage taker, 'I'm going to cut this little fucker's head off now.'

'It's on; the signal's back on.'

'Knife!' Nick Calvert shouted the word, alerting Ed to what he was seeing on the screen.

'I've been assured that the signal's on,' said Ed. 'Check your phone again before you do anything you might regret.'

Pause. Ed listened. There was silence in the cell. The temperature was rising. All the bodies were warming the room. Sweat bubbled up on his face, irritating his scar tissue.

Ed clicked off his headset and muttered, 'What's happening?'

'He's fiddling with his phone,' said Calvert. 'Now he's putting his knife away and moving back by the chimney stack.'

Ed exhaled slowly, trying to calm himself as he clicked back into the line again. 'Hello? Can you hear me?'

'I can hear you.'

'It's back on, right?'

'Right.'

The line went dead.

With his negotiation temporarily at a close, Ed knew he should address the situation that had arisen, namely his threat to resign from the negotiation. It went against all protocol and accepted standards of conduct. Once a negotiator was part of a negotiation, that was it: he or she was not going to go anywhere until relieved by the cell co-ordinator or incident commander. That he had so brazenly threatened to walk would not go unnoticed and gave him pause to consider his own mental state. He would never have behaved like that back in the old days, whatever the conditions of a negotiation. He should say something, speak to what had just happened, reassure his colleagues. That would be the right thing to do. But as the seconds ticked by and Serina Boise and Laura Massey started talking about the jamming facility that they had in operation and how they could isolate certain signals and block out others, he decided to let it go. If no one else wanted to talk about it then there was no point him raising the subject. It was more important to establish exactly what the military was planning, or whether, as Ed suspected, it was just reacting to events as they unfolded without any clear strategy.

There were voices – none of them directed at him – and one of them was Serina's. All the voices were modulated by nerves and the electricity of fear. The words came out fast and some of the phrases he could just make out. 'Line of sight' was one of them. 'Immediate threat' was another.

'What's happening now?' asked Ed. The atmosphere in the cell felt different from what he was used to. His position within the hierarchy of the negotiation felt compromised.

His standing was diminished, not just because of his recent behaviour but also because he was no longer on the force. In the old days, no one would ever have allowed a question from him to go unanswered, if for no other reason than out of respect for his disability. It didn't bother him unduly on that score; he had never sought or expected special treatment because of his blindness but, if nothing else, his unanswered question was an indicator that his new role as a consultant meant that he had been marginalised.

There were footsteps in the command centre and Serina Boise spoke to him from nearby. As she started to speak, he felt sure that the forced intimacy of the tone was a precursor to telling him that he had been relieved of his position as the number one in the cell, probably relieved of all negotiation duties.

'Ed, I've spoken to the other commanders and the commissioner.' He was right; he was being sacked. 'We're going to make no attempt to deploy the sniper at the present time. Not until such time as the hostage taker makes an attempt to harm any or all of the hostages. We'd like you to try to keep talking to him, establish what he wants and try to resolve the situation with no further loss of life.'

Like so many assumptions he had made that day, his judgement had been found wanting. A decision had been made to keep him in his post. But he knew that the decision could be rescinded at any moment. In the meantime, he had to stay focused – or as focused as he could – and needed to ensure that all possible communication channels with the stronghold and the hostage taker were deployed.

'We need to get a robot up there on the roof,' said Ed to the members of the negotiating cell.

'There's already one on site,' said Boise. 'Liaise with Laura, here.'

Ed never liked to be at the mercy of a phone connection during a negotiation, particularly when the subject was entirely in control of the communication. A robot, as it was known, was a remotely controlled vehicle most commonly used by bomb disposal technicians and was usually fitted with a loudspeaker, microphone, C.C.T.V. camera and some-times a shotgun for blowing up suspicious packages. The ones that were used by Scotland Yard negotiators had had the shotguns removed so as not to alarm hostage takers. With a robot in place on the roof, Ed knew he would at least be able to communicate via the loudspeaker, even if the microphone on the robot could not pick up the subject's responses due to the background noise of helicopters. Despite his fatigue and self-doubt, Ed knew he had to start to chip away at the subject's control of the situation. But before he could start to think of negotiation tactics, Des White said, 'We've got intelligence through from GCHQ. They're analysing all telecommunications signals into and out of the stronghold. It appears that Lily's got her phone on her.'

Ed considered this information – they all did. Nick Calvert spoke first. 'It's not going to help us, is it? She can't very well use it and, even if she could make contact with us, what are we going to say to her?' Calvert's rhetorical questions invited no answer and received none. He was right. Lily's phone didn't help them.

12:29 PM

Roof of 11 Blenheim Terrace, Belgravia

'Right, I'm going to cut this little fucker's head off now.'
The giant's demeanour had changed. It was the first time
he had given his aggression free reign. His body was a wall
of tense, taut muscle. He had the hunting knife held against
James's neck. The blade flashed in the sun, congealing blood
clearly visible on it. The knife was so vicious and the hand
holding it so muscular and powerful that it looked as though
the giant could take James's head off with the ease of
removing the end of a carrot. James's Adam's apple scraped
against the knife's razor edge as he swallowed hard, his eyes
clamped tight shut, his skin pale and oily with sweat. The
giant held his phone to his ear, then held it in front of him
and looked down at the screen, his thumb tapping at it.
Then he raised it back to his ear and said, 'I can hear you
. . . Right.' With that, he lowered his hand and, pressing on
the screen again to disconnect the call, put the phone back
in his pocket.

Taking James by the arm, he dragged him to his feet.

'Congratulations; you get to stay alive for now.' He gave James a shove before moving back within the shadow thrown by the chimney stack, spooling out the chain from around his wrist as he did so.

'Are you OK?' Lily asked James, watching their captor as she spoke, checking, after his recent outburst of aggression, that he was still employing his tolerant attitude to them communicating with one another.

'Yeah, I'm OK,' said James, resuming his position by Lily's side and putting his arm around her once again as though it was his duty to protect her.

'I don't think you should do anything to antagonise him,' said Lily.

'I think he's starting to lose it,' said James. 'Did you see him?'

'Yeah, I saw that he was about to kill you. I don't think you should mess with him.'

'Oh, I don't know.'

'What do you mean?'

'It might give us an opportunity.'

'What are you talking about?' Lily spoke more loudly than she had intended and looked up to check that the giant was still absorbed in his iPhone.

'We might be able to stop him doing whatever he's here to do,' said James, glancing from their captor to Lily.

'But he's twice the size of you,' said Lily.

'I'm not suggesting it should just be me. It should be all of us. There are four of us and one of him. If we get organised and rush him all at once, we might be able to disarm him or cut the chain to that thing around your neck.'

As much as Lily felt the need to discourage James from doing anything reckless, she hoped whatever plans he might be hatching would at least be ones that would stand some chance of succeeding. The thought of the four of them rushing at the giant and trying to overpower him sounded so ill-conceived and comically absurd that she found it impossible to formulate a response.

'I know you probably think I look like a bit of a weakling,' said James, pulling her closer to him as he did so. 'But I fight dirty.'

Lily looked at him. He didn't look like he was crazy. Whether he had always been like this or whether it was something that had been caused by him being taken hostage was impossible to say, but his talk of attempting to win a physical confrontation with the man in the balaclava was either extreme heroism or lunacy. Yet, however much his mental state might have been compromised, Lily couldn't help but think that his overall intention was a good one. There was every chance that their captor intended to harm one or all of them if his demands were not met and there was every chance that they wouldn't be. If they could attack him simultaneously, disarm him and disable him, then it might be the only chance they had.

'You need to try and keep close to him,' said James. 'That way he won't be able to pull the pin out of the grenade. If we rush him, you need to make sure that there's plenty of slack on the chain. The snipers will be looking for any opportunity to shoot him, so if they see that he can't pull out the pin then they'll have a go, I'm sure.'

It was clear he had given this some thought and, while any sort of physical confrontation with the giant was something that she felt acutely uneasy about – if not completely terrified – it was something that had to be considered. The giant clearly felt confident that no one was going to attack him. As far as he was concerned, his hostages' terror, and the ultimate compliance that it fuelled, was taken as read.

'So what do we do exactly?' asked Lily.

'We need to plan. We need to decide who is going to do what. When we go at him, each of us needs to aim at a different part of his body. We need to communicate all this to your parents.'

Lily turned to look at them standing next to her. Her mother was crying again; the tears had mixed with her mascara and created two grey tramlines down her face. Graham had his arm around her but there was little reassurance in his embrace. Helen kept glancing up at the hostage taker, her look one of venomous resentment that only her fear prevented her from voicing. Graham looked into the sky. This was all his doing and he seemed to realise it. His eyes were filled with tears too. Lily knew all about his crying fits. She had seen him a couple of times in the house in Zurich and realised that he had been weeping. One time, she had heard him sobbing late at night. He was a man on the edge, emotionally. It wouldn't take much to push him over it.

'Go on, tell your dad,' said James. Lily glanced over at the giant who was standing watching them from the shadow thrown by the chimney stack. There was no way he could hear them above the sound of the helicopters but there was something about the way that he allowed them to speak to one another that spooked her.

'Go on,' said James. His nervous enthusiasm for what may very well turn out to be a suicidal mission was beginning to worry her.

'Hold on. I don't want to antagonise him.'

'He said we could speak to one another, so we might as well do that.'

'OK.'

Lily didn't turn fully towards her father as she spoke and she kept her eyes on the giant.

'Dad?'

'Yeah.'

'We're going to have to try to attack him.'

'What?'

'There are four of us. If we all work together and go for different parts of his body then we might be able to disable him.' Lily had chanced a glance at her father but, when she looked back at the giant, he was looking directly at her once more. She looked away.

'No way, Lily. It's too dangerous.'

'He's threatening to kill us. How dangerous do you want it to get?'

'No, this is all about me. I'm going to speak to him. If he wants to harm someone – kill someone – then it should be me and me alone.' His words were bloated with self-pity and fresh tears formed in his eyes.

'We should stick together, Dad. If we move as one, he's not going to be able to stop us all.'

'Don't be so sure. He's a killer. I mean, look at him, for Christ's sake. No, sweetheart, I'm going to sort this out.'

'Don't do anything stupid,' said Helen.

'This is my mess,' said Graham. 'It's down to me now.' Lily's father wasn't a man who could stand back and do nothing. He was a problem solver. This was a huge, life-threatening problem but, as with all other work-related problems, in his mind there had to be some way of resolving it. That was part of his philosophy, always had been.

'I need to talk to you.' Her father was shouting at the giant. But the anger had gone from his voice. This was his negotiating voice. This was his I'm-going-to-level-with-you voice.

The giant looked across at him and said, 'Let's not talk. There's nothing you can say to me that is going to mean anything.'

'Let me speak to you just for a few moments. Please.'

'No.'

'You don't know what I'm going to say.'

'Yes, I do. You're going to make me an offer. Well, there's nothing you can offer me that I want to have.'

It was tough for Graham to find that his life's currency was no longer valid. He was stumped – bereft. A tear escaped from his eye and made its way down his cheek.

'You want some sort of revenge on me, is that right?'

'You don't need to know.'

'You want to make an example of me, right?' Graham was becoming more agitated.

'Stop talking.'

'You want a scapegoat, is that it? You want someone to blame for all the sins of the world, right?'

The giant didn't respond but took up the slack on the chain attached to the collar around Lily's neck. She could feel it tug against the pin on the grenade. She stepped forward to try to increase the slack, knowing she wouldn't be able to do anything to counteract a sudden yank.

'Dad, Dad! Careful. He's pulling on the chain.'

But Graham didn't look around; he was in a trance, focusing every part of his consciousness on the man who had taken his family hostage, determined to find some way to open his negotiation. 'So there's nothing I can do or say that will make you talk to me, right?'

'That's right, yeah.'

'You're sure about that?'

'I'd keep my mouth shut, if I was you.'

'But what happens if I do this?' Graham took his arm from around Helen's shoulders and started walking.

Helen shouted, 'Graham!'

'What the fuck's he doing?' said James.

'Dad!' shouted Lily as she watched him walk towards the edge of the flat roof, step over the low wall and stand on the brick lip at the front of the house.

'Stop or I'll kill her!' It was the first time that Lily had heard the giant shout. All semblance of self-control had disappeared; the words roared out of his lungs. 'Stop now!'

The chain was being pulled tighter. Lily stepped forward to reduce the tension, but the giant kept pulling back to take up the slack.

'Let my family go or I'm going to jump.' The voice that came out of her father's mouth was not the cowed, trembling voice she had heard him use earlier in the day, nor the one he had used these past few months after his very public woes had begun. It was a confident voice, a voice that demanded attention and, as much as she despised her father sometimes, especially when he used that voice, the fact was that in all the years she had known him, whenever Lily had heard him speak like that, he had never failed.

12:39 PM

Roof of 11 Blenheim Terrace, Belgravia

It felt good to be back in the game. But, now that Graham was, he needed to consider how to play it. The bastard was shouting at him, threatening him. The threats were about as bad as they could ever get. His daughter's life was on the line. But as long as he ignored the threats then he was free, no one could touch him. It was the same with his predicament at Stanmore Partners. Many of the fund's former investors were clamouring for their money, issuing writs, threats of writs; the legal machinery was lumbering towards him – private legal firms with exorbitant fees, the British government and all its agents, the media-fed court of popular opinion – and there had been nothing he could do about it. Until now. What he was doing right at that moment provided him with his first taste of freedom in months. This was the way out, the escape he had been racking his brains to find.

He looked down. On the railings in front of the house was the body of the security guard, now covered in a black tarpaulin. Beyond that, the colouring of the police vehicles provided a fluorescent mosaic on Blenheim Terrace. Police officers – some in uniform, some in plain clothes, wearing flak jackets and carrying guns – looked up at him. Everyone was watching him and waiting. For now at least, he was in charge of the situation.

Waiting for others to make decisions that would directly affect him had always been something for which he had a pathological hatred. He was only ever happy when he was in control. Helen often called him a control freak. It was one of her standard lines of attack. She was right, though: he was a control freak, but he didn't see anything inherently wrong with that. There was enough passivity in the world already, too many people who were only too eager to make victims of themselves. There was only a minute percentage of the population who had the imagination and the guts to take control and shape the future with their actions. Being a success and a winner was all about risk reward. To the victor, the spoils. That was his world and it was a world that others wanted to bring to an end. He and Bob Rushwood had played fast and loose, taken huge risks and with those huge risks had come huge rewards. They had been caught out, as so many others had been. But he wouldn't become a victim. It didn't suit him; it never had.

What had pained him so much over these past few months was his lack of choices. Once Bob had told him about the state of the fund, all that he could look forward to was humiliation and disgrace at the hands of the legal authorities. The public mood being what it was, people would revel in his downfall. Everyone, from the penniless losers sponging off the state to his former colleagues and business associates, would enjoy watching him receive what they perceived to be his just deserts. Banker bashing – call it what you will – had become something of a national pastime. His bleak future and its lack of options and possible means of escape had hypnotised him – traumatised him too. What had happened to him, falling into the clutches of this psycho who had taken him and his family hostage, was just another component in the machinery of his public humiliation and disgrace. It was more violent and placed his family in greater personal danger but it was all part of the same process. People hated to see others succeed and make something of themselves, especially when they made no apology for their success. This madman with his bombs and threats was just another of the scumbags who had decided to take it upon himself to hasten his demise.

As he stood on the parapet, teetering on the edge, with nothing between him and his own rendezvous with the railings down below, Lily started calling to him. Her voice, more than any other, clawed at his heart and his conscience.

'Dad! Stop! Don't!'

It could be over in a second. There would be a split second of agony and then nothing.

'Dad, don't do it! Please! Dad!'

He felt dizzy and he lost his balance for a moment but clawed it back. He knew he could jump if he needed to; part of him wanted to do it and that gave him strength.

'Let my family go now or I jump.' He shouted the words and no one could be in any doubt as to whether he meant them or not. Not even him.

People were shouting – the hostage taker, the kid who drove the delivery van, Helen – but it was Lily's voice that cut through them, Lily's voice that he was receiving loud and clear.

'Dad, if you jump, we're all going to die.'

As much as he loved her, he needed to blot out her words. Her pleas and entreaties would sap his will, drain his resolve. Without a clear intention to jump off that roof, he would cede control. At the present moment, he was a winner once more. Graham had found the hostage taker's weakness. His entire plan was based on the fact that his hostages – and Graham in particular – would want to stay alive. The hostage taker had been so sure of this that he had even left his hostages unbound with only the threat of one of them dying to ensure their compliance. But what if Graham didn't want to stay alive? Suddenly, the intricately constructed house of cards would come tumbling down. So long as Graham was prepared to kill himself and his family then no one could touch him. He had heard a terrorist talk about suicide bombers once on a news programme. The man said that the West could never defeat the jihadis because jihad meant that they were not only prepared to die for their cause, they *wanted* to. That mindset was inviolable. Despite this knowledge and the power that it gave him, however, his mind kept asking him the same questions. Did he want to die? Did he want his family to die? If it was Helen with the grenade around her neck, would it make things any easier? In the moment of brutal honesty in which he was trapped, he knew it would. But the questions were in danger of making his own house of cards wobble.

'Dad, don't!'

The voice stabbed at his resolve. He had to block it and state his intentions once more.

'Let them go now or I jump!' The faces looked up at him from down below. This must have been how rock stars felt when they were on stage and playing to thousands of people at a concert. As he waved his arms around for a second time to keep his balance on the thin parapet, he thought about performing in plays at school. It was something he had enjoyed, holding the attention of a crowd. He had the same feeling now. This show was all about him. He was the lead; he was the star.

'Dad!' She was screaming now. It tore at him; he had to think of something else, had to throw up a wall between himself and the horror of what was taking place to his family so close by. 'Da-aad!' She was being hurt now. He couldn't stop himself turning around. As he did so, he saw that the hostage taker had Lily by the throat with one hand, dragging her towards him and, with the other hand, he held taut the chain connected to the grenade.

'Don't come any closer.' Graham blurted out the words but gone was some of his former confidence. He had to try to get it back. The delivery driver remonstrated with the hostage taker for a moment but was pushed away and fell to the roof. Lily was dragged closer still.

'I'll jump!' But even as he shouted it, he could feel some of his conviction ebb away. He teetered once more on the parapet. All it would take would be a little push with his toes, a minute tilt of his body. All his reservations about dying, all his guilt over what might happen to Lily and Helen would be gone as he was swallowed up by the void. If he just shut his eyes and leaned back . . . That's all it would take. He shut his eyes but, before he could make the final, terrible decision, a massive hand reached out and grabbed him by the collar of his shirt, dragging him backwards with such force that he was sent sprawling. As he struggled to stand up, a boot crunched into the back of his knee with enough power to lift him off his feet once more and send him crashing to the ground. His impact with the lead roof was altogether more vicious and debilitating than the previous one and he didn't get up as Lily's screams blasted in his ears. For a few moments, he had felt a new sense of freedom and he had allowed himself to be liberated by it. But now, it was gone.

12:44 PM

Negotiating Cell, Blenheim Terrace, Belgravia

'Poynter is moving towards the edge of the roof at the front of the house,' said Nick Calvert, spitting the words out in a nervous semi-whisper. 'He's standing on the edge of the roof. Shit – he nearly fell off. He's shouting something. I think he's probably threatening to jump.'

Ed had sat resting his head in his hands for the past half minute, trying to empty his mind. He didn't like to think of it as meditation – it sounded too self-important. It was really just 'thinking of nothing'. And it helped, even if it was only for a moment. His breathing was more regular. He still felt tired; not physically – he had done nothing more than stand in negotiating command centres since he had been called to Muswell Hill that morning – but mentally, he was exhausted. He had suspected that Graham Poynter would attempt to wrest control back from the hostage taker. He was an alpha male; he wasn't going to face a situation like this without attempting to devise a strategy. Clearly this was the fruit of his labours. This was his plan.

'The perp's moving away from the chimney stack. He's wound the chain around his wrist and it's still tight on the girl. He's grabbing the girl by the neck and he's walking across to Poynter. The delivery driver's shouting at him and the subject's pushed him to the ground. Jesus – Poynter nearly fell again. The perp's dragging Poynter back now and Poynter's down on the ground. He's trying to get up but the perp's stamped on the back of his leg. That's going to hurt.'

Ed didn't appreciate Calvert's football pundit observations and asked him what he meant.

'He's kicked Poynter in the back of the leg and he's down now and not getting up.'

Ed stood up, letting go of the meditative feelings that had provided him with some respite from the collision of events going on around him.

'He's shouting at them now,' continued Calvert. 'He's making them all kneel and now he's going back to stand against the chimney stack.'

'We've just got the spec of the hand grenade around Lily Poynter's neck,' said Des White. 'By the looks of things, it's a Russian-made F1 grenade, which has an injury radius of about fifteen metres and a fatality radius of about five. That's very rough; some fragments can disperse as far as a couple of hundred metres.'

'So, even though it's strapped to Lily Poynter's neck,' said Ed, 'the chances are that, with a fatality radius of about forty-five feet, it's going to kill all of them, including the hostage taker.'

'What's the fuse time?' asked Calvert.

'Between four and five and a half seconds,' said White.

'You can run a fair way in that time,' replied Calvert.

'What about the chain?' asked Ed. 'Might it be possible for a sniper to shoot it and sever it?'

'Doubtful,' said White. 'But I'm sure it's being looked into by the military.'

'What about the media? Are they picking this up?'

'A couple of the helicopters are feeding images to the networks,' said Laura Massey. 'But COBRA are unhappy about it because of the potentially gruesome imagery if the grenade is detonated. They are talking about closing them down.'

'That's not a good idea,' said Ed. 'We need to find out who that guy is up there.'

'But he's wearing a balaclava,' said Laura. 'No one would be able to recognise him, anyway.'

'Not necessarily. Someone might be able to see a mannerism or an article of clothing that will allow them to identify him. If we can find out who he is, it allows us to work on him. We need to let this play in the news. Tell them it's essential.'

'OK; I'll run it past Commander Boise as soon as possible.'

'Do we have any leads on his identity?' asked Ed.

'Nothing as yet,' said Des White. 'We've got a number of

Geordie special forces soldiers, both past and present, but none of them specifically anti-capitalist or politically aggrieved.'

Ed rubbed at his neck, which felt stiff, rotating his head around, one way and then the other. 'So let's think about what the demands might be, seeing as this guy, whoever he is, clearly doesn't want to tell us. He's rational and aware enough to know that no one's going to give him safe passage out of here. So this has to be some sort of theatre. He is doing this to make an example of the Poynter family who represent something he hates and despises.'

'You still think it's a lone-wolf operation?' asked Calvert.

'It looks like it at the moment but I just can't get my head around the guy's motive. He clearly wants to bargain because he's brought an extra hostage up with him – the delivery driver – which he didn't need to do. So if he wants to bargain, then he's going to issue demands. If he wants something, then we need to think what it is. But that doesn't make sense either because he doesn't want to talk to us – or doesn't appear to want to.'

'I wouldn't be so sure of that,' said Des White. 'There's a call coming through from him right now.'

12:45 PM

Roof of 11 Blenheim Terrace, Belgravia

'Another stunt like that and people start to die,' the giant shouted at the four of them. Lily didn't want him to be upset. She wanted him to be how he had been earlier when he had been concerned about her catching cold. If he was angry, they were in greater danger. It was her neck with the hand grenade attached to it, after all.

'I didn't want to cuff you but I will if I have to.' He wound the chain tight around his wrist as he shouted to them. His anger was born of his need to reassert his authority. He had lost control of the situation for a couple of minutes back there and it had clearly shaken him.

'Get on your knees, now!'

This was a worrying development. Making them kneel dehumanised them. It reduced them, debased them, and what was killing someone but the ultimate debasement? Lily stared into the man's eyes, set in the holes in the balaclava, and considered whether they belonged to the sort of man who might kill her. Even in her most pessimistic moments, she couldn't see them as evil eyes. Even though she knew he had killed the security guards earlier, she didn't think he could kill her in cold blood. He had become calmer, although he was still agitated by the helicopters and kept glancing into the sky and across the rooftops. There were guns pointed at him from multiple locations. He might not be able to see them but they were there, they had to be. He was careful, however, and ensured that the tension on the chain was maintained at all times, winding it and unwinding it around his arm as he moved forward and back into the shadow cast by the chimney stack.

Lily turned to look at her father, who had caught his breath now but was gasping with pain from the kick he had received to the back of his leg.

'Are you all right, Dad?' She watched the giant as she spoke. He either didn't hear her speak or didn't care and continued to look around him, increasingly nervous and vigilant. She looked at her father. He looked more ashamed of himself than she had ever seen him. Kneeling was proving difficult for him because his leg hurt but, more than that, his posture had degenerated into a cower.

'I'm OK,' he said, without looking up.

'What were you going to do, Dad?'

'What do you think?'

'Would you really have jumped?'

'I wanted to. I wish I had.'

Lily's mother broke off from her sobs to mutter, 'Oh, Jesus.'

'So it's back to plan A,' said James.

'What the fuck is plan A?' said Graham.

'We need to get organised. We need to choose our moment and rush him. If we take a limb each, we can overpower him. He's already shaken by what happened before. We just bide our time.'

Graham sighed but Lily could tell that he was thinking about what James had said. Helen continued to snivel. Lily's mother was someone who could easily become seduced by procedure, with doing the right thing. She was obsessed with protocol. The dinner parties they hosted for people that Lily's dad did business with were events that could never be enjoyed in a relaxed atmosphere. Her mum always wanted everything to be just so. She hated to feel that she had missed something and that her understanding of social etiquette might be found wanting. And here, up on the roof, she was snivelling as though this was the right behaviour for the circumstances. This was what a hedge-fund manager's wife should do when held hostage on the roof of her house with a grenade attached to her daughter's neck. Snivelling was the order of the day. If, on the other hand, she could be made to think that attacking the man who had engineered this situation was also the order of the day then she might not be as useless as she appeared.

When Graham had walked across the roof and threatened to jump off it, James had told her to try to reason with him. When Lily had called to her dad, she had no idea what she should say to him but James encouraged her to keep going. 'You've got to stop him,' he had said. 'Keep going; keep trying.' It was the giant's intervention that had resolved the situation but there was something about James's demeanour that made her realise that if there was someone who might be able to make a difference, it was him. However much she and her family were terrified by their ordeal, James was strong. He was thinking clearly and trying to work out a plan. When Lily glanced across at the giant, she saw that he was speaking into his phone.

'How about we rush him when he's on the phone?' said Lily. James looked at the giant and nodded.

12:51 PM

Negotiating Cell, Blenheim Terrace, Belgravia

'This is Ed Mallory,' said Ed into his headset.

'Listen, Ed. We need to calm things down here.' Although still measured and considered, the hostage taker's voice sounded more rattled than before. 'I know this place is crawling with S.C.O.19 and special forces but everyone needs to relax.'

'I hear you. We're all as relaxed as we can possibly be.'

'You can get the helicopters to back off for a start. They're giving me a headache. I know you need to see what's going on here but they can use their zoom lenses, can't they?'

A potential strategy opened up to Ed as he heard this. As much as the proximity of the helicopters was bothering him, the hostage taker wanted them there none the less. He wanted everything to be captured for posterity. Ed decided to call his bluff.

'I can get rid of them altogether if you want?'

'It's up to you,' said the hostage taker and Ed knew that his bluff was being called in turn.

'I'll see if I can get them to move away a little, but you need to do something for me in return.'

'Leave them where they are then,' said the hostage taker. 'I don't care.'

'If I get them to move back a little, will you let me speak to the hostages?'

'What for?'

'I need to know they're OK.'

'The hostages are fine; you can see that for yourself.'

'I can't see anything; I'm blind.'

'So you keep saying but there are others watching the video link, I presume?'

'Yes.'

In his desire to forge a bond with the hostage taker, Ed had overplayed his disability. It was yet another sign that he was not on top of his game.

'Well, they can tell you that there are four very much alive hostages on their knees up here on the roof.'

'It would be good to speak to one of them, if possible.'

'It's not going to happen.'

Ed decided to change the focus of the conversation away from the hostages and on to the hostage taker himself.

'What about you? Are you OK?'

The man emitted a bitter, 'Ha!' and Ed felt sure that he was going to disconnect the call. But he didn't. Ed could just make him out above the sound of the helicopter engines, breathing into the phone. Under normal circumstances, Ed would try to avoid too much silence in an exchange – like a radio presenter trying to avoid dead air – but he left the question hanging for a moment and was rewarded.

'No, I'm not OK. I'm very far from fucking OK.'

'Are you injured?'

'No, I'm not injured.'

The way he said it, it was clear that he didn't want to be pressed on the subject. Ed needed another angle and quickly.

'Can I ask you something?'

'Fire away.' It was a positive response, albeit one that was expressed in a sarcastic tone. Ed needed to capitalise on this but first he needed to think what question he wanted to ask. It shouldn't be anything too provocative. He could hear a sense of frustration in the man's voice, a rise in tension which might be released violently if he was pushed too far. Then again, Ed knew that he might not have very long and needed to establish basic facts as soon as possible.

'When are you going to let us know what your demands are?'

'I thought we'd already been through this. You're presuming that I have demands.'

'So you're telling me that you don't have any demands?'

'At the moment, I have a request rather than a demand and that is that you should try to arrange for the helicopters to move a little higher in the sky because they're giving me a headache. It's not a threat or even a bargaining point, it's just that, if you don't move the helicopters away from me, I might get so pissed off with the sound of them that I'll just snap and kill someone.'

Instead of calming the situation and developing a relationship with the hostage taker, all that Ed had managed to do was incite him into making a threat of further violence. Although it was dangerous to ignore the hostage taker's threat too blatantly, he decided it was worth it and continued with his original line of questioning.

'All I'm asking is that you help me to understand what it is we're doing here.'

'Why?'

'Because, with the greatest respect, it doesn't make sense.'

'Today is not the day for making sense.'

It was Ed's turn to say, 'Why?'

'Today's a day for doing what needs to be done.'

'Can you tell me what you think it is that needs to be done?'

'You're not going to dig it out of me, Ed. You'll find out soon enough.'

'When might that be?'

'Soon.'

Ed was aware of the others in the command centre all around him, listening in to the exchange, relayed through the speakers. There was no way of knowing what any of them thought of what he was doing. Robbed of his ability to witness body language and facial expressions, he had had to rely on his enhanced powers of listening for the last fourteen years. Today, those powers were picking up his colleagues' reticence and concern about the way he was conducting the negotiation.

Roof of 11 Blenheim Terrace, Belgravia

The giant had to raise his voice to make himself heard on the phone but it was still impossible for Lily to hear what he was saying. Clearly some form of negotiation was taking place. He couldn't be speaking to an accomplice because the authorities would be able to intercept his call, listen to it and probably track it too. He would know that. Maybe he had already made his demands and she and James and her parents were not to be party to them.

'We need to choose our moment,' said James, watching him.

'What do you want us to do exactly?' asked Graham.

'Like I said, we each grab a limb. You can take his right leg. I'll take his right arm and try to disconnect the chain. If Lily takes his left arm, then you' – he looked at Helen – 'take his left leg. If we move together then we should be able to disable him long enough that the police can move in.'

'I don't like the sound of it,' said Graham.

Lily looked at her father. Gone was the tone of voice that he had managed to summon up when he was threatening to jump off the roof and, in its place, his whiny, defeated voice had returned.

'We have to do something, Dad.'

'Why? Why do we have to do something? We should leave it to the professionals.'

His behaviour was following a pattern that she had grown accustomed to over the years. Having attempted to carry out one course of action and failed, he would always swing to the polar opposite course of action. He had tried to wrest control back from the hostage taker and failed. Now, he would do the opposite and sit and wait.

'Have you given up?'

She knew this would rile him but she could tell how beaten down and emotionally wrecked he was when he said, 'No, of course I haven't,' and couldn't even bring himself to make eye contact as he did so.

'No, I agree with you, Graham,' said Helen. 'We shouldn't do anything that might make things worse. The authorities will have a plan, I'm sure.' That her mother could be so spineless came as no shock to Lily but it was good to see that James appeared to share her low opinion of her parents. He shook his head, wearing an expression of disbelief. Lily didn't want James's resolve to be weakened. He was their only chance.

'Are you telling me that you just want to sit and wait for whatever it is that this freak wants to do to us?' Lily spat the words at her parents. 'Neither of you two has a bomb tied around your neck. Don't you think I should be the one who makes the decisions here?'

'Shut up, Lily,' said Graham.

Even now, he thought he could control her with the same old lines. But their predicament – and hers, in particular – allowed her liberation from the usual rules of behaviour and, as their eyes met, she told him, 'Fuck you.'

Lily's mother had clearly decided where her allegiances lay and, even trapped up on the roof of their house, held hostage by a giant psychopath who had fixed a bomb around her daughter's neck, she managed to match her husband in boring predictability by saying, 'Lily,' in that admonishing manner she assumed when they ganged up on her.

Lily waited for her mother to look at her and, as their eyes met, she said, 'And fuck you too.'

12:53 PM

14 Spruce Road, Stockton-on-Tees

Jan made Emily's pasta as though she was an automaton. All she could think about was Danny and where he might be. If he had known he was going to be this late, he would have called. Whatever might have happened to him, he would have called – if he could. Maybe he had been involved in some sort of accident. Maybe he had been injured or attacked. It was always a possibility in his line of work. They had an unspoken agreement that she would never ask him about his job and he never told her. She had worried for a time that his secret life represented some sort of hole in their relationship but those feelings had waned when she had spoken to wives and girlfriends of other special forces and former special forces soldiers who had exactly the same arrangements with their partners. But he always called when he said he would. If he said he would be back on a certain day and time then he would be and if for any reason he was going to be delayed, he would let her know.

She stirred the tomato sauce into the pasta and took the bowl across to Emily. Usually, they ate at the table. She and Danny wanted Emily to associate mealtimes with time spent together as a family. Table manners were important. But today, Jan didn't care. She put the bowl of pasta on the rug and helped Emily with her first few mouthfuls, blowing on the food to help it cool.

She glanced up at the clock on the wall above the kitchen island: 12:59. Emily's cartoon had come to an end. Bugs Bunny had caused havoc with Elmer Fudd's hunting expedition once more. As the legend, 'That's all folks!' was doodled across the screen by an animator's unseen hand, Jan picked up the remote control and turned on the news. She didn't usually watch the news with Emily, in case there were some images of a terrorist attack somewhere in the Middle East or discussion of an unpleasant murder. But, being Christmas Day, she thought it would be fine and would probably just be cheerful reports of people enjoying Christmas, maybe footage of the royal family going to church. But she was surprised to see that the first item was concerned with a hostage-taking in central London. Fearing some unsuitable subject matter, Jan was just about to turn over when Emily kicked out with her foot and knocked over her cup of juice.

'Oh, Emily!'

Jan jumped to her feet and went to fetch a cloth from the draining board. When she came back and started dabbing at the wet patch on the rug, the newsreader was describing how the disgraced hedge-fund chairman Graham Poynter and his family were being held hostage on the roof of their central-London home by an unknown assailant. Jan glanced up from the rug and saw the blurred and slightly shaky footage of a large man dressed all in black and wearing a balaclava. He was standing by a large chimney stack while his hostages knelt nearby. The newsreader described how the hostage taker appeared to have attached an explosive device to Graham Poynter's daughter, Lily's, neck. The explosive was connected to the hostage taker by a chain, which he had wrapped around his wrist. But Jan wasn't listening to the newsreader anymore. Her hand that held the cloth was still dabbing at the stain on the rug. It was an automatic movement. Nothing could distract her from the close-up image of the man standing on the roof.

12:56 PM

Negotiating Cell, Blenheim Terrace, Belgravia

'Look, I'll ask if the helicopters can fly higher, OK?'

'If you like.'

'Can you at least give me your name?'

'You'll find out everything soon enough.'

Ed was getting nothing. The hostage taker didn't have any demands more pressing than asking if the helicopters could fly higher because the sound of their engines was giving him a headache. The purpose of his hostage-taking was no clearer now than it had been when Ed had first spoken to him nearly an hour and a half before. Yet he clearly wanted to communicate and that was a good thing and something that illustrated a potential source of weakness in his psychological armour. There were numerous angles that Ed could try to make him open up about his intentions, but he suspected that if he started to question him more closely on his exact motives and potential demands then the conversation would be terminated as it had been before.

'You don't make things easy for a negotiator.' Ed said it with what he hoped was the slightest hint at amusement, the tone of an opening gambit in a pub conversation between two men who don't know each other but might become friends.

'Sorry about that,' said the hostage taker.

Ed was pleased with the response because the tone he had attempted to conjure was reciprocated, albeit in a more fatalistic manner.

'I can't say this is the best Christmas I've ever spent,' continued Ed.

'Me neither.'

At any moment, the call could be disconnected so Ed needed to keep talking and make sure that whatever he was saying was distracting enough for the man to want to continue to communicate with him.

'I guess, in a way, we're both working,' said Ed.

'In a way,' said the man.

'I have a feeling that your day might turn out to be more successful than mine, professionally speaking.'

'How so?'

'Well, you've succeeded in doing what you set out to do, haven't you?'

'Not yet.'

'You've clearly been involved in work like this before.'

'Clearly.'

'You're not going to go away until you've done what you came here to do, right?'

'Right.'

'That scares me.'

Silence. After a few seconds, Ed was considering another line when the man said, 'It scares me too.'

An admission of fear – or an admission of any form of insecurity – from a subject in a hostage situation was nearly always a good sign, but Ed couldn't take this as such. It was strangely unsettling that the subject of the negotiation was opening up to him to such a degree that he was now admitting his own fears about what was to come. It was clear to everyone, not least the man on the end of the line, that no one was going to escape from the stronghold. The subject had murdered three security guards. He was either going to die or he was going to spend the rest of his life in prison. But Ed suspected that prison time wasn't in the plan; he couldn't shake the feeling that the subject was fully aware that he was going to be dead in a few hours.

'I'm not trying to trick you into giving up your identity or anything like that but you're clearly someone who has undergone advanced training and has been able to put that training into use on a number of occasions.'

'Sure.'

'Where've you worked?'

'Where do you think I might have worked?'

'We don't have to talk if you don't want to, but I get the feeling that you do want to.' Ed cursed himself in silence. It was a lame line and one that he felt sure the subject would punish him for by telling him to go to hell.

'I've worked in some of the leading shit holes in the world: Somalia, Nigeria, Saudi, Libya, Afghanistan, Iraq.'

Ed had spoken to enough would-be suicides to recognise the human need to unburden oneself. The ease with which he was managing to steer this man and make him open up was further proof to him that the subject knew that he would soon be dead. This was worrying in many ways – particularly for the plight of the hostages – but he would worry about that later. Now, he needed to keep the man talking. As long as the subject was talking, there might be an opportunity to establish his identity. As soon as he had an identity then Ed could really go to work. But something else that Ed would have to consider later on was the fact that this seemingly rational, intelligent man was on a suicide mission. It didn't make sense.

'You must be pretty good at what you do.'

'I'm the best.'

If any of the numerous subjects that Ed had spoken to over the years had told him they were the best at something – and some of them had, in differing ways – then he would have taken it as a sign of their inherent delusion. But this guy didn't say it in a conceited way; he said it as a matter of fact. Seemingly aware that he had said too much, however, the subject terminated the dialogue with a curt, 'I'll speak to you later,' and disconnected the call.

'He's not coming out of that stronghold alive and he knows it,' said Ed as he pulled his headset from his ears and let it hang around his neck. 'Have we got anything back from intel regarding possible disaffected former special forces soldiers?'

'It's on its way,' said Laura Massey. 'We're just having a few protocol issues with the revealing of the identities of ex-special forces troops.'

'Bollocks to the protocol. There can't be that many ex-S.A.S. or ex-S.B.S. soldiers who come from the North East who might have money troubles or specific reasons as to why they might have a grudge against someone like Graham Poynter.' Ed realised how he sounded. His voice was screechy and tense and betrayed his frustration.

'I'll get an update, see where we are with things.' Laura Massey was experienced and professional enough to know how to handle an antagonistic element in the negotiating cell. Ed felt sure it was only a matter of time before he was relieved of his role as number one. The only thing that was keeping him in that position was the fact that he had managed to make the subject open up, albeit briefly.

But Ed's state of mind was clearly something that Nick Calvert was referring to when he asked him, 'How's it going, Ed?'

'I don't think I can get through to him.'

'You just did; I heard it.'

'I might be able to get him to talk to me but I can't talk him down. He's on a suicide mission and what I can't get my head around is that it's not his mission. He's a puppet. A big, scary puppet, maybe, but a puppet nonetheless.'

01:00 PM

Roof of 11 Blenheim Terrace, Belgravia

'Just shut up, will you?' Graham hissed the words through gritted teeth, his face trembling with rage. 'Don't you fucking dare put me and my family in any more danger than we are already.' Lily suspected that her father felt he couldn't shout at her because of her uniquely horrible predicament, so he had decided instead to shout at James, the person who had so incited his rage and, in his opinion, set them all against each other.

'You couldn't be in any more danger than you are already,' said James.

Lily had to hand it to him, he wasn't easily intimidated, either by the situation that he had found himself in or by her father's temper. James had decided that the only option open to them was to try to overcome the hostage taker, and he wasn't going to be put off easily.

'Well, go on then,' countered Graham. 'If you're so big and brave, go right ahead and let's see you take him on.'

'I can't do it on my own. It needs to be all of us.'

'Well, you can count me out.'

Lily glanced at Helen as Graham growled the words. Lily's mother was a woman whose personality had been poisoned by money and privilege almost all of her adult life. All of the problems that she faced – her marriage, her unfulfilment, her loneliness – were the result. Her upbringing, however, had been very different. Her childhood was one of entitlement but it was also one of country living, the outdoors, riding and hunting. She was in tune with the physical side of her nature. Lily could read the expression on her mother's face. As much as Helen felt as though she needed to support her husband in his time of need, she also felt regret that he wasn't prepared to fight. Lily needed to work on that. But James hadn't finished with her dad.

'Listen to me,' he said, his eyes boring into Graham's. 'You're not the only one who's in the shit here. I've done nothing wrong. There I was, minding my own business, doing my job and now look at me. You may not want to save yourself but at least have the decency to try to help those who are directly affected by your actions.'

'If I thought for one moment that we could succeed,' countered Graham, assuming that supercilious attitude he so often employed, 'then by all means, sure, no problem,

I'd be right there beside you. But he's already killed three highly trained security guards. We're not going to stand a chance.'

'We won't if you just give up,' said James.

'I'm not giving up; I'm just being realistic.'

'We've got the element of surprise on our side.'

'Not really. As soon as we start to rush at him, he'll go for us. We'll never make it.'

Graham had a point and, as much as she admired James for even considering a counter-attack, there was no way they could overcome the giant without one or all of them sustaining major injuries or worse.

'What is it with you?' snapped James. 'You just don't get it, do you? If we don't do something now, we're all going to wind up dead. He's not keeping us here for fun. He's using us to bargain with and, if he doesn't get what he wants, he'll kill us. Let's face it, whatever he says he wants, whether it's the release of some murdering buddy of his or something impossible like world peace, he's not going to get it. So it's a simple choice we have here. It's either kill or be killed.'

The sound of helicopters filled the air; the giant's voice was just about audible above them as he spoke into the phone but it was impossible to make out what he said. When no one responded to James, he continued with his train of thought, although his tone had changed. 'Maybe it isn't a case of kill or be killed for you,' said James. 'Maybe you've got some vested interest in perpetuating what's going on here. Maybe you're part of all this.'

'What do you mean?' Anger flashed in Graham's eyes as he spoke.

'I know who you are. I've seen you on the news. You're that fella who ripped off all those investors and took all their money. Well, maybe you've set all this up. Maybe this guy's working for you.' James nodded at the giant still talking on the phone.

'Don't be fucking ridiculous,' said Graham, but as he said it, Lily saw something in his eyes. Lily's dad had done some incredibly risky and morally dubious things in his time, but not even he could have dreamed this up. Could he?

05:02 AM *(local time)*

1437 Park Drive, Sacramento, California

Abel had always hated Christmas. While his friends at school had enjoyed family time with their loved ones, with presents and turkey and Christmas decorations, he had been made to conform to his parents' twisted world view. In their eyes, Christmas had been something that was somehow fascistic and should be avoided and not even spoken about for fear of it poisoning their karma. Stupid hippies.

Abel readjusted his position in the chair. When he had been sitting there for a long time, his back sometimes ached a little. He'd inherited the problem from his father. It must have been a wonky gene. Some day, they would be able to fix it, amend the gene code just as he had so enjoyed amending the programme codes of corporate security systems and firewalls under the hacker handle of '4-Shore'. When he was going about his work – not that he had ever really thought of it as work – he didn't like to think of himself as either white hat or black hat. His hat was more of a light grey, neither malicious nor benign but morally ambivalent. It hadn't always been that way. As a member of the War Pigs network, named after his favourite Black Sabbath track, he had caused all sorts of cyber mayhem, stealing data and sometimes money from some of the most supposedly secure networks in the world and shutting down the websites of hostile organisations – national governments included – with D.D.o.S. – Distributed Denial-of-Service – attacks.

The sun was up and the milky light came between the slats of the blind. Abel felt a little shivery and pulled up the hood of his sweatshirt, a favourite black one that was too big for his skinny frame but all the more comfortable for that. When he glanced across at the mirror on the closet door, he looked like some sort of monk sitting at the desk, his face cast in shadow. He had spent his life embracing anonymity. At first, it was at school. He had created an entirely fictitious family background for himself in order to avoid the derision that he knew would be headed his way if he told the truth about the commune on which he and his family lived. His mother and father were second-generation hippies, their peace and love aesthetic having been handed down from their parents – his grandparents – who had been part of the original Haight-Ashbury scene of the late sixties. But Abel was only too glad to break the cycle. No way would any child of his have to live the hippy life

anymore. It was all just phoney bullshit and the entire movement needed to be consigned to the dustbin of history.

It had been a long night. He had only moved from his
seat three times: twice to piss out the Gatorade that he had
been drinking and once to smoke a J. Time just seemed to
ebb away when he was writing code. The code he had been
writing that night was for a new programme that would,
all being well, allow him to take a look inside some of the
Pentagon's most secure servers. But this was neither black-,
white- nor grey-hat work. This he was being paid to do by
the U.S. government in order to test its security systems as
part of a highly classified initiative. Some of those who had
been enlisted to undertake the work alongside him were
doing so in order to avoid prosecution, having carried out
less-than-perfect daisy-chaining and thereby failed to cover
their tracks, leading the federal authorities to close them
down and hold them to ransom. Not so with Abel. He had
offered his services, advertising himself as one of the finest
white-hat hackers on the planet, a boast that he could back
up with his abilities. What the authorities didn't realise –
and, all being well, never would realise – was that he had
managed to install back-door access into the networks that
he had gained entry to, so he could return and snoop about
at his leisure.

Abel took another swig of his Gatorade but it was warm
now and had lost its fizz. He clicked on to his web browser
and went to his email inbox to see that he had a handful of

messages: the usual spam. He was just about to select *delete all* when he saw a message from an Internet address, 'advo@cryptoblur.com', that had been sent the night before. Abel opened it immediately to see a single-line message that read, 'Operation #3. London. Happy Christmas.'

As Abel considered the meaning of the message he had received, another message dropped into his inbox, this one from a Russian hacker who had also been a member of the War Pigs collective. The message contained a hyperlink and a single word: 'Advo?' Abel clicked on the link and went through to a B.B.C. news page with the headline, 'GRAHAM POYNTER IN HOSTAGE DRAMA'. Abel hadn't heard the name before but, as he started to read the text, he was soon up to speed. Graham Poynter was the disgraced chief executive of a hedge fund in London called Stanmore Partners, which had come into some extreme financial difficulties and was now suspected of being, if not exactly a Bernie Madoff-style Ponzi scheme, something not far off. Poynter and his family had been taken hostage some hours previously and he was being paraded for the cameras on the roof of his expensive central-London home. It appeared there was only one hostage taker, but he had already killed three security guards who were employed to protect Poynter and his family following their recent return from a three-month, self-imposed exile in Zurich. As soon as Abel read the story, he could see that it had to be some sort of stunt. But the death of the guards pointed to the work of someone with murderous intent. Abel closed the window and there behind it was the Russian hacker's email and, 'Advo?'

Abel sat up straight, intensely alert. He reverted to the B.B.C. News page and scrolled down to see that there was an embedded video on which he clicked. Video footage showed an aerial view of the roof of a large cream house with some figures upon it. The camera zoomed in on the figures and there were four people, two men and two women, kneeling on the grey roof while a huge man dressed all in black and wearing a balaclava stood by a chimney stack nearby. There was clearly a chain or a piece of string running from his wrist to a collar around the neck of one of the women. The English news reporter explained that it was thought the collar comprised an explosive charge that the hostage taker had threatened to detonate in the event of any attempt to approach him. No demands had as yet been made.

'Advo' was an abbreviation of 'the Adversary', who had been a member of the War Pigs collective back in the old days. A clearly brilliant hacker, he had always stood out from the rest of them for his extreme views. The War Pigs were intent on pitting themselves against the Internet security of some of the biggest organisations in the world – governments, banks, multi-national corporations – and the Adversary was the same, the only difference being that he always spoke in violent terms. He never felt that succeeding in breaking into the most secure networks in existence and getting out again without detection was enough. On the War Pigs' message boards, he always talked about going further, taking the battle to the enemy and crossing the line between non-violent protest and targeted acts of violence. Abel and some of the other members of the collective had discussed his increasingly extreme views. The War Pigs were war-like only in as much as they were conducting a cyberwar. It would only ever exist in the virtual world. They had engaged Advo in debate but this had only served to increase the number of his posts in which he laid out, always calmly and rationally, his beliefs. It was time to draw a line in the sand, he believed. It was the responsibility of hacktivist collectives like the War Pigs to take the initiative. There were moments in history, such as the French revolution and the allied intervention in Europe following the Nazi invasion of Poland, when violence was justified for the good of humanity as a whole. Such a time, Advo believed, was now. He felt that what the banks and hedge funds of the world had propagated during the banking crisis was a big con, an inside job, a metaphorical land grab, which had succeeded in getting their organisations re-financed to the tune of billions. He saw this as nothing less than an act of war to which the only correct response was to engage in that war and target the worst perpetrators of hostile enemy acts with extreme violence. When Abel and others had attempted to draw Advo out on this last point, he had avoided specifics but had on one occasion replied to a message from Abel to say that a few public lynchings might just start to make the enemy give pause to think about their destructive behaviour. Advo reiterated his belief that as much as any violence was essentially abhorrent, very occasionally it could be justified. To illustrate his point, Advo boasted that he would 'execute' an enemy combatant.

It was a minor story in the media. A Wall Street banker by the name of Mark Walsh had been taken ill while at work just before Easter that year. It was the usual story: chest pains, shortness of breath. He ended up in the New York Presbyterian Hospital. There his condition worsened and he suffered a full-blown heart attack. He became unconscious and was put on a ventilator and life support. There he lay until Good Friday when the state-of-the-art life-support machine failed and he died. No one amongst the War Pigs collective had noticed the story until it was pointed out to them by Advo on the message board. He claimed to have learned about Mark Walsh's condition quite by chance while reading message boards on the web. Having dug a little deeper and done some research, he had found out that Walsh was due to be indicted in a major share-trading scandal. This was crime enough for Advo to act as his judge, jury and executioner. In his postings, he had explained how he had hacked into the New York Presbyterian Hospital's mainframe and tampered with the life support machine software so that it failed and Mark Walsh was killed. He claimed it as his first piece of direct action, the opening salvo of his new war.

No one believed him. Abel and others on the message board told Advo they felt that he was some sort of a prankster and he had seen the story of the life-support machine failing in the media and claimed ownership of it. This didn't seem to bother Advo. He was seemingly more concerned that his public execution – as he described it – was not public enough. He announced that he was going to discontinue his activities in the War Pigs collective and he was going to set about creating his own spectacular act of war against his capitalist enemy. As before, no one paid him much attention. There were some sarcastic farewells and suggestions that he was mentally deficient in some way, and that, for the time being, was the end of the matter.

Abel fully expected Advo to reappear some time later claiming responsibility for some other unfortunate incident that might have befallen a member of the banking industry. And so he did. But this time, he announced the specific details of what he was going to do *before* the incident took place. Avoiding the public forum of the War Pigs message board, Advo sent Abel a direct message which advised him to 'watch Tokyo tomorrow for attack #2'. Abel checked the news and, sure enough, the following day, there was a piece that was carried by most global media. A Japanese fund manager by the name of Yuki Takahashi had been killed in a car bomb explosion in Tokyo's financial district. Takahashi had recently been involved in a massive trading loss for the Tokyo Finance Corporation. The Nikkei was rocked by the revelations that such a massive loss could have been perpe-trated without safety mechanisms being alerted and rumours abounded that Takahashi had profited personally from the losses, rumours that were difficult to prove but had clung to him for months. The explosion that killed Takahashi was notable because it had been detonated using a mobile phone. Rather than activating the detonation via a phone call over a phone network, however, it was set in motion by an email. One Tokyo newspaper had run with the headline, 'DEATH BY WI-FI'.

Abel contacted Advo as soon as he saw the news. Advo was disappointed with the media reaction to his attack. Although it had been featured in news reports around the world, it had not made headline news. Advo signed off his message to Abel by saying that he would not be responding to further communications until his next 'operation' – as he called it.

Abel had done plenty of soul-searching and agonising over whether he should go to the authorities. In the end, he took the coward's way out and mentioned what he knew to other members of the War Pigs collective, thereby sharing his guilty secret. They discussed what they could do, but it wasn't much. All they had by way of evidence was a series of unverifiable messages from a completely anonymous Internet avatar claiming responsibility for two deaths. Abel couldn't help but be fascinated by what Advo was proposing, so he justified his reticence to notify law enforcement by telling himself that Advo was almost certainly untraceable. Abel tested this belief himself and spent many sleepless nights tracing the messages that Advo had sent him. But, try as hard as he could, he could only follow the threads of code so far via servers all over the world before he hit a dead end. If he couldn't trace Advo then it was extremely unlikely that the authorities would be able to do so either.

Advo had been disappointed with the dissemination of his media message but he had been pleased that the operation had proved so successful. What intrigued Abel was Advo's contention that he had facilitated the construction of the explosive device that was used and had deployed it 'remotely'. He wouldn't be drawn on exact details but Abel took this to mean that he had been on the ground in Tokyo, in person, to oversee the assassination.

Some of the other War Pigs members in whom Abel had confided continued to believe that Advo was a fantasist and had merely gained access to some third-party information regarding the planned attack via his hacking activities and set out to claim it as his own. But Abel felt otherwise. Over and above Advo's foreknowledge of the attack, there was something about his behaviour and the way that he phrased his messages and the intensity of his beliefs that had made

Abel think that he was for real. And now, the events taking place over five thousand miles away in London were proof. Advo was escalating his war.

01:17 PM

Negotiating Cell, Blenheim Terrace, Belgravia

'The van driver checks out,' said Des White. 'His name's James Watts. He's a twenty-two-year-old student at the University of Westminster. Working for the food company is a holiday job. Nothing untoward in his background: grew up in Shropshire, happy family. His parents have been informed.'

'Nothing new on the hostage taker?' asked Ed.

'Well, we've finally got clearance to check the S.A.S. and S.B.S. records but there's nothing definite as yet. Unfortunately, there are a number of current and former soldiers who hail from the North East. So, they're working on it.'

'Have there been any claims of responsibility?'

'Not yet,' said Des.

'Not even nutters?'

'No.'

'Keep us posted if there's anything. However seemingly mad or leftfield.'

'I will.' Des said it in such a way so as to indicate to Ed that he wasn't the only one who was feeling under pressure.

'I know you will,' said Ed in a conciliatory tone. He leaned back in his chair and sighed before enquiring, 'What's happening on the video feed, Nick?'

'Nothing,' said Calvert. 'The subject's hard up against the chimney stack and the four hostages are kneeling on the ground. They appear to be talking to one another.'

'They're talking?'

'Yeah.'

'What's their demeanour?'

'It's impossible to say. It looks as though they're shouting to be heard above the sound of the helicopters.'

'So the chances are that they can't hear what the hostage taker is saying when he's speaking to us on the phone?'

'Probably not.'

'But they're looking scared, right?'

'Even when the feed focuses closely on them, it's difficult to make out their facial expressions. Why do you ask?'

'I don't know.'

This wasn't enough for Calvert. He wanted to pursue Ed's line of thought now. 'What are you getting at, Ed?' Ed could hear Calvert turn in his chair to face him. There was something adversarial in his demeanour that hinted at a desire to spar – to test his own powers of reasoning and intuition against Ed's.

'Well, two things,' said Ed. 'Firstly, we have to ask why the hostage taker is allowing his hostages to speak. Either he wants them to – but I can't think why – or he just doesn't care. Secondly, and probably more importantly, we have to consider whether there is a degree of complicity between the hostage taker and his hostages.'

Ed could feel the collective focus of attention in the negotiating cell shift away from the video feed towards him. Heads were turned and postures altered in seats.

Calvert couldn't hide the impatience in his voice as he said, 'You really think that Graham Poynter could be in on this, do you?' Nick Calvert was a man who hated ambiguity, hated a proverbial grey area. He liked things to be clear and unequivocal. If Ed was suggesting something then he wanted to hear him say it.

'We have to look at that as a possibility. This hostage-taking follows no known pattern, as far as I can see. We've got a hostage taker who has no demands other than extreme visibility, even though this puts him in greater danger than if he concealed himself. In most situations, the hostage taker insists on total obedience and compliance from his hostages for fear that any form of insurrection might lead to an attempt to escape. They are his most precious commodities. They are all that stands between him and arrest or death. But this guy is letting his hostages have a chat. It's like all the natural rules of hostage-taking have gone out of the window.'

'But if, as you suggest, Graham Poynter has engineered all this,' said Nick Calvert, 'then I can't see his motive.'

'I don't know how it could work,' said Laura Massey, 'but maybe it's an attempt to clear his debts; maybe it's to do with life assurance. Possibly?'

'That's all well and good,' said Calvert, 'but it doesn't alter the fact that three security guards have been killed.'

'They are definitely dead, are they?' asked Ed.

'What do you mean?' Calvert's voice rose in frequency to accentuate his bafflement at why Ed would ask such a question. 'We saw the two in the garden on the video feed from the S.A.S. team. Both were taken out with extreme trauma to the neck. And the other bloke on the railings at the front of the house—'

'OK, they're dead. I'm sorry.'

'They're dead all right,' said Calvert who went on to describe the posture of the two guards' bodies in the garden and his theory of how they had been caught unawares by their attacker. Ed, however, wasn't listening. He was considering Laura Massey's comment about life assurance. Someone like Graham Poynter would have all sorts of financial instruments in place to hedge against his untimely demise. Ed didn't know much about finance; what he did know was that many life assurance policies would not pay out in the event of suicide. So perhaps Graham Poynter had engineered an elaborate hostage situation in which he would be killed, thereby providing for his wife and daughter as he faced ruin on account of the downfall of his hedge fund. Maybe this was all about him securing financial provision for his family.

'Maybe Graham Poynter is sacrificing himself for the good of his family,' said Ed. 'He dies but they get the life assurance payout, which is all they're going to have to save them from destitution when the authorities close down his business.'

'OK,' said Calvert, 'I can just about buy that. But what I can't understand is what the hostage taker is hoping to get from this. If he is Poynter's puppet and is being paid by him, he has still killed three men and he has no possible means of escape. Regardless of who it is who is pulling the strings, nothing, as far as I can see, explains what's in it for the big guy. Unless, that is, we're overlooking something completely fundamental.'

'Which is?' asked Ed.

'Well, maybe he has found a way to escape.'

01:25 PM

Roof of 11 Blenheim Terrace, Belgravia

There was only one other occasion when Helen had seen anything even approaching the intensity of expression now on Graham's face and that was, typically, business-related. It was the day back in September when everything had changed forever. It was the phone call from Bob Rushwood in which Bob had told Graham that the fund was effectively insolvent. Investors were trying to extract their money and there was no money to give them. Well, there was, but not enough and the fund was under investigation by the Financial Conduct Authority, who had also passed files to Scotland Yard for a full-scale legal investigation.

It was a Friday. Graham had been working from home when the call came through. He had been in the breakfast room with his laptop on the pine table, surrounded by papers and newspapers. Sometimes she thought it was as though he made a nest for himself when he worked. But, that day, his carefully nurtured environment of paper and electronics, which provided him with his economic world view, offered little comfort. Things were bad. They were worse than they had ever been. But he was unaware just how bad they were about to become. When his Blackberry had started to ring, he had answered the call from Bob Rushwood and paced the room as his partner had relayed the news to him.

Usually when he received bad news, he became flushed with anger – as though offended by it – and would respond with threats of confrontation, legal battle and the ultimate destruction of enemies or antagonists. Not so that day. Whatever it was that Bob Rushwood was telling him, this was different from the usual slings and arrows that came his way. Whatever it was – and at that stage she had no idea – it had him beaten, temporarily at least. At first, she had thought that perhaps Bob was telling him that he had a terminal illness or some such. Graham and Bob weren't exactly friends but their relationship was complex and went back to the beginnings of their respective careers. Although they argued constantly and were forever slating each other in private, their mutually assured loyalty was always solid. So, if it wasn't something related to illness or accident, Helen couldn't think what would render Graham so silent and seemingly bereft. Normally, when Graham and Bob spoke, it was Graham who did most of the talking, but that day he barely said a word. When he had finished the call, she asked him what was wrong. He might have been distraught about something but his love of profanity was still in full effect when he told her, 'We're fucked.' And that expression on his face was the same as the one he wore now as Lily tried to persuade them to fight back against the man who had taken them hostage.

Lily's argument had followed its usual trajectory for when she was trying to persuade them to do something. Except, that is, for one respect. Usually, Lily started off with what Helen liked to think of as the 'soft soap'. She would try to charm them and when that failed and they refused to yield to her demands – which might be anything from allowing her to go out for a night with her friends to heading off on an impromptu weekend somewhere – she would become abusive. But she had missed out the soft soap this time. It was made redundant by their circumstances. She had told them what she thought of them with no preamble. They were pathetic. They were cowards. They had failed her as parents. Lily had that tone of voice that she had employed so many times in the past. But this time she wasn't asking them to allow her to go out for the night with friends, or go to a pop concert, she was asking them to help save her life. Helen felt so alone. She wanted Graham to be angry, wanted him to rise to the challenge and lead them to safety but, the way he had behaved since his failed attempt to gain control earlier, it was as though he had finally acknowledged his frailty and had thrown in the towel. He kept telling Lily that by trying to attack their hostage taker, who was standing so close by, seemingly unconcerned by their ongoing communication, they were, in effect, committing suicide. Lily countered by telling him that if they didn't try to do something they were most definitely committing suicide. And she had a willing ally in the van driver. Graham didn't want to hear it. He was in a bad way; Helen had never seen him like this before. His ability to cope was crumbling.

Helen had a choice. She could either agree with Graham – something she had always done when faced with the strong-arm tactics of their daughter – and, in so doing, ensure that they remained at the mercy of their hostage taker, or she could side with her daughter and her new-found accomplice, James, and try to save them all by launching an attack. Lily was right. They had to fight. Looking at Graham and seeing how broken he appeared, she knew that it was the only thing to do.

Lily was starting up again, telling them how much she despised them for their weakness but Helen stopped her. 'OK, we'll do it.'

'What?' asked Graham, imploring, his eyes betraying his fear and confusion.

'She's right, Graham; we have to try to do something. We can't just let this person harm us.'

'But—'

'We have to do it,' Helen cut him off. Her husband's shoulders sagged yet further. Lily was silenced.

James took up the details of the plan. He explained what they needed to do. With typical youthful enthusiasm, he had over-complicated things with his strategy and she was only half listening as he repeated his theory that, if they were to take a limb each and attack it with as much ferocity as they could, they would be able to disable the man.

She watched her husband. He had closed his eyes; he was shivering. They all were. His frailty, now so apparent, opened up long-dormant feelings for him and she reached out and took his hand. He opened his eyes and looked at her. She nodded and mouthed, 'It'll be all right.'

'He doesn't appear to have a gun,' said James. 'So let's get ready. I'll go for his throat if I can. We have to go in hard. If the only way to stop him is to kill him, then we'll just have to do it.'

01:27 PM

Negotiating Cell, Blenheim Terrace, Belgravia

Nick Calvert was in full flight. Ed knew better than to try to stop him. He was taking Ed's hypothesis regarding Graham Poynter and his potential complicity in his own hostage-taking and trying to join the dots. But he was floundering. However he proposed it, there was no way of explaining the hostage taker's motives. If Graham was paying him to make it appear that he had taken him hostage then there was no way that he could collect on any payment unless he could escape. While Ed felt sure that the hostage taker was a puppet of other forces, he couldn't conceive of any workable escape plan. The entire area around the stronghold was sealed off by the police and the military.

'Unless,' said Calvert, 'there's some way that a helicopter can snatch him off the roof.' This was something that Ed hadn't thought of and it made him listen as Nick continued with his train of thought. 'What's to stop a helicopter with accomplices springing him? If he's got a hostage with him – the girl, most probably – and he manages to grab on to a rope ladder slung from a helicopter, then no one's going to try to intercept them, not over central London.'

It was a valiant effort by Calvert but it wasn't feasible. Even if the hostage taker could manage to hitch a ride on a helicopter with Lily Poynter as his hostage, the helicopter would be easily tracked and, wherever it attempted to land, whether on land or sea, the police would be able to intercept it. But he decided to keep his thoughts to himself. He didn't want to discourage Calvert from thinking aloud. He did, however, register his uncertainty regarding the hypothesis by muttering, 'I'm not sure.'

'Ed,' said Laura and he could tell from just that single syllable address that she had something important to tell him. 'Scotland Yard have been contacted by an anonymous hacker who claims to have a partial identity – or at least an online identity – of the person behind the hostage-taking. He claims it's a hacker by the name of Advo and it's not the first time he's taken direct action.'

'Was it a message or a call?'

'A call; he's still on the line.'

'I guess he's taking something of a risk, isn't he, making a call rather than sending an anonymous email?'

'I think he probably is.'

'Can I speak to him?'

'Sure; Des can patch him through.'

'He might be the first of the whackos to come out of the woodwork,' said Ed, while Laura asked Des White to patch through the call.

Nick Calvert, however, was continuing with his hypothesis regarding the hostage taker's possible escape plan. 'If he's got a helicopter, he could make out across the Channel to a cruiser from where he could escape to Europe.'

When he heard this, Ed knew they were now in the realms of a thriller novel, but he would try to be diplomatic. 'I think you'll find that all helicopters are fitted with a G.P.S. device but, even if it was disabled, it would be fairly straight-forward to track the helicopter's location. I can't see a helicopter being a viable means of escape for the hostage taker. I think we have to face the fact that he might not have an escape plan. Maybe he doesn't want to escape. Maybe up there on the roof with the Poynter family is meant to be the end of his journey.'

Calvert greeted Ed's opinion with a thoughtful murmur of agreement but, before he could respond, Laura said, 'We've got the hacker for you on the line, Ed. It's a web phone connection from an unidentifiable IP address and his voice has been distorted, presumably so as to prevent any attempts to identify him.'

Ed pulled on his headset and clicked into the line. 'Hello, this is Ed Mallory.'

'Hello.' The voice's bass frequency had been modified so as to greatly accentuate it.

'Who am I speaking to?'

'You can call me Abel.'

'Presumably Abel is not your real name.'

'You presume right, Mr Mallory.'

Ed could have done without the Bond villainy but he also suspected that it was an affectation and more than a little sarcastic.

'I've been told that you claim to know the identity of the hostage taker we have here.'

'It's Advo. He sometimes calls himself "the Adversary". We tried to track him but failed.'

'Who's "we"?'

'We *were* – we're not operational any longer – a collective of hackers who ended up getting compromised. Don't ask me for a name; I'm not going to give you one. Advo was one of us but he started acting weird. Said he'd killed a banker in New York by hacking into a hospital's network and fucking with the guy's life support.'

'Can you be more specific?'

'No, I can't. I'm trying to do you a favour so just listen to me. I thought, when he said about the guy in New York, that he was messing with us because he'd claimed responsibility after the event, but with his next attack – this was in Tokyo – he told us what he was going to do before it happened. Look it up on the web. It was a car bomb that killed a banker. "Death by Wi-Fi" was the headline. Well, Advo told us he was going to do that. And he did it. This morning I got an email from him saying, "Operation number three, London." And what do you know? This happens.'

'Is there any way we can find out his identity?' Ed thought that the Englishness of his own voice sounded so much more pronounced in comparison to the voice – albeit distorted – of the person to whom he was speaking.

'I've tried. So unless you've got someone on your govern-ment team who is better at what I do than I am – which I doubt – then I'm not so sure.'

'Can you tell me anything that you know about him? I'm thinking personal details, background, anything that might be relevant to a negotiation?'

'Advo is not the guy on the roof, if that's what you're thinking. I mean, there's no way out of there, is there?'

'You think that whoever has taken the family hostage is being worked by someone else?'

'Come on, man; you do, too.' Ed was glad to have his suspicions confirmed in front of everyone else in the cell listening to the conversation either through individual headsets or through the speakers on the walls.

'And you think that whoever is doing this is doing it because he wants to take his anti-capitalism protest to a new level. Right?'

'I know that's what it is; he's told me. He thinks that, at certain times, there is a moral justification for killing people. He seems to think that one of those times is now. And there are probably quite a few more people that agree with him than you think.'

'How do I know that you're not him?' It was the question that Ed had wanted to ask from the start of the conversation but had left it until now when it looked unlikely that he was going to learn anything more concrete about the identity of the person behind the hostage-taking.

'You don't, but you've got to question why I would be calling you at this time. If I was the one pulling the strings, I would probably have better things to do and why would I bother exposing myself to possible detection by contacting you in the first place? There's no reason why I would.'

'So what are your reasons for calling us, if there's nothing you can do to help confirm the identity of the person behind all this?'

'That's a very good question, Mr Mallory, and one that I can't really answer. I guess I'm easing my conscience. As much as I despise people like Graham Poynter and the other bankers that Advo killed, I don't believe in violence. As soon as you allow violence to be part of your methods then you've lost the war. Don't you agree?'

'I suppose I do.'

'So now you know the guy's avatar, maybe you can track him and find out his identity. Then again, maybe you can't, but at least I get to feel like I've done the right thing.'

'And that's the only reason for your call?'

'I guess it's all a matter of karma.'

'You're sure it's just that?'

'Yeah.'

'And if it is that, are you sure there's nothing else you could tell me? Make your karma complete?'

A distorted baritone chuckle thundered down the line. The laughter didn't fit with the impression that Ed had of the man.

'Goodbye, Ed Mallory,' said the voice.

'You don't have to go. I'd like to talk some more.'

'Good luck. You're gonna need it.'

01:30 PM

Roof of 11 Blenheim Terrace, Belgravia

The shivering was a constant. Even with James's jacket and socks, the cold seemed to radiate out from the clammy metal collar around her neck. The weight of the grenade pulled it forward at the front, making it dig into the skin at the back. Lily tried not to think about it and tried instead to focus on James's plan to attack the giant. The hope this engendered made her feel better than she had done all day. If she considered the grenade and what it might do to her, it made her feel nauseous. The only thing that concerned her about their plan was that putting it into effect could hamper an existing plan that the authorities might already have. She considered mentioning this to James but he appeared to be so consumed with the details of what he wanted them to do that she knew her reservations would be swept aside. Besides, there was no point waiting for a rescue that might never come. If there was one thing she had learned from her dad – and there was plenty that she had learned and would rather have unlearned – it was the need to seize the initiative rather than be passive and allow oneself to become the victim of events. The ghost of that belief had made Graham threaten to jump off the roof and now she could only hope that their plan to attack the giant might conjure up that ghost once again.

'I'll give the sign after I've counted down and then we just pile into him,' said James. 'We all got that?' Lily and her parents nodded their heads but her dad clearly didn't present enough enthusiasm for James's liking. 'I have to know that you're with me when I go for him,' said James. 'If it's just me on my own, he'll kill me. We can only do this if we all attack him at the same time.'

'I understand that,' said Graham.

'Good. Don't hold back. We have to try to kill him. Go into this with that mindset and we might just manage it.'

James's confidence and bravery was appealing, seductive even, but it also worried her too. Throughout the few minutes he had been planning his covert operation, he had directed his words – give or take a few comments – directly to her and Lily couldn't get over the feeling that he was attracted to her. He fancied her. She knew the signs. Despite the terrifying nature of the situation in which they all found themselves, she had the distinct impression that he was showing off. Whether that would make him more or less brave or more or less capable was something she couldn't answer. All she cared about was escape.

James raised his head and looked towards the chimney stack. He fixed the giant with a stare, nodding his head very slightly as though sizing him up and working out his chances. In that moment, Lily felt the fear rise up inside her and fuel her shaking. He was really going to do this. They all were. They were going to throw themselves forward at this monster and try to kill him.

'Keep with me, Lily,' said James. 'You need to make sure that he can't pull the chain tight. You got it?'

'Yes, I've got it.'

She felt sick. The shivering eased for a moment but she had been kneeling for so long and she was so cold that her legs felt numb.

'Are we ready to do this?' asked James.

'Yes,' said Lily.

'I think so,' said Helen, her voice rendered high pitched by her fear and emotion.

There was a pause while they all turned to look at Graham. Feeling their stares, he wiped his forehead with the flat of his hand. It was a nervous gesture. He had been doing it a lot lately.

'Yes,' he said.

'OK,' said James. 'When I give the word, we do it.'

01:32 PM

Roof of 11 Blenheim Terrace, Belgravia

It was time to start the endgame. Danny had gone over this so many times in his mind. He had visualised this very scene with his hostages kneeling in front of him. His powers of visualisation were as strong as they had ever been. He had always been good at summoning up the specific environment that he would find himself in during an operation. It was all part of the preparation. It was never exactly what he had imagined – occasionally it would be nothing like it – but, this time, he had it pretty much spot on. He had stood in this very place in his waking dreams for weeks, considering how it might look. He had been supplied with aerial photographs and satellite images; he had considered the amount of shelter that would be provided by the chimney stack. He had contemplated the view of the rooftops of central London that would be stretching away in the distance, had thought of the low cream walls on either side of the roof and the expanse of grey roofing lead.

The visual side of things had been easy in comparison with trying to prepare himself for the emotional side of things. It was always going to be extremely difficult from a psychological point of view. As much as he had tried, on a number of occasions, to consider and evaluate the intensity of the emotions that he might feel, he had failed. What he hadn't bargained on was the sensation of being exposed to the world. In all the other operations in which he had taken part, he had felt as though he was just one small component in the workings of a massive machine. But now he felt supremely alone and more vulnerable than ever before.

He had carried out various tests with the chain. Unfortunately, he had been unable to enlist anyone else to assist in his training and research. So he had had to rig up the chain and a disarmed grenade and put it on himself, attaching the other end of the chain to the door handle in the garage at home in order to evaluate the amount of pull that would be required to remove the pin. It was a laborious process and required him to make a number of modifications to the collar and also the weight and gauge of the chain so that the pin would remain in place until required to do otherwise. He knew that, as soon as the pin was out of the grenade, he was a dead man. That was the deal. Just as it was back in the old days, he was carrying out detailed instructions to the letter. Abdicating responsibility for his actions was something that he had always done in his professional life. Now it would be no different. This wasn't his war any more than those in Africa and the Middle East had been when he fought there. This conflict had been started by others and it would be finished by others. What he was engaged in was just one small part of an ongoing campaign of hostilities. He was just following orders and one of the orders that he had been given was that he should, at exactly this moment, separate Graham Poynter from the rest of his family – at gunpoint, if necessary – remove the can of petrol from his rucksack and pour its contents all over him.

01:35 PM

Roof of 11 Blenheim Terrace, Belgravia

Graham had always loved the smell of petrol. When he was a boy, he liked going to the filling station with his father. There was something about the smell of petrol that spoke of glamour and excitement. His father drove a Jaguar. It had leather seats that smelled sublime. His dad was a smoker too and the combined smell of Embassy Filter and leather upholstery always transported Graham back to the 1970s. He had sometimes accompanied his father on his numerous business trips around the country and often the smell of tobacco and leather would be joined by a blast of petrol fumes on filling-station forecourts. Recently, when he found himself reduced to tears, as he had been so many times of late, it was to this image of his childhood self, sitting in the car with his father, criss-crossing the country, that he returned. It was a time of innocence and the adult world was still a place of mystery and allure.

Often his father would bring him into his meetings at the factories that he visited rather than leave him to wait in the car. The meetings always seemed to follow a pattern. There were hearty handshakes and the exchange of pleasantries, discussions of holidays and children's schools. Graham would be asked a couple of questions about his own school by whoever his father had come to see and, with the small talk out of the way, he would be provided with a chair, a comic or a book, and forgotten about while the men – it was always men that his father met – had their meeting. Occasionally, one of them might swear or curse and an apology would be made on his account and Graham would pretend that he hadn't heard, keeping his head buried in whatever he was meant to be reading. But he wasn't reading. His attention was focused on the meeting every bit as much as the men who were part of it. He loved the discussion of contracts and orders and delivery dates and specifications. The men often smoked in the meetings and the smell of their cigarettes and sometimes cigars hung in the air, only joined from time to time by the aroma of the tea and coffee that was provided by their female secretaries. Sometimes, one of the men would make a suggestive comment about one of the secretaries before the conversation would turn back to business once more.

In his memory, the sun was always shining and his favourite records were always on the radio in his father's car. Occasionally, on a long trip, they would stay overnight in a hotel somewhere, and these trips Graham liked best of all. Even though they were often nothing more than mid-range executive hotels, sheds on the outskirts of big cities, to a young boy they were impossibly glamorous. And, in the mornings, they would set off once more to another manufacturing plant in that olfactory bubble of leather, cigarette smoke, the occasional blast of his father's after-shave and the petrol at the filling stations.

After the bastard who had taken them hostage had dragged him a few feet away from the others at gunpoint and undone the cap on the can, Graham was momentarily transported back to his childhood by the petrol fumes. Helen and Lily were screaming and shouting. The van driver was speaking to him but he couldn't hear what he said. It was as though reality was being transmitted to him from a long way away, as though he was encased within a giant fishbowl, locked behind thick glass. A spontaneous desire to flee made him try to stand up but the hostage taker pushed him back on to his knees. What Graham would have done had he been allowed to stand was impossible to say. Maybe he would have tried to run to the roof of another house in the terrace or even made good his threat of earlier to throw himself into the street below. As it was, he could do neither. His legs were numb from all the kneeling and, when he had tried to stand at the first sight of the petrol can, it felt as though they might give way under him. He was better kneeling; he was better doing nothing. Sometimes it was better just to wait and see. That policy had served him well in business over the years. Ninety-nine per cent of the time it was essential to be proactive, front-out one's problems and face them head on. But very occasionally it was worth doing nothing. That was what he needed to do now. Whatever was happening was happening a long way away. He was safe, locked in some quiet corner in his mind, back in the passenger seat of his father's Jaguar in the 1970s, speeding away along the motorway, the smell of leather upholstery and cigarette smoke in his nostrils and Jerry Rafferty's 'Baker Street' playing on the radio. He had always loved that record and, when his thoughts returned to the vision of his father and their numerous trips together, it was always playing on the soundtrack.

As the first splash of petrol hit him, he was surprised at how cold it felt. It soaked through his sweater and his shirt, right through to the skin. It made him shiver. The next splash caught him on the head, soaking his hair and making him splutter and sneeze. The stench of the petrol invaded his senses and shook him awake from his self-imposed reverie. Whether his trance-like state had been an attempt by his subconscious to blot out the horror of what was taking place or whether it was the onset of some psychological collapse was of no importance. It was gone now and reality was brought back into needle-sharp focus.

'No, please!' His voice sounded as desperate as he felt. 'Don't do this.'

'Stay down,' said the bastard in the balaclava. 'Don't stand up or your daughter dies.'

Another tide of petrol slapped against his torso and then another. The cold liquid spread out in the material of his clothes. It felt like liquid ice. He retched and a string of phlegm that dropped from his bottom lip was immediately washed away by another wave of petrol that caught him on his chin, neck and upper torso, making his clothes stick to him. By the time the hostage taker was finished and had discarded the petrol can, the only material on Graham's body that remained dry were the legs of his trousers below the knees.

'Don't do this,' he shouted. 'Please.'

'Just keep your mouth shut – all of you keep quiet – and nothing will happen. This is a threat. I'm going to threaten to burn you alive. So long as you do exactly as I say, it will remain just a threat. Have you got that? I want to see nodding heads. Is that clear?'

Helen had lost control and was shrieking indecipherable words.

'Shut her up. You two' – he was speaking to Lily and James – 'make her shut up.' Graham turned to see Lily and James remonstrating with Helen, who was curled up on the ground, sobbing.

'Don't be under any illusion; if any of you attempt to escape or harm me in any way, I will kill you without blinking an eye. If, however, you do exactly as you're told then no one gets hurt. Is that understood? Nod your heads now.'

The last splash of petrol had caught Graham in the mouth and some had gone up his nose. It felt as though his entire respiratory system was infused with petrol. He retched as he nodded his head. The others must have indicated their consent as well. Whether Graham could trust this man or not was not something that he had time to evaluate. All he knew was that he had to comply with his demands. The petrol fumes were making his head swim and, as he watched the man take the pistol from the side pocket of his jacket once more and, with it, a Zippo cigarette lighter, he threw up.

01:39 PM

Negotiating Cell, Blenheim Terrace, Belgravia

'Ed, there's something going on.' Nick Calvert's uncharacteristically deadpan delivery indicated that, whatever it was, it was serious. Everyone other than Ed strained towards the screen on which they could see the video feed from the roof. 'The subject's taking out a handgun. It's an automatic.'

It was almost inconceivable that, up until now, the hostage taker had managed to carry out this extremely complex and dangerous hostage-taking without using a firearm. The appearance of one now indicated that proceedings had entered a new phase. Ed felt his breathing quicken as he awaited the next part of Calvert's commentary.

'The subject's grabbed hold of Graham Poynter and he's moved him away from the other hostages and forced him back on to his knees.'

'He's still got the chain connected to the girl?' asked Ed.

'Yeah; it's tight – very tight. He's speaking to the hostages and there's movement. Now he's put the gun back into his pocket.' Ed could just make out the sound of Calvert chewing his lip, his teeth pulling at the skin, something that Ed knew betrayed his nervous state of mind. 'Now he's taking something out of his rucksack. Oh, shit; it looks like a petrol can – it is a fucking petrol can. He's taking off the lid. There appears to be a lot of shouting between the subject and Poynter. The others are shouting too. The subject's pulling hard on the chain connected to the grenade and he's holding the petrol can in his other hand. Poynter's trying to stand up. I think the subject must be threatening to pull the pin out of the grenade. Now he's put the petrol can down and he's pointing the gun at Poynter, who's getting back on his knees. The gun's been put away again now and he's – oh, Jesus – he's pouring the petrol all over Graham Poynter.'

'Try the subject's mobile again,' said Ed. 'I've got to speak to him. Where are we with the robot?'

'Yes, it's on the roof of the adjoining house,' said Laura, her voice cracking with nerves and suppressed emotion.

'Patch me through to the speaker on it, in case he doesn't answer his phone.'

'Ed, you need to hear this,' said Des White. 'Scotland Yard have got a woman on the line from Stockton-on-Tees who's claiming to be the wife of the hostage taker.'

Before he even had time to consider the implications of this statement, Nick Calvert was leaning in close and telling him, 'Ed, he's taking out the gun again and he's also got something else in his hand. They need to zoom in closer. Ah, there it is; it's a . . . It's a cigarette lighter.'

Hours, and sometimes days, of waiting and planning interspersed with moments of frantic activity. That was how Ed described the nature of hostage negotiation in his lectures and seminars. That was a fairly accurate summary of his experiences but he had never been involved in a negotiation in which events had moved so rapidly, seemingly competing with themselves to befuddle his reasoning and torture his mind. A decision needed to be made and everyone was waiting for him to make it. He didn't have time to speak to the woman who was claiming to be the subject's wife. All he could do was try to stop the man setting fire to one of his hostages.

'OK, I need the woman's name and I need her husband's name immediately and you need to patch me through to the loudspeaker on the robot. What's happening on the roof?'

'He's taking out his phone,' said Calvert. 'I think he might be answering our call.'

'Hold it with the robot,' said Ed. 'I need those names.' He could hear White speaking to someone on another line.

'Yeah, OK; all right. Thanks.' His call concluded, Des White said, 'The wife's called Jan McAteer and her husband is Danny McAteer, ex-S.A.S.'

'I need everything on him,' said Ed as Des White, in his haste to stay ahead of the rapidly unfolding events, spoke over him.

'We've got a call coming through from the subject.'

'OK,' said Ed as he pulled the headset into place and clicked into the line. 'This is Ed Mallory.'

'I know you can't see what's going on but presumably you know what I've just done, right?'

'You've just poured a liquid over Graham Poynter.'

'It was a gallon of unleaded.'

'I have to warn you,' said Ed, trying to maintain an even tone of voice, 'that in the event of you making any attempt to ignite the petrol, you'll give us no choice but to launch a rapid intervention.' Ed didn't know that this was definitely the case anymore – he had no idea what the military options were because he had been excluded from the circle of communication – but it was important that the hostage taker knew that any actions he might take would have very specific consequences.

'If I see any sign of an intervention,' said the hostage taker. 'I'll kill Poynter and his daughter.'

Ed might have told him that if he did carry out his threat then he would die too but it seemed pointless; as a former member of the S.A.S., Danny McAteer – if that was his name – would know that already. Now was not the time to be making threats; he needed to test the intelligence he'd been given while he still had the chance. As much as he knew that the robot with the loudspeaker on it was in position, he didn't want to be forced to use it. In his experience, negotiations through loudspeakers on account of a subject's reluctance to use a phone were rarely successful.

Ed had not had time to prepare what he was going to say now that he had been given the potential identity of the hostage taker. If he could have introduced it into the conversation at a much less volatile moment then he would have done but he didn't have that luxury.

'We have been contacted by a woman who claims to be your wife.'

'I'm not married.'

'Her name's Jan and she tells us that your name is Danny McAteer.'

'She's winding you up.'

'She seems pretty sure.'

There was silence on the line and Ed waited for the man – who he now felt certain was this Danny McAteer – to speak.

Ed clicked the mute button on the headset and said, 'Get her ready on the other line. I want to patch her straight through.'

'We won't have prepped her,' said Calvert.

'We don't even know that she is his wife,' said Laura.

Ed chose to use the ongoing silence from the hostage taker to say, 'He's Danny McAteer; you can hear it in his voice. So, if she is his wife, then she might be able to make a difference.'

01:41 PM

Roof of 11 Blenheim Terrace, Belgravia

Danny had always known that this might happen. Jan might turn on the television, see him on the news and realise it was him. He had always hoped that, if it were to happen, it would be after the mission was complete. It was the one eventuality for which he had not been able to prepare. He knew the emotional burden of having to speak to her at a time like this was going to be impossible to bear and might compromise the entire operation. The right decision was to stonewall Ed Mallory, get the password information from Poynter as planned, then make the statement as instructed and say goodbye. Jan would know what he had done for her soon enough, when the letter arrived that he had posted the day before.

He had handwritten it with a shaky hand. It hadn't felt right to type it out on his laptop, not something as important as that. And he didn't want it to be traced, anyway. He had said goodbye to his family. There was no point turning back now. But, try as hard as he could to block it out, the knowledge that Jan was there on the line and wanting to speak to him was a whole new kind of pain. There was nothing he could say at this moment that would help her understand what he had done and why he had done it. There was nothing he could say that would make this any easier for either of them. All that mattered was that she and Emily would be provided for. He could do nothing else for them.

But his usually stoical and resilient thinking was starting to crumble and emotion was seeping into the cracks. If he spoke to Jan, he could tell her that he loved her, if nothing else. It was sentiment – pure and simple – but could he not allow himself a moment of that on today of all days? He could speak to her after he had secured the password from Poynter and after he had made the statement. By that stage, his job would be at an end. If he spoke to her then, it might help them both deal with what was to come. But, even as he thought this, he knew he was in danger of falling victim to his emotions. He knew he needed to keep a clear head and finish what he had started.

'Come on, Danny; I can hear it in your voice that it's you.'

There was no point denying his identity. The others – the architects of the day's events – had also realised that it was a very real possibility that Danny would be confronted by his wife in any attempted negotiation and they had suggested that he should use the possibility of speaking to Jan as a bargaining point. Logistically they were right, but they hadn't taken into account how he might be feeling.

He raised the iPhone to his ear and said, 'OK; this is Danny McAteer. Now listen to me very carefully. I will speak to Jan in a few minutes' time but, in order for that to happen, you have to guarantee that no rapid intervention will take place beforehand.'

'I can't make that guarantee. You know how this works, Danny; there's more than just me in charge here.'

'And I also know that everyone else of any importance will be listening to our conversation. So I want to make it clear that I'm happy to negotiate with you for the safe release of the hostages and also to speak to my wife but, in the meantime, you have to give me a few minutes. Is that understood? Do we have a deal?'

01:45 PM

Roof of 11 Blenheim Terrace, Belgravia

He was weak; he was greedy and sometimes, if it furthered
his own ends, he was devious. He probably deserved all the
disgust that was directed at him in the media. Lily knew all
of this only too well. But he was also her dad and, despite
everything they had been through as a family, he was loyal
and he loved her. At least, she thought he did. To see him
on his knees, doused in petrol, possibly only minutes –
maybe even only seconds – from a horrific death was almost
too unbearable to contemplate. That he deserved to be
punished for what he had done and the recklessness with
which he had exploited people's trust was not in dispute.
But this? This was sick and depraved. No one wanted to see
a man burned to death, or even threatened with it. Did
they?

Since they had been out on the roof of the house and
James had spoken of his plan to attack the hostage taker,

she had managed to keep her emotions under control, but now she found it impossible and the tears streamed down her face.

'Dad, I love you,' she called to him. She hadn't said it in a long time. Probably not since she was a little girl. He looked across at her and he had a strange expression on his face. It was neither broken nor anguished. It was almost animalistic, as though he had been stripped of everything that made him a man. This was Graham Poynter in his most basic form: a lonely, middle-aged man, kneeling on the roof of his own home, a starring role in someone else's morality play. He didn't respond to her; maybe he didn't hear. She wasn't going to say it again. She had more important things to consider, like when they were going to launch their attack.

The giant was standing with his back against the chimney stack, talking into his phone. Held in the same hand as the phone was the cigarette lighter that he had waved around a few moments before. That he had not used it yet had to be a good sign. There was still an opportunity for negotiation. Whatever it was that he wanted, she had to hope the authorities would give it to him. He appeared relatively calm, albeit deep in thought. He certainly didn't look like a man who was about to commit a horrific murder. In his other hand – the one whose wrist the chain was connected to – he held the pistol, which he pointed in the direction of Lily, her mother and James.

'You just say the word,' she said to James, glancing up at him. But he didn't respond, just continued to stare at the hostage taker. 'I said—'

'I heard what you said.'

'Whenever you're ready, let's rush him.'

'Now's not a good time.'

'Why not?'

'Can't you see what he's got in his hand?'

'That doesn't make any difference. It's no more dangerous than it was before.'

'Of course it is. He's got a gun.' The expression on his face made her feel desperate. While James was strong and determined, she still had hope, but the change in his demeanour made it begin to ebb away. James was her last line of defence, both physically and emotionally. 'If we run straight at him,' he said, his voice sounding hollow, 'he'll open fire. We'll never even get close enough to try to overpower him.'

'Please, James; we can still try.'

'Let me think.' He didn't even look at her as he said it. His eyes were locked on the giant. The sun was shining but it provided little warmth. Her feet were frozen and numb, her hands the same. Shivers continued to emanate from the metal collar around her neck and her legs and back ached from kneeling for so long.

'You haven't given up, have you?' she said to James, not caring that her voice had a childish petulance to it.

'No, of course I haven't. You think I want to be up here any more than you do?'

'Well, you don't sound so sure of things anymore.'

James turned to look at her and she could see the fear and uncertainty in his eyes. There were moments earlier when she had thought his bravery was born of a foolhardy desire to try to impress her. But now she could see that he was every bit as afraid as she was. Lily reached out, took his hand and squeezed it.

'I'll do something, Lily,' he said. 'Trust me. It's just, if we move on him now, one of us is going to die for sure. We need to find the right moment.' He held her hand long after she had squeezed his. It was the only part of her body that felt warm.

01:47 PM

Negotiating Cell, Blenheim Terrace, Belgravia

Danny had said he would speak to his wife and negotiate for the safe release of the hostages so long as he had a guarantee of no immediate intervention for the next few minutes. That was what he had said. But what did it mean? He needed a window in which to do something. He needed to know that he was safe for a short while – or as safe as he could ever be in the theatre of terror that he had created. Why?

In terms of the immediate negotiation, this development provided Ed with a commodity with which he could trade. He could tell Danny that he needed to speak to the powers-that-be and find out whether it would be possible to provide a guarantee; he could stall, even if it was only for a few minutes. But he also knew that, as a former member of the S.A.S., Danny McAteer's knowledge and understanding of hostage situations would be, in its own way, possibly the match of his and he would know that Ed had little with which to bargain. By rights, he should have taken advice at least from Laura, who, as the cell co-ordinator, had ultimate seniority in Serina Boise's absence. Ed had made the decision, however, that keeping the subject talking was more important.

'Look at it from our point of view, Danny.' Ed made sure that every time he addressed Danny at the start of a new phase of the conversation, he used his name. Even with the limited amount of time available to him, he had to try to build a degree of familiarity and trust. As a blind man, Ed knew the value of names. By using a subject's name, language has a greater resonance and is directed in a more personal way. 'You've allegedly killed three men—'

'Not allegedly; I did kill them,' broke in Danny.

'You're putting this family in danger, threatening them with extreme brutality and, on top of that, you want us to provide you with a window of time in which to do something.'

'Listen, Ed.' Just as Ed overused Danny's name in an attempt to foster an atmosphere of honesty and openness, so too was Danny doing the same to him. Ed had never negotiated with someone who was as calm and stoical as this. Subjects in hostage negotiations were almost exclusively desperate people who found it difficult to control their emotions. Danny was different. To Ed, it didn't feel like talking to a subject. It was more like talking to a colleague. 'I just need a few minutes before I speak to Jan,' continued Danny. 'So listen to me, I'm saying this so that no one can be in any doubt as to what my intentions are here. I am going to release the hostages, unharmed, in a few minutes' time. I'll speak to my wife and everything will be resolved. However, if any attempt is made to move on me then I'll kill everyone up here.'

It was a difficult call to make. Theoretically, Ed should have continued to stall him. Most negotiators would have argued that this was the best course of action. He might even have agreed with them, sitting in a meeting room somewhere, in a seminar, discussing hypothetical scenarios. But he could feel Danny's impatience; it bled into his headset every time Danny spoke to him. If he allowed Danny this concession, it might play to his advantage. What he mustn't do was give away the concession too easily.

'OK, we'll guarantee that there will be no rapid intervention in the next ten minutes. You have exactly ten minutes but after that, if you don't release the hostages, the military option will be back on the table.' It was probably way too bullish but Ed didn't care. The thought of Graham Poynter drenched in petrol kept him aware that they were seconds away from a public spectacle the likes of which the television viewers of the world would struggle to forget.

'Nice try, Ed, but you're basically saying that I've got ten minutes, then I'm a dead man. You don't get to have that much control. You know as well as I do that, if they come for me, I'll start killing people and take as many with me as I can. Added to which, you'll have missed the chance to talk me down by using my wife to appeal to me.'

Back to square one. The hostage taker wasn't going to cede any ground. Danny was fully aware that he had contrived a situation which presented the authorities with a uniquely difficult problem and he wasn't going to squander his advantage.

'Can I ask you a question, Danny?'

'Go ahead.'

'Why do you want a few minutes before you talk to your wife? Why can't you speak to her now?'

'If you call me in ten minutes, I'll speak to Jan. If you call before then, I won't answer. Understand? Actually, I don't care if you understand. That's the way that it's going to be.'

Danny terminated the call. To Ed, he sounded like a man in a hurry, which was yet another bad sign.

Ed pulled off his headset. 'Have we got any more intelligence on this guy?'

'They're working on it,' said Des White.

'They should go for his medical records first.' As random thoughts came to him, Ed barked them out to the cell. 'Someone needs to find out how long it takes for petrol to evaporate. If there's a single communication into or out of the stronghold that isn't accounted for, we need to be able to monitor it and identify it immediately. Oh, and someone needs to keep an eye on the time. We need to know exactly when the ten minutes is up so we can put a call straight back into him.'

It took him a moment to realise that the voice that was directed at him belonged to Serina Boise. He had never heard her sounding so lacking in self-belief. The crisis was getting to her.

'Ed, we're under a lot of pressure from on high to close this down now.'

'Don't tell me – the sniper's back on the cards.'

'There's a plan being put in place to make an intervention across the roof from the neighbouring house, using the cover of the chimney stacks. The S.A.S. O.C. is planning to send in a four-man team who can disable the subject and cut the chain with bolt croppers before he has a chance to set off the explosive.'

It wasn't that Ed resented the intervention of special forces. If they could succeed in a mission like the one that Boise had outlined, then he would have been all for it. It was the fact that his being made party to the details of such a mission jolted him out of his contemplation of what he as a negotiator needed to do to resolve the situation.

'You did hear all of that just now, right?' asked Ed, failing to conceal his truculence.

'Of course I did.'

'I've given him ten minutes.'

'I heard that.'

'Well, if the military are going to ignore that and just go blazing in, then let me know and I'll stop torturing myself with how I can try to talk him down.'

'No, they're not going to be ready for a while at least, so the subject can have his ten minutes.'

Ed couldn't be bothered to tell Serina how distracting it was to be provided with operational details like this in the midst of a negotiation. Sometimes it was better not to know what was going on behind the scenes. It just made it harder to concentrate and contemplate a potential resolution.

'Well, I'm going to carry on as normal then, until such time as you tell me otherwise.' Ed's tone had softened. It was difficult to contain the frustration. He knew that as well as anyone.

'You do that,' said Serina and she put her hand on his arm and squeezed it. It was an awkward gesture but it was meant well. They were both on the front line. They both needed to be at the top of their game. There was something in the touch of Serina's fingers that hinted at a shared intimacy and understanding, something of a mutual acceptance that they could only ever do the best they could and sometimes it might not be enough. It was the sort of unspoken contract, thought Ed, that a man and a woman enter into before they make love.

What Ed couldn't tell Serina – couldn't tell anyone – was that he had heard something in Danny's voice that made him sure that, either with or without his ten-minute window, it was extremely unlikely that he was going to release his hostages. Danny was lying to him.

'Do we have Jan McAteer on the line?' asked Ed.

'Yeah; I can patch her through,' said White.

It was going to be a difficult conversation. He had to speak to a woman whose husband was very possibly going to be killed in the near future, a woman who was more than likely still in the early stages of shock. Ed pulled on his headset and clicked into the line.

'Hello, this is Ed Mallory.'

'Hello.' Her voice had that same Teesside accent as her husband's. There was every chance that they had been together since childhood but it was a detail that he didn't need to contemplate. Ed had a matter of minutes to try to find something, some piece of information – however minute – that might provide him with the psychological insight to unlock Danny McAteer. He didn't feel confident.

'I'm the lead hostage negotiator and I'm the one who's been speaking to Danny. May I call you Jan?'

'Yes, go ahead.'

'We haven't got very long here, Jan. Now, you know what it is that Danny is threatening to do?'

'Yes.' The voice was wobbly. Jan had clearly been crying and there were more tears on the way.

'I want you to try to think why Danny might be doing this.'

'I'll try.'

'Has he ever given any hint that he might want to cause harm to someone who works in the world of high finance?'

'No, not that I know of. He swears at the television when the news is on and there's talk of bankers' bonuses. Same as everyone else.'

'Have you ever had any money troubles, been turned down for a loan or had your house repossessed – anything else that might have triggered this?'

'Nothing I can think of. He's been strange for these past few months.'

When the line went quiet and it was clear that Jan wasn't going to provide any further information, Ed chose to push her a little. 'What do you mean by "strange"?'

'Kind of distant. Not his usual self at all. It was like he was sort of depressed.'

'Did you talk about it?'

'No; I tried a couple of times but he changed the subject. I thought it might be to do with lack of work.'

'But you weren't struggling financially?'

'Not especially. No more than most people.'

Ed could feel the seconds ticking by and, as they did so, he felt his sense of frustration ratcheting up.

'If you could think of anything that might stop Danny harming himself or someone else, what would you say it was?'

'I don't know. I don't know why he would want to hurt

someone that he doesn't know like this. I heard that he killed three security guards—' Her voice cracked.

She was on the edge. Ed needed to steer her away from her husband's murder spree. 'What's the most important thing in Danny's life?'

'His family. Without a doubt.'

'How many children do you have?'

'Just the one. Her name's Emily. She's two.'

'Does she ever speak to her daddy on the phone when he's away from home?'

'Very occasionally.'

'He's crazy about his little girl, right?'

'Of course, but—'

'If I asked you to speak to him to ask him why he's doing this and to ask him to stop, would you do that?'

'Yeah, of course I would.'

Ed came straight back at Jan at the end of her statements, closing off any attempt she might make to think of reservations. He needed to get her onside as fast as he could and he knew that the next question would be the one that might arouse some dissent.

'If I was to ask you to put Emily on the line to speak to her dad, how would you feel about that?'

'I don't know. I don't want to upset her.'

'Presumably she doesn't know what's going on here?'

'No, but she can see I'm upset. She's with my mum at the moment – her gran – in the next room.'

'Jan, I think it might make all the difference if you can tell Danny that Emily wants to speak to him. Maybe she wants to wish him a happy Christmas?'

'I don't know.'

'Jan, I respect the fact that you don't want to upset your daughter but I think the only way we can stop Danny from doing something stupid is to play on his love for you and Emily. So it's very important that, if I can manage to get Danny to speak to you, I know that you'll try and put Emily on the line if needs be.'

'It's like emotional blackmail.'

'That's exactly what it is. In a situation like this, sometimes emotional blackmail is all we've got. What do you say?'

'OK, I'll try; but what do you want me to say to him?'

'I just want you to say what you want to say. Presumably you want to tell him that you love him and you want him to come home to you and Emily.'

'But he's not going to, is he? If he doesn't end up dead, he's going to have to spend the rest of his life in prison for what he's done.'

As much as he felt that brutal honesty was nearly always the best course of action during a negotiation, sometimes it was better to be more pragmatic. Jan had faced enough today already. 'We don't know what he's done yet. All we really care about at this moment in time is getting Danny safely down off that roof along with all the hostages.'

But this wasn't enough for Jan. 'He's never coming home, is he?'

'I don't know. There'll be an investigation and all of that will be dealt with then. There's nothing I can say to provide any consolation, but the question that you need to ask yourself at this stage is do you want Danny to live?'

'Of course I do.'

'Well, let's work towards that and, when I say the word, I'd like you to come on the line and talk to him and, if at all possible, have Emily speak to him as well. What do you say?'

'OK; I'll try my best.'

'Good. Thank you. Now hold the line and my colleague will be back to you in a moment.' Ed pulled his headset down and asked, 'How long have we got until the ten minutes is up?'

'Almost exactly five minutes gone,' said Nick Calvert.

'What's happening on the video?'

'McAteer is speaking to Poynter. He's still got the gun in one hand – the hand with the chain attached to the wrist – and in his other hand he's holding the phone and what looks like the cigarette lighter.'

Calvert modulated his voice from its announcing tone to one that was more familiar as he addressed Ed directly: 'I don't think he's got any intention of letting anyone go.'

'No, me neither.'

'I think this is looking more and more like a suicide mission.'

Ed turned to his colleague and nodded. 'Yup, I think you might be right.'

01:50 PM

Roof of 11 Blenheim Terrace, Belgravia

The look on the doctor's face when he tells you that you're going to die. Pancreatic cancer. You've got six months to live. I'm very sorry.

It was so far beyond Danny's frame of reference, so absurd, that he almost felt like laughing. It had started with pains in his stomach, and his skin didn't feel right – it itched and trembled. He knew he was ill, had suspected it was something nasty from the way the doctor behaved. Then came the test results and that was that. Six months. Maybe nine, at a push. There was something in the bloke's expression that spoke of a sense of relief. It was a relief to unburden himself of the news. He must have been nervous. However many times you have to tell someone they're going to die, it can never be easy. You could never get used to it. Maybe some doctors sat and looked at themselves in the mirror and studied their appearance by way of rehearsal. Maybe they had training workshops. But you could never prepare for it completely. Facial expressions are sometimes involuntary. And his doctor couldn't help the look of relief on his face. It suggested that his subconscious was cheering and whooping that it was someone else dying and not him.

Danny had thought about death. As a member of the S.A.S. it was a constant presence. He had always thought that, if he were to die young, it would be at the hands of a suicide bomber, a sniper or a roadside I.E.D. He had never considered an illness. He was fit and healthy – as fit and healthy as any man he knew. He couldn't tell Jan; he had nearly told her when he was going for the first tests but something had stopped him. He realised when he had been given the final diagnosis that deep down he had never really accepted that it could be something terminal. Even when the doctor had sat there with that strange expression on his face, he had not been able to believe it. He wanted a second opinion and he got one: pancreatic cancer. Six to nine months. There was no ambiguity in the two separate diagnoses. The disbelief turned to anger fairly rapidly. It was on his final visit to his doctor, the final visit he had made to any doctor, that he had felt the rage inside him almost explode. The doctor had worn that same expression on his face as when he had first delivered the bad news. And, for a moment, Danny had felt like killing him. It would have been so easy. So wonderfully easy. In that brief moment when the doctor would realise he was being attacked, and just before his neck was snapped and he slumped dead to his desk, he would know that his life was equally as fragile as Danny's. More so.

The rage didn't subside. He couldn't speak to Jan, found it hard to spend any time with Emily without crying. A couple of times, he had openly wept in front of the little girl when Jan wasn't there. When Emily asked him what he was doing, he had told her he had something wrong with his eyes. Even at two years of age, he got the feeling that she didn't believe him. It was the injustice of it that made him so angry. He had managed to stay alive in some of the most dangerous places on earth and now he was going to be killed by his own body turning against him. He would miss out on his life with Jan, miss out on seeing little Emily grow up.

There was so much to think about and all of it desperately depressing. As the days grew into weeks, he came to a decision. There was no way that he could face a slow, lingering death. He could throw himself into the most dangerous situations in the world but he couldn't face that. His thoughts were invaded by an army of doubts and fears, all of which he chose to keep from his family. But despite all the trauma he suffered, life still had the ability to surprise him. He had been in a dark place, had taken to sitting up late at night, trawling the Internet. He didn't know what he was looking for but he couldn't stop searching. What he didn't realise was that, just as he was searching for someone or something to offer meaning to him during his dire predicament, someone was also searching for him. When they found him, they explained how they had done it.

Once Danny's condition had entered the digital realm on a medical database, a cross-reference could be made with his former profession on another compromised database and this specific combination – a special forces soldier with a terminal illness – was a perfect fit for a unique employment opportunity.

Danny was eventually presented with an unusual job offer. But not at first. When he first started to correspond with a man who called himself Advo, it didn't feel as though he was being groomed. Cunning tactics were at work. At first, he was just someone that Danny could talk to. There were long night-time Skype calls as Danny poured out the truth of his medical condition and Advo listened to all his fears and frustrations. This anonymous character who had sought him out from the millions of chattering voices on the Internet became his confidant, the only person to whom he could unburden himself. It was an intense relationship. Here was a man who was clearly much younger than him, had barely lived, but seemed to have an instinctive understanding of life, which belied his years. Danny was sucked in – he could feel it happening – but it felt as though it was his only escape. He was faced with a very simple choice: he could either give up and die or he could provide a large amount of money for his family, securing their future when he would not be around to do so. He had always been thoughtless with money, permanently living to the extent of his overdraft and credit card limits. Work was hard. As he had grown older, it took a greater emotional toll on him. He had turned down a lot of jobs. People remembered. His capabilities were never in question but his reputation suffered. His desire to spend so much time with his family made some people suggest he had gone soft.

When his relationship with Advo started to change, so did his finances. Large sums, by Danny's standards – ten grand at first and then another twenty – appeared in his bank account. He was assured that this was the tip of the iceberg. As though to prove it, a hundred grand was paid into his account. It was at this stage that his ongoing conversation with Advo began to take on a more subversive tone. Advo would have made an excellent politician and the success of his pitch to Danny lay in his ability to unite all Danny's feelings of injustice and frustration and channel them in one specific direction.

His family was all that Danny had left. Did he not want to provide some security for them after he had gone? Of course he did. When he was told the details of the proposed mission, it was in such a way that it had played on his sense of injustice and united it with all other injustice in the world. When the mechanics of the operation were discussed, an intense debate had ensued. They did not know at this stage what level of security Graham Poynter would have put in place in his London property. But there had been every chance that it would involve bodies on the ground. Advo insisted that Danny would need to kill them. Danny told Advo it was a deal breaker. He agreed with Advo's principles and motivations up to a point. Western society's moral compass did need recalibrating but he didn't see why innocent people had to die for it. But even when the debate and discussion fell over into an argument, Danny knew deep down that this aspect of the operation was not a deal breaker. He was in too deep now. When Advo had told him that he could walk away – no hard feelings – Danny had finally agreed. Five million U.S. dollars would be paid into a numbered account in the Cayman Islands in two instalments, half at the start of the operation and half on completion. Jan would be notified of the money at the necessary time.

As the pains in Danny's stomach and his headaches became fiercer and more intense, he knew he had to fight. He couldn't fight his cancer but he could fight bad people. It was all that he was good at. He would not go gentle into that good night. Not for him, wasting away in a hospital bed with tubes sticking out of him. Now he had a cause and he was going to die for it.

Danny had entered the last hour of his life. It frightened him how fragile he felt and how much he wanted to speak to Jan and Emily just one more time. Saying goodbye to them the day before had been one of the most difficult things he had ever had to do. He had barely held himself together and he knew that Jan had noticed this. It had probably preyed on her mind ever since he left. To hear her tell him that she didn't care what he had done and that she still loved him, was a craving he was finding hard to deny.

Danny looked at Graham Poynter kneeling, shivering, his petrol-sodden clothes sticking to his body. The final part of the operation had begun and, in a few minutes, he would assign both himself and Poynter to the hereafter. The smell of petrol caught in his throat as he leaned down to his sacrificial offering and spoke into his ear.

'This is what you have to do in order to save yourself, OK?'

Poynter managed to control his trembling long enough to nod his head.

'You need to give me your password for the Anchorage account.'

'What?'

'Don't even try to mess me around by giving me the wrong password because, you know as well as I do, there are two passwords that are required. We already have the first from your partner, Bob Rushwood. So, once you've handed over the second password, I'll be checking it and, if it's not the right one, I'll burn you alive and then I'll shoot your family. Do you understand me?'

'Yes, but how do I know you won't do all that anyway?'

'You don't. But be aware that, if you don't give me the password now, you and your family are going to die. It's a risk that you have to take. You got that?'

'Yes.'

'Good; now fire away.'

01:53 PM

Roof of 11 Blenheim Terrace, Belgravia

There was no point lying. Even if he could manage to stay alive without giving up the password, it was clear that the secrecy regarding the existence of the Anchorage account had been compromised. His and Bob's safety net, their 'ace in the hole' as Bob had called it, was lost either way. Some safety net it had turned out to be. The bastard was right: this was his only chance to save himself. Graham's trading days had come to an end.

He was always terrible at remembering passwords but this one was embedded in his mind. It was the only one that really mattered and he had made a point of making it easy to remember. It was his daughter's name. What name would he be least likely to forget? He didn't worry about people hacking into the account; it had an extra layer of security in that it required two independently held pass-words in order to extract or transfer money from it. Bob

Rushwood held the other password and he was meticulous in such matters. Graham's password started with his daughter's name and finished with his mother's birthday, the 26th May.

'It's "Lily2605". That's Lily, L, I, L, Y, with a capital L at the start, then two, six, zero, five.'

The bastard held his phone to his ear and started shouting the letters and numbers into it. He didn't want whoever it was that he was speaking to to be in any doubt as to what he was saying. He repeated the password three times, reciting it slowly each time, enunciating as clearly as he could.

Graham Poynter felt strangely liberated that he had finally been able to unburden himself of the spectre of the Anchorage account. The knowledge that he and Bob had salted away a few million in case of the fund's collapse had never really provided him with much comfort. Certainly not as much as it had Bob. The fact of the matter was, it was all fantasy. After the nightmarish scenario at the fund with its gradual mutation into nothing more than a Ponzi scheme, the Anchorage account was always going to be discovered. As soon as they started to draw funds from it in order to avert their own personal collapse, questions would have been asked. At least now it might actually serve a purpose and save his and his family's lives. If this man and whoever he was working with wanted money then it meant that, once they had the money, they might just leave him alone. For the first time in years, Graham felt as though he had done the right thing and he made a decision that, if he was to survive this ordeal, he would start over again. His life would change. Things would be different.

01:55 PM

Roof of 11 Blenheim Terrace, Belgravia

'What do you suppose all that's about?' said James as the giant shouted into his phone the letters that spelled her name along with some random numbers.

'It sounds like a password,' said Lily. 'My dad always uses my name or some version of it for passwords – I know that because he told me – and then he adds the birth date of someone in the family. Two, six, zero, five is 26th May. It's my grandmother's birthday. Maybe it's the password to a bank account. Maybe that's what this is all about. He's telling whoever's on the other end of the line a bank password and they're going to steal Dad's money, whatever money he's got left.'

'You think this is all about money?'

'It could be; why not?'

'Because I can't see how the guy who's taken us hostage can ever get to collect. There's no way he's getting out of here alive, whether we try to stop him or whether someone else does.'

Helen had been weeping for the past few minutes, traumatised by the sight of her husband doused in petrol. She looked across at Lily and said, 'We have to do something. We have to do what you said; we have to rush at him and attack him all at once.'

Lily looked from her mother to James. Try as hard as he could to summon it up once more, his gung-ho spirit of earlier had dissipated.

'Come on, James,' said Lily. 'I'm not going to let him burn my dad alive. If he goes to use that lighter then I'm going to try to stop him, whether you help me or not.'

James turned to look at her. He looked wounded by what she had said. 'You think I'm scared. Right?'

'We're all scared.'

'I'm just not sure we should try anything for the time being. He's clearly managed to get some sort of password from your father. Maybe that's all he wants.'

'God knows what he wants. You said yourself there's no way that he can collect any money personally.'

'Lily, you know I'll do whatever it takes, but we can't afford to screw this up. For all our sakes. You know I'll do whatever I can to get us out of here. Trust me, OK?'

James put his arm around her as Lily looked up into his eyes.

'OK,' she said. 'I trust you.'

01:57 PM

Negotiating Cell, Blenheim Terrace, Belgravia

'He's speaking into his phone. It's like he's reciting something,' said Calvert. I can't see how he thinks he can get away with that. He must realise we're going to be monitoring everything that goes into and out of the stronghold.'

'Is this the first time he's spoken to someone other than us from his handset?'

'Yeah, I'm pretty sure it is,' said Calvert.

'Definitely,' said White.

'How long will it take to get the details of who he's speaking to?' asked Ed.

'Longer than we want it to be,' said White.

'We might not get anything in time to save the negotiation but finding out who he's talking to is going to help us discover who's behind all this.'

'I'm on it,' said White.

'In the meantime,' said Ed, 'is there any way we can find

out what it is he's saying into the phone. We need to see if it's being picked up on the microphone on the robot. If it isn't, maybe we can we get a lip reader to analyse the video footage. What's the time?'

'Nearly ten minutes have gone,' said White.

'All right, let's try to speak to him.' Ed pulled his headset back into place.

'Putting in the call,' said White. There was silence in the command centre until the ringtone was audible. It was answered immediately.

'Yes,' said Danny McAteer.

'This is Ed Mallory; the ten minutes is up.'

'Not quite.'

'Well, I'm told you've finished your phone call.'

'I have.'

'Presumably we won't be able to trace it.'

'That's for you to find out.'

'Danny, can't we lose all the cloak-and-dagger? You don't want to be doing this. Why don't you let everyone go now? This is over. You've done whatever it is you came here to do.'

'Not quite. I need to make an announcement.'

There was an urgency to his voice. He needed to unburden himself and Ed couldn't help but think that this was a worrying development. Danny sounded as though he needed to deliver a pre-rehearsed speech before proceeding with whatever else it was he had come to do. Dousing Graham Poynter in petrol and brandishing a cigarette lighter indicated only one thing. Ed needed to slow things down and throw obstacles in his path. He needed to stop Danny making his announcement. So he chanced an interruption and spoke across him: 'Jan wants to speak to you, Danny. She wants to hear your voice.'

'I need to tell you something first.'

'Please, Danny, just speak to Jan, then you can make your announcement.'

'That's not going to happen.'

Ed gave the pre-arranged signal – a thumbs-up – to indicate that he wanted Danny's wife, Jan, patched through to the robot's loudspeaker on the adjacent house. Des White had been speaking to her, priming her in readiness for a conversation with her husband. She was an intelligent woman. She was fully aware of the magnitude of the situation. She knew that what she or Emily said to Danny might represent the only chance they all had of keeping him alive.

Ed was convinced that Danny was carrying out the hostage-taking on behalf of a third party. Whatever his reasons for doing so, they were heartfelt and unshakeable. They were not reasons that could easily be broken down by a hostage negotiator who had only minutes in which to work. But now that they had his wife on the line, someone who could communicate with him on a completely different emotional level, this represented about the only opportunity they had to break through Danny's psychological armour.

Facilitating the conversation was going to be difficult. Connecting Jan to the loudspeaker on the robot was not something with which Ed felt comfortable. Hearing his wife's voice suddenly amplified across the rooftops might spook him. He might be a powerful physical presence but there should be no underestimation of his emotional fragility.

'Danny, I want you to speak to Jan. She's here on the line and she's desperate to speak to you.'

'Tell her I love her but I'm not speaking to her.'

'Danny she's here on the line.'

'No, I'm going to disconnect the call if you put her through.'

Ed was in dangerous territory now as he knew that he was faced with no alternative but to make a threat.

'If you won't speak to her on the phone, she wants to speak to you via a loudspeaker—'

'No.'

'It's all in place on the adjacent house.'

'No!'

'Danny, please speak to Jan.'

'If you put her on loudspeaker to me, I'm going to start killing people. You got that?'

'Danny, this is the time to stop what you're doing. Jan wants you to stop; Emily wants you to stop—'

'Don't you fucking dare bring my daughter into this.'

Ed was getting through to him, landing big hits, but

whether they were working to the benefit of the negotiation, it was impossible to say. A resolution was a long way
off and he had the feeling – he had had it before, during
other negotiations – that it was unlikely to materialise. He
was pushing Danny hard and there was every chance he
might snap.

'Danny, I think I know why you're doing this.'

'You have no idea.'

'You're doing this for the right reasons. You want to
provide for your family. You want to help them.' Should he
mention his additional suspicions that it was a suicide
mission? No, it was too much. 'We all want you to stop and
give yourself up here but nobody more so than Jan and
Emily. They love you, Danny. Jan and Emily love you and
they want you to stop and they want you to talk to them.'

'No way.'

'We're going to put Jan on the loudspeaker, Danny. She
wants to speak to you; she wants you to know something
very important.'

'Don't fucking do it, or I'll kill someone. I need to tell you
something first. I'll speak to Jan but you need to hear this
first. OK?'

Ed could keep pushing or he could accept Danny's asser-
tion that he would speak to Jan after he had imparted
whatever message it was that his handlers had instructed
him to deliver. Danny's voice was a mess of conflicting
frequencies and tones. He was fired up on adrenalin, which

was masking his fear with urgency and anger. Whatever the final intended outcome of Danny's mission, it involved imparting this message and to refuse him that at this stage might be counter-productive.

'Danny, you're moving the goalposts here.'

'No, I'm not.'

'You said you'd discuss the release of your hostages if we guaranteed your safety for ten minutes.'

'And I will, but first I need to make this announcement.'

'So you're telling me that if you can say what you want to say then you'll speak to Jan and release the hostages?'

'I didn't say that. I said I would speak to Jan then discuss the safe release of the hostages.'

'That's not giving me much reassurance, Danny. It suggests that you're happy to talk and no more. That's not giving me anything in return for allowing you to make your speech.'

'Let me speak, Ed. Once I've said what I need to say then I'll talk to Jan and talk about releasing the hostages. If you won't let me speak then it's you forcing me to kill a hostage.'

'No one's forcing you to do anything, are they, Danny? Are people forcing you to do this?'

'Don't play games. I've agreed to speak to Jan and discuss the hostages, now you've got to let me speak.'

'All right, Danny, but I need to hear you say that we have a deal here, that if we let you make your speech you'll speak to Jan and set in motion the release of the hostages.'

'It's a deal.'

Hearing Danny say this didn't provide Ed with much comfort but there was no point stalling him any further. 'Go ahead, then; tell us what you want to say.'

'Graham Poynter is the Lord of Misrule. He is the Archbishop of Dolts, the Abbot of Unreason, the Pope of Fools . . .' Danny trailed off. He was trying to remember his script. Ed could have interrupted him, could have jumped in to his recitation and rattled him but it would have served no purpose. Danny needed to say what he had been sent there to say and, if he was stopped from doing that, there was every chance he would lose control. 'In the ancient festival of Saturnalia, a lowly peasant would be chosen to become the Lord of Misrule. For the few days' duration of the festival, this man would enjoy a reversal of his fortunes and live like a king. But, like all kings, his wealth and power were illusory and would be claimed back by the people on the final day of the festival, Christmas Day, when he would be slaughtered as a sacrifice.'

There was a moment of silence both from Danny and the members of the negotiating cell. Ed spoke first, knowing that at any moment Graham Poynter could die and knowing also that this might be all it took for a decision to be reached that the four-man special forces team should be deployed. There was no time to consider psychological tactics; Danny needed to know the unvarnished truth.

'Danny, listen to me. If you make a move with that

cigarette lighter, they'll kill you. You know that. You'll miss your chance of speaking to Jan and Emily. You'll condemn your wife and daughter to replaying this moment over and over for the rest of their lives. Don't do that to them, Danny. We can sort this out.'

'I haven't finished.' Danny sounded like an automaton.

'You've said what you wanted to say. You've completed what's been asked of you. The symbolism of what you've done is complete. Yes, Graham Poynter has done some awful things but he doesn't deserve this.'

'It's what the people want, Ed, you know it is. They used to turn out in their thousands for public executions.'

'Not like this.'

'They're all sitting at home watching this unfold on the news and they want this to happen.'

'No, they don't.' Ed didn't sound convincing. He sounded as though he doubted himself and that was probably because he did. Not all, not even most, but many people would feel little sorrow for Graham Poynter's passing and may even derive secret pleasure from it.

'Ed, you need to let me finish.'

'Danny, you need to speak to Jan now, otherwise they're going to take you out.' Ed tried to maintain an even tone but he couldn't help the high notes in his own voice.

'Let me say what I need to say.'

'Not if it means you're going to harm someone after you've said it.'

'I've told you that I'll speak to Jan after I've said this.'

'I only have your word for that, Danny, and your little speech is suggesting that, rather than speak to your family, you're actually going to do something very different.' Danny went to speak but Ed bulldozed over him. 'If you go for that cigarette lighter, you'll be dead before you can light it. Come on, Danny, you know how this works.'

'I'll speak to them once I've said one more thing.'

'OK, Danny, but the more words that come out of your mouth before you speak to your family, the less likely it is I can guarantee your safety. Come on; buy yourself some time by speaking to Jan and Emily now. Speaking to them is the only way you're going to prevent special forces coming for you and, you know as well as I do, they're not going to take you alive. You're still in control here, Danny, and you can stop this. You've still got your family and you need to know they don't want you to continue doing what you're doing.' Ed was going to keep talking until events dictated otherwise.

Danny stopped him by continuing with his prepared speech. Speaking over him was an option but it was a dangerous one. Ed could hear Serina's voice nearby as she spoke into a phone. Decisions were being made to which he would not be party. All he could do was rely on his instinct and that was telling him to allow Danny to finish what he had been contracted to say and, if he was still alive afterwards, then try to connect him to his family.

'Graham Poynter has lived like a king for years,' said Danny, his voice returning to a monotone. 'Now it's time for the people to reverse his fortunes. This is a warning to all the bankers, hedge-fund managers, industrialists and so-called entrepreneurs whose lives are built on exploitation without a care for the people they exploit, without a care for the damage and the misery they cause. Their final, ultimate reversals of fortune are long overdue. They can run and hide, as Graham Poynter did with his houses overseas. The governments, the politicians and the legal system won't help us; they're part of the disease. But we will find those individuals whose crimes are judged by the court of public opinion to be truly criminal and we will see justice served in the name of the people.'

At any moment Ed expected to hear shots as Danny was engaged by special forces. But the shots didn't come. Maybe there were problems with the logistics or maybe it was something as simple as a desire on the military's part to hold back until Danny actually made a move with the lighter or the chain attached to the grenade on Lily's neck. Either way, it gave Ed some time to keep working.

'According to the ancient rites of the feast of Saturnalia, Graham Poynter has enjoyed all of life's great pleasures – his very own feast of fools – but now that his corrupt ways have been exposed, he must die to appease the will of the people.'

These were not the words of a man who intended to discuss the release of his hostages. There was a profound disconnect between the words and their delivery. Now was the time for Ed to jump in and work on Danny's self-doubt.

'Those aren't your words, Danny. You're saying what you've been told to say.'

'They're the words of the people.'

'I don't think you believe that any more than I do.'

'I don't care what you think, Ed; there will be plenty of time for everyone to ponder on what I've just said when all this is over. This message will be distributed far and wide by the media.'

'OK, Danny, you've said what you needed to say, now you need to speak to Jan.'

Danny said nothing and, just beyond the squall of helicopter engines amplified through his headset, Ed could make out Des White speaking to Jan on the other line, his voice calm and reassuring. Ed heard him say, 'We really need you to do this,' followed by, 'Thank you.' She was as ready as she would ever be. Now was the time to put her on the line. Ed thought Danny's subconscious was probably screaming out for the opportunity to hear his wife's voice but he was having to suppress it in order to carry out his instructions to the letter. But his hesitation was a good sign. It showed there was still a part of him that was reluctant to go along with the pre-arranged strategy. When he reverted to knee-jerk admonishment – 'Fuck you, Ed Mallory' – and disconnected the call, Ed noticed that he didn't tell him not to put her through. As much as he was expressing his displeasure at Ed's behaviour, he was not telling him to desist, and cutting the call when he did was – if Ed could allow himself a moment's optimism – a sign that, even if it was only unconsciously, he wanted to hear what his wife had to say.

'OK; put Jan on,' Ed said as he slipped off his headset. 'Can we get audio from the roof?'

'We can get audio directly from the robot,' said Laura and, in immediate confirmation of her statement, the sound of distant helicopters and street sounds burst through the speakers in the command centre. There was a squeal of feedback.

'Danny? It's me.' Jan's voice sounded self-conscious and wary. She also sounded scared and emotionally confused. But Ed couldn't listen to her; there was another voice louder and more insistent of his attention from within the cell.

'We've got Danny McAteer's medical records through,' said Laura. 'He's got stage-four cancer. He's dying.'

'Danny, you mustn't hurt anyone else.' Jan's voice was gaining in confidence as it was relayed through the speakers. 'You need to give yourself up. I want you to talk to me and tell me what this is all about.'

02:00 PM

Roof of 11 Blenheim Terrace, Belgravia

'That must be his wife,' said Lily shouting to make herself heard above the sound of the woman's voice, amplified through the speaker on an adjacent roof.

'I guess it must be,' said James.

While Helen cowered with her head bowed, seemingly reluctant to face the horror of the situation that was unfolding in front of her, James and Lily watched the giant intently as he stood next to Graham in the shadow of the chimney stack. The woman whose voice was being relayed over the loudspeaker sounded desperate. She was crying and her voice kept faltering. She had a North-Eastern accent too, just like her husband. Unless she was an extremely accomplished actress, what her husband was doing had come to her as a profound shock.

'Please, Danny,' said the woman, her voice choked with emotion. 'Stop this. Think of Emily. Think of us.'

There was a gunshot. The giant had taken the gun from his pocket and was shooting across the rooftops. Every time he moved, there was a pull on the chain. Lily moved forward to try to find some slack. Hearing his wife's voice on the loudspeaker had agitated him. He reached up and peeled off the balaclava. His face matched his build. The features were large. His nose looked as though it might have been broken at some stage and it lent him the appearance of a boxer. The forehead was wide and square; his jaw was solid and muscular. He looked like an action-movie star, complete with the stubble and the short, cropped hair. But there was something about his face that was incongruous with the remainder of his hard, inscrutable appearance. It was the kindness. This wasn't a face twisted with malice or evil intent. If someone was casting the role of a dangerous hostage taker in a movie, this Danny – if that was his name – wouldn't get the part on account of his face. As he raised the pistol once more to take aim, there was something else to his expression – despair. He peered along the barrel of the pistol and fired again. The target he was aiming at was the loudspeaker that broadcast his wife's voice and, every time he missed it, his angst ratcheted up another notch.

'I'm going to put Emily on the line, Danny.'

Bang. Another shot. James appeared to be more agitated than he had been all day and, with his shoulder pressed against hers, she could feel him trembling. Even though he flinched each time a shot was fired, he kept his eyes trained on Danny.

The voice of a little girl came through the speaker.

'Hello, Daddy.' She was young enough that she had no idea of the significance of the conversation. She had obviously been told that she needed to speak to her father and was completely unaware of the circumstances. In her two-year-old, maybe three-year-old, mind she was just talking to her dad as she had done a thousand times before. 'Daddy coming home soon?' The voice of pure innocence rang out across the rooftops, cutting through the background thrum of the helicopters. It was just possible to hear the mother whispering to her, prompting her as to what to say. 'Daddy, come home now?'

Danny's face was even more twisted than before and there were tears in his eyes as he levelled the pistol and fired again. There was another tug on the chain – a sharp one, as the gun kicked. He had appeared so controlled earlier in the day. Although Lily had been terrified and traumatised by the situation in which she had found herself, she could at least feel assured that the hostage taker was calm and thoughtful. That calmness was gone now and he was in danger of losing control. The jerks on the chain were coming one after the other with seemingly little concern for their effect on the grenade on her neck. Not even James seemed to care as he watched Danny with a stare of laser-focused intensity.

Bang. Another shot was fired. Another pull on the chain.

Lily moved forward but, feeling the slack on the chain, Danny wound it a half turn around his wrist.

'He's going to set off the grenade!' shouted Lily.

'Don't worry,' said James in a voice that offered little by way of reassurance. 'If he tries to pull out the pin, I'll grab the chain.'

'I'm worried he's going to do it by accident.'

'No, he won't.'

He sounded very sure – carelessly so. It felt as though she was losing her only friend and ally. He had been sucked into the drama of the moment, leaving Lily all alone once more. Her mother was a sobbing wreck; her father was catatonic with fear. Only she and James were functioning human beings and now James's focus was elsewhere. What worried Lily was that events were moving so fast that someone would try to kill Danny at any moment, or attempt to intervene in some way when they thought he was distracted by his wife and daughter, and, in the ensuing mayhem, the pin would be pulled from the grenade and she would die. She had seen stories on the news about attempts made to release hostages in the Middle East and, so often, despite all the best intentions of the soldiers, the hostages were killed. Another shot was fired.

'I love you, Daddy,' said the little girl.

Danny paused for a moment, looking momentarily bereft, his eyes hollow and swimming with tears, before he gritted his teeth and fired three more shots in rapid succession across the rooftops. The chain pulled on her neck, harder this time than ever and it felt as though there was definite movement on the contraption around her neck. She felt like shouting at him to keep still but her mouth was impossibly dry and her throat was choked with fear.

Another voice came through the loudspeaker, which was functioning despite the shots that had been fired at it. It was a man's voice, the voice of some sort of negotiator. 'Danny, this is Ed Mallory again. I need to speak to you as a matter of urgency due to new information that has come to light. Please answer your phone when we call. It is very important that we speak.'

Danny raised the pistol and appeared to be about to take another shot when he thought better of it and put it back into his pocket.

'What the fuck is going on?' asked James. 'They could just take him out now.'

'James, I'm scared.' As much as it was an attempt to grab his attention, it was also a statement of fact. The waiting had been bad enough but the feeling she couldn't shake was that she was moments from death – a death that would be caused as much by accident as by design.

James tore his attention away from Danny and looked at her. He looked more agitated than he had done all day but, as he spoke, he put his arm around her once more. 'Don't worry, Lily; it's going to be OK. I'm not going to let anything happen to you.'

02:07 PM

Negotiating Cell, Blenheim Terrace, Belgravia

While Jan and Emily spoke to Danny through the loud-speaker, Nick Calvert had provided Ed with a detailed commentary of what was taking place on the video feed from the roof. It was clear that Danny was beginning to lose control, and that benefitted no one. Once Ed had been patched through to the loudspeaker on the robot, he had no idea what he was going to say, but he knew he had to make it as compelling as possible. He had said that new information had come to light. It was true: they now knew that Danny was dying. Beyond that, however, they had nothing, certainly nothing that might force him to stop what he was meant to do. All Ed could hope was that he could drive a wedge between Danny and his paymasters and somehow compromise the contract between them. So, when the call came through from Danny on his phone, he knew it might be his last chance to engineer a resolution.

'This is Ed Mallory.'

'You're really fucking pushing it now,' said Danny. 'Any more of this and there are going to be a lot of dead people up here.'

'Danny, we know about your health. We know you haven't got long to live.'

'Then you'll also realise that I've got nothing to lose.'

'Even now, you've got plenty to lose. You must know that. You're doing this for your family, right? You're being paid—'

'No, no I'm not. I'm doing this to strike a blow against the parasites of this world. I'm striking a blow for the ninety-nine per cent against the one per cent. Graham Poynter will die, just as the Lord of Misrule would have died in days gone by, because that's what everyone wants, deep down.' Danny spoke quickly, reciting the thin justification he had clung to and blurting it out, maintaining his momentum so Ed couldn't respond, couldn't start picking holes in his carefully constructed façade. But he could only speak for so long and when he drew breath, Ed took his chance.

'No one wants to see this, Danny. No one.'

'Ed, you underestimate the hatred people feel for men like Graham Poynter.'

'Danny, this isn't your war. You're doing this for others and any benefit you may derive from it will be discovered and compromised.'

Danny had been stuttering his objections, trying to find a moment when Ed would allow him to speak but, now that

Ed had made his point, there was a pause in the stuttering and he knew his words had found their target. It was time to press his advantage. 'If you go through with what you're being paid to do, there's no guarantee that Jan and Emily will collect your payment. Danny, I know this is tough. I can't imagine what you're going through but you have to consider your actions. You have to think about what you're doing.' Ed had to choose his words with extreme care. At any moment, Danny might disconnect the call, set fire to Graham Poynter, pull the pin out of the grenade and go down in a hail of bullets. 'Think about this, Danny; think of Emily – does she really want to grow up knowing what her father has done? Does she want to spend her life being constantly reminded of the vicious and cruel act that her father carried out?'

'It's too late for that now.' Danny's voice had changed. The anger and the rage were gone. The tone was more calm and thoughtful.

When Ed spoke, he tried to emulate it. 'It's never too late, Danny. If you stop this now, then everyone will always know you had good intentions at heart. But if you burn Graham Poynter alive, any sympathy they may have felt for you will have gone.'

There was activity in the command centre. Ed could hear excited voices. He could only think that there was some development in the planning of the rapid intervention. It was something he had to try to blot out: him knowing what they had in mind served no purpose. He was getting through to the subject. It may not be enough but if he were to stop his interaction with Danny, even for a moment, in order to try to prevent whatever intervention was on the cards, the moment would be lost.

'You don't know what you're talking about,' said Danny. 'You're way off the mark.' This was bluster and Ed could sense that Danny's anger was on the rise once again.

'Danny, we both know you're not some big anti-capitalist crusader.'

'Don't presume to know anything about me.'

'You need to stop this now. If you continue with your actions, no one will benefit from this. Not you and not your family. The people who are paying you to do this don't care about you.'

'Stop. OK? Stop. I don't want to hear it.'

'We need to talk, Danny.'

Silence. The sound of the muttering and conversation in the command centre beyond his headset was increasing in volume and Ed found it difficult to concentrate.

'If you want to talk to me so much, Ed, then why don't you come up here and talk to me, face to face?'

The suggestion caught Ed off guard and clearly had a similar effect on the others in the command centre, who quietened down. Ed didn't stop to think of the implications of what he was about to say. Matters of safety were for others to consider. As a stalling tactic and a means of reducing the emotional temperature of the situation, this was a potential game changer.

'OK, Danny, if that's what it's going to take to make you give yourself up then—'

'I'm not going to give myself up.'

'So why do you want to speak to me?'

'I just do.'

'So, let me get this straight. You want me to come up on to the roof with no agreement in place that you're going to release all or any of the hostages?'

'Yes, that's right.'

'I'm not sure I can do that.'

'If you want any chance of resolving this then you need to come up here on to the roof.'

'You know how this works, Danny. You need to give me something in return. You need to release a hostage.'

'No one's going anywhere.'

'If you agree to let one hostage go, Danny, then I promise I'll speak to those in charge to see if it might be possible.'

'No; either you come up here now or I'll bring this all to an end.'

'Danny, you know how mad this sounds. Negotiators do not enter strongholds. Only in movies.'

'I'll make this easier for you then, Ed. I'll give you ten minutes to sort this out and if you're not on the roof here with me at the end of that ten minutes, I'll kill everyone.'

02:21 PM

Roof of 11 Blenheim Terrace, Belgravia

They say that every man has a price and Danny's had been five million U.S. dollars. He had always known that the only thing that could carry him through all he had to do was the knowledge that he was providing for Jan and Emily. Five million U.S. dollars was over three million quid. Jan could hide it in offshore accounts and dip into it only when she needed it. The logistics of how Jan might be informed of the money and have access to it had consumed his thoughts, particularly in the last few days. He had decided to keep things simple and had written her the letter he had posted the day before, which had explained everything – including his reasons as to why he felt he couldn't speak to her about his condition. Throughout the planning of the operation, he had been beset by doubts both of a practical and moral nature. Advo's rhetoric had resonated with him and he had agreed with his ultimate aim of punishing the wrongdoers in the financial industry. Danny had worried, however, that in one respect – that of salting away a large sum of money to provide security for his family – he was no better than Graham Poynter.

Danny had finally overcome his doubts and agreed to the mission. So long as he could be certain that he had provided for his family after he was dead, then he could face his death – and all that he had to do before it – with a clear conscience. Ed Mallory, however, had him spooked. Had the negotiator sussed him out? Did he know about the five million dollars? Or was he just airing his suspicions about Danny's motives by firing shots in the dark in the hope that one of them might find a target? It made him feel sick to think that he might have done all this, killed those three men and subjected Jan and Emily to this torture, all for nothing. If the authorities had uncovered the exact details of what was taking place then they might intercept the money, Jan might never collect and all this was a brutal waste of life – his own short remaining life included.

Danny knew he had to find out the truth. It would be too dangerous to question Mallory on the phone connection to the negotiating command centre. If he could speak to him face to face, however, he would be able to see his expression – albeit the expression of a blind man – and he would be able to know if he was bluffing or not. And if they wouldn't allow Mallory to come up on to the roof – something that was a very real possibility – then he would make good his threat and kill Poynter. After that, he would just keep shooting until they shot him. He had to do this; Advo would understand. He would have to and, besides, there was nothing he could do about it anyway.

Replacing the phone in the side pocket of his jacket, Danny glanced at his watch. Ten minutes. They would seem like the longest ten minutes of his life and, while the seconds ticked away, there was every possibility that his former colleagues in the S.A.S. would attempt to intervene. But he also had the feeling Ed Mallory would do all he could to make the face-to-face meeting happen. Danny could hear in his voice that he felt he could talk him down. He would argue for the right to enter the stronghold to at least try. There was a determination to the man and the same steely resolve that he recognised in himself. What Ed Mallory didn't know, however, was that there was nothing he could say that would make him give himself up. Whether his financial arrangement with Advo had been uncovered or not, there was no way Danny was leaving that roof alive.

02:22 PM

Negotiating Cell, Blenheim Terrace, Belgravia

'You've got to be fucking joking, Ed,' said Nick Calvert. 'Have you got some sort of death wish?'

If the question had not been rhetorical, Ed might have replied that, since his blinding, there were occasions when he had worried that he might have a death wish. It wasn't as though he actively went out of his way to put himself in dangerous situations, it was just that, when a dangerous situation presented itself to him, he had always felt drawn to it, almost compelled to take himself nearer to the danger. But it was more than some possibly latent desire for self-harm that made him want to go up on to the roof. He knew it was the only chance they had. The only alternative was the military going in and that was something that, as long as he was still on the front line, he wanted to try to avoid.

'He's killed three men today already,' continued Calvert. 'Do you really want to be number four?'

'I think me going to talk to him is the best chance we've got.'

'He's dying, anyway. There's nothing you can say to make that go away.'

'No, but he'll want to die right. Everyone always does. It's my belief that him wanting to die right and do the right thing by his family is what this is all about.'

'I think you've lost it.'

Ed always liked Nick Calvert's bluntness. You always knew where you stood. There was no artifice or agenda. Under normal circumstances, this comment might have stung. Not today. For the first time since he had entered the command centre and put on his headset, he felt in control. His senses came into focus. Serina Boise was over by the door, staring at him, Laura Massey was seated at the opposite desk, directly in front of him. Nick Calvert was boiling with mute frustration next to him on his right. Des White was sighing next to Nick. They were all of them evaluating the situation, processing it in their minds, weighing up the plusses and minuses. Calvert had already made his feelings known. Which way would the others go? All their opinions counted, but none more so than Serina's. If she sanctioned his intervention then he was in. If not, then he would be left all alone in the command centre while control slipped away from him.

When Keir, Ed's cell co-ordinator at the hostage negotiation that morning, had told him that he hadn't received clearance to go in and talk to Raymond, Ed hadn't argued. Maybe his desire to be allowed in to speak to Danny now was some residual guilt over his easy compliance earlier. If he had fought harder and dug his heels in then Raymond might still be alive. Ed wasn't sure he could make a difference with Danny McAteer but what he did know was that it had to be worth a try. This was more than just a decision regarding how best to bring the siege to an end. It was a verdict on his abilities as a negotiator and, alongside those, his value as a person. He had to fight. There was no point ranting and raving; he needed to use all his strategic powers of persuasion to make this come out in his favour. One of the voices in the cell had already aired its opinion. Calvert thought that his going up on the roof to talk to Danny McAteer was a crazy idea. Ed was one–nil down already. He could go straight to Serina Boise and ask her opinion but immediately she would have to confront the preceding negative opinion. Her decision was too important to solicit straight away; he needed to leave her until last to cast the deciding vote. Laura was a different proposition. Being probably the most thoughtful and intuitive cell co-ordinator he had ever worked with, she would give a reasoned answer, uncluttered by emotion.

'Laura, what do you think?'

The exhalation of breath before she spoke was a good sign. It was for Calvert's benefit and Ed could tell she was about to disagree with Nick's damning prognosis. 'I'm not sure. It's very dangerous.' This was another positive expression; she was qualifying her decision. Yes, it was dangerous, everyone knew it was dangerous. It was insane. But she sounded as though she was attempting to soften Calvert's negativity. 'The thing is,' continued Laura, 'I tend to agree with Ed that, if special forces go in, Danny's not going to be taken down easily. He could kill a lot of people. If Ed' – she was talking about him in the third person, addressing her comments to Boise in the doorway – 'thinks he can talk to Danny from close proximity and try to develop a bond that might allow us to come to a resolution without a violent confrontation, then I think that has to be explored.' Ed couldn't have put it better himself and, in her calm insouciance and considered judgement, Laura Massey's comments far outweighed Nick Calvert's knee-jerk bluster. Even so, within the democracy of the cell, it was still only one–one with all to play for.

Nick was about to come back with another objection but Ed spoke over him to elicit an opinion from the number three in the cell, Des White. 'Des. What do you think?'

Des exhaled hard – not a good sign. It was a preparatory gesture; he was preparing Ed for bad news. 'I tend to agree with Nick here. It's incredibly dangerous, Ed. Danny McAteer's dying; he's got nothing to live for. Psychologically, he's already crossed the line with the three security guards. He's going to think nothing of killing you and the others. We still don't know what's caused him to do this. If he is, as we suspect, doing it for money to provide for his family, there is still the possibility that he has been paid to try to kill as many people as possible. This is a terrorist act. The more deaths he can cause, the more terror he can create.'

'OK, Des. Thanks.' He didn't know whether Des had finished his train of thought but Ed needed to stop him. The argument was all too cogent and – unlike Calvert's – thoughtfully expressed. Ed was two–one down. But it counted for nothing until they had heard what Serina Boise thought. Which way would she go? Her judgement of Ed's abilities had already been confirmed that morning by choosing him to be number one in the cell. But a lot had happened since then. She had asked him to play it all by the book and, in wanting to go into the stronghold to talk to the hostage face to face, he was taking the book, burning it and dancing in its ashes. He should not have threatened to quit earlier; he had allowed his emotions to get the better of him. Serina would have seen this. She already knew he was struggling with fatigue. But there were also the political issues to consider. If Ed could resolve the situation with no further loss of life then there would be huge kudos for her command. Ed didn't really believe she was that mercenary and self-interested but Boise hadn't reached the position she had without considering all angles. Added to which, he did have a good track record. His statistics as a negotiator were healthy. People had died on his watch but if you had handled as many negotiations as he had over the years it was impossible to avoid that.

'Ultimately, Ed, this negotiation is my responsibility. Your safety as a negotiator is part of that responsibility.' Serina emitted a sigh, the implications of which Ed couldn't read. But before she could continue, she was interrupted by a man's voice that muttered something Ed didn't manage to catch. 'OK; all right,' said Serina before she cleared her throat. 'The S.A.S. team are in place. They can go in before the ten-minute deadline is up. They've had clearance from COBRA; they're making a final consultation with us.'

Ed knew it would be so easy for her to say yes to the intervention but he also knew that her decision would have far-reaching implications. It would be pored over in inquests and inquiries. In saying yes to the intervention, she would be absolving herself of further responsibility. It would be a strong, positive decision and she would be applauded for it in some quarters. However, if Danny McAteer were to take a number of lives before he was brought down, she would face accusations of heavy-handedness – more so when it was discovered that the negotiator had not only been invited into the stronghold by the hostage taker to discuss the release of the hostages, but he was also very keen to accept that invitation, believing that he could make a difference.

'I can do this, Serina; I can talk to him. If I fail, you can send in the military then. All I'm asking is for a few minutes.'

'I don't know, Ed. We've given him long enough already.'

'I don't agree,' said Ed. 'If this was a standard house siege, we wouldn't have even set everything up by now. We'd be hunkering down for the long haul. It's only because of the media and the political implications involved here that people want to close it down so quickly. Let me have a few minutes with him.'

'Ed, imagine how this will look if he takes you hostage too and kills you. Imagine how that will make us all look.'

'Either we do the right thing or we worry about our public image.'

Serina came straight back at him: 'Worrying about our public image is part of doing the right thing.'

Ed said nothing, allowing the silence to provide Serina with his response.

'I don't even know if I can stop this,' said Serina.

'Well, just tell whoever will listen that your number-one negotiator thinks he can still bring this to a conclusion without further loss of life.'

'And that he may very well die in the process,' chipped in Nick Calvert.

'Just give me a few minutes,' shot back Ed.

'You'll never get there in time, anyway,' said Calvert.

'I can get back on the phone or loudspeaker and negotiate a few minutes more with him. Maybe I can; maybe I can't. We won't know unless I try. We can buy some time that way and try to calm him down. Then I'll go in and talk to him.'

'You really think you can do something?' Serina was speaking directly to him. She didn't care what Calvert – or anyone – thought. She wanted to hear it from Ed.

He had no idea if he could do anything, but now was not a time for indecision. It was time for a tactical untruth. 'I do.'

'I just don't know, Ed.'

'Remember, I'm not on the force anymore.'

'You're still my responsibility.'

'I'll agree to sign whatever waivers of that responsibility you want me to. If I go in, there will never be any suggestion that you ordered me to do so.'

'You have got a death wish,' said Calvert. But, even as he said it, Ed could feel the mood in the cell shift his way and this was confirmed by Serina.

'Ed, I'll speak to them and see if we can hold fire on the rapid intervention. You get on the line and find out if Danny will agree to an extension to his deadline.'

'Sure,' replied Ed as his stomach churned with nerves. Serina left the cell, speaking to someone as she walked away. Ed turned to Des White and said, 'Put me through to Danny's phone.'

02:23 PM

Eversholt Street, Camden

What he enjoyed most about driving around central London at lunchtime on Christmas Day was that it was so quiet. Everyone was sitting down with their family, overindulging. It was easy to be cynical about Christmas. There was nothing wrong with kicking back and relaxing for a couple of days. It was all part of human nature and if people wanted to do it in the name of their man-made god, then so be it.

Lucas parked up the motorbike but he didn't dismount, just put the kickstand down and rested his feet on the asphalt. Taking out his iPhone, he tapped on the pictures folder and clicked again on the video clip he had made earlier. It had been awkward to film. If he had planned things a little better – and next time he would – he would have used a small video camera and a stand. As it was, he had been forced to prop the iPhone up on one of the work surfaces in the kitchen and it had taken a couple of minutes of trial and error before he had managed to get the right angle. What made things more tricky was that he had already told Bob Rushwood what he was going to do to him. He had toyed with whether this was a good idea but he wanted the footage to have as much impact as possible so it was important that he created the necessary drama.

Knowing what was to come had supplied Bob with all the motivation he needed to make plenty of noise. There was a lot of swearing and pleading. Bob had tried to crawl across the floor to reach the panic button and Lucas had been forced to drag him back so that he was in frame. This was one aspect of the day's events that he should have prepared for more thoroughly. After this operation was finished, he would make himself into a one-man film crew. In future, he would be prepared.

As he sat astride his motorbike, Lucas turned up the volume on the iPhone and clicked *start* on the video file. There he was on the screen, his face obscured behind the crash helmet visor as he looked into the camera lens.

'This is what happens when you misbehave.' He had had to speak loudly in order to ensure that his words were audible above the sound of Bob's shrieks and protestations. There he was, holding up the skillet and the bundle of cash in his hands. It was all rather melodramatic, like something out of a pantomime. Then he approached Bob, who was lying on the floor. He dragged him back towards the kitchen island in order to ensure they were both in shot. Then he said, 'This is a warning to all you parasites out there.'

Bob had screamed and pleaded. He had played his part well. Thanks to this little piece of footage that would be distributed far and wide, he would achieve more fame and recognition than he had ever done during his life. Bob's hands had been all over Lucas, trying to push him away, trying to hit him, but he had little strength left – it was sapped by the pain from the bullet wounds in his foot and his leg. Lucas had beaten him around the head with the skillet a couple of times to make him more manageable and, by the time Lucas was forcing the cash into his mouth with the handle of the skillet, Bob's body was still and inert. Lucas made sure that there was plenty of bloody cash spilling out of his mouth. It was important to get the imagery just right. Lucas had propped Bob up against the kitchen island and tried to angle his head towards the camera. The dead man wore an expression of resignation, as though this was something that was all part of his destiny. Which Lucas supposed it was. All his professional life, Bob Rushwood had shafted people and screwed as much money as he possibly could out of the markets, spreading his poison and to hell with the consequences. All of it had been building up to the moment when he would choke to death on money.

The footage came to an end and there was a frozen image of Bob's face. It was a good image, a defining image, which would go viral throughout the world and, along with what

was about to happen to Graham Poynter, act as a warning
to all the other cheating, lying bastards out there who might
think they could wreck people's lives with impunity.

02:28 PM

Negotiating Cell, Blenheim Terrace, Belgravia

'I just need a little more time, Danny.'

'No way.'

'Come on, Danny. I can't be up there in two minutes.'

'You can. You're just outside.'

'I'm blind, Danny; it's going to take me more than two minutes to walk all the way up there. There's protocol; there are systems. Come on, you know this. You have to give me more time.'

'No.'

Ed could feel the exasperation grabbing at him. He had come this close to giving himself and Danny another chance; he had done what he thought would be the hard part, which was to persuade Serina Boise to allow him up there, and now he was going to be foiled by Danny's intransigence.

'This hasn't been easy. I didn't even think I would be allowed to do this but I think I've managed to persuade them. At least now we've got this far, give me the time to actually get up there to talk to you.'

'If it's the wire they want you to wear that's taking the time, tell them I'll be checking you. If there's a wire on you, you're a dead man. You got that?'

'I get it. I'm not going to wear anything.'

'You've got another ten minutes from now. But that's it. I'm timing. If you're not here by then, it's all over for everyone.'

'OK, Danny; I'll be there—' Danny had cut the connection before Ed could finish.

'Someone start the clock,' said Ed.

'We can put a wire on you that he'd never find,' said Des White.

'No, I'd rather not; you heard what he said.'

'I can't help feeling,' said Calvert, 'that we're providing him with another hostage. We already know he's trying to increase his hostage quota. That's why he took the delivery driver. So now we're giving him another.'

'Maybe you're right,' said Ed. 'But I don't think so. I genuinely think he wants to talk, don't you?'

'Maybe. I don't know. I can't tell from what he's saying. All I know is that he's dying, so he's got nothing to live for. He's already killed three people, he's threatening to kill two more, possibly three or even four, and he clearly knows that he's only coming down from there in a body bag. And you're going up to talk to him.'

'OK, Nick, you've made your point. We know where you stand on this.'

'Something that neither of you has taken into account,' said Laura, 'is that we still haven't had the go-ahead for you to go in. This is going all the way to the top. If COBRA say no to Commander Boise, there's nothing we can do.'

'They won't say no. They can't.' Ed didn't care if he sounded overconfident. Nick Calvert might be right. He might be walking into some sort of trap. It might be the most stupid, foolhardy thing he had ever done but it might also make a difference. It was a gamble. The members of COBRA would know that, but they would also know it was a gamble worth taking. Dead soldiers were always more politically difficult to deal with than dead freelance hostage-negotiators.

Ed turned to Calvert as he spoke. 'Are you going to take me up, Nick, when the time comes?'

'Of course, Ed; I can do that.'

Calvert couldn't help the disapproving tone in his voice. Ed was breaking all the laws of negotiation strategy. But more than that, he felt that Ed was making a mistake, was putting his life in danger and he didn't want to see him get hurt. Calvert's disapproval was born of his desire to protect him, Ed knew it, and maybe because of that knowledge it rankled even more. It *was* stupid to go up there. Danny's stage-four cancer meant there was little Ed could do to persuade him to stay alive. What did he have to live for? Six months in the cells with the guilt of having killed innocent people and put Jan and Emily through hell. It wasn't much of a contest. All that Ed could hope to do was persuade him of the destructive effect his behaviour would have on his family. He needed to make Danny consider how his wife and child would feel if he made good his threat to burn Graham Poynter alive. His family meant everything to Danny and it was their perception of him that was all that Ed could work on. There was no moral justification Ed could turn to – Danny had gone too far for that already. It was all about his own flesh and blood now.

'I've got some details for you about the feast of Saturnalia,' said Des White.

'Sure,' said Ed.

Des read from some notes on his computer, fleshing out the bones of what Danny had spoken of earlier. Pagan Romans reversed the norms of society so that no one would be punished for stealing or damaging property throughout the duration of the festival. Masters waited on slaves and the people and authorities would choose a Lord of Misrule, a victim who was forced to experience all the pleasures of the festivities before being brutally killed as a sacrifice on the final day of the festival, 25th December, thereby defeating the forces of darkness. Ed was only half listening. It sounded as though whoever was behind this entire operation – Advo, if that's who it was – had chosen the festival of Saturnalia as a convenient peg on which to hang his murderous fantasies, and nothing more.

Nick Calvert had moved away to the far side of the Porta-kabin that housed the command centre and was talking to someone on his phone. Ed couldn't make out what he was saying above Des White's narrative about Saturnalia but he could tell from his tone of voice that it was something important.

'In England, an imitation of the Roman festival of Satur-nalia was the Feast of Fools,' continued Des White. 'This accentuated the social reversal aspect of the celebration.'

'Sorry, Des,' said Nick Calvert, interrupting. 'We've got word back from GCHQ. They've analysed the video footage of Danny speaking into his handset. As we thought, he was reciting what had been said to him by Graham Poynter. It appears that Danny was repeating a combination of letters and numbers. They think it was L, I, L, Y and the numbers two, six, zero, five.'

'It's got to be a password for a bank account,' said Ed, breaking in. 'This isn't about some pagan festival, that's just some hokum that's been tacked on to provide symbolism. This is a robbery. They're stealing Graham Poynter's money.'

'I didn't think he had any money left,' said Laura Massey. 'I thought they'd proved that his fund was a fraud.'

'Someone like Poynter always has money. He'll have spent some of the money he's taken from his investors but there'll be plenty he hasn't spent. If we can find out who it is that Danny McAteer was speaking to on that call, then we can unravel this thing once and for all.'

'They're still working on it,' said Calvert. 'But there's something else you ought to know. Graham Poynter's partner at Stanmore Partners, a guy called Bob Rushwood, has been found dead at his rented house in Hampstead. Someone forced a load of cash down his throat, causing him to asphyxiate.'

The statement was greeted with silence from the rest of the negotiating cell. As much as they had all suspected that Danny McAteer wasn't a lone wolf, the fact that he had accomplices out on the streets of London, killing people with such savagery, gave them all pause to think. Ed was so deep in thought that he missed the telltale sound of Serina Boise's shoes on the linoleum floor as she entered the command centre.

'You've heard the news about Graham Poynter's partner then?' Grunts of affirmation encouraged her to continue. 'We've been given the go-ahead for you to go into the stronghold, Ed. There were a number of voices of caution amongst the members of COBRA but they've managed to achieve a consensus that it would be better at this stage to continue with a negotiation rather than press for a rapid intervention, particularly given the experience and military capabilities of the hostage taker. But they want me to make it explicit that you are under no duty to undertake this operation. You are entering the stronghold to speak to the hostage taker entirely of your own volition.'

'I can sign something, if that's what you want.'

Serina Boise would have detected the hint of sarcasm in Ed's voice but she let it go. 'That won't be necessary.'

'Nick's taking me up.'

'Fine,' said Serina.

'Don't wish me luck.'

'I won't,' said Serina. 'You'll be wearing a flak jacket, I take it?'

'I wasn't intending to.'

'You must.'

'Let me do this my way. Please.'

Ed didn't like the petulant sound of his own voice but he knew that he didn't want to wear a flak jacket and he didn't want to have to argue about it as the seconds ticked by. It was more important that his mental preparations were not compromised by a pointless argument about the efficacy of wearing body protection. Nick Calvert exhaled in frustration. Serina was about to object so he needed to push things harder.

'I'd prefer not to wear a flak jacket. Please respect that.'

Nick Calvert and Serina Boise were looking at one another, making non-vocal exchanges the likes of which Ed would never know.

'Take care, Ed,' said Serina, as she patted him on the shoulder. She was trying to be reassuring, and the fact that she felt she needed to be unnerved him.

'Thanks, Serina. I will,' said Ed, as Nick Calvert took his arm and they walked to the door and down the steps into the cold December air. It was a relief after the warm, musty environment of the negotiating cell which stank of breath and coffee.

Nick Calvert spoke to someone, said, 'Hi.'

A man's voice responded. 'Hi, Ed; I'm John.' His use of a first name – probably not his real one – made Ed realise he was a member of special forces. 'We're going to take you into the stronghold behind a bulletproof shield, OK? We'd like you to move quite fast, just in case.'

Ed nodded. He would do as he was told but he knew there was no chance that Danny was going to start firing at them. It would have been completely counterproductive.

With Nick Calvert guiding him by the arm, they moved across the street. Other men's footsteps were tight around them, probably either S.C.O.19 officers or other special forces soldiers.

'Steps here,' said Calvert, and they made their way up the steps and in through the front door, which was closed after them. The squeak of boots on the marble floor indicated there were a number of people already in the house. 'Flights of stairs here,' said Calvert, and they started to make their way up, Ed's shoes sinking into a luxurious carpet. This was the home of someone with expensive tastes in interior decor, although it didn't have the aroma of a beautifully furnished house – the reek of cordite from the earlier explosion lingered – it smelled more like a war zone.

'What's the layout of the roof terrace?' asked Ed.

'I can only really tell you from what I've seen on the video,' said Calvert. 'It's about twenty feet by twenty feet with a low wall about two feet high all around it. The sections of wall at the front and back of the house provide a barrier of sorts between the drop into the street at the front and the drop into the garden at the back.'

'What's the orientation?' asked Ed, as they turned around a landing and up the next flight of stairs.

It was John that responded. 'The back of the house looks out over the garden and the conservatory extension that houses the swimming pool. That's facing due north. The front of the house faces due south.'

'So the chimney stack in the shadow of which Danny is standing is on the north side of the roof terrace?'

'That's right,' continued John. 'It's in the top right-hand corner. The door you'll be coming out of is at the front of the house.'

'Which means,' said Calvert, 'that as you walk out of the door, you'll be heading north towards Danny and the hostages. To your left will be Graham Poynter, to your right will be Lily and Helen Poynter and the delivery driver.'

'So, if I'm to talk to Danny,' said Ed as they turned around another landing and made their way up to the second floor, 'which side of the chain that's attached to Lily will I be on?'

'The chain will be to the east of you, to your right, running almost exactly north–south between the hostage taker and the daughter. Narrow attic steps here.'

They climbed a flight of stairs up into the attic, which felt spacious and had a lacquered wooden floor. It was unlike any attic he had been in before. They walked a few feet and Ed could hear the helicopters up above on the other side of the roof tiles and timber joists. There were people all around him – soldiers, most probably. He could hear their movements and mutterings.

'Here we are,' said John, their guide, as they came to a stop next to what must have been a door. 'We've got a loudhailer for you to speak to the hostage taker.' Ed reached out and the handle of the loudhailer was pushed into his hand. 'You press this button here to speak,' said John, sliding his finger over Ed's and pressing down the button for a moment to the accompaniment of a burst of static and a faint screech of feedback. 'It's all yours. Just let us know when you want us to open the door.'

Ed turned to Calvert and asked, 'How long until the deadline?'

'It's just gone nine minutes,' came the response. 'Are you going to keep him waiting?' Nick Calvert had been on enough hostage negotiations with Ed to know it was habitual for him to leave deadlines until they had just expired in order to exert an extra psychological element of control over the situation.

'Not this time,' said Ed. 'I want to be as straight with him as I can be. Open the door.'

Nick Calvert leaned in close to Ed so that his whispered

words would be audible to no one but him. 'You don't have to do this,' he said.

'Yes, I do,' said Ed.

'Don't get killed.'

'I love you too,' whispered Ed, and Calvert chuckled.

The door was opened and the sound of the helicopters rushed at him. He could understand how the hostages could speak to each other without anyone even close by hearing what was being said. Pressing down the talk button on the loudhailer, Ed raised it to his mouth and pointed it into the source of the cold air and the swirling sound.

'Danny, this is Ed Mallory, the negotiator.'

The voice was amplified by a loudhailer and came from the doorway to the attic. The door was only partly open and no one was visible through it. Lily turned back towards Danny and saw his gaze fixed on the source of the voice. He shouted, 'You can come out.'

'Put the gun down and then I'll come out.' Whatever the nature of the negotiations that had led up to this moment, Danny clearly hadn't anticipated this. He remained silent as the metallic voice continued. 'If I'm going to come out there unarmed, you must give me something in return. Please put down the gun.'

Danny put the gun in his pocket but, as he withdrew his hand, the polished brass of the cigarette lighter glinted gold between his fingers. Whoever was monitoring his movements – someone, presumably, via a camera on one of the helicopters up above – it was deemed enough of a concession for the man with the loudhailer to open the door.

The negotiator was in his forties; he was about six feet tall, dressed all in black – black slip-on boots, trousers, crew-neck jumper and sunglasses – which accentuated his straw-berry-blond hair, which was cut short and spiky. There was something about his face. Once handsome, now it was scarred. As he turned and handed the loudhailer to someone who took it from him in the doorway, he stepped forward and Lily could see from the way he moved that he was blind.

The door was closed after him, leaving only a few inches gap between it and the doorframe. That a negotiator was there on the roof in person allowed her to dare to hope there might be some sort of impending resolution. If Danny was going to harm them as he was so clearly threatening to do, there was no reason why he couldn't already have done it. He clearly felt the need to communicate. This had to be a good sign.

'What's going on?' asked James.

'You heard what he said; he's a negotiator,' said Lily. She glanced at James to see that he was deep in thought, trying to work out the significance of this development.

'So we don't do anything for the time being, right?' said Lily.

'I don't know,' said James, watching the blond man take a step forward before stopping.

'Move towards my voice,' shouted Danny.

'I can't hear it clearly enough,' shouted the negotiator. 'I could fall off the roof.' He was standing not ten feet from them and, to approach Danny, he would have to walk past them.

'Oi! Delivery boy!' shouted Danny at James. 'Bring him over.'

James looked across at him questioningly.

'Yes, you; come on, bring him to me.'

'Oh shit,' said James to Lily. He took his arm from around her and he pulled himself up from his kneeling position and approached the negotiator. Taking his arm, he led him across the roof, past Graham, who was still kneeling, soaked in petrol and trembling. Once the negotiator was standing alongside Danny, James resumed his position kneeling next to Lily, putting his arm around her once more as he did so.

'What do you think is going on?' asked Lily.

'I have no fucking idea.' James appeared to be annoyed that he had been denied an opportunity to make some sort of intervention himself. He was brave, she had to give him that. And so cute. Warmed by the glimmer of hope that the negotiator's appearance afforded, Lily leaned into James, enjoying the warmth and wiry strength of his body.

'It has to be a good sign, doesn't it?' said Lily.

'No, I don't think so,' said James. 'In fact, if this goes on much longer, then we revert back to plan A and run at him.'

02:44 PM

Roof of 11 Blenheim Terrace, Belgravia

Ed couldn't remember the exact height that Calvert had read to him from the notes but it was obvious that Danny was considerably taller than him because of the angle of trajectory from which his words were delivered into his ear.

'Stand here. Don't make any sudden movements. I thought you'd be wearing a flak jacket.'

'I was kind of hoping I wouldn't need one.'

'I bet you were told to wear one.'

'I've always been a rebel.'

Danny coughed out a chuckle, then said, 'I'm not going to take your word for it that you're blind, I'm afraid.' Ed's sunglasses were removed as Danny inspected his face. In the few seconds the glasses were off, the thirty per cent light sensitivity in Ed's left eye registered the vague glow of the sun, low in the sky to the south-west. Over the years since he had been blinded, the fact that his left eye had maintained some light sensitivity had not provided much comfort. If anything, it taunted him, giving him a faint glimpse into the world he had left behind, reminding him that he would always miss it. The light was extinguished once more as Danny replaced his glasses.

'Satisfied?' asked Ed.

'You got pretty messed up there,' said Danny.

'Bomb blast,' said Ed, but Danny didn't respond. He had started checking Ed for wires and listening devices. His huge hands patted him down and reached into pockets. The search provided Ed with further time to consider what he was doing up there on the roof. His eagerness to come there was born of more than just a desire to resolve the situation. It was more than just the motivation that drove people to conquer ever higher mountains, dive deeper in the ocean, push themselves to greater feats of endurance in extreme sports. If he could have done, Ed would have been content to attribute it to that and that alone. But there was something else that had made him want to come up and speak to Danny face to face. It was something that had maybe always been there, something that had perhaps driven him to work in the world of hostage negotiation in the first place and had been accentuated tenfold when he had been robbed of his sight. He would never admit it to another living soul but he had to face up to the fact that he felt strangely drawn to suicidal people. It was like vertigo suffers seeking out high places in order to indulge their perverse fascination with the possibility of falling. It was as though he was daring himself. Continuing the negotiation up on the roof had presented him with an opportunity to get as close to a man facing imminent death as he had ever been before. However dangerous the encounter might prove to be, it was an opportunity he felt compelled to take. Standing in front of him, checking every fold and crevice of his clothing, was a man who would most likely be dead very soon. Ed was up close and personal with a dead man walking. And, accompanied as it was by the smell of petrol rising up off Graham Poynter, he found it intoxicating. Ed had been close to death before on a handful of occasions during his years on the force, but nothing like this. Nick Calvert had been right: it was lunacy to go up there and confront a man who had nothing to lose. Ed would have provided a similar observation regarding the wisdom of entering a stronghold, if called upon to do so. Never had Ed felt less in control of his own behaviour in a negotiation. It felt as though a line had been crossed and he knew that he needed to steer his own thoughts back to the job in hand. He needed to start talking.

'Danny, who's making you do this?'

'No one's making me do this. I'm doing this myself. I told you.'

'Are they bribing you or are they blackmailing you?'

'Neither, Ed. That's not what this is all about.'

He was denying it but Ed knew that he was really asking him to stop. There was no point pushing this line any further. But what line could he push? Now that he was in position, face to face with Danny McAteer, he worried that his instinct as a negotiator had deserted him.

'Has this got anything to do with a hacktivist by the name of Advo?'

A hesitation and a slightly choked delivery as Danny said, 'No, I don't know who you're talking about.' Danny knew exactly who he was talking about. It was extremely unlikely he would have ever met him face to face; their relationship would have been played out across the wild frontier of the web with its boundless anonymity.

'We've been provided with very detailed intelligence that Advo – or the Adversary, as he is sometimes known – is behind this entire operation and the net is closing in on him.'

'I have no idea what you're talking about.'

'Danny, I know that's not true. I can hear it in your voice.'

'I don't care what you think you can or cannot hear.'

'Danny, there's no one listening to us up here. This is completely off the record. Please, talk to me.'

'The fact is, you don't know anything.'

'They'll bring him in, Danny. They'll throw everything they've got at it. These hackers always make a mistake eventually. Whether it's now or ten years' time, he'll screw up and then whatever deal you've done with him will be compromised.'

'I knew that whoever conducted the negotiation would

tell me I was a puppet and the true architects of the operation would be found. But you don't know who you're dealing with. There's a new world order rising up out of the wreckage of capitalism.'

'Are those your words, Danny?'

The question went unanswered as Danny continued with his diatribe. 'All the law enforcement and intelligence agencies throughout the world are working to the wrong agenda. They're using the wrong tools. The people they are fighting are not criminals in the traditional sense. Some don't even see them as criminals at all – myself included. They employ different methods; they employ a different philosophy. The only way that the authorities will be able to catch them is if they fundamentally change their own philosophy and working methods and by the time that happens, their enemies will already have won. All you need to know, Ed, is that I'm not alone. We're everywhere.'

This was about as close as Ed was ever going to get to a confession from Danny. The tension in his voice was gone. The truth made his words sing through the drone of the helicopter engines.

'Presumably, you're being paid?'

'We're all being paid, Ed. In one way or another. Payment is relative.'

Ed could have done without the grand platitudes but he didn't want to antagonise Danny any more than necessary. 'Your payment is going directly to your family, right?'

'Ed, this is over now. I wanted to speak to you because I wanted to know how much you knew. But you know no more than I would have expected.'

Ed was about to tell him that it didn't matter how much he knew at that moment in time; he would learn more – they would all learn more – as the wheels of the investigation started to move after the day's events had come to their conclusion. But a man started shouting nearby.

'What the fuck is going on?'

It wasn't Graham Poynter's voice asking the question – couldn't be – so it had to be James. It was a voice charged with nervous adrenalin, a voice that was foolhardy, young and arrogant, pumped up on the sort of youthful heroics that were always at their peak of intensity when delivered in the close proximity of a pretty girl.

'Shut up and calm down,' shouted Danny in response. Whether a gun was pointed to accompany the dialogue, it was impossible to tell but it succeeded in silencing the young delivery driver.

'What you have to realise,' said Danny, his voice modulated once more to a loud speaking volume, directed at the side of Ed's head, 'is that there's nothing you can say that's going to make me stop. Even if I thought maybe you were right, that maybe you might catch my accomplices, I still have to do this because there's a chance that you won't, a good chance, a strong likelihood, in fact.'

'Your family don't want money,' said Ed. 'They don't want

dirty money that's been earned from other people's misfortunes. They want you, Danny. They want to hold you and tell you that they love you.'

'No, Ed, the time for that has past. Holding hands through the bars in a prison visiting room is not my style. I've already said my goodbyes. I've got to finish what I started – whether it's right or wrong. I've already done the hard part. Killing a scumbag like this bastard is going to be easy.'

02:51 PM

Roof of 11 Blenheim Terrace, Belgravia

Lily knew she had to try to make James calm down. The
negotiator's presence on the roof was the only chance they
had. She knew that James didn't share her optimism but
shouting at the hostage taker when he was brandishing the
cigarette lighter could do none of them any good. She looked
at the negotiator. He was above average build but he was
dwarfed next to Danny. Yet, despite the size difference and
his disability, he didn't appear to be cowed by the situation.
He looked like the only person on the roof who wasn't
frightened.

'Don't go shouting, James. Let him talk.'

'Oh, Jesus,' muttered James. 'This is getting so fucked up.'

'Not necessarily.'

'What's happening?' asked Lily's mother, her face streaked
with eyeliner-dyed tears. She looked lost, bereft. Lily had
always thought of her mother as being a woman who had

kept her true nature under wraps for the sake of her husband. She had always thought that, beneath the façade of the banker's trophy wife, there was a woman of strength, a woman who, if called upon, would fight to defend her family from attack. Lily still believed that, under the right circumstances, her mother might show some true grit. But this scenario, with its violence and cruelty, was so far out of Helen's frame of reference that she could not compute it and it had left her tearful and broken.

'The negotiator's talking to him,' said Lily to her mother.

While James and Lily had watched the new arrival speak to Danny, trying to work out what was going on from one moment to the next, Helen had stared at the roof, as though trying to avert her gaze from the source of her terror. But now she looked up at the two men talking nearby. As she did so, she gasped and her face twisted into a mask of desperation. Lily followed her gaze and saw Danny flick open the lid of the Zippo lighter and hold it out towards her father.

02:56 PM

Roof of 11 Blenheim Terrace, Belgravia

The time for negotiation was over. Ed had felt sure that Danny's invitation to join him on the roof was a sign that he wanted to reach out to him and discuss his predicament. He had known that Danny was eager to find out how much he knew about his arrangement with his paymasters but what Ed hadn't realised was that this was the only reason Danny had wanted to speak to him. The realisation that there was nothing he could do to stop Danny setting fire to Graham Poynter sent a rock of confusion and despair barrelling into his solar plexus. As he heard the unmistakable sound of a Zippo lighter being flicked open, he knew that the graph that plotted his chances of resolving the situation had fallen away to nothing. But to be a hostage negotiator is to be an optimist. Even in the bleakest moments, you have to believe that what you are going to say can make a difference. Without that optimism, a negotiator cannot function. Ed had time for one final shot at trying to stop Danny from completing his mission.

Graham Poynter was shouting, 'Stay away from me, you fucking madman!'

'Stop! Danny, there's something you need to know,' said Ed.

'Tell me.'

'Put down the lighter.'

'Tell me now!'

'Don't fucking do that!' Graham Poynter's voice carried every tonal nuance of his terror and desperation.

'Tell me what it is, now,' demanded Danny.

Ed had no idea what it was that he had to tell him. He was thinking as fast as he could. Danny's voice was screechy and pained; Ed had heard the tone before and it was not a good note to hear. There was only one name Ed could invoke that would have maximum emotional resonance.

'It's Emily,' said Ed.

'What about her?'

'Put down the lighter and I'll tell you.'

'No!' Danny was losing control. Ed's mention of his daughter only added to his suffering. He just wanted the pain to stop.

'She wants to speak to you. She needs to tell you something.'

'She loves me. I know she loves me; she doesn't need to tell me.' His voice had risen almost a full octave as the emotion took hold. His composure was disintegrating.

'It's not that, Danny. She wants you to stop. She doesn't want you to do this.'

'Good try, Ed, but I have to do this, don't you see? Without this, everything's lost. At least with this, there's a chance that some good will come.'

Even as Ed spoke the words, he knew they were pointless. But he said them anyway: 'Stop, Danny; don't do it.'

Graham Poynter was shouting again but Ed could still just make out the sound of the flint wheel on the Zippo lighter as Danny spun it. The talking had come to an end. But Ed was wrong about something: he hadn't run out of options. The negotiation was done. There was nothing left to say. There was, however, the reality that he was there, standing on the roof of the house next to Danny. There was no way he could intervene physically. He couldn't fight him. That would be pointless. But there was something else.

All of them were shouting now, screaming. Danny's first attempt at creating a flame had failed but, as he spun the flint wheel for a second time, there followed the telltale *whoomph* of igniting petrol, which was followed by an intense heat that scorched Ed's face. Reaching up with his right hand, he knocked off his sunglasses and the bright orange glow of the sun registered on what remained of his retina. But there was another light source, closer to hand, emanating from the ball of flame in front of him. He dived forward towards the heat. Slamming into Graham Poynter's burning, screaming body, he threw him backwards. Their feet tripped against one another's as Ed's momentum sent them stumbling into the low wall that Nick Calvert had told him bordered the flat roof. Poynter had clearly stood up as the petrol had ignited but he was going down now as his legs crashed into the wall and he tripped backwards over it and Ed went with him, falling through the air, his hands still locked around Graham Poynter's shoulders. Their bodies turned over and over as they plummeted ground-wards, smashing through the glass roof of the swimming pool annexe. In a shower of breaking glass and splintering wooden joists, they hurtled into the water below, the height from which they had fallen sending them crashing against the bottom of the pool, rising slowly from it in an expanding fog of blood, the taste of which was unmistakable.

Roof of 11 Blenheim Terrace, Belgravia

Everyone had recoiled from the flames except the negotiator. It was an automatic reaction for everyone but him. Knocking off his sunglasses, he dived at Lily's father and pushed him backwards, the two of them locked in an awkward stumbling embrace until they fell together over the side of the roof. Lily looked into Danny's tear-filled eyes. He mouthed, 'I'm sorry,' and pulled on the chain. There wasn't time to move forward fast enough to prevent the pin from being pulled from the grenade. It clattered to the roof with the chain snaking away behind it. Danny threw his arms wide as though opening them up to welcome the red laser dots on his chest that erupted into bloody entry wounds as the bullets struck him. His lifeless body fell hard against the roof. Lily reached up to the grenade against her throat. She pulled at it but the clammy cold metal was solid around her neck. The direction of her mother's shrieks changed and Lily turned to look at her. Helen's mouth was screaming, the spittle-flecked lips stretched open, her eyes wide as she started to move away from her daughter across the roof as the seconds ticked by. Lily knew she couldn't loosen the collar but her fingers clawed at it nonetheless. There were figures, appearing from behind walls and chimney stacks on neighbouring roofs, their black paramilitary clothing and balaclavas making it seem as though, at the moment of his death, Danny had spawned an army of clones.

All of them kept their distance. She turned to James. He hadn't moved. There were tears in his eyes but also an expression of conviction and she knew instantly that, whatever was going to happen to her in the next few seconds, he wasn't going to leave her.

'Go! Get away from me,' shouted Lily, but he moved forward, throwing his arms around her and holding her close. There was no uncertainty in his grip; he knew where he wanted to be and that was right there with her.

'I'm not going anywhere without you,' he said. For the first time in Lily's life, she felt secure. This was unconditional self-sacrifice, the likes of which she had never experienced before. They would die together. She didn't feel lonely anymore. One day, this man might have become her lover or her husband. Now all that had been stolen away from her. But in these last few moments of her life, as her head swam and she waited for the explosion, she knew what it felt like to be loved.

But the explosion didn't come. It had to be at least ten seconds now, more like twenty. They were still standing there. James reached down to touch her chin and raised her face to look at him. He wore a hopeful expression. He turned around to the figures of the special forces soldiers, keeping their distance on the neighbouring roof. Her mother was long gone, sobbing uncontrollably while being escorted away by a man in black.

'Hurry! Come on! We need to get the collar off,' shouted James. But the figures kept their distance. 'You've got to help me!' James's increased desperation made no difference. The men were shouting to each other but it was clear that none of them was going to approach Lily when there was every chance that the grenade could go off at any moment.

'For Christ's sake, throw me some pliers or something.' Even when he was shouting at them, begging them for help, he didn't let go of her. 'Help me!'

A pair of pliers was thrown and clattered on to the lead roof from where James picked them up and went to work on the collar. He was breathless with exertion and the adrenalin that was coursing through his system. As he wrenched at the metal, cutting at it and twisting, Lily stared into his face, which trembled with concentration only inches from hers. He muttered and cursed and finally the collar came away in his hand and he threw it away from them, sending it arcing against the blue sky to come to land on the lawn in the back garden.

Figures were making their way towards them, shouting orders. It was difficult to make out what they were saying. A helicopter moved lower and soldiers climbed down a rope from it and on to the roof. James put his arm around Lily and held her close as they looked down into the garden. The metal collar and the unexploded grenade lay on the lawn, but their eyes were drawn to the big hole in the glass roof above the swimming pool, and to the two bodies in the pink water.

03:00 PM

Blenheim Terrace, Belgravia

Ed was disorientated and struggled to find his feet on the bottom of the swimming pool. By the time he had done so and stood up, water had entered his lungs. There were footsteps all around him, people were shouting but he couldn't make out what they were saying. His entire being was focused on trying to prevent himself from choking to death. He struggled to fill his lungs as he gagged and coughed and retched up water. Finally, he managed to draw in some air but continued to splutter as his breathing began to equalise. There were others in the water by now and he could start to make out what they were saying. Graham Poynter wasn't breathing. They were going to attempt emergency ventilation on him; it sounded as though someone was doing mouth-to-mouth and C.P.R. Being clearly conscious and breathing unaided, Ed was low on the paramedics' list of priorities, although he did hear a voice, directed at him, ask, 'Are you OK there?' But, before he could answer, someone else was calling to him. It was Nick Calvert.

'Mallory, you fucking mad bastard.'

'What happened to Lily, Nick?' Ed's voiced was strained and hoarse from coughing.

'She's OK. Danny pulled out the pin. Special forces shot him but the grenade didn't detonate. The delivery driver managed to get the collar off her and threw it away.'

'Danny's dead, right?'

'Right. Multiple wounds.'

'His poor wife and daughter. Tell me what's happening with Poynter.'

'They're working on him.'

Ed waded in the direction of Nick Calvert's voice. Calvert crouched down on the side of the pool. The paramedics' conversation betrayed an escalating tension. They were struggling to revive Poynter. Ed's attempt to save his life may well have been for nothing. What had happened would have been beamed around the world and there would be many people out there who didn't want Graham Poynter to survive, who had foisted on to him all their mistrust and hatred of the mendacity of the one per cent and all that it had come to represent. Ed wanted him to live for purely selfish reasons as much as anything. His negotiation had been a failure and saving Graham Poynter would help ease the soul-searching heading his way in the coming days and weeks, not least because of his motives for his journey up to the roof and his descent from it. As he had fallen into the void, he had felt free, released from his life of perpetual darkness. For the briefest of moments, he could see again.

'Ed, you're bleeding.'

'Where?'

'Side of the head, there.' Calvert lifted up Ed's hand and pressed his fingers against a jagged gash above his left temple. 'It's going to need stitches.'

'We'd like to take a look at you, if we may—'

'Hold on,' said Ed, cutting across the fraught voice of the paramedic, who was clearly trying to sound workmanlike to mask his own nerves in the face of Graham Poynter's dire prognosis. 'I just need to know what's happening here.' He pulled himself from the water and sat on the edge of the pool. He could feel and smell the blood as it dribbled between his fingers but he could also feel that the gash in his head, although deep, was no more than a couple of inches long. It would need stitches, for sure, but its deleterious effect on his appearance meant nothing. It would be just one more scar among many.

It was a strange noise, somewhere between a burp and a convulsion. No one who was conscious would make an involuntary sound like that. It had to have come from Graham Poynter and, even before a voice said, 'We've got him,' Ed knew that he had survived. This man, who had so enraged the media consumers of the country – the world – this man who had stolen people's money and, with it, their hopes of a secure future, was going to live. Maybe the visual evidence of his wounds would augur some sort of rebirth. Only Graham Poynter himself would be able to decide that and, right now, he was in no fit state to do much other than cough and splutter and fight for breath, just as Ed had only moments before.

'Looks like you saved his life,' said Nick Calvert.

Ed didn't respond. His thoughts were no longer focused on Graham Poynter. Despite all that had taken place in the past few minutes, they were no nearer solving the mystery of who was set to benefit from all that had happened.

'Nick, you need to contact the command centre and ask Des White if we've had anything back from GCHQ on who it was that Danny was giving that password to.'

'I already know.'

'Who was it?'

'It was no one.'

'What do you mean?'

'They analysed all the web and phone activity and there was no call. He wasn't speaking to anyone. He must have been speaking into the voice recorder on the handset.'

'Why would he do that?'

'I don't know, Ed.' Nick Calvert's frustration was palpable. It was a question that had no answer. What possible benefit could Danny derive from leaving the details of a bank password on his phone's voice recorder?

'Where's his phone now?'

'It'll be up there on the roof, either on him or nearby. The whole place is in lockdown. It's not going anywhere.'

It didn't make sense. Danny had died without communicating to an accomplice the password he had extracted from Graham Poynter. Why would a man as meticulous as him do that? Despite his thumping headache, Ed's mind raced. Danny's death was all part of a story that had been written by an unseen hand. Ed thought about the American hacker, Abel, and what he had said to him on the phone earlier. 'Advo is not the guy on the roof, if that's what you're thinking. I mean, there's no way out of there, is there?'

Blenheim Terrace, Belgravia

The entire area was locked down; no one was going to get in or out. Lucas steered the motorbike as close to the perimeter of the police cordon as he could get. Photographers and reporters milled about trying to decode the meaning of any movement around the stronghold. They all seemed isolated in their own little worlds, staring at their laptops and tablets. Their physical proximity, only yards from the epicentre of the news story, was no match for the multiple points of view beamed at them via the Internet. There was a big police presence within the perimeter but the serious people, the people who made up the government's front line, were elsewhere, hidden away, poised and ready for violent deployment.

'Poynter survived. He's fucked up but he's alive.' The hack that stood only a few feet away from him spoke in a matter-of-fact voice. He almost sounded disappointed, as though the story that he would write up later on had been compromised in some way by the survival of the lead hostage. Lucas, too, felt disappointed, but it wasn't worth dwelling upon. Bob Rushwood's mutilated body would have been found by now. The point had been made. The symbolism had been created whether Graham Poynter lived or died. The threat was implicit. If you don't behave as you should, we will come looking for you. This was the opening salvo of the war. He and his fellow combatants would discuss it; they would learn from it, adapt and move on. They were warriors. Lucas liked the analogy. It made him feel valiant and brave.

'Can you please stand back here?' The voice was hassled, a couple of clicks down from angry. Lucas turned around and saw that a flat-bed lorry, complete with car crane, was inching its way towards the perimeter and the armed police officers were beginning to make an entrance for it. Some of the cars were going to be cleared from Blenheim Terrace to make way for more police vehicles. No doubt the van he had parked there earlier in the day would be one of the vehicles they wanted to clear. But, as Lucas reached into his pocket and his fingers closed around the remote control device, he knew the van was going nowhere.

11 Blenheim Terrace, Belgravia

'Come on, Ed, let's get you patched up.' As always, Nick Calvert's voice was a barometer of his mood. It was clear he thought the situation was at an end. All that remained was the mopping up, the grand post-mortem that every hostage scenario had to go through. The investigation into what had taken place and who was responsible would start now. One chapter had closed while another one, a less violent and dangerous one, would begin. Ed, however, didn't share his feelings.

'Hold on a minute, Nick.' Ed pinched together the wound on his forehead to stop the bleeding. What he was thinking about had taken place only minutes before but it had already taken on a sheen of unreality. He tried to concentrate while shards of pain were jabbing at his head wound. He was up on the roof with Danny. He was lost in the negotiation, fighting a losing battle to get through to him, scouring his brain for anything that might prevent Danny from setting fire to Graham Poynter. 'What the fuck is going on?' That was what James had said to Danny. Ed had barely registered the question at the time and had put down the cocky, confident tone of its asking to adrenalin and youthful arrogance.

'Shut up and calm down,' Danny had said. It was not the response one would have expected from a hostage taker to a hostage. There was a lot about the way that Danny had undertaken his duties as a hostage taker that had perplexed Ed throughout the day, but none more so than that. It denoted a familiarity between the two men. He would obsess about the minute details at another time, but now, all he needed to imagine was that Danny and James knew each other. That was enough.

'The password,' said Ed.

'What about it?' said Calvert.

'I still think he was telling someone that password. Him speaking into the phone makes us think he was doing it via that. But he wasn't. You've watched the video feed right?'

'Yeah.'

'You told me he was shouting the letters and the numbers that made up the password.'

'Seemed to be.'

'He was shouting them to someone else on the roof. Where are Lily and James now?'

'They'll be brought out of the stronghold fairly soon, I would have thought, so we can preserve the crime scene for forensics. Why?' The 'Why?' was the only indicator that Nick was beginning to register the nuances implicit in Ed's question.

'It's James,' said Ed.

'James? What do you mean?' Calvert's tone had changed. His falling adrenalin levels were reversed.

'He's the one working Danny.'

'But he checked out,' said Nick. 'He's just a student, just a kid.'

'I don't care what intel told us; it's him. He's a clean skin.'

Ed pulled himself to his feet and immediately wobbled. Nick put his hand on his arm to steady him.

'I think you'd better stay here, Ed, and get some medical attention.'

'No way,' said Ed. 'We need to stop him.'

'Stop him from what? He can't go anywhere. The place is in lockdown. It's swarming with police and special forces.'

Ed wasn't arguing; he grabbed Calvert's arm and said, 'Come on.'

03:30 PM

11 Blenheim Terrace, Belgravia

James had shown her more commitment in the past few hours than her parents had in ten years. That probably wasn't entirely true, but it was something that she could imagine saying to them during an argument. Her new-found freedom was only a few minutes old and already she was considering her parents' objections to her relationship with James. All she knew was that she would allow nothing to stand in the way of her being with him. He had stayed with her when no one else would. Facing certain death, he had held her close. The bond between Lily and James, forged as it was in the white heat of acute danger, was unbreakable.

When they told her that her father had survived the fall and his burns were only superficial, it had made her cry. For a couple of minutes, she was convulsed with sobs. She couldn't control them. A psychologist would probably be able to explain why that was. Something to do with the release of tension, no doubt. The news had the same effect on her mother but, while Lily's emotions were soothed by the outpouring, Helen walked behind them and continued to sob all the way down the stairs. Lily wouldn't have been surprised if she was having some sort of nervous breakdown. She couldn't blame her mother for backing away from her when it looked as though the grenade was going to explode. It was a perfectly natural instinct. She would probably have done the same if the explosive collar had been on her mother's neck. There was no point dying for someone who you didn't love, or rather, someone you didn't love enough. James, on the other hand, had risked everything for her and she would never forget it.

Special forces soldiers accompanied them as they walked across the hall. Some of them were as big and scary-looking as Danny. She felt no feelings of hatred or animosity to him. He had paid for what he had done with his life. Lily felt sorry for his family and friends, just as she felt sorry for the families and friends of the men who Danny had killed. But her own life and those of her family had been saved and, in the process, she had found someone so special that she never wanted to be apart from him.

The clear blue sky above the rooftops of the houses opposite was framed in the doorway up ahead. She no longer felt cold. Her feet were numb inside James's socks but she didn't care. In a few moments she would be swept inside a warm vehicle and driven away. With James.

Lily turned to look at him and they shared a smile. It was a strange sensation. She felt as though she had known his face for so much longer than the few hours they had spent together. Already it was indelibly etched into her mind. When she had been with boys in the past that she liked, she had always been wary of showing her true feelings for fear of being hurt. She felt no such fear now. The normal rules no longer applied. She felt renewed and she knew that her life had entered a new phase. Her life would be forever divided into before this day and after this day. Before James and after James.

They moved towards the doorway, towards the light and a whole new world. James squeezed her hand and she squeezed his hand back. They stepped out and she turned to look at the vehicles that filled Blenheim Terrace. There were police everywhere. Many of them turned to look at Lily and James as they appeared in the doorway. She found herself smiling. It was an involuntary reaction and, as soon as she realised she was doing it, she stopped. It wasn't appropriate. People had died. Her home – her former home now, perhaps – was a crime scene; there had been multiple murders in it. Yet even this thought did nothing to sully her feelings of hope. She turned to look at James once again, only this time, he wasn't smiling. There was a strange expression on his face, one she hadn't expected. He was looking out across the police lines into the distance and, for no apparent reason, he raised his arm in a clenched-fist salute. No sooner had he done this than he lowered it again and turned to Lily, all evidence of his gentle demeanour now gone as he grabbed her roughly by the shoulders and threw himself against her so that they both fell to the ground.

Positioned along Blenheim Terrace with police and soldiers and emergency vehicles close by it on all sides, was a white van. Inside the van, a small chemical reaction was taking place. This had been set in motion fractions of a second earlier by the remotely controlled activation of an electrical charge within a cannon fuse and detonator. With the first part of the process complete, the second part – the ignition of the ammonium nitrate that filled the back of the van – ensued and the van was torn apart at an explosive velocity of thousands of miles per second.

James lay upon Lily, protecting her from the objects that were hurled down upon the two of them. The roar of the explosion hammered against her eardrums; the shock of the blast rendered her disorientated and confused. She thought that perhaps the explosive collar that had been around her neck had finally exploded, but it couldn't be. As much as she knew next to nothing about explosives, she knew enough to know that a grenade couldn't cause such a big blast. Whatever this was, it wasn't a grenade. As the roar faded, Lily's thoughts turned to issues closer to home. James had taken the force of the missiles and rubble that had rained down upon them. He wasn't moving.

'James?' His ensuing silence had her spooked. 'James!' He moved and she felt some of her rising panic level out.

'Shit, my head.' His voice was croaky and weak.

'Are you OK?' asked Lily.

'I think so.'

He rolled off her and Lily looked up into the smoke from which came shouts and screams and the sound of car and house alarms. They had survived a second ordeal together and, as with the last one, James had been there for her. He had shielded her, protected her and made her safe. When James dragged her to her feet, however, he did so with an urgency that hinted at further danger.

'Come on,' he said and, gripping her hand, he pulled her down the steps at the front of the house, weaving in between the semi-conscious special forces soldiers who had, until a few moments previously, been escorting them out of the house. James pulled her close behind him and they dashed out of the gate. Lily could see the effects of the blast through the thick smoke that shrouded the street. Flames spouted from vehicles nearby and one in particular that was almost unrecognisable. The ground was littered with charred lumps of smoking detritus. Some people were dragging themselves to their feet; others remained motionless. In a few seconds, the street that she knew so well had been transformed into what looked like a war zone. It felt as though reality had had a hole ripped in it and through the hole had come a roaring blast of hell. The socks on her feet snagged on objects in the road on which she couldn't help but tread. A sharp piece of metal dug into her heel making her hobble as she ran, but still she ran, sprinting alongside James between the burning vehicles and wounded people.

It felt as though the air itself was on fire and it scorched her throat and lungs as she sucked it in. She couldn't avoid breathing in some of the black drizzle of charred material that fell all around, making her cough. It was the same smell as the one earlier after the explosion in the house, only so much stronger. Her streaming eyes made navigation in the dense smoke difficult but she continued to hurl herself forward after James. Whatever it was they were running to or from, it no longer mattered. Her destiny was with him and if he felt they needed to run then run they must. The ground was sticky and hot beneath her feet. For a moment, it felt as though they were surrounded by walls of fire and James pulled her forward with increased urgency, shouting, 'Jump!' as he did so. She threw herself forward, emulating his leaping stride. They came through the fire but she landed on something, part of an engine perhaps, and she twisted her ankle. Despite the pain, she kept up with James.

Up ahead, Lily could see the smoke was starting to clear and she could even see the blue of the sky. There were fewer obstacles in their path and Lily had to run faster to keep up with James. It felt as though they were accelerating towards a finishing line.

Through the smoke came a motorbike, the metallic scream of its engine cutting through the sounds of chaos all around. It was heading straight for them until, with only a few feet between them and it and without even slowing at its approach, it skidded through a full one hundred and eighty degrees and came to a halt. James let go of Lily's hand and, utilising her continuing forward momentum, swung her up on to the back of the bike behind the rider, clad in black motorcycle leathers.

'Hold on,' said James, and before Lily could even begin to formulate a question as to what was going on, he jumped on to the back of the bike behind her and shouted, 'Go!'

The motorbike surged forward but Lily was held firm, sandwiched between the two men. She pulled her stinging feet up on to the foot pegs as they accelerated away from Blenheim Terrace, hurtling through the streets.

03:31 PM

Blenheim Terrace, Belgravia

All the windows at the front of the house were shattered, blown inwards by the force of the blast. Even though Ed Mallory and Nick Calvert were standing at the rear of the hallway when the explosion came, they were showered in glass fragments.

After any bomb blast – as Ed knew so well – there is a moment of complete silence once the apocalyptic roar of the explosion has subsided. Lost in that fleeting stillness, Ed was transported back to the Hanway Street siege fourteen years before, when a bomb blast sent a shower of glass fragments into his face and his eyes. But this explosion was different. The explosion in the Hanway Street siege was caused by a grenade, powerful enough to kill and maim but an altogether different symphony of destruction. It was the last thing he heard as a sighted person and the first as a blind one. But it was puny in comparison to this. This was much bigger. Anyone within the vicinity of its epicentre would be killed; those nearby would be badly injured. It was all part of the script, and the man who had written that script was about to start the final act.

'Jesus!' shouted Calvert, staggering back from the doorway. Ed held out his hand and they steadied themselves against each other.

'Are you OK, Nick?'

'Shit!' Calvert was reacting to what he was seeing. Ed could only imagine the scene. But what needed to be done now – over and above anything else – was to catch the perpetrator of this chaos.

'Listen to me; this is the getaway,' said Ed. 'If we move fast, we can stop him.'

'This is so fucked.'

Ed had never heard Nick Calvert sound so rattled.

'Nick,' he said, trying to stop himself from coughing as the stench of the explosion reached his nostrils. 'We need to concentrate. James can only have gone one of two ways down the street.'

'I can't see him,' said Calvert. 'There's too much smoke.'

'Let's move,' said Ed. 'Hold my hand and run. It's a fifty-fifty chance. They can't be that far ahead.'

Calvert did as he was asked and took Ed's hand, setting off down the steps. Ed followed him, his feet stumbling as they collided with obstructions. He allowed Calvert to pull him along. His shoulder caught on the gatepost as they turned into the street, where the smell of the explosion was stronger still. Calvert came to a standstill and Ed was about to ask him to keep moving when he said, 'I can see them! They're over there.'

'They?'

'James and Lily.'

They set off running once more, Calvert steering Ed between the obstacles. There were burning vehicles. Ed could feel their heat and the brightness of the flames registered on the few still-functioning light receptors in his left eye. Nick Calvert stopped suddenly and Ed came up hard against his shoulder.

'What is it?' asked Ed.

'They're getting on a motorbike,' said Calvert. 'Both of them riding pillion behind a big bloke in leathers.'

Ed could hear the engine as it accelerated away from them. 'We need to go after them,' he said.

Any worries that Ed might have had that Calvert's faculties were impaired in any way by the shock of the explosion were banished as he listened to him speak to someone close by.

'Hey, I need the car,' said Calvert. 'Here's my I.D. You need to get medical attention for that straight away; you're bleeding badly. Are the keys in?'

Calvert bundled Ed into the passenger seat of a car which smelled of cheap air freshener. The door was slammed after him and he listened to Calvert's footsteps as he went around to the driver's door, opened it, climbed in and started the engine. Nick Calvert's advanced driving techniques were immediately apparent as the door slammed and the car lurched forward into a tight manoeuvre around whatever obstructions were in its path and was off, tyres screaming against the asphalt. Ed pulled on his seat belt and wiped his left eye, which was being liberally doused with blood from the wound above it.

'Where's the radio?' asked Ed and Calvert pushed a handset into his hand. Ed pushed the talk button down.

'This is Ed Mallory and D.I. Nick Calvert; are you reading me?'

Ed's question was greeted with the sound of static which was relayed through speakers into the interior of the car. He clicked the button and repeated the question. More static. Ed was about to ask for a third time when a voice broke into the flow of white noise to say, 'Yes, reading you.'

'I realise all hell has broken loose in Belgravia with the bomb, but you need to stay with us on this. We're in a police vehicle – you should be able to ascertain which one from this signal – and we're in pursuit of James Watts and Lily Poynter, who are riding pillion with an unidentified motorcyclist. We're heading' – Ed lowered the handset for a moment – 'Nick, where are we heading?'

Calvert broke off from his muttered profanities to say, 'North; Hyde Park Corner up ahead.'

'North towards Hyde Park Corner,' said Ed into the handset.

'We've got your G.P.S. location,' said the radio operator.

'You should also be able to get the G.P.S. location of the target from the mobile phone signal of Lily Poynter's phone. The negotiating command centre at the stronghold is probably messed up, but you should be able to get the number of the phone from G.C.H.Q.'

'That may take a short while,' said the operator.

'We don't have a while so please do what you can.'

Throughout the entire exchange, it didn't occur to Ed that he was no longer a member of the force. The interaction was second nature. As they swung on to a more open stretch of road, Ed heard the pedal slap against the vinyl interior of the car as Calvert stamped it down against the floor and the engine growled its accompaniment to their brutal acceleration.

03:41 PM

Hyde Park Corner

Whoever was sitting in front of her, driving the bike, cared nothing for the rules of the road. He didn't even seem to care whether they lived or died. They shot across road junctions and through red lights, the engine screaming in her ears, almost but not quite drowning out the blaring car horns that heralded their reckless manoeuvres. No one spoke, not that she would have been able to hear them above the engine if they had. She could feel James turning around in his seat from time to time to look back over his shoulder. The man in front remained motionless, apart from leaning into the bends around which they sped. As they turned off Hyde Park Corner and headed north on to Park Lane, he opened up the throttle and they moved through the traffic on either side of them as though it was stationary.

There were cars waiting at the red light on the slip road that cut across the southbound Park Lane traffic to turn right. Lily knew they weren't going to stop and she felt sick. She closed her eyes for a moment, trying to blot out the approaching red lights and the stationary vehicles between which they shot. She opened them again to see they were flying across the junction. There were no car horns this time, just the screeching of rubber against asphalt as drivers made desperate attempts to avoid them. Brakes on the motorcycle were applied only momentarily – the only hint of an evasive manoeuvre – before the throttle was opened once more and they roared past the Connaught Hotel and into the narrow streets of Mayfair. Any hope that they might reduce their speed was banished as they swerved around a dog-leg bend and accelerated so that the buildings on either side of them became a blurred tunnel of colours. It was a strange sensation; the cold air of their slipstream made Lily's arms feel numb while her front and back were shielded and kept warm by the bodies on either side. Her heart was pounding as the adrenalin flooded her system. It felt as though she was falling off a cliff.

It was a part of London she knew only too well. When she was younger and she still spent time with her mother, they would sometimes walk up here from Belgravia. They might do some shopping on Bond Street before lunch in Nobu on Berkeley Square, then a cab home with their shopping bags. Approached at such speed and with such recklessness, these streets lost their familiarity and appeared strangely alien as they bled across her vision. The events of the day were surreal on so many levels that Lily had had no opportunity to consider what exactly was taking place. All she knew was that James had saved her; he was the only one who cared for her and she felt safe with him, his chest pressed against her back, keeping her warm as the motorbike roared through the streets. Wherever they were going, it was where he wanted them to go. That was all that mattered.

Her reasoning – shocked and startled as it was – had told her that she was safe and secure with James. But the growing unease in her subconscious couldn't help but prompt a physiological reaction to the unfolding events. She felt sick with fear. This was not how she was meant to feel. The danger was meant to have passed. Her father was still alive; the grenade around her neck had not exploded; Danny was dead. James was her future. The bomb had changed all that. The day's lunacy had entered a new phase. But James was keeping her safe. He was looking after her. He was keeping her from harm. That's what it was, right? That's what it had to be. She couldn't ask him now, hurtling through the London streets, but she would ask him soon enough. When they stopped, he would explain. It would all be fine.

When they came to Regent Street, they were lucky: the lights were green. As they shot across the street, Lily could see the huge, sparkling Christmas decorations strung between the buildings up above them. The sun shone down from the cold winter sky and then it was clicked off as they entered the narrow streets of Soho, the bike's driver sitting in front of her refusing to reduce his speed, despite the sharp corners they navigated. On Berners Street, the driver opened up the throttle and the bike surged forward. When he pulled on the brakes, she was thrown against his back as they turned into a narrow side street and skidded to a halt at the kerb. There were only a few cars in the street and the sound of the motorbike's engine echoed off the façades of the buildings. The driver killed the engine, kicked down the stand and jumped off..

'What's happening?' asked Lily as James helped her dismount. She hated the way her voice made her sound so frightened and childlike.

'I'll explain in a minute,' said James. 'Get in the car.' His manner had changed from earlier, when everything he had said and done seemed to be predicated on his concern for her well-being. Now he was much more blunt. The motorcyclist had the boot of a Lexus saloon car open and was changing out of his leathers into jeans and a jumper. He pulled off his crash helmet to reveal a face that belonged to someone much younger than she had expected.

'Get in, Lily,' said James. Any hint of affection or even kindness was gone from his voice now.

'I want to know what's—'

'Get in the fucking car!' James took her by the arm, his fingers digging into her skin as he pushed her into the back seat.

03:52 PM

Berners Street, Soho

Lucas steered the car out into the street and drove away, his style of driving the complete opposite of that which he had employed on the motorbike. As planned, he would drive within the speed limit, observing all the rules of the road, until such time as events conspired to force him to do otherwise. Lucas had done well. There had been times during the operation's planning stage when James had worried about his abilities. He wasn't worried about him getting the job done; he knew that Lucas was committed to the cause and perfectly capable on that score. What concerned him was that he knew there was a deep-rooted psychopathy at work in Lucas's mind and this might expose them to danger. There had been so much for Lucas to do. So much intricate planning had been involved and there had been so many opportunities for something to go wrong. Just as there had been so many opportunities for his own side of things to go wrong too. The whole Radcliffe & Penny part of the plan had been fraught with difficulties. Having found out that the Poynters had ordered their Christmas dinner from the company by tracking Helen Poynter's emails, James had managed to pass the interview procedure and been hired as one of a number of extra Christmas drivers that the company took on every year. But what had not worked in his favour was the company's delivery schedule. One of the other drivers had been assigned the Poynter drop. For the plan to work, it was essential that James was at the wheel of the van that brought their food on Christmas morning. Hacking into the company's computer system was easy but re-assigning the Poynters' delivery to himself from another driver was something else entirely. He had managed to break into some of the most secure networks in the world, but reconfiguring the delivery schedule of a busy fine-foods company on Christmas Day had proved to be far more difficult. Thankfully, all of that was in the past and the fact that they were sitting together in the car now was confirmation that, so far at least, all his planning and strategising had been a success.

Danny had been more of a loose cannon than Lucas and, in this regard, James's fears had been well founded. On balance, Danny had screwed up, allowing Graham Poynter to survive the sacrifice. But James knew he had to be pragmatic about this. The implicit threat that had been made to Graham Poynter and its subsequent execution, even if he hadn't ultimately been killed, was all the symbolism that was needed. They were painting pictures, banners behind which people could rally. This picture was now complete. The enemy would have plenty of time to keep looking at it on the rotating canvas of the twenty-four-hour news media.

It was the first opportunity he had had to speak to Lucas since they had both set out that morning.

'All OK?'

Lucas turned to him and smiled. 'Everything's perfect.'

James put his hand on Lucas's shoulder and gave it a squeeze. It was a gesture of thanks and also a farewell.

Now he must deal with Lily. It was always going to be a risk to bring her with them. But, such were the risks to which they were already exposed, it seemed like only a minor one in addition to all the others. And he couldn't help himself. He was intrigued by her and, if he was honest, more than a little obsessed. She was so rich, so privileged, but also so sad. James's obsession with Graham Poynter's public sacrifice went hand in hand with his obsession with Lily. He wanted to free her from her imprisonment. Faced with the thought of leaving her behind after the bomb had gone off, he had always known what he would do and had told Lucas about it right from the operation's preliminary planning stages. If he was going to lead a new underground movement, he would have to live his life in hiding from this day onwards and he would need someone beside him. Spending time with her earlier had done nothing to make him worry that he had made a bad choice. She was beautiful, intelligent and, most importantly, she was brave. With Lily by his side, he knew he couldn't fail. But he also knew that one of the most difficult tasks that he would have to complete in the course of the day was persuading her to see it that way too. 'Lily, I'm sorry about shouting at you just then.'

'Are you going to tell me what the hell is going on?'

'Yes, I'm going to explain everything. Now, please, put on your seat belt. It's absolutely crucial we don't arouse any suspicion from here on in.'

'And what if I don't?'

'Lily, please don't be like that. I promise you, I'm going to explain everything. Now put on your seat belt; it'll be safer that way.'

James was relieved to hear the seat belt being clicked into place.

'I can't help feeling I've been kidnapped,' she said.

'You haven't been kidnapped. I just want you to come with us.'

'Us? Who's us?'

'Lily, there's a lot I need to tell you, a lot we need to talk about.'

'Who are you, James?'

It was a question he had been asking himself for years and it was only recently that he had found the answer. It wasn't as though he had changed. He was the same James

Watts who had grown up in Shropshire and moved down to London as soon as he could to attend the University of Westminster. He was the same James Watts who had grown to hate the injustices in the world; the same James Watts who wanted to make a difference and became a true cyber-warrior: Advo, 'the righter of wrongs'. Nothing had changed, all that had happened was that he had realised his destiny: he was going to be instrumental in the onset of a war between the one per cent and the ninety-nine. As Thomas Jefferson had said – and he loved to quote – 'Sometimes the tree of liberty must be watered with the blood of patriots and tyrants.' Jefferson might have added, 'and bankers.' James would add that for him. Times had changed; the political landscape had changed but the sentiment still rang true.

'I'm your friend, Lily.'

'You tried to kill my father.'

'Your father is an enemy combatant; it was nothing personal.'

'You see yourself as some sort of soldier?'

'It's not what I see myself as; it's what I am.'

'You're a fucking psycho, that's what you are.'

'I don't think you believe that at all, Lily. I think you're torn between family loyalty and the truth.'

'You had me going; I'll give you that. All the shit about launching an attack on Danny; you were just making sure we didn't.'

'Lily, come with me.'

'Fuck you.'

She spat the words with an anger that surprised him. She was unlike anyone he had met before. She wasn't intimidated by danger any more than Danny had been. Danny; poor Danny. He had done what he was being paid to do and – apart from the wobble at the end, which resulted in the blind guy saving Poynter's life – he had done his job well. He would be paid – if he could be. And that was something that James knew he had to discover before he did anything else.

'Have you got the iPad?' he asked Lucas.

'It's under the seat.'

James reached down and found it. He tapped the screen and opened up the web browser. He typed in the address in the box and it opened up into the bank's dashboard. He tapped on the login window and there were the two boxes for the corresponding passwords.

Just as he was about to ask Lucas what Bob Rushwood's password was, Lily spoke across him. 'I'm not going anywhere with you. You need to let me go.'

'Lily, please understand, there's no point us discussing this now. There will be plenty of time later.'

'Why? Where are we going?'

'Somewhere far away.' He turned back to Lucas and said, 'What was Bob Rushwood's password?'

Lucas reached into the top pocket of his shirt, took out a piece of paper and passed it to James, who opened it and

read the letters and numbers written on it in Lucas's pecu-
liarly neat handwriting: '2312Tomkins'.

'You checked it, right?' asked James as he tapped the password into the dialogue box.

'Yeah, it was fine.'

'So you did all of this just to steal some money?' Lily's
self-righteous tone was understandable. She was young. He
couldn't expect her to grasp what they were doing in a
matter of a few hours. Gradually, however, she would learn
about the true nature of the war in which they were engaged.

'No, that's not what this is all about. Now keep quiet for
a minute.' It wasn't all about the money. It was about so
much more than that. But as he typed in the password that
Danny had shouted to him on the roof – Lily2605 – the
money, and their successful procurement of it, seemed more
important than ever. It would be proof of his abilities as a
tactician and strategist. The symbolism of what they had
done to Bob Rushwood and Graham Poynter was important,
but so was this. He pressed return on the screen and waited.

'Let me out of the car.' She had the seat belt undone and
was reaching for the handle to open the door.

James had activated the child lock himself on both rear
passenger doors, so he knew that she wouldn't be able to
climb out. However, he didn't want to risk any behaviour
that might alert the attention of a passing police car. Tearing
his eyes away from the iPad screen for a moment, he reached
into the glove compartment and took out the pistol. He

didn't want to get heavy-handed; he had hoped that it wouldn't come to this but, during the next few minutes, he knew that they had to be extremely careful. He unclipped his seat belt and swivelled around in his seat, pointing the gun at Lily. 'Lily, I don't want to hurt you.'

Still she pulled at the door handle, muttering and cursing to herself.

'Lily!' He pushed the barrel of the gun against her shoulder, forcing her back into the seat. He hated having to do it but it was necessary. It worked. The fight went out of her for a moment and she sat still, staring up at him with hatred burning in her eyes. 'Listen, Lily, I don't want to hurt you but you mustn't be under any illusion here. If you jeopardise our operation then I will kill you. I don't want to have to do that because I love you, but I will if you force me to.' He had said more than he had intended and couldn't hold Lily's gaze a moment longer. 'Put your seat belt back on.'

James spun around in the seat and looked out of the window to check there was still no sign of the police. He listened as Lily clicked her seat belt back into place before he pulled on his own and replaced the gun in the glove compartment. His eagerness to get back to the iPad and confirmation of the success of the mission made him nervous. But he needn't have worried. On the screen, the view had changed and, with both passwords accepted, the account had been opened successfully and there it was: all eighty-five million U.S. dollars of it. His hacking over the past couple of years had earned the movement some big hauls of cash, but nothing like this. This was the 'ace in the hole' that Rushwood and Poynter had discussed in their emails to one another, those same emails that they had convinced themselves were private and safe from prying eyes. Advo had been reading them for months. Here was their safety net in the event that everything fell apart at the fund. Only scumbags like these two could have been greedy enough to think that they couldn't survive on less than eighty-five million U.S. dollars. Even in their attempt to provide some secret funds for themselves and their families in the event of the authorities catching up with them, their greed was obscene. Much good it had done them. James had already set up an account at the Cayman Island Banking Corporation from where funds could be transferred to various other accounts throughout the world. Danny's widow would get her cut. She would be notified covertly in due course and given the details of the account into which the second instalment of Danny's fee would be paid. James wished he could have provided for the families of the security guards who had been killed by Danny, not to mention the police, military and emergency services who would have been caught in the blast outside the Poynters' house. Maybe if he could find out their identities, he would try to do something for them. They were, after all, members of the ninety-nine per cent too.

James couldn't help feeling a twinge of pride in his

abilities and his benevolence. It was a stupid notion and one that could only ever have come from Lucas, but maybe his comparison to Robin Hood was not such a bad one after all. Romantic nonsense possibly, but it did have a sort of mythic charm. People responded to myth. All the great leaders shrouded themselves in it to achieve a resonance with their followers. James would do the same.

04:03 PM

Shaftesbury Avenue, Piccadilly

'They're heading east on Shaftesbury Avenue.' The radio controller's voice filled the car. Ed could hear the nerves in it. The man was frightened. The authorities were in a state of panic. There had been a massive deployment of police, special forces and emergency services to a location that had subsequently been transformed into the epicentre of a bomb blast. But, while others dealt with the fallout from that, Ed knew that he and Nick Calvert had to focus on catching the perpetrators – or some of them, at least – before they escaped. If James was Advo and he had accomplices, or if James and his accomplices were Advo collectively, then it would only be a matter of time before they resurfaced elsewhere with a similar or possibly worse attack. They had to seize the opportunity to catch these two. Or was it three? Was Lily involved? Had she provided the inside information they had required to carry out the siege? Ed doubted it, but what was not in question was that James and whoever had helped him were mass murderers – terrorists who thought nothing of creating multiple casualties to further their cause. Despite their intricate planning, however, not to mention the audacity with which they had carried it out, they had screwed up. The secrecy of their location had been compromised. They were on Shaftesbury Avenue, up ahead. They were close.

'Do we have air support?' asked Ed.

'It's on its way,' said the controller.

'Can you give me an E.T.A?'

'No. Sorry. Everything's messed up on account of the bomb. I'm getting you all the backup I can, as soon as I can.'

'Motorbikes?'

'We're giving you everything possible.'

The theatres being dark, because of Christmas, Shaftesbury Avenue was quieter than usual but there was still a line of traffic and the car lurched and swayed as Calvert threw it in and out of the oncoming lane and slammed his foot from accelerator pedal to brake pedal and back again. Somewhere ahead of them, out there beyond the shattered flesh of Ed's unseeing eyes, was their target, and Calvert drove as though he wanted to throw the car straight into the centre of it.

04:08 PM

Shaftesbury Avenue, Piccadilly

It felt like a family. James was his brother. James had given him a cause, something to believe in. Lily was – what was Lily? – his sister-in-law? Maybe, in time. Lucas had never had much of a family when he was growing up; no one that he cared a damn about. James was more of a family to him than his mother and father had ever been. For the first time in his life, he felt as though he belonged.

The traffic was light. There were sirens. But there were always sirens. This was London. Nothing appeared to be headed their way. They were just a group of friends making their way across London in an unremarkable car, moving at an unremarkable speed.

Lucas had worried that James was being too hard on Lily earlier, telling her to shut up and pushing her into the car. When she was trying to open the door, however, he was glad that James had pulled the gun on her. They had come too far for their mission to be screwed up by an hysterical girl. Thankfully, she had calmed down. It always amazed him the effect that James had on people. Within minutes of being in his company, Lucas had fallen under his spell and known from that moment onwards that his and James's destinies were inextricably linked. James was charismatic. There was no other word for it. He had the ability to make you agree with his point of view and make you feel that, deep down, it had always been your point of view as well.

It was James's charisma that had been instrumental in enlisting Danny McAteer. Lucas had thought that it couldn't be done. Here was a man who had spent his life devoted to the British establishment. His loyalty to his country was unshakeable. Lucas had witnessed first hand the way James had befriended Danny and made him open up about his health. All the while, he was working on his fears for his family and his inability to make financial provision for them after his death. The final piece of the jigsaw was Danny's resentment regarding a certain sector of society – a resentment that, James persuaded him, he had always had. These people stood in direct opposition to everything in which he believed. Why should they enjoy a rarefied exist-ence when their behaviour was not only criminal but morally repugnant on every level? Danny had worked hard all of his life. He had served his country. His family deserved some of the security that only money can buy, even if he couldn't enjoy that security with them. James had played on all of Danny's resentment and provided it with a focus. He had channelled it directly at the inherent corruption of the super-rich, something that was perfectly embodied by one Graham Poynter. A warning needed to be given to others who might think they could behave in a similar manner. A line must be drawn. Governments weren't going to do anything. Some of them were in collusion. It was a sustained narrative that James had maintained and, while he had presented his thesis to Danny, he also allowed Danny to talk. He needed to talk and James had listened to every word. It was this that had made all the difference and had eventually persuaded Danny to join the movement. It was quite something; James had succeeded in turning a former S.A.S. soldier, a man with ultimate loyalty to his country, into a renegade freedom-fighter. Now James would have to turn the focus of his charismatic charm on to Lily Poynter. Knowing James as he did, Lucas had no doubt that this part of the operation would be as well planned and no less successful than all the rest.

James needed someone close to him. As much as Lucas felt that he was James's confidant in all things, James had emotional needs that he could not satisfy. It was a thought that had come to him a few times over the past few days and it made him smile. If James was the king of this new underground resistance movement then maybe Lily would become his queen. And Lucas? Well, maybe he was the prince. It was as though they were some sort of covert royal family. It was crazy to think like that, of course. James was forever cautioning against pride and unchecked ego but Lucas couldn't help it. What they had achieved that day would go down in history as the moment when war was declared. It was James's strategic brilliance that had brought them to this place but Lucas knew that he had also played his part – a big part – and, while the road stayed clear and the sirens remained distant, all he could think was that the first battle was won.

04:11 PM

High Holborn

It wasn't that she had forgotten about her phone. She had been aware of it all day, hanging there against her leg in the lining of her tracksuit bottoms. But it had meant nothing to her. It wasn't as though she could use it. Now, however, it might make all the difference. The authorities could trace its signal. Or, better, she could alert them to her whereabouts and a rescue mission could be launched that would trap James and his accomplice. She had heard people talk about the thin line between love and hate and she had never really experienced it before. But, looking at James, she knew exactly what they meant and that line was so much easier to cross than she might ever have imagined.

She hated James for what he had done to her family, especially what he had done to her father, and she hated him for what he had done to all the others – including Danny.

She hated him for all those things but, despite all of it, she might have been able to forgive him. But what she couldn't forgive him for was destroying her dream. It had felt so real. He had been her saviour. But the turning point had come when he had shouted at her and pushed her into the car. He had shown who he truly was. Those few moments when he had made her think he was trying to save her life when everyone else had given up on her would stay with her; they would never go away. But it had all been a lie. She wanted to look him in the eye and for them both to know that she had brought about his entrapment. He would never be able to forget her.

Lily put her hand into the pocket in the front of her tracksuit bottoms and held the phone. Was it even working? She hadn't charged it since the night before, in Zurich. It might have run out of juice. As she slid it out of her pocket, she looked up to check that she wasn't being watched and, as she did so, her eyes met James's.

'Oh no, Lily.'

Whether he had grown suspicious on account of her silence following her outburst of a few minutes previously or whether it was just her bad luck, it was impossible to say. Before she could even articulate a response, he reached out and snatched the phone from her. Opening the window, he threw it out of the car.

'You'd better speed up, Lucas; she had a phone.'

'Oh shit.'

James and Lucas became agitated, peering through the windows and glancing back over their shoulders. When James spoke to her she thought he would be angry. But he wasn't.

'Lily, I want you to come with me.' He turned around in his seat, wearing an expression she had seen before. It was the same expression he had worn when they were on the roof together. He looked afraid but he was masking his fear with bravery. It made him look like a child who was standing up to a domineering parent. It was an expression she had probably worn herself many times over the years.

'What if I don't want to?'

She had meant to tell him to go to hell but, as much as she hated him for destroying her dream of a new life, she couldn't close the door on that dream just yet. It gave her a thrill to perpetuate it, to play with him. He wanted her. He had told her that he loved her. If nothing else, this provided her with an opportunity to hurt him as much as he had hurt her.

'You do want to come with me, Lily; I can see it in your face. We were meant to be together.' He unclipped his seat belt, took the pistol from the glove compartment and climbed into the back to sit next to her. That he had brought the gun with him made her think that perhaps he was going to try to coerce her into agreeing to go with him by threatening to kill her. But he kept the gun lowered and stared into her eyes. 'Lily, you've got to come with me. There's so much I need to tell you. I know you hate the fact that people had to die and we had to make threats to your family.'

'You tried to kill my father.'

'And we would have done, if we could. I won't lie to you. But I know you, Lily. Don't be angry about this, but I've read your emails and texts. I know you don't want the life that your parents have mapped out for you. I know that, deep down, you're a good person and you want a different life, a life with truth and honesty in a world where treating people fairly counts for something.'

'That's the life you lead, is it?'

'That's the life I'm fighting for, Lily, and if a few people have to get hurt along the way then so be it.'

'I think those sirens are for us,' said Lucas from the front seat. 'What do you want me to do?'

James spun around and looked out of the back window. Lily didn't turn to look but it was clearly an approaching police car. She watched James as the blue lights reflected in his eyes. He turned back to her and put his hand on her shoulder.

'Come with me, Lily.'

'What do you want me to do?' shouted Lucas.

For a moment, James looked lost, broken, like a little boy who has been caught doing something he shouldn't have been and the shame is all too much for him. He looked as though he might cry. But as the police siren became louder and the blue light bounced off the rear-view mirror around the interior of the car, he gritted his teeth and seemed to come to a decision.

Lucas began to speak. 'What are we going—' But he didn't get to finish the question before James had raised the pistol, pressed it against the base of his skull and fired a shot through his head. Gouts of blood erupted from the exit wound in Lucas's face and splattered across the windscreen, which was now cracked from the bullet that had passed through it. James leaned forward and grabbed the hand-brake, pulling it hard. The car hadn't been travelling fast, probably about twenty miles per hour, but the sudden application of the brake sent it skidding into the kerb, off which it bounced and spun through ninety degrees, coming to rest at a right angle to the flow of the traffic. The sound of screeching tyres drowned out whatever it was that James was shouting at Lily as he fired a shot through the rear passenger window, which frosted over with tiny cracks but remained in place until he smashed it out with his elbow, reached through and opened the door from the outside. Taking hold of Lily's arm, he dragged her out after him. The police car was a few places back in the queue of cars which had now formed behind them. There were voices all around but, when James spoke to her, his words were loud and clear as though beamed straight into her consciousness.

'Come with me, Lily. This is our last chance.'

Even as she went so speak, she didn't know what she was going to say. She wanted to go with him. She felt drawn to him despite everything. But she knew she couldn't. He was right; she did want a different life, but it wasn't the one that he wanted to provide for her. She listened to her words as she said them and it was as though they were spoken by someone else.

'Fuck you,' she said.

James raised the pistol and pointed it at her head.

04:11 PM

High Holborn

'Mobile phone coming out of the window of a black Lexus up ahead,' shouted Nick Calvert.

'It's got to be them,' said Ed. 'Are you armed?'

'No.'

'Should we wait for backup?' Ed hoped Calvert would say no and he did. Nick Calvert was a by-the-book copper only up to a point and that point had been reached. Ed knew that his former Met colleague, whether armed or not, would do whatever it took to stop James from escaping.

'We've got a visual on the car up ahead,' said Ed into the radio handset. 'It's a black Lexus. A phone's just been thrown out of the window so you should see the G.P.S. signal remain static.'

'That's confirmed,' said the controller.

'That's them then. We're not close enough for the number

plate but will keep you posted. You'll see that we're—Where
are we Nick?'

'High Holborn.'

'High Holborn, heading east,' said Ed into the handset.
'You need to get us all the backup you've got.' Ed lowered
the handset and said to Calvert, 'Can you see the number
plate?'

'No. Shit!' Calvert jerked the wheel and pulled out from
behind the car in front but no sooner had he done so than
he had to pull back in. Whatever was coming towards them
– a bus or lorry, perhaps – was too big to get out of the way.
Ed despised his blind isolation. He wanted Calvert to
commentate and answer all the questions that were jumping
into his mind but he knew it was better to allow him to
keep the car they were pursuing in a clear line of sight. He
remained silent, locked away in his own dark box, trying
to solve a puzzle that was forever changing just as he was
about to crack it.

'Come on, that's it. Get out of the fucking way. That's it!
That's it! *Come on!* No you don't!' As Calvert maintained his
stream of consciousness, reacting to the vehicles and obstacles in their way as though they were sentient beings who
might understand what he was saying, he worked the pedals
and the steering wheel and the car rocked from side to side
as they cut out from the line of traffic and shot back in again.

'Oh my God!' There was a change of tone in Calvert's voice
that denoted a game-changing event but, before Ed could

ask exactly what it was, Calvert provided him with the answer. 'The car's skidded to a halt across the road.' He stamped on the brakes and the car came to a halt.

Ed was thrown forward against his seat belt. 'What's happening?' he asked.

'Hold on; James and Lily are getting out. Shit – he's pointing a gun at her head.' All the angry tension and volume had gone from Nick Calvert's voice when he said, with a calmness that was chilling, 'I think he's going to kill her.'

'Have you got a clear run at him with the car?' asked Ed.

'I don't know; maybe.'

'Go! Just drive straight at him.'

Tyres screeched as Calvert stamped on the accelerator and the car surged forward.

04:13 PM

High Holborn

If she was going to die, she wanted to be looking into his eyes, defiant to the last. But inside, she was crumbling. She felt as though her legs might collapse at any moment. The businesslike way that James had killed Lucas was a sickening precedent. Even though it was now clear that James was behind the entire ordeal that she and her family had suffered throughout the day, it was horrifying to see him kill someone as easily as wiping his nose. And now he was going to kill her with the exact same carelessness. When he had asked her to come with him, she could have suppressed her true feelings and said yes. She could have told him that she loved him too. But, no; with the same pig-headedness that she had faced the previous seventeen years of her life, she had told him to go to hell. And now she would die for it.

She was close enough to him to see his finger tighten around the trigger. The roar of an engine, however, distracted him. Spinning around, he pointed the pistol at an approaching police car and started firing at the two figures in the front seats. The windscreen cracked and frosted as the car skidded to one side. Unlike their car, which had not been travelling as fast when it went out of control, the police car was possessed of enough speed that, when it smashed into a van on the opposite side of the road, the front third of the car became misshapen and displaced.

Lily threw herself at James. She tried to reach for the gun but, when her fingers closed around the barrel, he pulled it out of her grasp. She went for his face with the intention of gouging at his eyes but, despite his slim build, he was much stronger than her and he pushed her back against the car. She rushed at him again. He stopped her with a straight-arm punch, his knuckles connecting with the bridge of her nose as shards of pain stabbed her face and she went sprawling to the ground. Looking through streaming eyes, she watched as he reached into the car, leaning across his accomplice's body to retrieve a small rucksack into which he had placed his iPad. Swinging this over his shoulder, he walked across to the police car, whose ruptured engine had now fallen silent. He lowered his head and peered in through the front passenger window.

04:15 PM

High Holborn

'Nick? Nick!' Ed reached for Calvert with one hand while he unclicked his seat belt with the other. The fact that Ed was still alive was testament to the fact that the bullets had been aimed at the driver of the car and not him. There was silence from the big man, still strapped into the driver's seat. Ed found his neck and pressed his fingers against it, trying to find a pulse.

'It's you, Mr Negotiator. We've got to stop meeting like this.' The voice came through the car window. It was the same voice he had heard earlier, asking Danny, 'What the fuck is going on?' It was a voice that was part youthful rebellion, part adrenalin-soaked idealist with a screech of fear turned up high in the mix.

'Come here; let me look at you.'

Ed found a pulse on Calvert's neck but it was slight and irregular. He needed urgent medical attention. Ed turned his face in the direction of the voice and said, 'Hadn't you better make your getaway?'

'I will. Just wanted to look at you. Jesus! Your face . . .'

The sirens were getting louder and Ed thought he could just make out the sound of a helicopter. If the guy was going to kill him it would be in the next few moments before he fled. Ed could try to stall him and give the police a better chance of catching him, but this would also increase his and Calvert's chances of dying. Ed had nothing left with which to bargain. 'I guess you won,' he said, in the direction of the window.

'Maybe the battle,' said James. 'But the war has only just begun. You did well to save Poynter. Nasty to burn to death, right?'

As soon as he heard this, Ed knew what James was going to do. It was as clear to him as if the words had been shouted into his ear. As each bullet struck and pierced the petrol tank, the car rocked as though struck by a sledgehammer. Ed waited for the explosion after each shot and it came after the fourth one, lifting the car up on its axles before slamming it down once again. They were on fire.

04:15 PM

High Holborn

Lily was seventeen – little more than a child. As far as her parents were concerned, she still was a child. But she felt old. It had been a long seventeen years – the past few months, especially. Maybe it was enough; maybe this was where it was meant to end. Her friends all seemed to have a clear vision of their futures. They knew what they wanted to do. They knew where they were going. All that Lily knew was what she didn't want to do. She didn't want to be like her mother and father and live a life that had no value. All that she had ever really hoped for was that, one day, she would do something that made a difference, something that wasn't based on exploitation, something good, something worthwhile. Her father would have told her that she was being naïve. What could she possibly know about life? 'All of life's a competition,' he had said to her on many occasions. 'It's survival of the fittest.' This comment had always left her stumped. What could she say to that? There was no denying it. It *was* nature's way, although, the last time that her father had come out with his pearl of wisdom, she had managed to retort that the fittest weren't always the ones who based their degree of success on the size of their house and car and how much money they had in the bank.

Lily sat on the ground in the middle of the street, blood streaming from her nose as she waited for more events, over which she had no control, to take place around her. Her entire life, she had been a victim of the decisions of others. It wasn't just the choices that had been made for her, like school, clothes, home, friends; it was more than that. It was the decisions people she didn't even know had made about her. She was the little rich girl, the spoiled brat. As the events of that day were filtered through the news media, this perception of her would only be reinforced. There was no escape. She would never be free and, if she couldn't be free, she would rather be dead.

Before the car had collided with the van, Lily had seen that the man in the passenger seat was the blind negotiator who had managed to save her father. Whether it was to him or whether it was to the driver, she couldn't tell, but James was speaking to someone through the shattered driver's window. Then he stood up straight and, pointing the pistol at the rear of the car, he started shooting until the petrol tank exploded. Spinning around, he pointed the gun at Lily but the shot didn't come. He stood, silhouetted against the flames, and as the beginnings of a smile began to form on his lips, he lowered the gun and ran.

There was movement in the burning wreckage and Lily could see the man in the passenger seat struggling with the door. But the impact of the crash had realigned the body of the car and he couldn't push it open. Lily dashed forward and grabbed the door handle, using all her weight to pull back on it until the door flew open and the negotiator burst out, dragging the unconscious driver of the car with him.

04:17 PM

High Holborn

A second explosion, bigger than the first, erupted from the car, but they were far enough away that the flames didn't reach them. Ed's throat was already sore from coughing up the water from the swimming pool earlier, and now he was convulsed once more, hacking to clear the smoke from his lungs.

'Are you OK?' It was a young woman's voice.

'Lily?'

'Yes.'

'This guy,' he gestured to Calvert. 'Is he alive?'

'I don't know.'

'Is he breathing?' Ed lay on the ground gasping at the cold London air.

'I can't tell. He's been shot in the head and the chest.'

'Where's James?'

'He ran.'

'Which way?'

'Towards the Tube.'

Through the wail of the sirens, Ed could just make out the sound of approaching footsteps. He propped himself up on his elbows and shouted in their direction. 'There's an officer injured here needs urgent attention. Armed assailant heading towards Holborn Tube: James Watts; white male, twenty-two years old.'

The flesh on his face felt scorched and his scars felt like acid burns but he could tell that his injuries were only superficial. He had been lucky. Without Lily to pull him from the car, he and Calvert would have died. Calvert might still do so. There was shouting for assistance; to the sound of sirens were added footsteps, traffic and helicopters. There was nothing else he could do. A man's voice asked him if he was OK and he said, 'Yes, I'm fine.' But clearly his response did not tally with his outward appearance – bruised, bloody and singed – and he was told he would be checked out in due course.

'Lily, are you there?'

'Yeah, I'm here.'

Ed sat up and pulled himself to his feet. He didn't want to lie next to Nick Calvert and listen while they tried to save him. He felt the need to move away and he reached out to Lily.

'Let's go.'

'Where?' asked Lily, as she took his hand.

'Anywhere.' She led him on to the pavement. Ed felt a lamp post brush against his shoulder and leaned against it. 'This'll do,' he said, letting go of Lily's hand and pressing his forehead against the cold metal of the pole.

'Will they catch him?' asked Lily.

'They'll catch him eventually,' said Ed. 'Let's face it; we nearly got him this time.'

'This time?'

'It's not the first time he's done this. He's killed others. But we'll get him. He's human; he needs to interact with people, whether on his computer or in the real world. And every time he does that and every time he attempts something like this, he's putting himself in danger. At some point, just as he did with your phone, he'll fuck up and then we've got him.'

Even though his police days were long gone, he said 'we', still feeling part of a body of people whose mission it was to stop individuals like James, the Adversary, or whatever it was that he wanted to call himself.

'Thanks for saving my dad.'

'Sorry I couldn't try to save you.'

'I didn't need saving. I wasn't in danger.'

'We didn't know that at the time.'

'But we do now. He fooled me, made me think he was for real and I fell for it.'

'Don't beat yourself up about it.'

'I thought he was a hero.'

'I'm not convinced there are any heroes, Lily, but if there are then you came pretty close a couple of minutes ago. If it wasn't for you, I'd be dead. So would my colleague. Never forget that.'

'I won't.'

They were lifting Nick Calvert on to a stretcher – Ed knew the sounds. He and Lily stood together in silence for a moment before he felt her lips against his scarred cheek as she kissed him.

04:55 PM

Minicab

They would see him on footage from cameras mounted on the street as he ran past Holborn Tube station. For a moment, he had thought that he might jump on a Tube train, but the station was all closed up for Christmas. The footage would show a man in a hurry, a man who was troubled, desperate even, but ultimately in control. Cameras would have also picked him up as he pointed a handgun at a man at the wheel of a Volkswagen Golf, into the passenger seat of which he climbed. He would have provided the authorities with all the separate pieces to the puzzle of his escape. But once they had taken the time to assemble them all, he would be long gone.

The driver of the car he had climbed into had been scared but also compliant. James could tell that he wasn't going to do anything silly like try to be a hero. About the same age as James, he had kept his fingers curled tightly around the steering wheel as he drove through the deserted streets of the City. James had kept the gun trained on the driver as he took the clothes from his rucksack. He had been forced to move the gun from one hand to the other as he put on a new jacket, baseball cap and glasses, but the driver hadn't even turned to look at him. In South London, in the quiet suburban street that James had said they should park, he had struck the man twice across the back of the head with the gun, knocking him unconscious. The man had groaned but stayed still, his head pressed against the top of the steering wheel. James had stepped from the car and walked away.

The minicab company was one of those that stayed open three hundred and sixty-five days of the year. Neither the controller behind the desk in the dingy office that smelled of rotten carpet, nor the driver who was sitting beside him now, driving the car, looked as though they cared much for Christmas.

James leaned back in the seat and tried to keep his nervous energy at bay; the adrenalin made him jumpy. Things had gone wrong during the day – there was no denying it – but he had adapted, strategised and moved on. That pleased him and gave him hope for the future. He would only ever be caught if the enemy was smarter than him and he knew it never would be.

As they pulled up at some traffic lights on the outskirts of London, James looked across at the car that pulled up next to theirs. In the car was a young family. There was a mother and father in their thirties: working Londoners, by the looks of them. They were on their way either to or from relatives, most probably. There were two children, a girl and a boy. The girl was seven or eight and the boy a couple of years younger. They were excited. It was Christmas Day, the best day of the year. Their childish excitement as they sang along to a song on the radio made James smile. They were untainted by the realities of adult life, unsullied by the greed and arrogance of a tiny minority that was allowed to exert such power and influence over them. What James had done earlier, he had done for them and all children, so that one day they might live in a world in which decency and fairness actually counted for something. The time had come to stop the bad people from winning.

Read on for a sneak peek of the explosive
DCI Ed Mallory thriller

BAPTISM
MAX KINNINGS

THE COUNTDOWN HAS STARTED.
EVERYTHING IS ON THE LINE.

10:02 AM

*Tunnel between Leicester Square
and Tottenham Court Road stations*

From the train, Glen could just make out the faint sound of voices, passengers talking most probably. Sweat dribbled down his face and his heart thumped against his sternum. Remember the training. It was like a mantra that had been instilled in him. If he remembered the training, everything would be all right. As a member of CO19, he was at the sharp end of one of the world's most elite police special operations groups. They had earned a bad reputation in the past due to a couple of high-profile mistakes. The media had made a lot of those while playing down the successes. Glen felt proud to be a member of CO19, proud that he had passed the psychological tests and been invited to attend the eight-week training course at the Metropolitan Police Specialist Training Centre to learn about firearms, methods of entry, fast rope skills, scenario intervention, rescue techniques and potential terrorist attacks. His colleague, Rob, was one of the top specialist firearms officers in the country and by being chosen to be on operation alongside him, Glen knew that he too must be held in high regard by the powers-that-be.

The voice was relayed into his headset: 'Can you see anything?'

'Nothing,' said Rob.

'OK then, move in closer and keep talking to me.'

Rob stood up first and moved past Glen, who followed him, aiming his 9mm Glock 17 pistol at the train. This was not the most dangerous part of the mission but it was close to it; they were in the open, approaching a static target, with no cover. But they had darkness and the enclosed space of the tunnel on their side. It was unlikely that a night scope would pick them up at this distance. A few feet further on, Rob crouched down on one side of the tunnel and Glen did the same a few feet behind him, careful not to touch the live rail.

'OK, we're about twenty feet away from it now,' said Rob into his mouthpiece. 'There's nothing moving and all is quiet.' But just as he said these words, something did move. There was a flash from the cab and a soft popping sound. Glen felt a spray of warm liquid and grit on his face. He glanced at Rob but there was something wrong with him. The upper right-hand quadrant of his head was completely missing, leaving a jagged fringe of shattered bone fragments and ruptured brain in its place from which blood sluiced freely as his legs gave way and he collapsed to the ground.

'Rob?' Glen didn't know why he said it. It wasn't as though Rob could hear anything.

'What is it?' came the voice over the headset.

'Shit.' It wasn't an exclamation. Glen spoke the word softly. He looked at the train and suddenly felt very lonely. The rules of engagement seemed so far away now. He knew what he had to do but he also knew what would happen when he did it. He raised his pistol and took aim at the rear cab of the train, from where there was another flash followed by a pop. Before he could fire off a shot, the entire top of his head, from the bridge of his nose upwards was sheered off and he fell backwards onto the sleepers between the rails.

'Someone talk to me.' The calm, flat voice came from the bloody remains of two radio headsets. But no one was listening.